all one universe

all one universe

Poul Anderson

TOR

A Tom Doherty Associates Book
New York

ALL ONE UNIVERSE

A Tor Book
Published by Tom Doherty Associates, Inc.
175 Fifth Avenue
New York, NY 10010

Tor Books on the World-Wide Web:
http:// www. tor. com

Tor® is a registered trademark of Tom Doherty Associates, Inc.

ISBN 0-312-85873-6

Printed in the United States of America

Copyright
Acknowledgments

Parts of this book have been previously published, sometimes in slightly different form, and are copyright as follows:

"Strangers," *Analog Science Fiction/Science Fact*, January 1988. © 1988 by Davis Publications, Inc.

"Neptune Diary," *New Destinies*, vol. 9 (Baen Books). © 1990 by Poul Anderson.

"Requiem for a Universe," *The Universe*. © 1987 by Byron Preiss Visual Publications, Inc.

"John Campbell" (as "Campbell in Memoriam"), *The Diversifier*, March 1978. © 1978 by C. C. Clingan.

"In Memoriam," *Omni*, December 1992. © 1991 by Omni Publications International, Ltd.

"The House of Sorrows" (as "In the House of Sorrows"), *What Might Have Been*, vol. 1 (Bantam Spectra). © 1991 by Abbenford Associates.

"Uncleftish Beholding," *Analog Science Fiction/Science Fact*, mid-December 1989. © 1989 by Davis Publications, Inc.

"Losers' Night," *Pulphouse Short Story Paperback #1*. © 1991 by Poul Anderson.

"Science Fiction and History," *Amazing Stories*, January 1989. © 1988 by TSR, Inc.

"Rokuro," *Full Spectrum 3* (Doubleday). © 1991 by Poul Anderson.

"Rudyard Kipling" (as " 'Beyond the loom of the last lone star . . .' "), *A Separate Star* (Baen Books). © 1988 by Poul Anderson.

"The Forest," *Moonsinger's Friends* (Blue Jay Books). © 1985 by Poul Anderson.

"Johannes V. Jensen" (as "The Fantasy of Johannes V. Jensen"), *Procrastination* #15. © 1981 by Darrell Schweitzer.

"Fortune Hunter," *Infinity Four* (Lancer Books). © 1967 by Lancer Books.

"Wolfram," *Homeward and Beyond* (Doubleday). © 1975 by Poul Anderson.

"The Visitor," *The Magazine of Fantasy and Science Fiction*, October 1974. © 1974 by Mercury Press, Inc.

"Wellsprings of Dream," *Amazing Stories*, June 1993. © 1993 by TSR, Inc.

"The Voortrekkers," *Final Stage* (Chilton). © 1974 by Edward L. Ferman and Barry N. Malzberg.

Introductory material © 1996 by The Trigonier Trust.

To
Robert L. Forward
who's exploring it

Contents

Introduction

I T'S ALL ONE UNIVERSE.
Maybe others exist. There could even be infinitely many, some more or less like ours, some where the very laws of nature are alien. They wouldn't really be like bubbles in a vast sea or pages in a space-time book. The concepts are both more precise and more unearthly than that. For such ideas these days do not come from dreamers, mystics, or science fiction writers. They are the speculations of sober, well-regarded physicists and cosmologists.

Speculations only, of course. Probably most scientific opinion still denies them, or at least thinks they must be forever unprovable. Maybe someday—and the someday is perhaps not so distant—we will learn otherwise; maybe not. What is certain and wonderful is that they can no longer be ruled out of court. The cosmos we live in has proven to be so rich and strange, so full of mysteries and paradoxes, that the presence of others would be just one more surprise.

Besides, it would simply expand a whole that we already know is greater than we can imagine. We would see the *total* universe as having many different facets, aspects, avatars, however we name them. But the one immediately around us does by itself!

We are among them. Together with the comets, planets, stars, galaxies, black holes and dark matter and every enigma, space to the uttermost wave front of the oldest light and time from whatever the beginning was to whatever the end will be—if words like that mean anything at all—we belong here. The atoms of our bodies were born of the primordial fireball and later great suns. Our race is a twig, our spirit a leaf on Yggdrasil, the tree of life that has grown, ever-changing, through billions of years to overshadow its world.

Einstein said once that the least understandable thing about the universe is that we can understand it as well as we do. This hints at some tremendous oneness in the foundations of reality. The findings of science do likewise, seeming ever more the misty outlines of a single, though endlessly and miraculously diverse, creation.

Through science fiction we do not explore it; that is the work of science. I'll have a few remarks to make about the relationship of the two, as I see it—at any rate, as far as the kind of science fiction that tries to deal with authentic science is concerned. For now I merely propose that such stories help us feel our kinship to the rest of the universe, past, present, and future, close to home or abyssally remote, grim or grand, bleak or bright, always fascinating.

The tales and occasional essays in your hand put into human terms, as well as I am able, a little of that variety in unity. They differ from each other, often wildly, because things and events throughout space-time do. Nevertheless I'll try to show how the matters they touch on are parts of a singleness. At the end we'll see if we can bring them together.

Lest this look too solemn, let me add that the purpose is to entertain and I hope you'll enjoy.

Strangers

We begin with a motif traditional but ageless, space travel and the beings that might live on other worlds.

This story is "hard" science fiction, meaning that it assumes nothing a present-day scientist would consider physically impossible. True, in it humans have reached a distant star, but they did not necessarily travel faster than light. Perhaps their ship got close to that speed, giving them the benefit of time dilation, or perhaps they passed a voyage of centuries in some kind of suspended animation, or perhaps—? Questions like this lie beyond the narrator's horizons. What questions lie beyond yours and mine?

Really hard science fiction implies more than a certain conservatism in the postulates. The details should be worked out to the best of the author's ability. I went to some trouble about stellar type, planetary masses and orbits, precession effects, evolutionary biology, and the consequences of these parameters. If, even so, the tale has a mystical quality, it's because that's how the narrator thinks, and because science itself opens our eyes to wonders and mysteries.

LAST NIGHT AS I stood on the clifftop at Hrau, seeking dreams, a ghost sailed by. The moon was well aloft, full, so bright that it flooded most stars out of heaven, for clouds had whitened nearly all its face. The light shimmered over darkful waves as if to make a path to Lost Motherland. Afar on my left, the northern horizon flickered with the campfires of the dead.

Wind lulled and ruffled my fur. It was cool, and full of salt odors to which my tendrils quivered. The surf broke utterly white, so far beneath me that the sound came low and steady, like the murmur of First River on its way to the sea when I was young. Here was a good loneliness in which to hope for dreams that would help me understand what this life has meant that now nears its end. I had not thought myself to be the kind that does—I am no saint or familiar of the Unseen—but the Watermother says I should, because of what happened long ago. Aia, how long ago!

Then as I waited, something glimmered yonder. It might have been a leaf, pale with autumn, which the wind hunted along the foam-crests. Yet it was too large, and fared too steadily, and it came not down the wind but across, from the east. Was this the form of my guide into sleep? A shiver and a shiver passed through me.

Still it neared, until suddenly it swung about. By that time it was so close that I could see what was below, the knife-lean shape cleaving its way, with a wake behind on which the moonlight shattered and swirled. My fin, already lowered, shut itself hard against my back. That was no canoe of ours passing by. That was a boat of the Night Folk.

Why have they come to seek us out, after these many years? What has changed in the Forest or in Lost Motherland, and is it of horror or of hope? Almost, I called out, but fear choked me and I crouched down, not to be seen against the western stars and the Sky Flow.

The ghost boat sailed in its swiftness and silence, following the shoreline but well clear of the breakers. As it moved away, dread left me. Might those be aboard whom I had known? I leaped to my feet, raised my fin to the full that moonlight might gleam off it, shouted and sprang about.

The boat sailed on. I do not know if they saw me. Surely they could have, as great as their powers are; but I do not know. The boat vanished southward. Grief welled up in me. I dropped to all fours, my tail lashed to and fro, I wailed for my loss, if it was indeed a loss.

No dream would come to me before dawn. Presently, though, calm did. I rose again and sang the song of farewell. After that I went home. Today I tell you of this that I have seen.

Most of you are young. You have heard the tales and learned the songs, but you do not know Lost Motherland as we few aged do who were born there and once walked on the downs and offered at the ancestral tombs. And I alone remain of those who ever saw the Night Folk. I alone sought them out in the Forest. We who remember have paid that price and suffered that loss which mortals must who deal with them; but mine was the sacrifice over and above this. Therefore you others do not know what you believe you know. I must try to tell you. Hear me.

It may be that the ghost boat was bound past on its way to some mystery beyond sight. It may be that the Night Folk have many times flitted about these islands unbeknownst to us. Did I only chance to see last night, or did they want me to see? That may have been the sending I sought, to make me ready; and after I am in my dolmen they will come by moonlight and whisper to me. Who can say? If they do seek you out, you will need the awe, the wariness, and also the eerie gladness that were ours, not as words but deep in your dreams. It is for your children and their children, who will not have countless ancestors to watch over them as we did, but merely us. Though you believe you have heard my story before, you have not really. Hear me.

◦   ◦   ◦

For two days, people at home saw smoke drift up in the distance above Gneissback Fell. Ktiya had been a large thorp; it and its crop-lands were long in burning and longer still in smoldering after the Charioteers torched them. The sullen sight brooded behind us through our return to Oaua and haunted the following sunrise. At last it grew thin and the merciful winds scattered what was left. They could not blow the memories out of us, nor the forebodings. Ktiya was large, I say, and it had gotten the help of such other Wold People as spied the beacon fires that meant Charioteers were on their way to it. Nevertheless Ktiya perished. Oaua was small; and belike it would stand alone when next the destroyers came, for our kindred around the land would be in despair.

"But we drove them off, Ak'hai'i," my oath-comrade Izizi pro-tested when I forced myself to utter this. "We killed several and hurt more—as you know better than anyone else among us—until they wheeled about and lashed their ehins to full speed eastward."

"They were a small party," I answered. "We had thrice the count of them, I think. Even so, they left our dead and wounded wide-strewn. They withdrew in good order, taking their own fallen along, except for those two it happened we surrounded."

"You should sing of that, Ak'hai'i," he said.

I might well have, for it was I who led the charge that split the enemy line. We cut a single chariot off from the rest, and Ngi of Thunder Bay put a spear in the driver but it was I—I—I who sprang up over the rail and killed the warrior himself. My ax smashed his head before his blade gave me more than a shallow slash, and now that blade rested sheathed upon my breast.

But darkness had risen in me with the smoke of Ktiya. "They rallied at once," I said. "They could have cloven us asunder and hunted us down one by one as we fled. They did not, because it was not worth their trouble. They had done what they meant to do, and longed back to their horde."

We lay in the Male Lodge, we who had gone forth to battle and lived. Soon we would seek the females and their wisdom, but first we must come to terms with those of us whom we had carried home for burial, and with ourselves. Afterward we would explain as best we could to the females, and take counsel, and all together try to come to terms with the Unseen. Thus did the Wold People do in the old times. It is different today. Everything is different.

Coolness dwelt within the thick clay walls. Sunlight filtered through the matting in the doorway to make dusk for us. The thatch smelled of nightwort and dry forage, a peaceful smell. Our gaze we kept on the lampflame on top of the Block.

"What was it, then, that the Charioteers came to do?" asked Ngi. He and his family lived by themselves, strandfishing or venturing out into the bay on a raft more than they worked the soil. Therefore he had not heard as much as we did in our thorp, and until this moment, time and breath had been lacking for him to learn.

"To lay waste," I told him. "They have cleared that vale of people and crops. Naught will meet them when they return but the whistlewing above and the wanderbeast on the ground. Naught will be growing but forage for their herds. In this wise, piece by piece they take the world away from the Wold People."

"What drives them to such deeds?" Izizi cried.

I shrugged my fin. "Who knows? Maybe not even themselves. Or maybe the years have worsened still more in the far east than they have here, as the sun slips from her rightful path."

"They fall on us who never harmed them!"

"A flippertail may think the same of me when my net hauls him from the water," said Ngi harshly.

"They have the power, true," breathed from me, "the chariots and the iron." So did we call the terrible material that cut and stabbed, unbreakable, keener than the finest-knapped sharpstone. Nobody knew who first named it. The Watermother said the word might have come from the users. Sometimes they bore off captives, and maybe a very few of these had escaped over the years and made their way back.

"If I did," rumbled Ngi, "I would use it against them just as they do against us."

"But the fate is otherwise," I replied. "Now let us be silent, mingle our spirits with the lampflame, and find peace."

Stillness fell. It did not in me. I lay there with rage on my right side and grief on my left. What to do? At heavy cost, we had slain four or eight of a raiding party and I had brought back a weapon of theirs. What good was that when the horde had blades like stalks in a swale and we knew not how to make a single one?

At last I drew mine. The others were rapt and did not see. I looked at it and felt of it as I had done whenever we stopped to rest while homebound. It was almost as long as my arm, but at the middle no more thick than my outer thumb. A stone blade shaped like that could only be for ceremony, would shatter in use; the iron did not even chip. It sheened darkly, ice-smooth. The edges, which drew blood if I stroked them, had the beautiful curve of a sunseeker leaf. There was a guardian crosspiece at their top. The haft beyond was not merely shaped, it was a thing to itself, carven hardwood somehow fastened on and wrapped with leather, flaring out to a knob in which was set a crystal. When I lifted the weapon, it was heavy as stone, but so balanced that it came alive in my hand. The crystal gleamed in the dusk, an eye that watched me like the eye of a beast of prey.

For I was the prey. My people were. Surely I was not the first who ever won an iron blade for himself. It must have happened here and there, as our kind met the invaders. But what was the use? Unskilled, its possessor would fare worse in his next battle than if he bore familiar arms. Better he leave his prize behind in the tomb of his ancestors, to wait for him. Better still, maybe, that he sink it in a pool or thrust it into a hilltop. The Unseen might accept such an offering and grant peace of soul, or the Night Folk might take it and be pleased enough to give his kindred some small help.

The flame on the Block wavered. It called me, and my spirit followed. I came back to my body knowing what I must do.

In those days the Watermother of Oaua was Riao, old, wise, and deep in the mysteries. When I told her of my intent, we two alone in her house, she said more quietly than I had awaited, "This is a wildness in you."

"It is a hope," I answered. "I see none other."

"You are likeliest to find death or worse, you who have wife and children."

"I go because I have them."

"What is your plan?"

"None. How can I make any when I know naught? I will seek until I find the Night Folk, then I will beg of them or try to compel them, whatever seems best. There are tales of ancestors who had to do with them. My own grandmother saw one."

"They flit from the Forest, across the Wold, sometimes—oftener than we know, I think," Riao agreed. "Most people who have a glimpse are afraid to tell of it afterward. If you must venture this, why do you not rove the darkness closer to home?"

"How can I be sure I will meet any, though years pass in waiting? They come and go like the wind. Or they may well spy me and stay clear of me. Also, should I catch one, their anger may fall on the whole thorp; they may blight the crops and put a murrain on the livestock. By myself, off in their own country, I may well draw them to me, and they should understand that any offense against them is mine alone."

"That is well spoken," she said, "and you have hunted in the fringes of the Forest, at least. Depart, keep silence, and let me dream on this."

I left that dim hut behung with strange things and went to my home. When I entered, Hroai looked hard at me and sent our young outside. "Your fin is nearly white," she whispered. Waves of violet pulsed between the ribs of hers.

"It is in my mind to brave a certain danger," I told her.

"Again?"

"This is not another battle. It would be unlucky for you to hear more. Have I your leave to fare?"

She was a long while mute, though her fin darkened and lightened and darkened, her tail twitched, her fur stood briefly on end. At last she said, "I believe I know what you intend. For the children's sake, I will not speak of it. For good or ill, there is a fate in you. Let us have each other while we still may." And that night she loved me often and fiercely.

In the morning I went back to Riao. "You shall go," she declared, "but first I will teach you and give you that which may help."

And so I abode with her for three days and nights. What she taught me I may not reveal, only that certain signs I could watch for and certain spells I could cast were therein. At the end she took me to First River, where it cascaded into a shadowy coomb otherwise forbidden to males, and purified me. After that she gave me a lasso. "The groundvine whose fiber is in this grew on the tomb of my ancestors," she said. "I twisted it together by night, singing moonbeams in among the strands. It may bind one of those whom you seek. Be on your way."

"Let me return home and make my farewell," I asked.

"You dare not," the Watermother said.

Dawn was breaking above the mist and clangor in the hollow. I prostrated myself before her, rose, and climbed out to begin my journey.

From a hilltop I looked widely across the land. That sight is before me as I tell of it, clearer and more colored than this around us; but I was young then.

Shadows reached long and blue in the morning light. They brought forth the strong curves of the Wold, the downs rolling away and away on every side until I saw a thin gleam in the west that was the sea, the vales between their slopes, the river winding and shining through a web of lesser streams that trickled or tumbled to mingle with it. Autumn-tawny the land was, save where cultivation made small dark patches. A few scattered trees stood northward, stunted and wind-gnarled, forerunners of the Forest. Dolmens and passage graves brooded gray on heights.

Tiny and very dear was Oaua, the round huts clustered close together, hearthfire smoke seeping up out of their thatch. Hurdle-fenced pens encircled it like a lover's arms and legs. I knew the bustle and clatter of awakening, I knew that Hroai was already out in our fleshroot field with her digging stick while little Uo fed the animals and littler Lyang cleaned house and cared for the infant yet nameless, but none of this could I hear or see from where I was. I whispered, "Farewell" and started north.

The weather was chill. Even in the afternoon I needed only half unfold my fin to stay cool. Clouds drove low on blustery airs. It should not have been so. The sallowness of forage and shrubs recalled a wet, cold summer. When my mother was a child, snow seldom fell in winter; now most years saw several nights of black frost.

Late that day, following the river upstream, I came upon the Henge. I did not linger; those standing stones were too grim. The Wold People no longer met there for rites, as my grandparents had told me they once did. It was not that we believed a curse had fallen on the halidom. But when a watcher stood on the Flagstone at solstice, the sun did not rise above either Altar of the Seasons. Sacredness had gone after the heavenly paths turned awry; and weather bleakened and presently the Charioteers began arriving.

Nevertheless this remained a good land, Motherland, and I

would keep it for us if my fate had might enough. So did I vow, then.

At eventide I made camp. My plan was to enter the Forest when the moon was full. Belike it would give more power to the Night Folk, but it would give sight to me. Meanwhile, though, I would use the dark for resting. I cut some withes, fashioned a weir, and staked it in the stream hoping my breakfast would be there at sunrise. I kindled no fire, which would have been troublesome to do and might draw a heed I did not yet want. Instead, I found pebbles to serve as a henge around me, within which I unrolled my blanket hide and ate of the dried provisions I carried.

Besides these things, I bore a casting spear and my ax: the weapons in my hands, the skin and pouch on my shoulders. A knife hung on a cord at my throat. Should any of my gear break, I could readily replace it, for sharpstone was plentiful on the Wold. Moreover, across my chest lay the iron blade, with Riao's lasso wrapped about its sheath.

I slept lightly, and my dreams were of home. I did not know what that meant.

Trees became more and taller as I trotted on. By the third day I had truly entered the Forest.

Most that grew around me were stonewood, their ruddy boles soaring aloft till the branches arched in leafage that tented off the sky. Sunlight filled the shadows overhead with flickery turquoise and the shadows beneath with white flecks. Distances reached boundless, for sight soon lost itself yonder. In places I saw bluecap blooming upward, low nightwort, moonfruit aglow, a tangle of groundvine, fangthorn crouched cruel; but mainly it was clear between the trees, except for old leaves that rustled underfoot. Sometimes a whistlewing flew from a bough, a redflit piped, a buzzbuzz blundered past; and when I stood still a while and listened closely I might hear scuttering go through the brush. Such noises hardly broke the stillness. It was warmer here than out on the Wold, and full of earth odors.

I had ventured this far in the past, hunting uk'ho or trihorn. Thus I had once come upon a field of the Night Folk. Others had done likewise. Always we called aloud that we purposed no trespass, and veered off. Today I must do what I earlier denied. I touched the rope that encoiled the blade and hastened onward before courage should bleed out of me.

My course took me from First River and the comfort of open sky above it, for here the land began to climb. The fields had been in damp, shady places. I followed a tributary brook up its own stream. It glided slow, dimly aglimmer. Shadows thickened. Evening was nigh when I found what I sought.

All those clearings were small. I think this was to have trees close around, that they might keep full sun off the witch-plants. Much water was needed too; the brook ran through the middle. High and strange and in straight rows grew the plants. When last I saw them they were brilliant green, but that was in a different season. Now they were nearly white, had dried out, and bore long berries encased in husks. Four trees rose in their midst, dwarfish and gnarly. Leaves of a paler green and large red fruits clustered upon them.

I touched naught. Stories told of reckless hunters who had stolen from plots like this. They hoped the trophies would bring luck, but only misfortune came to them. A child of one ate, and although the taste made him spit it straightway out, he was sick for days. And then there are tales of Night Folk who visited wise females, talked with them, sometimes warned that something people were doing was unwise, but refused any food offered, or any drink save water. It alone may pass between the worlds without bearing death.

Casting about, I found what I had not found earlier, when I merely stared and fled. A trail ran along the farther side of the clearing, in easy curves that soon went beyond my sight. It was no game track, but wide and hard-packed, kept clear of growth. Peering close, I made out marks in the dirt, grooves that ran side by side about two tailspans apart. Wheel marks? Who had taught the Charioteers?

I flinched from that question and looked for a blind. A cane-brake at an opposite corner of the field seemed best. I settled myself within to wait.

The sun sank until its beams speared through rare breaks in the wall of woods, as long as my thoughts. When would the Night Folk arrive to see to their harvest? Could I abide for that? What should I do? What would they do? The songs and the stories told how ill it was to cross them. Yet tales also went of kindnesses they had done, wonders they had worked, when the mood blew into them. These happenings took place in olden times, when they came out more

freely upon the Wold and it was not unheard of for people to encounter them. No living person in Riao's knowledge had done so,
aside from glimpses. She knew not what had changed or why. One
story said that a powerful Watermother grew overweeningly proud
and took such a visitor captive by spells and force; she met a frightful
end when others appeared in the doorway, and afterward they never
guested anyone. Many more stories said that to have anything to do
with the Night Folk, even though it was help they gave, cost heavily;
some said the price was half one's soul.

Nonetheless I meant to dare it, for next year the Charioteers
would be back.

The sun went down. The moon rose, but the Forest shut it off.
Darkness weighed on me. Its creatures hooted, chirred, and thrice
from afar howled. I sat on my tail as moveless as I was able. At last
I dozed.

A new sound brought me fully awake. For a moment I was
aware of thirst. Time had worn on until the moon was over the
treetops around the clearing. Fear thrilled everything else out of me.
What I heard coming from the west was the beat of ehin hoofs.

The moon stood huge. Its clouds covered entirely the mottlings
on its face. Light frosted leaves, poured down them to drench the field
and melt into the brook. The edges of things were stark, the shadows
they cast were dappled. Air had gone cool and still. The water whispered of secrets.

Hoofs thudded. He of the Night rode forth from under the
trees.

Rode. His ehin did not draw a chariot but stepped as proudly
and gracefully as if in the wild, with him upon its back. Bewilderment
whirled in me. How could this be? Then I remembered that the
Night Folk have no tails.

Tall he was, tall as I am long from muzzle to tailtip, and slender.
The moonlight revealed him moon-pale, without fur; but hair grew
in a fallow mane on his head and in a bristle on his lower face. That
face was flat, save that the eyes were deep-set (and no tendril fronds
above) and a beak jutted outward. The ears were small and round.
No fin grew from his back. You have heard weird rumors of how the
Night Folk look. This is the truth.

He came to the edge of the field and drew on cords he had
fastened about the ehin's head. The animal halted and he sprang

down to earth. I saw that he had bound a kind of seat to the ehin's back. . . . Aia, I forgot most of you have never seen such a beast. Like many large four-footed creatures of the mainland, instead of a real fin it has a low ridge of ribs and membranes along neck and back. A pad flattening part of this is harmless; the female does it to the male when she mounts him in breeding season.

My gaze went wholly to the rider. He stood as straight as he sat, needing no tail to balance himself. Through me flitted a wondering: what did he use when he must strike a heavy blow and had no ax? At once I asked myself: what would dare attack him?

I would, if I must.

The rope felt slippery as I unwound it and made a coil to carry in my left hand. My right was empty, ready to snatch out the blade, for my stone weapons were surely of no avail here. Did cold iron have power against Night Folk? Or had they made a pact with the warriors of the east, teaching them about iron and wheels? That thought stiffened my will.

He entered the field, handling the witch-plants like any farmer who wants to see how the crop ripens. Somehow that made it all the eerier. What would his harvest be? I raised my courage and trod forth into the moonlight.

He heard, turned about, stood for an instant as though startled. I lifted my right hand. "Hail to you, strong one," I heard myself call. "Forgive that I trouble you. The need of my people is great."

I stopped. The ehin stamped and whistled. For what seemed a very long time, he of the Night stayed moveless. Finally he walked toward me. You or I could never do that gait. A tailspan away he paused, and we were silent before each other.

"I am Ak'hai'i of Oaua," I said when I became able. "Lately the Charioteers came as near us as Ktiya and laid its territory waste, in spite of the Wold People who live within sight of its beacons sending males to help. Next year or next, they will be upon us. After that, year by year, they will take all for themselves. The last of us will lie untombed and none be left to light the ancestors' home on Hallows' Eve. To come to you was my choosing and nobody else's. But I beg you, help us."

His mouth, below the beak, opened. The teeth that gleamed in the moonlight were like none I had ever seen before in person or beast. As he spoke, his mouth writhed around them. His voice was an eldritch singing, full of overtones and sounds we cannot make; and it changed the sounds we can make until I barely knew what they were meant to be. When I was small, my father had a tame redflit that could say a few words. They were less alien than what I now heard.

And these words stumbled. I hear them anew, even as I see that moon-washed space, the light like rimefrost on the crowns of trees and in the murmurous water; even as I feel the cold that went through and through me. "You . . . people . . . never come . . . so."

"Death drove me," I pleaded. "You know us of old. Our ancestors remember you. Help us, lest we die!"

He spread his hands. Each bore an extra finger, and only one of the curiously shaped five was a thumb. Or thus it seemed. "No can help," he said. "You go."

I braced myself foursquare. "You must."

He pointed at me. "Go."

I stood where I was. No lightning blasted me, no curse withered me. He backed off a step. Was he afraid? That could not be, could it? He was immortal.

Yet the tales told of bounds upon what they did when they might well have done much more. And why did they shun daylight?

He moved toward his ehin. Belike he had wand or weapon tied to the animal. If I did not act at once, I could soon be dead—unentombed—or stricken mad or turned to stone.

Before fear froze me, I whipped the charmed lasso upward. It whirled about my head and pounced. I am a hunter. I noosed him by the legs, hauled, and brought him to earth.

He shouted and struggled. I leaped close and tossed coil after coil around him, snugged them taut, made him lie trussed like a taorhi for slaughter. I secured the bonds and had him.

He glared. Moonlight glistened off the white that was in his eyes. "Let me go," he panted. "No can help."

"I think you can but will not," I answered. "Or your folk can. We shall see."

He stiffened and defied me. "What you do?"

Dismay winged through my spirit. How indeed could I compel the Night Folk? What doom had I already brought on myself?

Nevertheless . . . he lay there snared. He spoke poorly, must be ignorant of speech, he, the lord of lore. None of his brethren had come on the wind to save him.

Through the awe that held me glided a thought. "You shall lie where you are till daybreak," I told him.

He gasped. Emboldened, I bent low to look closer at this that I had, incredibly, captured. What I had taken for skin wrinkled and folded with his movements. I forced myself to feel. It was covering, like a cape we put on in the bitterest weather, though this was woven so fine that warp and woof were lost within it, and was fitted to his limbs.

I drew the iron blade. Its living heaviness became my own will. "You shall have no shade from the sun," I threatened. Carefully, I slashed. His true skin shone bone-pallid under the moon. When I tugged at the fabric to get it clear of the rope, it ripped. I peeled him from shoulders to hips and left his belly naked to the sky.

What I then saw struck me with such astonishment that I dropped the blade and sprang back. "But you are female!" I cried. What evil had I been about to wreak?

His mouth twisted upward. A wild barking noise broke from him. "I male," he choked.

I mastered myself again and looked harder. Indeed that which sprouted between his thighs did not much resemble the female organ. Were the Night Folk wholly deformed?

It came to me how unwise he had been. Had he let me believe him female, I might well have released him. The Charioteers kill everyone, but the Wold People respect the Life Power.

Or would I have set him free? He was not of my people, and their need was great. I did not know, and it did not matter. He *was* male; and he was not clever, regardless of what he knew. He was mine, unless and until his vengeful rescuers arrived.

He keened words in his own language, if that was what they were, and strained against his bonds. I stood by. Dawn was still far away. Patience was my single strength. I must be the rock that outlasts the night wind.

But it was just a short while before he calmed. His uncanny gaze met mine. I compelled myself not to look away. "Sun kill me," he said. "Sun, fire, burn. I dead."

"Unless you help my people, they are dead," I answered.

"Not know how."

"There are those among you who do." I must believe that. "Take me to them."

Silence brimmed the well of moonlight that was the clearing. My spirit was cold. At last he said, "I take you."

The cold became a rushing tide. "Will you swear to that?" I asked. "By the honor of your ancestors, will you bring me unharmed to the home of your folk and will they hear me out?"

He bobbed his head up and down. "I take you, I take you."

That was no oath. Maybe the Night Folk could not swear any. Maybe, immortal, they lacked ancestors. Well, if he intended treachery, my hope was lost anyway. "We will go," I said. Stooping, I undid the knot.

Meanwhile I commanded, "Hold still." He obeyed. I kept my blade lying ready to stab while I drew the lasso off him and used it to tie his hands behind his back. He rose, and for a little while we stared again at each other.

"I . . . Sten," he said, "Sten Granstad."—as nearly as I can make the sounds.

Did he offer me his name for a hostage, as I had offered mine? My throat shut tight. It was a moment before I could repeat, "Ak'hai'i" and his gesture.

His mouth curved, though he did not bark. "Come, Ak'hai'i," he said quite softly, and turned about.

I did not risk breaking the spell by fetching my gear from the canebrake. If ever I started back home, it would be easy to chip out a hand ax, and that would be enough for the journey.

We walked west down the broad trail. He had me lead the ehin by the cords. My other hand held the enchanted rope that leashed him. As time and distance passed, my grip eased. He had made no trial of escape, nor done anything else to alarm me. He gave no sign of wrath at my binding him and spoiling his garment. Rather, he went by my side almost as a comrade might.

Of course, we were bound for his kindred, and once among them I would become the captive. What I had gained was, at most, the right to speak with them; and my gain could well prove to be no more than death, and helpless homelessness forever afterward.

Only our footfalls and the ehin's hoofbeats spoke while we followed that moonlit path. The shadows shifted, shortened; dew began to glitter on boulders and fallen trees; coolness deepened toward chill; stars trekked across heaven. My thoughts were few and dream-like. I had gone beyond myself as well as beyond my world.

We passed more stands of witch-plants, and once a shelter. It was of wood, timbers shaped to a fineness no sharpstone adze could achieve. The form was square-sided, altogether foreign. And yet that was ordinary naoi wood.

My dream broke apart like dawn-mists when suddenly hoofs tramped ahead of us. Sten's ehin whistled. We halted. I stood stiff, awaiting my fate.

It happened the boughs here were thin above us. The moon hovered enormous behind their lattice. Its light poured over the trail. Around a bend, out of the speckled shadows, another mount came into that hueless brilliance, and upon it another of the Night Folk. Behind paced two beasts of unknown kind. Four-footed, they stood about as high as my hip. Thick hair covered them from long muzzle to short tail. When they sensed me and growled, fangs gleamed.

The rider stopped, stared, reached for something. "Nadia!" Sten called. The rider drew a hollow cane of iron from a sheath and pointed it. Sten spoke fast in a lilting language that no throat among us could ever form, unless partly and brokenly. The rider replied. I stood awaiting my fate.

Sten turned to me. "Nadia Zaleski," he said, and made a gesture with his head. I cannot speak it any better than that, but I knew it was a name. He barked and added, "She female."

In truth? I stared. She too had covered her body, but I could find some differences. Her mane was black, longer than his. Apart from the thin lines of hair the Night Folk have above their eyes in place of tendrils, none grew on her face. Her form was smaller, slighter, rounder, with twin swellings at the chest. Had they not told me, I would have taken her for the male, him for the female. But they did give me this knowledge into my hands, and therewith a brightening of hope.

I stepped behind Sten and loosed his arms. "Is she your Water-mother?" I asked unsteadily. "If so, I will beg of her."

Nadia spoke from her seat. Although she could not make words of ours sound right, they flowed much more readily, in a voice more high and sweet, than his. "We have no Watermother," she said. "You have wandered far from your world, Ak'hai'i."

"But surely you have traveled into ours, mighty lady," I had courage to reply.

She moved her head up and down. The mane rippled about her shoulders. "I have that. What is your home, Ak'hai'i?" When I told her, she murmured, "It is long since I was in Oaua. You cannot have been born. But I met with its Watermother—secretly seeking her out, lest fear of me make her people dread her too—and we spoke of many things. She was Kiluo."

I shuddered. "Kiluo is in her tomb. Riao now deals for us with the Unseen." Bracing myself: "But why should this be strange? You never grow old, you Night Folk."

A sound like a breeze through darkness blew from her mouth. Did I hear sorrow? "We do not grow old as fast as you, Ak'hai'i."

At that, somehow, the hope within me turned from fire to ice. I had trapped and tricked Sten. I had made him guide me here, because else I would have made the sun burn him alive. Now Nadia said they also must someday die. "Have you no power to save us?" I howled.

They talked together.

"I will go," I said dully. "Forgive my people that I troubled you. They knew naught of it."

Nadia raised her hand. "Wait," she called. I turned back. The blood knocked in my head. "You have dared what none before you ever did, Ak'hai'i," she said low. "We would help you because of that, if we can. I make no promise. And I fear the price to you must be heavy, whether you win or lose. Are you willing?"

"I am, I am," I sang.

A moment she sat quiet. Her teeth gnawed her mouth. "Can we bring ourselves to this?" she wondered.

"I think we must, whatever it costs us," replied Sten, likewise in my language.

She commanded her ehin to go west. "Follow," she said.

He mounted his. I came behind. The hunting beasts loped at my tail.

Of what happened thereafter I can say very little. We lack the words. We lack the eyes and the thoughts. Do you understand? A thing may be so strange that you cannot *see* it. You do not know how to look. It is like a mist where colors go swirling, now bright, now dim, never the same. Sometimes the mist rolls aside somewhere, and for a breath a shape stands forth, but it is an icicle or a lightning bolt; and what you hear is voices in a dream that seem to have meaning until you awaken and cannot imagine what the meaning was.

We three had fared a ways when Sten gaped and stretched and mumbled something. Nadia spoke back to him before she explained to me—how kindly they both had become!—"He is weary."

By that time my surprise could only be dull, but she observed it. Her mouth curved as she said with a ghost-wind of breath, "We grow weary and must sleep the same as you. Sten has been traveling on his rounds since sundown."

"Was it a hard journey?" I asked, wondering what dangers he might have encountered.

She barked a tiny bit. "Not until he met you. He was just seeing if all was well with our fields. But it has been a long wakefulness for him." She was quiet a spell. The hoofs of the ehins thudded, the leather of the seats upon them creaked. "In the place where we should be, the days and the nights are but half as long as here."

"Why do you not stop and rest?" I blurted.

"We must be sure to return before dawn."

"Is it true the Night Folk cannot endure daylight?"

Her head moved up and down. "Your sun burns too cruelly bright for us."

Bewilderment silenced me.

I was tired myself when we ended our journey. But what I found there took from me every sense of mortality. I was like the spirit of one unentombed, a bodiless awareness in a world no longer mine. This world, though, had never been mine; I had not even a memory of it.

The stronghold of the Night Folk stands on high ground above the sea. Forest is at its back and trees grow around three sides of it. The fourth looks down into a bay that was then a broken path of light under the sinking moon. Mightily rear those walls, stone and timber, beneath a roof that is also of cloven wood. The windows are filled with clear ice that never melts, and dawn-soft yellow light glows through it. Nearby are the worksteads. Of them I can say naught, except that I saw flames flicker and heard iron ring upon iron, with undergroundish noises as of whirring and tramping. I was brought to the house.

Forth they came to meet us, the tall Night Folk, and more from the woods and the worksteads, carrying lights in their hands that I thought at first, seeing them at a distance, were stars descended upon earth. By this and the shining windows I saw how garb upon the Night Folk was colored, fire-red, sunseeker-orange, springleaf-yellow, gem-green and sea-green, heaven-blue and sea-blue, blood-violet, the white of snow and the black of oracular pools. Their speech caroled and surged about me. I believed some were angry and would have stricken me dead with the iron things they bore, but maybe I was mistaken. Sure it is that the will of Nadia and Sten prevailed; and who had better right to spare my life than Sten? The first brightening was above the Forest when they led me within.

And there—I cannot say what was there. I am not forbidden, but I am not able. No mortal would be. I may speak of soaring rooms and rainbow hues and music that bore me on its tide, but how shall I conjure this up out of the passage grave that is my memory? That I can never share the miracle has set me apart forever.

They gave me a place to be by myself. They brought me food I could eat, and pure water. They heard me out, questioned, listened, talked one with another, went off and left me alone, came back and questioned further. Sometimes they named names I remembered, Wold People, though all whom I had ever heard of or known as a child were dead. Indeed the Night Folk had gone among us.

"Mostly we sought to learn about you, to understand you," Nadia said once. "Certain things that happened were bad. I suppose that is inescapable, when races are altogether unlike. We cherished hopes—But they came to naught, and now we seldom leave the Forest."

Day broke. The dwellers drew into their great house of many rooms. They closed wooden slabs over the windows. When any of them must venture out, he went muffled and shaded, with pieces of black ice masking his eyes.

"This is not our world, you see," Nadia told me.

"Whence came your forebears?" I whispered.

"It was far away, beneath a gentler sun," she said. "They fell from the sky long ago, long ago . . . as you reckon lifetimes. Since then we have made what we could out of what we have."

In my puzzlement I could not ask further.

The day wore on. About noon, I met with one who seemed

almost a Watermother, though male. The hair on his head was white. "Did the Charioteers learn their arts from you?" I made bold to question him; for I had seen ehins drawing wheels.

"They did not," he avowed. "We knew no more about them than that there are herders on the eastern plains. Nor did we know, until you bore us the tidings, that any have moved this far west."

"They ravage and slay," I said. "In the name of whatever friendship ever was between the Night Folk and the Wold People, help us. Else we perish."

"What would you have us do?"

"You can tell better than I. Give us iron weapons and chariots of our own, and school us in their use?"

"The invaders are too many for you, I fear. That is an enormous country which bred them. Also, would you gladly become what they are?"

"Then go against them yourselves," I urged. "Ride to their camps in the dark, strike them with the lightning that the stories say you can wield, drive them back from us."

"Nor can we do that," he said, gentle and merciless. "They have their own right to life. Drought holds the plains, and will not let go for generations to come."

My anguish lashed at him: "How can you know this?"

His straightness sagged a little. "We do know. We always did. Your heavy sun and your huge moon pull so hard upon this world of yours that its spinning changes swiftly . . . as the stars reckon lifetimes."

Thus he said. The words echo in me like words from a Hallows' Eve dream, never to be understood, never to be forgotten. In my later years, I have thought that maybe he meant the skewing of the heavenly pathways.

I crouched down in that dim room full of gleaming things, tail raised as if for battle, and screamed, "But have *we* no right to live?"

He turned and went from me. His garb billowed with his haste. Did he flee? I sought the room that was mine, lay there with eyes shut, and tried to call Hroai and our children to my spirit. They could not come. I had wandered too far, into a land too other.

The sun trudged west.

Sten entered my refuge, which had become my cage. The times we talked had given him a better command of earthly language. His voice wavered. "We may have discovered what we can do for you," he said.

You may think this is the end of my story. The rest you have heard, since first you could listen, until it is woven into flesh and bone. I say to you, it was not the end. Through the rest of my life grew a slow understanding, for whose fullness I strove last night when I stood on the clifftop and the ghost boat sailed by. Today I would give you what understanding I do have, if I am able, for you may have need of it after I have gone home to my Hroai in our dolmen.

You know how I went in another ghost boat, on the tide that followed the sunken sun, with two of the Night Folk. Nadia and Sten, they were. The wind filled the sails and we bounded over long, murmurous waves, across which the moonlight flowed in rivers. Smells of salt and the deeps filled my tendrils. Great creatures broached and wings skimmed low, but we fared unharmed across the waste, and at dawn we raised the easternmost of these islands.

I went about it during the day, while Sten and Nadia sheltered in a tent on the strand. "It is good country," I told them. "The soil is rich and the springs are fresh."

"We are glad," Nadia answered. "We knew simply that it was here."

"But it is lonely," I said.

"That is well," Sten replied. "None will dispute your settlement. None will pursue you."

He spoke truth. I could not bring myself to say it was barely half a truth. Where were the tombs? How could we remain one with our ancestors if we forsook Motherland?

At darkfall we three set homeward. Winds were ill-humored, and morning found us still at sea. The Night Folk stretched the larger sail across the hull and huddled. For me that might have been an empty day, rocking on an endless gleam of waters. Instead it became a time of magic; for we talked freely together, we three. I came to learn a little, little about the Night Folk. Sten said they knew how to make a thing that would drive a boat without sails or paddles, but had never found time to build it, they being few in a foreign world—

Well, this is not what I mean by understanding. It is merely words. Water and words may pass between the worlds without carrying death; water, however, quenches, while words raise a thirst that can never be slaked.

We landed early in the dark and found that the Night Folk in their stronghold had the canoe ready. Often have I had to make clear why this was what they made for me, instead of a boat like their own. I will tell you again. To make a ghost boat and to handle it are craft, wizardry, beyond us people. We might have learned how, but it would have taken more time than we had. For us the Night Folk devised the simple dugout with paddles and square mat sail that you know. In the next few days in the house and darks in the open, they taught me well how to make more and how to bring them over the sea to the islands.

And then they sent me back. I returned with my hands empty but my spirit full. I prophesied and I taught—the help of Watermother Riao and the strength of Hroai upbore me—and those months were bitter, for who would willingly leave Motherland? We did at last, we Wold People, thorp by thorp, with our homes aflame behind us; and here we are, and *this* is your home and you are happy in it.

But our ancestors are all alone.

That, and a memory of dawn stealing over the downs, are the price that we, your mothers and fathers, must pay. Will you and your children and your children's children repay us, care for our tombs and call on our dreams? Or will there be only the Night Folk whispering to us?

And I, I gave more. Half my soul it was, as the old songs warned. I have been in the house of wonder; it will always haunt me. None else will ever know what I have known, and so I too am forever lonely. Yet I remember the look upon Hroai when I brought hope to her.

And also the Night Folk have paid. I have not understood what it was they must give up to the Unseen because of what they did. But as we said farewell, Nadia caught me in her arms. "When we were beginning to know you!" she cried softly, and laid her mouth upon mine. Water welled from her eyes. It tasted salt.

Neptune Diary

The discoveries of science and the achievements of technology have not come about through the waving of magic wands, nor will this happen in the future. We feel our way step by step, we build stone by patiently shaped stone. The great illuminations guide us, those that have come to the likes of Newton, Lavoisier, Einstein, Planck, Schrödinger, Darwin, Watson and Crick, but they are few and we have just as much need for the lesser lights kindled by many and many a lesser worker. Popular accounts of science are all very well, but we can't really begin to understand the universe until we have some idea of how people go about seeking the knowledge.

Besides, it's far from dull. I've been as thrilled by a spectrogram, an electron micrograph, or the excavation of a prehistoric site as by the awesome liftoff of a Saturn Five, bound for the Moon. Here's an eyewitness account of one event in one years-long endeavor. It relates unimportant, day-by-day, personal happenings, because I want to convey a sense of the scientific enterprise as an integral part of our everyday modern world—and also, to be sure, a sense of the "why," of science as a quest.

Monday 21 August 1989

THE PLANE SETS DOWN at Burbank about 3:30 P.M. Karen's right foot is temporarily in a cast, and she can barely struggle along a few yards at a time by leaning on a walker, but attendants graciously wheel her out of the terminal, as they did in Oakland. She waits while I collect our baggage and rent a car. We make our way over the freeways to Pasadena through square miles of concrete, poisoned air, and vicious traffic—a blasphemy against the stark beauty of the background mountains. Never mind Mars or Venus; when will greater Los Angeles be terraformed? Our motel room is a cave of refuge. It has a small refrigerator, for which I obtain food and, above all, beer.

The bad mood evaporates once we have proceeded to the California Institute of Technology campus. The writers' club at the Jet Propulsion Laboratory has organized a panel of science fiction writers here this evening. Various young people scurry around being helpful to us, and Voyager project historian Craig Waff appears with a wheelchair he has borrowed for Karen. Besides us, the speakers are Larry Niven, a fellow dealer in the hard stuff, and Robert Forward and moderator Tom McDonough, both working scientists who have written topflight fact as well as stories. Our topic is supposed to be the future of science fiction, but of course, like every such panel, we wander over the whole map, mainly wondering aloud about the future of humanity itself. Our audience is SRO, interested, and full of excellent questions. Afterward some of us go around to the Burger Continental for a late, huge dinner. On the whole, an auspicious beginning.

Tuesday

In the morning I rent another wheelchair and start learning how to push my wife around. Naturally, I was never opposed to such aids for the handicapped as ramps, graded curbs, and reserved parking spaces; but this makes me appreciate what an advance in civility they represent.

We drive to the Jet Propulsion Laboratory. It's a sprawling complex of buildings, housing any number of space-related endeavors, operated by Caltech for NASA. We've obtained press credentials for the meeting of Voyager 2 and Neptune, as we did for virtually every Voyager encounter plus the Viking landings. Assuredly, we didn't want to miss this one. It will be the last of its kind in our lifetimes. Oh, yes, Magellan is off to Venus and Galileo is to start its long-way-around Jupiter journey in a couple of months, and they will be boundlessly revealing and exciting, but what is now drawing to a close was unique.

Also because of our friends. There's nothing like being on the spot as the data come in day by day, hour by hour, and the scientists try to puzzle out what each astonishment means. It's brought forth its own groupies, who have come to know one another over the years, sharing the wonder of it. Some are journalists, whose favorite assignments these have been. Some are science fiction writers like us. After all, during the long quiet times between the spectacular events, mainly they have kept the vision shining. We've earned our front-row seats.

We reach Von Kármán Auditorium as the daily ten o'clock press conference is finishing. A couple of the team, the investigators who maintain the principal liaison, Norman Haynes, Bradford Smith, Edward Stone, Charles Kohlhase, are still on hand, still buttonholed by the newsfolk who swarm around. We meet, once again, science fact writers Patrick Moore and Joel Davis, artist Joel Hagen, old-time fictioneer Dwight Swain. Jonathan Eberhart, more or less the dean of the press corps here, is also perforce on wheels, in his case an electric cart. He easily crosses a thick TV cable that gives me some difficulty. "Well, he has more power than you do," says somebody to Karen. "I resent that!" I exclaim.

We've come to witness the discoveries, but not to write about them especially. Given our publisher's lead time, when our piece appears the readers will know far more about Neptune than we do today, or will even at the end of the week. What we'd like to do is convey a sense of the people, the place, what goes on, the Earthside reality.

The remembered Voyager prototype still occupies a wall of the auditorium. One is apt to think of it as "the little spacecraft that could"—that, a dozen years en route, most of its equipment obsolete and some incapacitated, has nevertheless sailed through the solar winds, adventuring past three great planets with their moons and rings and now a fourth, humanity's questing small avatar—but actually its size is quite impressive. Opposite it is a model of the latest flyby orbit, a blue globe and a curving luminous tube. The choicest of the pictures already transmitted and recreated are posted on a bulletin board. After the mysterious blandness of Uranus, Neptune seems nearly homelike, with clouds and a dark spot perhaps akin to the red one on Jupiter.

Another project historian conducts a brief film interview with us. That department must really be thoroughgoing.

The adjacent press room is jam-packed. So is the main cafeteria when we go for some lunch. This occurrence has drawn even more than its share of reporters from around the world. Is this partly because August is notoriously a news-empty month? We hope and believe the public is genuinely interested, and that the remarks we keep hearing about "What does this mean to Joe Sixpack?" are mere snobbery. A man from CNN opines to us that this is so, provided there are pictures; words alone won't do.

A section of the cafeteria has been set aside for the press. Thus we can eat in relative peace and quiet, watching real-time transmissions on an outsize screen. Streamers of white cloud trail past the dark spot, as if wind-blown around a terrestrial mountain.

Memories . . . Here we sat thirteen years ago, among our sort, throughout a long night until that first picture from Mars unrolled, line by line, before the eyes of Robert Heinlein. . . . This time, we seem to be very nearly the only members of the tribe on hand. To be sure, the actual encounter is days away.

After lunch, weariness overtakes me and I catch a nap in the shade of a grassy hollow. A plaque records that in an arroyo nearby, Theodore Von Kármán and a few of his students long ago tested the midget rocket motor with which this all began.

Later Karen wants to visit the employee shop to buy souvenirs. The hill to whose top I must push her was not the longest and steepest this side of San Francisco, but soon becomes so. Stiffen the sinews, summon up the machismo, and *get* her there.

A four o'clock, back in the auditorium, we attend an informal press conference, where everybody simply clusters around several scientists who discuss their work and answer questions. The topic today is Neptune's rings. They're still a riddle. Is the outer one actually complete, or is it a set of arcs, and what do you mean by "arc," anyway? No doubt in retrospect, when the truth is known, this won't seem like much; but at the moment it's emotionally tremendous. "To travel hopefully is better than to arrive."

Wednesday

Coolish overcast weather, a blessing to wheelchair horses. We are in time for the 10 A.M. briefing. Unlike previous encounters, this one is so crowded that those who don't have daily deadlines to meet are requested to stay out of Von Kármán and follow the proceedings on the big screen in the cafeteria. A telephone hookup allows us to ask questions too. More and more stuff has been coming in. Ed Stone describes the oddly skewed magnetic field of Neptune, the ring arcs—fewer than were hitherto thought to be—and the mapping of the planet's weather. Brad Smith says that the images newly received had his team jumping up and down. They show a lesser dark spot, the cloud patterns change remarkably fast, this is a lively world indeed. It has a tenuous inner ring, and the "arcs" do seem to be clumps in a continuous outer one; but what causes the bunching? Triton has become a mottled disc with dark areas and a section whose blueness may be due to light scattering by tiny solid particles. May be. We'll wait and see!

Somebody asks about Voyager 1, which headed north from Saturn. Stone explains that it's some twenty astronomical units off the ecliptic, therefore not much help in predicting the solar wind at Neptune. But Pioneer 10 (memories of that first astounding news from

Jupiter) is still in the planetary plane, and what it has learned gives clues to understanding what Voyager 2 now reports. Our argosies out yonder.

When the conference is over, we go look at the latest pictures. Two or three are utterly beautiful by any standard. At lunch we fall into conversation with Dwight and Joyce Swain, and catch one of the hourly televised updates, interviews with selected scientists about their specialties. Al Hibbs MCs it, another familiar face, though this time he doesn't do all of them. We hear that he came out of retirement for the occasion. Voyager has not been long under way in historical time, and in cosmic time it's been less than an eyeblink, but for humans the years add up fast.

We feel our own a bit, and no four o'clock is scheduled, so we decide to go back to our place and relax. As I remark to a couple of journalists on our way out, nothing much will be going on for the rest of the day, just detailed views of entire worlds never before beheld like this.

In the evening we meet Rick Foss and his wife. He arranged our trip to Perú and the Galápagos several years ago, and is working on one to Hawaii for the 1991 solar eclipse. Dinner is at the Parkway Grill, highly to be recommended. Greater LA does have some places, besides JPL and the County Museum, worth a pilgrimage.

Thursday

The mild gray weather continues. We take it easy in the morning, but catch the tail end of the ten o'clock and the update that follows. Word is that a number of press badges have been lost and others forged; everybody must be reidentified. While waiting in line, I find myself giving a verbal interview to a reporter who must be hard up for copy. No, I do not believe that the surface of the Uranian moon Miranda was so strangely rearranged by aliens as a message to us. The new tags are less attractive than the old and my name is misspelled, but what the hell.

More grumbling arises from the fact that Vice President Quayle will come here and speak tomorrow morning. Now we know why that stand is being erected on the grounds. The Secret Service will be everywhere and, we hear, will block off all the convenient freeway exits. A disruption and distraction; soon a cartoon circulates and a placard appears in the press room, neither one complimentary. I daresay he means well.

At lunch, I meet an engineer who's on the Magellan project. We last saw each other at one of those magnificent parties Joe Green threw after the Apollo launches. (There too we science fiction types went as journalists. The press box is a better viewing site than the VIP section.) He likes my writing, and I'm an ardent fan of his kind of work, so we're both happy.

At the four o'clock, among the team members fielding questions is a geologist from the Vernadsky Institute in Moscow, a pleasant and witty man. We'll take this as a favorable omen.

Charles Sheffield has arrived, and now Greg Bear does, our son-in-law, together with Astrid. What will her unborn daughter think of having been here today? This night's the climax, when the spacecraft passes over the north pole of Neptune and close to Triton, before lining out for the Big Deep.

Ron Williams, who chairs the JPL writers' club, has left a message. He has kindly assembled a schedule of activities, inside and outside the lab, for us. I toil uphill to his office and collect it, alone. Karen was warned she'd get just a single trip to the store. However, it's close by, and I obtain the mug she failed to remember. Coffee from it will taste special.

Joel Davis joins us and the Bears and we go out to dinner at a Hamburger Hamlet. Good food, and ah, that schooner of Bass Ale! No alcohol on the JPL premises, obviously.

Returning there, we hang around Von K., gabbing with people and watching the updates, which hour by hour grow more stirring. Eventually we seek the cafeteria, which is open late, for a soda and the big screen. Triton is already looking wonderfully weird. Time was when we'd have spent the night, as many do; but we are no longer young, and even the Bears at last call it quits. About 2 A.M. we make for bed. The remaining marvels can wait till tomorrow.

Friday

Avoiding politicians, we take a swim, then go downtown for Danish sandwiches and the Planetfest. This has been organized by the Planetary Society in the Pasadena Center, three days of exhibits, movies, lectures, and more, including the updates and real-time transmissions. Karen in her wheelchair can't well see much, though, and presently we shift to JPL, where we listen to some tentative explanations of the fantastic Tritonian landscape. Thereafter we catch a nap in our motel. We'll need it.

Jerry and Roberta Pournelle are giving a party this evening. We arrive early, only Harry Turtledove ahead of us, but soon the place is abuzz. Virginia Heinlein is looking great. Fred Pohl and his wife Elizabeth Hull, Gregory Benford and his wife, his twin brother Jim, David Brin, Vernor Vinge, Marvin Minsky, John McCarthy—the list could go on for a long paragraph, including people already encountered. Gary and Ann Hudson tell me how their space launch company is faring. Robert Bloch tells me he's fed up with screenwriting and back to doing real stories. Publisher Tom Doherty says enthusiastic things about my forthcoming novel. Well, he's a natural-born enthusiast. Jerry recalls our sailing days of long ago and suggests a trip to the desert or someplace; we aren't really old, not yet. Why, look at Jack Williamson over there, damn near immune to time.

It's a grand occasion, but Karen and I leave before midnight. Tomorrow will be another long day.

Saturday

Yesterday a lot of VIPs were at JPL, more or less in connection with Mr. Quayle's visit. Today others have been similarly invited, including the science fiction folk. We have the better bargain.

At the entrance we're issued special badges and a lady escorts us some distance to one of the new cafeterias. Its cavernous interior has been equipped with a multitude of chairs, a podium, giant screens, and tables where a breakfast and later a lunch buffet are offered. As Karen and I enter, a speaker has begun to recount the history of the Voyager mission. He's excellent, and no matter how often beheld, the slides are stunning. Then the ten o'clock conference comes on, and lasts for nearly two hours. Our readers will have seen it all by the time this comes before them, the amazements and splendors, but for us today they are newborn, full of fire. I never leave my seat.

The conference gives way to images from afar and I go fill a plate. Joe Haldeman says he has some beer in his car, out in the parking lot. He is a gentleman and a scholar. I walk there with him,

Jack Williamson, and Charlie Sheffield, and we stand around drinking it and talking good talk.

After our return, excitement comes only in spurts, when something new appears on the screens. Mostly we're all in various conversations. A charming young electrical engineer, an employee doubling as a hostess, occupies much of my time and that of several other men. Karen renews acquaintance with Terry Adamski, whom we first knew as a wide-eyed kid in the Los Angeles Science Fantasy Society. Now his title is spacecraft operations manager, and he's helped keep Voyager on course for all these years. Gossip turns to those scientists who've been prominent on television and in the papers. The press has its own favorites among them, but staff members say that, while X's people will do anything to make him happy, Y is too full of himself. Humans questing spaceward remain obstinately human.

The last holdouts among the guests are politely dismissed at five.

Not far away, Neola Caveny and my quondam backpacking partner Paul Turner are holding open house. We find Paul and Jim Benford in the hot tub; the view is equally Californian, rugged hills and canyons, reaching out to Catalina Island on a clear day. Jim, Vernor, and I are soon arguing about Fermi's question ("Where are they?") and the future of life and machines in general. Later Paul shows us an elaborate chart of the interacting factors likely to prove important to space development, and later still I meet its creator. A quiet party but a fine one, the perfect ending to our venture.

Sunday

It wasn't quite. The JPL writers' club has a brunch at a Mexican restaurant, which we and the Bears attend for an enjoyable couple of hours. The lady who sits across from us has also been with Voyager, in charge of the scan platform's troubled motor. She tells us that when she entered college she was interested in aerospace engineering but didn't know that it existed as a major. Since in science fiction the heroes were oftener physicists than engineers, she went into physics. It qualified her for this. Hers is not the only such case. We do not live or work in vain.

Afterward Karen wants to pay a final visit to the lab. When we get there, Brad Smith is holding forth before a small group of reporters, describing the newest interpretation of the newest findings about Triton. Nitrogen geysers! We look at the pictures. Neptune may have as many as five rings. We chat with a couple of friends, catch a couple of updates. The last one, before we say goodbye, consists of technical material, spectra, impact counts, temperature profiles, the kind of hard data from which knowledge grows—such stuff as dreams are made on.

Requiem for a Universe

Everything is linked to everything else. (At least, it is within any given light cone, and conceivably even beyond, if certain new ideas about causality violation turn out to hold some truth.) Consequences have consequences. Quantum theory suggested the possibility of what we now call the transistor, which presently brought on the computer revolution. That is still going on, for better *and* for worse, and in fact accelerating. We do not know when or where it will finally level off, or what transformations it will have wrought. I don't believe anybody, no matter how well-versed and boldly imaginative, can predict it.

Here is one suggestion about one possible development, in itself probably rather minor, but touching on our theme of human interaction with the rest of the cosmos. Again, I regard the story as fairly hard science fiction, however far-fetched it may seem.

T HIS IS NOT MY story, but David Rhys can't tell it. Nor can I, except in a ghostly way. The words are lacking, and still more is the understanding. Maybe that's as well. He understood, just a little, and it sent him over the edge. Even so, humankind needs to hear.

Is the story true? He who replies to that is either a fool or wise beyond all wisdom of our race. The question forever haunts us: "What is truth?" Certainly these things did not happen as your birth has happened and your death will. Think, though, of a mathematical theorem. Its truth, its meaning, exists apart from any material reality; it is false only if, somewhere, it contradicts itself, disavows the logic from which it sprang. Then there are the truths uttered by poetry and by music. I think Rhys' story comes nearest to those; but you must judge for yourself.

It entered my life through a call in the middle of the night. I didn't hear, being too heavily asleep. No matter exercise regimen and biochemical control, the body takes much time to regain full strength after a year in space. Laura woke, and left our bed immediately to answer. After that separation, we wanted to be together in peace, and had set the phone to respond exclusively to messages that the program deemed we must receive. Among the codes for that was the name "David Rhys."

The image was another woman's, Marie Fontenay, neuropsychiatrist in Paris, calling from Grenoble. While I talked with her—we found we did best in Spanish—Laura made coffee. We two had taken a primitive cottage away off on Kauai, to be alone with sea and sand, flowers and sun and rainbows. It felt good to do things for ourselves. Especially it did to me. A linker lives mostly among abstractions. Laura teaches history at an elementary school in California. No computer yet built, no program yet written can do for children what a living person can, if she has the gift and their parents can afford her salary.

"Thanks," I said to her. "Much needed. I'm off for Honolulu in an hour."

She studied my face a moment before she murmured, "Bad, hm?"

"Bad enough that they're sending a suborbital to bring me to France. 'They' being the Institute of Holothetics, and the rocket lent by the Peace Command."

"Why *you*?" For an instant her question hurt, then I realized she wasn't implying I was merely a linker. After all, my sort aren't many either. But the few, few holothetes do differ from us not just in degree, but in kind. If we linkers are like high priests in the temple of science and technology, they are like its gods; and often what they have to tell the faithful is perforce Delphic.

The kona was rich and reviving on my tongue. "Well, since I am an old friend of Dave's and we've worked together in the past, Jeanie—his wife, that is, not their daughter—thought I'll have some chance of guessing what went wrong and what can be done about it." Grimly: "If anything can. He's—catatonic? Fontenay, the doctor, says the brain scans show no organic damage but every trace of a traumatic, absolutely devastating impact. And Dave was—he's always had more psychic strength than most people." Otherwise he could not have done what he did, been what he was, my thought went on.

"Why must you go in person?"

"Same reason I had to be in space. They couldn't build the Galactic Analyzer and get it operating properly without a linker; and the communications channels weren't adequate to connect me across fifty astronomical units. . . . I'm sorry. I'm still too dazed to know when I'm quacking forth the obvious."

"You're on Earth now," she protested.

"And the channels aren't adequate either. Fontenay said a technician on the project told her. You see, I'll have to examine Dave's program."

"It's too complex for transmission in a reasonable time?" She shook her head and whistled. Sudden terror struck. She grabbed my arm. "Be careful! It could hurt you too."

"Fontenay thinks not." I'd have been more honest to say she hoped not. "They haven't called in another holothete because she is afraid of what it might do to him or her. A linker can't have the same experience." What song the sirens sang could not lure mariners who were tone-deaf.

She clung to me. "I've got to go," I told her: in friendship and in my pride.

So she talked with gallant merriment while our car flew us to Honolulu Interplanetary, and kissed me fiercely before I boarded the rocket. Oh, I had reasons aplenty to be careful.

Acceleration was tough on flesh not reaccustomed to Earth gravity, but the arc was altogether soft. I floated in my harness, hearing silence as if it were a presence, hearing the blood pulse within me, and looked at the outviewer. Stars gleamed multitudinous and winter-cold through a crystalline darkness. When I touched a control, vision swung toward the planet. We were coming around to dayside, and heaven was a blue-and-gold coronet on swirling vastnesses of cloud. Below their virginal white I saw land on ocean, malachite set in turquoise. How beautiful is this world our mother. How far from her had the soul of David Rhys wandered?

The crew saw I wanted to think and left me undisturbed. My thoughts were not of programs, however, nor in computer language. They dwelt on Rhys.

The popular mind supposes holothetes are all cold fish. It's true they are apt to be a little awkward socially, and over the years some grow eccentric to the point of what looks like madness. You cannot work with, live in, the Absolute, which is inhuman, and leave the strangeness of it wholly behind when you uncouple from your machine. But not the less do you remain a child of Earth. No less than your sisters and brothers can you know pain, jubilation, fear, wishfulness, anger, love.

Apart from those rare gifts which made it possible for him to become a holothete, Rhys was simply a decent man. Off work, he enjoyed gardening, carpentry, a half-liter in the pub after a day's hike in the woodlands around Snowdon; he played violin in an amateur chamber orchestra; he voted Constructive and worried about too much loss of national autonomy to the World Union; no linguist, he had trouble with his Spanish on international hookups but slogged good-naturedly ahead anyway; his artistic idols were Shelley, Monet, and Berlioz, though most commonly projected in his house were astronomical images and old folk tunes. I'd several times been a guest in that house. It held a happy family.

Now and then he did drift out of touch, into lordly half-memories; and he admitted that the great psychological writers left him wondering what the shootin' was for. ("An Americanism, in your honor, Jack," he'd laughed; and I'd replied, "Hey, while the shooting was going on over there, my ancestors were picking cotton in Alabama.") The price did not seem overly high for being at one with everything science has learned. I tried hard not to envy him. He must have sensed that, for once in conversation he quietly pointed out that the demands on linkers are as hard in their fashion, and the need for us is basic. "Your eyes process more data, but your ears hear what people say, and that matters most."

Had it been his humanness which made him vulnerable to whatever the thing was he encountered?

A car with an attendant waited for me at Lyon and flitted me to Grenoble. That man was employed at the Institute's laboratory there, but knew nothing about the disaster. Since it wasn't in the news, I realized powerful persons wanted it kept secret for a while. Well, when you have a problem subtle and frightening, you're better off without journalists.

The man took me to a suite in the residential building, helped me settle in, and advised me to rest before reporting. "No," I said. "My impression is that this won't keep. It's early afternoon here. Thank you, señor, and good day."

I did ache. My head and eyelids felt full of sand. An antifatigant took care of that, but it was blessed to lean back into a lounger's embrace and sip a cup of bouillon I'd sent the errand cart to get me. While the phone searched for Marie Fontenay, my gaze went out the window. The compound occupies a hill with a view over the medieval city, the river, green countryside, distant Alpine snowpeaks. Even stronger than seeing Earth from space, a scene like this brings to me the sense of home, that here is where we belong.

Fontenay was in conference at the hospital when the communications found her, but left as soon as she heard I'd arrived and called me from an office. Her head nearly leaped out of my screen, haggard with stress, vivid with purpose. "Ah, Sr. Henry," she greeted almost brusquely. "Welcome. Are you prepared to commence?"

I nodded. "How is Rhys?" My throat tightened up.

"I will show you. He is in a private room in the neurological ward." The hologram transmuted itself.

It was a full scan. The thin blanket did not hide how stiffly my friend lay, not quite straight, congealed in a convulsion. I touched for a closeup. His face was white and likewise locked—against what? His eyes were open but blank—staring at what? I reached forward as if I could stroke the time-faded blond hair. But that was for Jeanie, when she visited yonder hushed place. Surely she kept vigil somewhere in town, or soon would.

I switched back to Fontenay, and was grateful to her for continuing the impersonal tone: "It is a state of total fugue. He had an experience he could not bear, and fled from awareness. We have completed the molecular tests and found no genetic predisposition. Therefore the experience must have been terrible indeed."

"What, uh, prognosis?"

"I do not know. His brain has full capability but refuses to use it. That is clinically well-known, but the form it has taken here is unique." She scowled. "Studying the encephalograms and other indicators, I have been tempted to diagnose the condition as active rather than passive—part of him desperately threshing about in search of what might save him—It is childish of me, at least in my present ignorance."

"You can't haul him out of the trance? Drugs, electropulses—"

"I am afraid to try. It could destroy him completely. This *is* a defense mechanism. And we know little yet about the psychodynamics of holothetics. Remember, he was stricken while in the program." Fontenay drew breath. "On the other hand, if we do nothing, that probably means just a slower destruction. He cannot long maintain such tension and—yes, I will say it—grief. The indicators of overwhelming sorrow are unmistakable. He will become either a madman or a vegetable. My rather wild hope is that you can find a clue to what might help."

"What happened, exactly?"

"We'll make full recordings available to you, audiovisual as well as computer. Briefly, he had been engaged for about seven hours— that seemed unduly long, but it was an unprecedentedly ambitious undertaking and he had expected several lengthy sessions—when he began to show distress. At first, irregular breath; soon, moans and small jerky motions; all at once, screaming and flailing about. A linker was present and in circuit too. He did not participate in the actual program, which would have been distracting to Rhys, but stood guard on the electronics. A microvariation in line voltage, anything like that, would have disrupted the intricate process, he tells me. Nothing untoward had occurred. Being thus only partially engaged, he observed the trouble, cut off the entire operation, and called for help." Sternly: "Yes, he knew that may harm a person in the circuit, but after watching the tapes—that is a wise routine, making them—I agree the emergency justified his action. Rhys' tetany became rigidity, and in it he remains."

"I'll judge for myself," I said with care. "First, however, have you anything more to tell me? Anything you can imagine might be significant?"

Fontenay sat quiet until: "Look closely at the last few seconds before the shutdown. Was—is Rhys a religious man, Sr. Henry?"

"No, except that, well, he scarcely ever talked about it, but I have heard him say he walked in awe. And—let me think—yes, he told me his parents were churchgoers, and took him when he was a boy. Why do you ask?"

" 'The living God!' " she answered in English. Returning to Spanish: "That was what he cried out. His only real words. After them, coma. Does this suggest anything to you?"

"No," I admitted low. "But—you know, you haven't told me what he was working on, and I haven't thought to ask. What is it?"

Again she hesitated before she made response. "The biography, from beginning to end, the origin and fate, of the universe."

I spent the rest of that day familiarizing myself with the huge new mainframe computer at the heart of the laboratory. Nothing less could have made possible the project the Galilean Society commissioned and Rhys undertook. Strange it was to lie back in the same lounger he had used and adjust on my head the same helmet.

Electromagnetic induction joined my brain to the machine, and for a time beyond time I lost any forebodings. I almost forgot why I was there. The power of intellect that was mine outshone and overrode all else. In the words of a writer, among the many who have tried to describe what linkage is like, I was drunk on sanity.

The instrument and I were one. We shared its world-spanning nanosecond access to every datum ever entered in molecular memory units; its nearly light-speed scan, selection, and integration of what we needed; its quadrillionfold mathematical and logical operations within an eyeblink; . . . my human creativity, flexibility, initiative, awareness. *I* was our program, which continuously rewrote itself, which had no hidden flaws to take us astray because it was not composed beforehand by an outsider but evolved in action. Not that I was conscious of this. I did it. I was it.

Think of a man running. That is so intricate and changeable a set of motions, within a context of circumstances so enormous and unpredictable, that we have never built a robot able to do it half as well. Even our organics are poor, clumsy parodies. But the man runs. He doesn't know how; he doesn't have to; his entire body knows for him.

Like such an athlete, I strained toward my goal and exulted in my strength. And today I was mighty beyond anything I had known before. For the span of this linkage, mine was the greatest intelligence in the whole of humanity.

Warming up, I calculated a few hundred Bessel functions to several hundred decimal places. It was trivial, done in an instant. Rather than take the information out of the database, I decided for myself the exact configurations that various large protein molecules must needs have, and put them through their chemical paces. I became conversant with neurology and related disciplines. Thereupon I dismissed them, aside from a small amount left in my brain in order that I could later talk seriously with Fontenay. More congenial was a problem in astrophysics, practice for efforts to come. I established arbitrary initial conditions—gas and dust distributions, galactic location, ambient force fields—and ran off the development of the system that resulted. Matter condensed, nuclear fires kindled, a new star brightened; planets formed; geology did its work; atmospheres brewed each its special weathers, and also altered with millions and billions of years; and these happenings were inevitable from the beginning. Yet often and often as I watched the unfolding of my logic, I was surprised.

Does God feel thus? I don't presume to guess. I didn't look into life, though one of my imaginary words was bound to engender it. To this day, too much is unknown about that. I could have imposed conditions more detailed, but following out their consequences would have taken time we could ill afford, when Rhys lay in hell.

Disconnecting at last, returning to mere flesh, always leaves me with a sense of desolation, unutterable loss. I have to remember what is best in my days, such as Laura, and go out and savor the world around me, before I can again be content with what I am.

"Frankly, I consider the project lunatic," Fontenay declared when I phoned her in the morning. "An ancient Greek would tell us your friend was stricken down for his hubris."

"No, it's a perfectly respectable scientific idea," I replied. "Something went ghastly wrong, but that was unforeseeable."

"Exactly! What can we, for all of our proud instruments and theories, foresee? Without a solid basis of facts, thought is empty, mere noise. And what do we actually know about the universe, as immeasurably huge and old as it is?" She spread her hands and shrugged her shoulders in the French fashion. "Nothing!"

"That isn't true. Pardon me, but it isn't. We have instruments throughout the Solar System, farther than Pluto. Their precision is limited only by quantum uncertainties built into nature. They study planets of the nearer stars, supernovae in the remotest galaxies, and everything between. Since the unified field theory was worked out, and that was over a century ago, we've had a clear understanding of the structure and behavior of matter, energy, space-time, and the dimensions beyond. The fact that hardly any people are able to learn it in its entirety just proves that the Ultimate is not like the everyday environment our evolution has fitted us for. In linkage, I've employed the theory easily. It predicts what our physicists and astronomers observe, and nothing that contradicts their observations. So we're being entirely reasonable when we use it to make deductions about things we cannot observe, such as the distant past or the far future."

"And?" The note of scorn lingered.

"Well, we know the universe originated as a quantum fluctuation about twenty billion years ago. We know the primordial fireball expanded, that the cellular distribution of galactic clusters was the work of energy concentrations we call strings, that most matter is nonluminous particles in space. Nevertheless, the mass is insufficient to close the universe. It will expand forever."

She stopped me with an impatient chopping gesture. "I am aware of this, Sr. Henry. Every educated person is. But the totality of galaxies, those mutable energies and particles you speak of, in a space-time whose wave front has been expanding at the speed of light for twenty billion years—no, you *cannot* handle it. Could the sheer volume have overloaded Rhys?"

Not bothering to correct her physics, I shook my head and answered, "No. We do have our failures, we computermen. Usually they're due to inadequate data, but occasionally the problem proves to be too big—or, rather, inappropriately formulated. We realize that after a while and quit. It's scarcely worse than a similar frustration in ordinary life."

"I spoke figuratively. Of course I have an acquaintance with your profession, as far as a nonlinker can. In fact, I wonder why he wrestled as long as he did with his nonsensical, impossible task."

"Because it isn't. Certainly nobody supposes we can deal with countless individual stars—or galaxies or clusters. In linkage yesterday, I reviewed the entire project to date, from the original proposals and studies to the final schematics. It requires a lot of mathematics to follow. In essence, though, the plan is, was, to take our theoretical structure, plug in what relevant empirical data we possess, and compute the consequences. Not in detail, obviously. On the broadest scale, the cosmos as a whole. We don't need to know what single molecules in the air are doing to understand the weather. The dynamics of the mass suffices. Likewise for the universe. That's what the instigators, the sponsors, and David Rhys intended."

Fontenay frowned. "But the objective?"

"Why, to check out our knowledge. To see if the calculated course of events made sense. If it didn't, if it yielded an absurdity, we'd know there was an error somewhere in our concepts." I attempted a smile. "Then, as we say in America, it would have been back to the drawing board."

Perhaps the archaic phrase puzzled her, for she began to ask, "What—" and broke off with: "Thank you. I suspected something like this, but wanted clarification. Now what do you suggest we do?"

I gathered courage to tell her: "What I am going to do is link

with the record Rhys left. I mean to follow him down whatever road
it was he walked."

I couldn't really, and was glad of that. A linker is not a holothete.
It's hard to explain the difference, immense though it be. Every
linkage involves creativity; that is the reason for it. Through his or
her peculiar, intensely trained gift, a holothete has such mastery as
to confer on the system a creative imagination.

I can dream the seed of a planetary system and apply the mathematical laws of physics to make it flower. I cannot change those
laws if they seem faulty—not, and continue making sense. Rhys
could. Analogy: I am a competent professor of the subject, he was
Einstein.

Another analogy: The world outside our skins is real, but what
we directly experience is our sensory impressions. From those we
infer—we construct—sunlight, trees, lovers, everything. We do this
on so deep, instinctive a level that we can properly say we experience
these things themselves. But an atom or a galaxy is too alien, too
remote from what our race has evolved amidst. Such must always be
abstractions, consciously formed, never felt or understood as we feel
and understand our dear immediate realities—unless we are holothetes in linkage.

From the molecules of the database I would summon up the
vast program Rhys had written as he went along. I would replay it
and dimly, partially, distortedly know what had passed through him.
My purblindness was my armor. This I must hope.

Creation began.
From emptiness, the fireball bloomed. It was not the first, nor would
it be the last. Limitlessly throughout the omnicontinuum, indeter-
minacy brought forth universes. No two of them were akin. That was
the most I knew. Necessity made them be, but they were unreachable. Nothing whatsoever could pass between. I was alone in this
cosmos which was mine.

Outward and outward the energy storm raged. Yet there was
never a primordial chaos. In that supernal surging, the very laws of
nature changed, like foam on the back of a wave. Unity broke asunder; dimensions twisted, cast themselves wide or shrank toward nul-
lity; the single force became four; the speed at which attainable space

fled from itself dwindled to that of light, which was flung into existence like spindrift blown off the crest of the wave. And all, all was contrapuntal, its majesty wholly foreordained.

Billions upon billions of nanoseconds passed. The fundamental particles formed. Antimatter went its way; the imbalance that would drive the future was manifest. A seething sea of hydrogen and helium mingled with darker material. It cooled as it widened until its radiation roar was a whisper. One-dimensional cables hauled it on the currents of their dissolution. It gathered in monstrous many-layered configurations, millions of light-years apart from each other.

Quiescence fell.

The cold and the dark entered into my spirit. Creation had ended.

No. Not altogether. Glimmers awoke, faint and tiny. The gas was falling in on itself. Galactic clusters coalesced, proto-galaxies, the earliest stars. From their atoms, gravitation evoked the other three forces, and light was reborn. The suns were furnaces forging the higher elements, as high as iron. The greatest of them exploded in supernova glory, and out of their deaths came nuclei new and strange. Dust lanes dimmed a little the shining spirals; but this was dust that went into younger suns, and worlds of theirs, and upon some of those worlds, life.

But how feeble this was, how swiftly the gigayears fell away. Time is not a fixed, marked rod; it is events. Harking back to those first furious hours, I now found only the gasps of a thing that was dying. While old stars burned out and ever fewer came into being, I meditated on the paradox that a closed universe, fated to reach an ultimate size and then contract until the fireball blazes afresh, gives any dwellers in it an infinite future: for the closer it draws to the end, the more manyfold, diverse, and swift are its changes.

Huge stars collapsed to black holes, which light itself could no longer escape. Whole galaxies did, and devoured those around them. After a trillion years, the last members of the last generation of energy-hoarding dwarfs flickered out. And there was darkness.

Space expanded onward into silence. Perhaps weird forms of life huddled near some few black holes, drawing nourishment from the infall. I could not know, nor did I care. They too were doomed.

Flashes in the night—Black holes must also perish. Quantum

tunneling erodes them: the smaller they are, the faster. Finally these death-rattles likewise ended.

Matter itself was vanishing. Quantum accident made black holes of atoms, and photons of those. Wavelengths stretched as they wearied until radiation guttered toward its own extinction. It took time, oh, yes, for any such event was an unimaginably seldom thing; but because of that sparsity, a billion billion billion years were to me as a solitary heartbeat.

When a black hole was entirely gone, the singularity at its core strayed naked. There natural law was annulled and anything could happen. Nothing did, for nothing was left. It was simply that law was going out with all else.

What meaning had the whole thing had? It was a senseless upwelling of randomness, sinking back to the zero whence it came.

If ours could have been a closed universe! They existed. The same blind chance made that certain. But ours was too small, and therefore condemned to grow infinite.

Adrift in frozen doomsday, I knew what shattered Rhys. It was hard enough on me; an infinitesimal part of my mind thought I'd need Fontenay's help to rid me of nightmares. And I was like a boy listening to a man tell of a war he has suffered. Rhys had *known*, had *been* this hopelessness. It overcame him in a rush, before he could comprehend and break free, as a black hole drinks light. This was our fatal arrogance, that we supposed a man can behold our destiny and live.

Almost, I released myself. I might be at hideous risk. But— something had come to him. I could not imagine what, here where everything had happened that was ever going to happen. Maybe it was no more than his flight from the unendurable. But while I was able, I would endure.

It came to me.

And the universe ended.

That is an arsenal powerful and delicate which Fontenay has at her command. Within hours I was sitting up in bed and talking rationally with her. She'd sought me in person, for wisdom is hers as well.

"His associate had the best of intentions," I said. "No way could he have realized that the worst possible thing was to stop the program. That's always hazardous, you know; the shock is considerable. This time it interrupted what might have saved him."

"Are you sure?" she asked in a subdued voice. "It seems . . . fantastic."

"No, I am not sure, and yes, the whole affair is fantastic," I answered. "What I have discovered is that there is, in fact, something missing in our cosmology. The logic showed this as inexorably as it traced the entire pattern that went before."

"His mind was disintegrating under stress. Hallucination—"

"That doesn't occur in linkage. If it could, and if it did in this case, I'd have recognized it as such—I, the detached observer, not the directly involved holothete." Which was not quite true of myself, I thought with a slight shudder. "Of course, logic is only as good as its postulates, but what we've found out is that ours have implications we never imagined. I'm not saying that whatever appeared is necessarily a construct corresponding to reality. I do think that probably it is. And at least it gives us a possibility of healing my friend."

She raised her brows. "How?"

Doubtless she anticipated what I'd say: "Put him back in circuit. I'll be in parallel, guiding his injured brain till it resurrects what it alone was able to . . . deduce, create, envision . . . and completes the sequence—draws the full conclusion that it was prevented from drawing—solves the riddle—whatever the answer may be.

"I admit the attempt may fail. It may permanently ruin his mind. But he hasn't much to lose, has he? And my hope is, from the glimpse I got, that going through with it can save him."

Marie Fontenay is an almighty brave person. She staked her reputation, her career, when she agreed to my counsel. Naturally, first she studied and thought. She got a holothete to analyze the neurology. Results were ambiguous. I have an idea that what persuaded her was what I had already related of that which Rhys met at the graveside of time.

Triumph. Splendor. Joy.

This is not my story, but David Rhys can't tell it. After his long convalescence he's eager to take up his work—more than eager, considering what we both believe is a revelation that logic gave unto him. However, he isn't an especially articulate man, outside of his profession. Nor can I find words that will serve. They don't exist. I must simply try.

I must simply proclaim that there in the abyss a flame appeared, and somehow it smiled and its spirit said with unbounded love: "Go home to my forebears and tell them all this was mistaken. They forgot about themselves."

John Campbell

I like to think John Campbell would have approved of that story. Although he wrote a few downbeat ones early in his career, and as an editor published some others, on the whole he was the great optimist. In his view, the scope of humanity included absolutely everything.

Already he is being forgotten; many readers have never heard of him. Yet he saved and regenerated science fiction. When he took over at *Astounding*, which he eventually renamed *Analog*, the field had fallen into a dismal state. With a few shining exceptions, it was the product of hack pulpsters. By his editorial policies and the help and encouragement he gave his writers (always behind the scenes), he raised both the literary and the intellectual standard anew. Whatever progress has since been made stems from that renaissance.

So at this point it seems right to pay him a small tribute. After all, it is our dreams that drive us, in our private lives, our work, our politics, our arts, and our science. These days, especially among the young, science fiction begets and nourishes dreams about the universe and the future.

IT IS NOT LIKELY that people who have entered the science fiction field within the past ten or fifteen years, whether as professionals, fans, or simply readers, will ever quite understand what John W. Campbell, Jr., meant to those of us who came earlier. Writers in particular will never again have the experience that we did. Though there may well be other great editors—in fact, there have already been two or three—still, nobody is going to create modern science fiction all over. That job has been done, and John Campbell was the man who did it.

I am not the best one to describe his impact. A person like Jack Williamson, who began working well before him but then came under his influence, would have the longest perspective. Equally valuable would be a study by one of the writers who developed under Campbell's aegis and went on to shape the Golden Age, such as Isaac Asimov, L. Sprague de Camp, Robert A. Heinlein, Theodore Sturgeon, and A. E. van Vogt. (Those names are by themselves ample support for my contention that *Astounding* and *Unknown* from about 1938 to about 1943 constituted the Golden Age of science fiction.) Unfortunately, none of them did, as far as I know, except sometimes in passing, and most of them are now gone from among us, so I must try.

Actually, I should doubtless be considered as belonging to the next generation, since my first published story appeared in 1947 and I didn't really start hitting any kind of stride till around 1950. While beginning with Campbell and, unlike some others, staying with him till the end, I soon came to do increasing amounts of work for different editors, of whom Anthony Boucher was the most important to me. Thus my qualifications to discuss this man are limited, and I propose to do it in a personal rather than scholarly vein.

As a lonely farm boy avidly reading his magazine, dreaming of writing professionally myself someday but never daring to imagine I might be good enough for him; later as a new recruit to his team; even later still, when most of my effort was directed elsewhere: I, like so many, found in John Campbell a towering father figure. It was he who assembled all these marvels, month after month, his editorials far from the least among them. It was he who bought or bounced my submissions to him, the latter usually for reasons that I had to admit were sound. It was he whose infrequent requests for changes always meant improvement, and who was an incredible fountainhead of brilliant ideas for new stories, which he gave away with both hands to whomever he thought might be interested. In short, since my real father had died young, Campbell equalled my mother as a shaping force on me in adolescence and early adulthood; he helped set the course of my life.

We hadn't had much contact, just short letters back and forth concerning manuscripts I'd sent in, when at last I met him in person. That was in the fall of 1951. Homeward bound after several months abroad, I stopped off for a while in New York. The hope of visiting him in his office was a major reason for that. He responded heartily to my diffident phone call and invited me over. A big man physically, who seemed to bulge out the walls of the cluttered cubicle where he and Kay Tarrant worked, he received me with his wonted cordiality and then, as was also his wont, plunged directly into his latest enthusiasm, which at the time happened to be psychology. "Here's a question for you," he flung at me around his Rooseveltian cigarette holder. "It requires a snap answer. Everybody dreads going insane, but people fear it for different reasons. What's yours?" When I in my astonishment mumbled something about the helplessness of that condition, he nodded with satisfaction. "What a person tells you is the opposite of what's most important to him," he said. "In your case, it's achievement." I don't know about that, and of course it's really just a parlor trick, but it's an interesting one to spring on your friends, and the responses are apt to be surprising.

Campbell couldn't give me his entire attention while I was

there; he had a job to do, after all. I well remember how an artist came in with the rough of a cover painting for a serial, which turned out to be set in a totalitarian future society. It showed an armed man in a spacesuit. Though he wasn't officially the art director, Campbell had cogent things to say, including: "Move the figure up so the logo will cover his face. That'll take all individual personality out of him." It was exactly right for that particular novel.

It chanced that during the next year and a half I was selling elsewhere. I didn't reappear in *Astounding* till January of 1953, but that was with a novella, "Un-Man," and there followed a fair number of other stories, among them "Sam Hall." I name these because they were written in the middle of the so-called McCarthy era and were both very "liberal," internationalistic, and vatic about the danger of American fascism. To my present way of thinking, this helps show that the McCarthy era was not quite the reign of terror that intellectual folklore maintains. However, fear did lead to some suppression, even in the tolerant realm of science fiction. Campbell might conceivably have gotten in trouble with his bosses for printing my tales and, indeed, giving them the cover. (In the event, he didn't. Street and Smith Publications seems to have exercised censorship only in the matter of sex, profanity, and the like. He might have, though.) Furthermore, he was himself a political conservative whose main objection to the Republican Party was that it no longer espoused social Darwinism.

The fact is that he never, never tried to impose his views on his writers; at most, he would turn down an offering because it contained a premise he believed was not merely unlikely, but flat-out absurd. Rather, he rejoiced as much when we writers came up with fresh sociological ideas as when we did with new speculations about science or technology.

As examples of how broadly this might range, consider the American theocracy and the libertarian order that succeeds it in Heinlein's "future history"; the foreign agents who are deliberately allowed to escape after they have almost managed to detonate an atomic bomb in New York, in Chan Davis' "The Nightmare"; forgiveness of the enemy as a national policy in Sturgeon's "Thunder and Roses"; any number of pieces by Mack Reynolds, who came to specialize in creating a variety of offbeat near-future worlds; harking back to my own case, the feudalism implicit in *The High Crusade*, the ultra-libertarian society of "Starfog," and chattel slavery as an accepted institution in *The Long Way Home*.

That last evidently touched off something notorious, which nevertheless typifies the man and how he often operated. In the novel, a born-and-bred slave, intelligent and well-educated, argues about it with the hero. He, an American from the distant past, is shocked to his guts at finding that humans are once again property. She replies that there is much to be said in favor of it, spells out her reasons, and ends by challenging him to tell her who is *not* a slave, one way or another. To me, this was simply a characterizing touch; I'm an Abolitionist from way back. However, it struck Campbell as a new insight, or at any rate a new heresy, such as he loved to come upon or create on his own. He wanted to stir his readers up to question everything, take nothing for granted, always think, in the true Socratic tradition.

Thus for a time he was pushing the idea that for many persons, in fact for many entire societies, slavery works better than universal freedom. I argued it hotly with him in our correspondence. Others, who saw a chance to make a quick sale, adopted it for narrative purposes, and readers got quite a rash of stories on the theme until, I presume, he decided it was used up.

You see, though he had keen literary judgment, of which more later, in his opinion the idea mattered above all else in science fiction. He'd buy an otherwise marginal thing if he felt it contained an interesting notion. Besides, he had a magazine to fill every month, and there aren't that many masterpieces produced annually. As a result, in his later years, when his was no longer the sole attractive market in the field, certain writers were doing little more than selling him back his editorials, and things often got dismal. Yet his personal creativity remained unabated, and toward the end he was again developing bright new talents and steering bright older ones in fresh directions.

He was an authoritarian only in the sense that he maintained, with his customary vigor, that some individuals are better fitted to lead than others. He delighted in argument, whether face to face or by mail, and then he was unfailingly courteous, in his bluff fashion, a good listener as well as talker. It pleased him boundlessly to see somebody take a position he'd taken, stand it on its head, and turn it inside out.

Among the ludicrous charges leveled against him was, once, anti-Semitism. Robert Silverberg and he had a good laugh about that, when the former was his most frequently selling writer, and worked out a new Silverberg pseudonym: Calvin M. Knox, with the world never told that the "M." stood for "Moses." Actually, Campbell's idea about the Jews was that, as the survivors of centuries of hardship and persecution, they must as a class be superior to the average human stock.

He seldom touched alcohol, just a little wine when a meal was special. At conventions, he didn't chase women or sing bawdy songs like several I could name. For many years his magazine was so chaste that it got to be a game among us low-minded types to see what violations we could smuggle in. George O. Smith's line about the original ball-bearing mousetrap—the tomcat—lives in fond memory because success was so rare. All this gave the editor the reputation of being a prude. He wasn't. His publishers were. As soon as he moved over to Condé Nast, the censorship lifted. Long before then, he'd printed and chuckled with me at the occasionally risqué Nicholas van Rijn stories.

The truth is that he was perfectly frank and relaxed about such things. If he didn't go in for the wild partying common in those days, it was because he found more interesting ways to spend his time. If he didn't throw around the coarse four-letter words, it was because, unlike today's young literati, he had a vocabulary large enough and precise enough that he didn't need to.

Most often, especially after he began taking up eccentric causes such as dianetics and psionics, he was called a crank. No doubt he did go off the deep end now and then—but a mind so widely and energetically exploring was bound to, by sheer statistics. He never claimed infallibility.

Rather, he demanded what he considered a reasonable amount of evidence, and when he had that, he simply advocated further research. For instance, there was his conduit dowser. I had been heavily skeptical of his claim that about half the population can locate buried pipelines with this rudimentary gadget. When I visited his home, he took me out in the back yard and asked me to try it. As I walked along, the freely swinging L-shaped wires suddenly clicked aside into alignment. It happened consistently at the same place. Afterward he showed me a dropoff at the end of the lawn where a drainpipe came out along that precise line. I have since made it work elsewhere. (To my wife's disappointment, she can't.) Yes, of course these aren't controlled experiments, but don't they suggest that it would be interesting to find out what is going on?

Meanwhile Campbell stayed fully abreast of the established sciences and had an extensive acquaintance among their leaders. In astronomy, physics, chemistry, biology, he was totally sound, merely feeling that we can't already have mastered everything nature has to teach us. The current revolution in them—ranging from phenomena associated with black holes and singularities to the newest upset in our figures for the geological age of the hominids—seems to bear him out. A long-time radio ham, he was highly skilled in electronics. Where it came to disciplines with less well-defined terms, such as anthropology and psychology, his suggestions could get quite radical. However, he knew what the specialists were doing. History was another interest of his. It is of mine, too, and we discussed it frequently and at length. While I was more apt than not to disagree with a particular interpretation he made of it, he had his facts straight.

In the rest of the liberal arts he was probably less well educated, but he was no ignoramus there either, and what the hell, nobody can learn everything. Certainly he had a wonderful sense for the English language. It seems obvious that Don A. Stuart (a pseudonym in his pre-editorial writing days) would, but I also remember, for example, how once in conversation he observed that all good prose has metrical structure and added casually that more than half of Heinlein's *Methuselah's Children* is in blank verse. An amateur photographer, he showed me pictures he had taken—no, composed—which really deserved to be in a gallery. His sensitivity to landscapes and the people in them caused him, in spite of his determined Scottishness, to fall in love with the Irish countryside.

His correspondence was fantastic. This was my chief contact with him, since for most of those years we had a continent between us. He is said to have sent letters rejecting stories which sometimes were longer than the stories themselves, stating his reasons and then happily pursuing whatever line of thought this had started up. I know he'd often mail me page after page of single-spaced commentary, ending with the famous oscillographic signature, whether he bought or not. He'd also pass on ideas that had occurred to him which he thought I might like to use in fiction. (Indeed, though he never took credit for it himself, many of the classics of science fiction originated as Campbell suggestions.) Once he even gave me an excellent, biting idea for a crime story, confessing that he could see no way to apply it to his magazine but thinking I might enjoy it anyhow. A lot of our correspondence, though, was just that, exchange of thoughts and facts for their own sakes, knock-down-drag-out arguments about things like politics, scientific and philosophical speculations, all fascinating and stimulating to me. Needless to say, I was far from the only person granted this extraordinary privilege.

John Campbell the human being I was slower to get to know. There was that geographical separation; there could be conflicting demands on his time when we did meet; there was a dearth of small talk, since he preferred impersonal topics. Nevertheless, year by year—

My wife and I visited him and his at their home in the course of a cross-country trip way back in 1959. They received us and gave us dinner with gracious if informal hospitality. Family business brought him out to our area once and he was briefly in our place; as he was leaving, our little daughter offered him her hand and I saw he was touched, though he took it with grave respect for the child's dignity. I was there—in fact, it happened I was a combatant—when he witnessed his first medieval tourney staged by the Society for Creative Anachronism, and his unabashed pleasure at the pageantry was moving to see. Sometimes at conventions, a few of us would get away from the tumult by dropping up to the Campbells' suite for some hours of conversation which might prove relaxed instead of challenging. And then, well, you can't exchange many thousands of words in letters with a person, over a couple of decades, and not start to glimpse the person himself.

Thus I gradually learned that beneath the forceful, prickly exterior was a warm, gentle, even shy soul. I began by being in awe of him, and ended by loving him. I am not ashamed to admit that when news of his death reached me, I wept. Then I went out and got a bottle of scotch—Teacher's, of course—and came home and put a pipe concert on the record player, and Karen and I waked him.

In Memoriam

He would probably not have liked this one. However, in human eyes the future is a sheaf of possibilities, and some of them are dark. The universe will go on regardless.

THE LAST MAN ON Earth knew not that he was. Nor would he have cared. He had met very few other humans in his life, and none since his woman coughed herself into silence. How long ago that happened, he did not know either. He kept no count of years, or of anything else. She lay blurred in his memory, but so did most that was more than a few days past. Day-by-day survival took all his wits and strength, such as they were.

She had not been the last woman. That one had died in Novosibirsk. To her it was nameless; the crumbling buildings simply provided dens and fuel against the winters, with a stock of rats and other small game for her to trap. Her family had laired there until, one by one, sickness or accident overtook each and they became food for the rest. A brother lived long enough that his feeble attentions got her pregnant, but it was a stillbirth and she ate it also. Nevertheless it left her weakened. When she fell and broke a leg she was helpless and starved to death. The small creatures cleaned her bones.

The last man was likewise born in what had been a city, in his case Atlanta. He fled it when a gang of cannibals arrived and settled in to stalk its streets and hallways for meat. Several generations ago their sort had been common, but the prey dwindled fast. These few soon perished in various ways. By that time the last man was elsewhere, and thus missed the satisfaction of learning about their fates.

In his wanderings he came upon a girl, equally footloose. She fled, terrified. Having eaten more recently, he was able to run her down. But then he was not ungentle, and afterward she accompanied him willingly. He meant a slight added measure of food and protection.

She had no name and few words, which she seldom used. His childhood had been more fortunate, leaving him with some language and scraps of tradition. Those led him to grope east across sun-seared barrens until, lurching and croaking, he and his mate found a swamp. Although risen sea level brought a salt tide upstream twice a day, the water was not too brackish to drink. In and around it, fish, frogs, snakes, insects, worms, roots, tubers, and leaves furnished a meager diet if the pair worked hard at their gathering and trapping. They were unaware of the lead, mercury, and organic toxins not yet broken down.

Indeed, had anyone spoken to them of contamination, they would have stared uncomprehending. Plankton, krill, soil requirements, ecological balance, the food chain, its broad and vulnerable base, ozone, greenhouse effect, famine, nuclear warheads, positive feedback, mass extinction were noises they had never heard. Their world was what it was, hot, harsh, mostly parched and bare, scoured by rains that turned the rivers to mudflows and uncovered bedrock to the sky. So had it been and always would be. Once upon a time children had heard their parents say, "Once upon a time" and relate stories of a fabulous age; but as life grew harder and people scarcer, such tales seemed gibberish and were forgotten.

The girl became a woman before she really took sick—neither had ever been healthy—and died. Her infrequent couplings with the man had had no issue. He mourned in a mute fashion. Unsure what to do about the body, he finally dragged it behind a fallen tree at a distance from the brush shelter in which they had dwelt. Whenever he revisited the site, he would squat silent and shyly stroke her skull. In time, boggy ground and thorny overgrowth hid the skeleton, but he continued to eat the grubs he picked out of that log with a certain reverence.

Otherwise he lived dumb. His name and most else dropped out of memory. Gaunt, rachitic, rotten-toothed, plagued by recurrent fevers and jaw-clattering chills, he endured for years. He made crude tools, traps, snares out of wood, bone, gut, what sharp stones he could find. Fire was a lost art, but on the rare cool nights he kept warm between layers of bracken. He paid no attention to the mosquitoes that beclouded and feasted on his nakedness; as for ticks and leeches, he plucked them off and swallowed them, ignoring the festering sores where their heads were stuck.

In due course his skin cancers shed their seed into his bloodstream and devoured him from within. All he knew was that he felt increasingly wretched, until he could not crawl more than a few of his own lengths in any one day.

Yet at the end a delirious yearning came upon him. Just outside the shelter was a small boulder. He had, in fact, chosen the location because this was a convenient surface on which to crack shells and crania or split reeds for their pith. Now he crept there on all fours. The sky burned pitiless blue overhead. A cypress, dead and bleached white, offered no shade. The edge of the swamp, which was shrinking, glimmered scummily, unreachable yards away. Rain had fallen during the night and a depression in the cracked red clay held a little water. The man sucked its siltiness dry. His thirst still smoldered, he was crusted and he stank, but his eyes cleared somewhat and he dragged his carcass onward to the rock. Several stones that he had collected lay around it. He took a wedge-shaped one in his left hand and a blunt one in his right. Blow by blow, he chiseled a mark into the boulder: as it happened, an X, unless it was a cross falling down. He could not have done this were the material not soft limestone, and even so, the mark was barely visible. For a spell he stared at it. The breath rattled in his lungs. He crumpled, sprawled, and breathed a while longer, then no more.

The undertakers sought to him, ants across the ground, insects from the air. They too had no way of knowing that this was the last man on Earth.

Life went on in vigor unabated. The continents were more brown than they were green; rare was the sight of silver slenderness cleaving the seas; but the desert appearance was deceptive. Only the least hardy animals and plants were extinct. They included the larger sorts and those that humans had considered beautiful, but this was of no serious biological consequence. Bacteria, protozoa, and other microscopic organisms had always outweighed as well as outnumbered everything else alive. Some parasites and disease germs died out with their hosts, but most species found the new conditions to their advantage and proliferated. Tough, scrubby grasses, shrubs, and trees made do. Freed of their warm-blooded predators, many invertebrates underwent population explosions. Amphibians had suffered badly, but various kinds of fish and reptiles survived and started to increase. The same was true of certain birds and lesser mammals, especially rodents. Conspicuous among these were the rats. They had declined after the civilization that nourished them ceased to be, but adapted well to the wild, for they were intelligent and tenacious and could eat practically anything.

Earth and moon wheeled on their ancient ways. Rain torrented, light blazed, oxygen and acids gnawed. In every crack or corner where a bit of dirt had drifted, seeds arrived, rootlets thrust forth, stalks lifted, and within a year masonry was breaking apart into finer and finer fragments. Termites and dry rot fungi feasted for a century or more on wood, but when a house fell down it was lichen and moss, grass and thistle that reduced the harder parts.

Of course, much resisted. Steel-framed buildings reared as before, perhaps hollowed out but their exteriors merely blotched. The Pyramids of Egypt withstood the flood when the Aswan Dam broke, and defied every weather. An explorer would have seen a few other such anomalies scattered around the planet. Small objects held on in large numbers, gemstones, goldwork, ceramics, inert plastics.

Time passed. Within a century the bones of the last man were gone, dissolved, taken back into nature. The mark he scratched on his headstone had already blurred to nothing.

Time passed. Chemistry proceeded. Impurities were transformed or diluted to harmlessness. The ozone layer thickened again. Excess carbon dioxide reacted with exposed rock to form carbonates. Resurgent plant life took up more. Greenhouse effect diminished and Earth cooled.

This actually happened rather fast. High temperatures had evaporated vast quantities of ocean water. Much of this fell as snow on mountains and the polar regions. Not all of it melted in summer. The glaciers grew. They locked up most of the water vapor that is also an important greenhouse gas. Temperatures dropped further. Geologically speaking, the new Ice Age came overnight.

Glaciers penetrated Europe until they had buried what was left of Bordeaux, Berlin, Warsaw, and St. Petersburg. Local sheets in the Alps accounted for their share. In North America, ice engulfed the reaches once called Alaska and Canada; the Great Lakes froze to make a foundation for cliffs sheer above the sites of Detroit and Chicago. Except at high altitudes, Asia was too dry for this, though its northern half went bitterly cold. Africa stayed clear, like South America apart from the Andean heights. The Pacific experienced mainly a fall in sea level sufficient to rejoin Australia to the Indonesian islands; but icebergs often hove above the Tasmanian horizon.

At its mightiest, the glacier in Europe or North America bulked a mile thick. Wind whistled over its wrinkled emptiness, driving snow or a glitter of crystals; crevasses shone a lovely mysterious blue; but the sun alone beheld. In summer at its edge, streams rushed down the cliffs and out of the caves, down to gurgle among stones, make the ground a bog, and lose themselves in the tundra that stretched on southward. Here grew lichens, mosses, now and then a tussock of grass or a clump of dwarf willows. Mosquitoes bred their billions, darkened the air and sawed it with their whine. Then the brief season ended, pools stiffened, snow fell anew, stars crowded darkness out of utterly clear nights.

Interstadial periods occurred, when for millennia at a time the glacier retreated for hundreds of miles. The tundra lay warm, mist baked out of it, life swarmed in from the south, wildflowers, berrybushes, evergreens, seeding, growing, spreading, until a forest stood with its crowns like an ocean beneath the wind and flying creatures clamorous above. But the glaciers returned, froze the woods to death, crushed them underfoot, ground and scattered further the works of man.

This Ice Age lasted three million years.

They were by no means evil years for living things. On the contrary, Gaia flourished as she had not since the Pleistocene. Rain belts, forced equatorward, quickened the deserts. The erosion that washed soil down the rivers into the seas nourished them. Meanwhile its forces weathered rock and carried in organic matter to make loam, which roots anchored. Plants and animals multiplied, died, decayed, formed humus to support a life more rich. Volcanoes and ocean trenches brought minerals up from the depths; currents and winds spread them, microbes concentrated them, larger species used them. The waters filled with fins, the land with feet, the sky with wings. Below the tundras and beneath the ranges, forests ran from shore to shore, save where grass billowed or marshes choked on their own abundance.

Evolution worked onward. Species diversified, more and more as increasing fertility opened opportunities. Those that were gone never came back, but new ones took their places. Sometimes, to some degree, they resembled the old. Broadleaf trees bore nuts and fruits, flowers bloomed like bits of rainbow, creatures had descendants bigger than themselves, such features as horns or fingers reappeared. However, an anatomist would have found essential differences; the likenesses were as superficial as those between fish, ichthyosaur, and whale had been.

After three million years, secular changes in Earth's orbit and axial inclination, together with geological and geochemical action, terminated the Ice Age. The glaciers withdrew to the poles and mountaintops. The woods advanced northward and southward over the tundras. They demolished the few shards of human artifacts above ground which the ice had not milled to powder. What roots and rain and frost did not finish yielded to natural acids or the microbes that had "learned" to eat otherwise resistant synthetic materials.

The middle latitudes kept a little evidence of man. The violence of earthquake, eruption, and tsunami had brought many works low, but this was as nothing compared to the patience of weather. There were hills, though, some quite big, where burrowing animals still came upon things that nature could not have made; in them, the soil usually had a high iron content. The Sphinx was long gone but identifiably artificial stumps of the Pyramids stood in the desolation that had encroached again after the rain belts moved back north. Early on, several tombs in the Valley of the Kings had filled with sand, which during the wet epoch hardened into stone. It preserved their contours and hints of their murals. Similar freaks of circumstance persisted in other corners of the world, far apart.

And then there were the fossils, not simply bones and teeth but manmade objects that by chance had been buried and petrified. They existed both ashore and at sea; countless minor items and several almost complete ships lay deep in the silt on ocean bottoms. Other remnants were not, strictly speaking, fossils. A coffee mug, a jade ornament, a metate, a faceted diamond, or the like could stay as it was, encysted in stone, indefinitely. Not every relic dated from historic times. Strata held fugitive memories of the Neolithic, the Paleolithic, or eras even older, a jawbone, a brainpan, a flint pounded to shape by Neandertal or perhaps Pithecanthropus.

Beyond the clouds were clearer traces.

No artificial satellite or piece of debris had continued in orbit around Earth past a century or two. Residual friction dragged them down, to flash as meteors or drift as dust. Whatever struck ground fell to the forces that gnawed at everything else. A few bits had escaped the planet, to course about the sun on eccentric tracks of their own, but collisions with asteroidal gravel annihilated them piecemeal.

Cosmic infall had also wiped footprints and wheel tracks off the moon. Crashed probes, abandoned vehicles, used-up robots, and discarded gear were left, untouched by air, water, or life. The stony rain wore them away, but slowly, slowly, perhaps one really damaging strike in a hundred thousand years. Destruction went a little faster on Mars, which kept a wisp of atmosphere and was nearer the asteroid belt, but only a little. Jupiter had almost instantly reduced all that reached it, and Venus had done so within decades.

Time passed. Occasionally during the next thirty million years the ice advanced, but never very far, and each retreat went deeper back. At last none remained except on Antarctica and the tallest mountains. Swollen, ocean drowned many islands and coastal plains. Otherwise it was benign, the source and guardian of climates that held steady from tropical rain forests to the mild northern and southern fringes of the continents.

Life forms evolved, had their day, and yielded to successor breeds. Some lines of descent died out altogether, but some radiated into fresh kinds while some kept virtually unchanged for periods that ran into the hundreds of millions of years. From the rats arose creatures that grazed, creatures that preyed on them, creatures that took to the air and became raptors more fearsome than any bird. One branch of the rat family went into the trees and developed hands of a sort. Certain among these returned to the ground and grew large and brainy. None ever put fire to use nor any tool more complex than a carefully chosen stone or a stick sharpened with the teeth. Another branch became aquatic and gained flippers; but the truly gigantic sea beasts were originally birds.

A variety of octopodidae got to outliving their own procreation, and thence to caring for their young and a life span that lengthened as generation followed generation. Ultimately there were beings whose tentacles worked rock, shell, bone, and coral. They had language, although its symbols were gestures and color changes. They hatched ignorant and weak, but learned from their elders and from experience as they matured. They created societies which practiced religious rites and subtle arts. Yet being confined to salt water, they never went technologically beyond their equivalent of the Stone Age. One by one, in different manners around the world, their cultures adapted so well to local conditions that innovation ceased; caste systems congealed; the biography of an individual was predetermined within narrow limits and in elaborate detail from the egg to the disposal. Having abolished natural selection for itself, intelligence atrophied. The species grew less and less able to cope with any change in environment. Twelve million years after it came into existence, it was extinct. To be sure, this was a considerably longer run than humankind had had.

As for the vestiges of that earlier race, geological vicissitudes pursued them. A river would change course, a land mass rise or sink, a fossil come to light and thus to erosion. For example, a set of footprints was once laid down in muddy ground that got covered over and lithified as shale. After fifty million years this was laid bare and broken open. Rain filled the prints, algae greened the puddles, the stone flaked and crumbled. In less than a century it had completely lost those traces left by the shoes of George Washington.

A few things stayed entombed and lasted immensely longer, fossilized tools or teeth, roadbeds or graves. But the planet querned. Crustal plates shifted ponderous about. When Africa sundered from Asia, the marks of the Pharaohs disintegrated. North America, colliding with northeastern Asia, raised a mountain chain and ground every token of man in those parts to molecules. Seabed relics slipped down subduction zones to be cycled through moltenness. So it went, while the years mounted into the billions.

No living things witnessed the end. Since first it condensed from primordial gas and dust, the sun had been brightening. Temperatures on Earth kept remarkably stable. In part this was due to chemistry and physics. More heat evaporated more water, much of which recondensed as clouds and deflected sunlight. Rock exposed by falling sea level or by geological uplift reacted with that other major greenhouse gas, carbon dioxide, and bound it. Life was a potent force too. Plants tied up their own carbon, which often stayed in place when they died, were buried, and turned into peat or coal. Plankton exuded substances that contributed to cloud formation. Animals helped maintain the balance, cropping vegetable matter and each other lest one kind overrun the world.

Yet at last the input became overwhelming. The tropics steamed dry, wildfire consumed their jungles and savannahs, scorching winds blew the ashes off and left hardpan desert. Soon the higher latitudes went the selfsame way. Vertebrates died rapidly beside the vegetation that had sustained them; the toughest insects hung on for a span; finally the microbes succumbed.

Primitive, sorely depleted life lingered in the oceans, but not for long. The concentration of water vapor in the atmosphere passed a critical point, and a runaway greenhouse effect set in. The seas began to boil. It took a little time, but by one billion A.D. Earth was totally dead. Ascending, the water molecules encountered ultraviolet photons that split them apart. Their hydrogen escaped to space, the oxygen united with materials below. Carbon dioxide, roasted out of limestone, stoked the furnace further. The planet did not quite change into a twin of Venus, but the difference was trivial.

Volcanoes continued to vomit huge quantities of water from the mantle. It too was lost. Deprived of that lubricant, plate tectonics ground to a halt. Besides, the radioactive elements whose energy had driven the process were giving out.

You could not say that continental drift ceased. Lacking oceans, Earth really had no more continents, just massifs in the basins. Unblocked by ozone, actinic radiation spalled them; wind sanded them; sometimes a large meteorite smote them. Without water, oxygen, and life, erosion went very slowly. Even after four billion added years, a few mesas stood above silicate wastes. A few rocks contained a few fossils, including bits of degraded organic matter, that an observer who knew what to look for might have identified as of human origin.

When the seas departed, the sun and moon generated less tidal friction. Earth turned more leisurely than aforetime, but it did not go into locked rotation with either body. The distance of the moon varied according to the interplay of celestial mechanics, now greater, now lesser, but it neither crashed into the planet nor wandered free. By A.D. five billion meteoritic bombardment had completely, unrecognizably mingled all human-fashioned things on it and on Mars with their regoliths.

That was the approximate time when the sun left the main sequence and swelled to gigantic size. Surface temperature declined until it shone red, like a dying coal, but the whole output was monstrous. At its greatest radius, it ate Mercury and Venus and filled almost half the sky of Earth. The globe glowed, sand fused into glass, the last faint fossils melted and the last biotic molecules broke into their olden elements.

Now the sun collapsed. It ended as a white dwarf, hellish hot, its mass crushed into a volume scarcely larger than Earth's, gradually cooling toward oblivion. But this is epilogue and incidental. Nature had already erased from the Solar System every spoor of humanity. We might as well never have been.

Many light-years away, on widely divergent courses, Pioneer 10 and 11, Voyager 1 and 2, and perhaps some small sister spacecraft fared among the stars.

The House of
Sorrows

The future is unknown to us. The past we think we know somewhat. Do we really?

In general relativity, an event that one observer perceives as having already happened, can lie in the future of another observer. This suggests that past and future are equally fixed, unchangeable; and indeed relativity is deterministic. "And the first Morning of Creation wrote/ What the last Dawn of Reckoning shall read."

On the other hand, quantum mechanics (at least in its widely accepted Copenhagen interpretation) seems to indicate that we construct, or decide, a great deal of reality ourselves. The observer influences the outcome of the observation, not because of poor laboratory technique, but inescapably. To what extent may history be a construct, dependent on how we view it? St. Thomas Aquinas declared that God Himself cannot alter the past, for this is a logical impossibility, a contradiction in terms. Perhaps, though, our logic does not reach to everything. Certainly Gödel showed that it has its limits.

Alternatively, in the Everett interpretation, which quite a few physicists have now adopted, reality does not change, it branches. Whatever can happen, does. It would be incorrect to take this too literally—at present. But perhaps further study will show that there is in fact a boundless array of worlds, all of them as tangible as ours, in which events have taken as many different courses.

THAT IS A VERY old land, full of wrongs that will not die. They weighted me like the noontime heat, and with the same stillness, but the names of many I had never known. My horse's hoofs made the loudest noise, beneath it now and then a creak of saddle leather, once the twitter of a shepherd boy's pipes. Dusty green, orchards and kitchen gardens dappled summer-brown hills. Dwellings, mostly sun-baked brick, strewed themselves likewise. They grew thicker along the road as it wound upward. Men in shabby kaftans stared at me from doorways, women and children from deeper inside, speaking no word. A few times I met laden camels, donkeys, oxcarts. The lips of their drivers closed when I came in sight.

It had been thus for the past day. Some news had flown abroad. Riding, I had glimpsed restlessness in the villages and between them. No longer did anybody hail me, rush forth to offer wares or beg for alms. Thrice I stopped to water my mount, my remount, and myself, and sought to ask what went on, but those I spoke to gave short, meaningless answers and slipped away. That was easy for them. I had little of either the Aramaic or the Edomite tongues.

That night I deemed it best not to seek a caravanserai, but rolled up in my saddle blanket in a field well off the highway. At sunrise I ate what cheese and pita bread were left me, and quenched thirst with the last water in my flask. It's hard for a Marklander to be without his morning coffee, but dead man can't drink anyhow.

Now the walls of Mirzabad rose before me. Afar, they had shimmered hazy through the heat. Close, I saw the pockmarks of former wars in their gray-white stone. A flag drooped from a cross-armed staff above the gate. The Lion and Sun of Persia slackened a little the tightness in me. At least that much abided. My gaze sought after the hues of Ispanya and did not find them. However, I told myself, belike they were not seeable from here.

Lesser buildings, shops and worksteads, crowded the roadsides. They should have been alive with the racket of the East, hammers on iron, hoofs thudding, wheels groaning, beasts lowing and braying, fowl cackling, folk shrilling. Smells should have thickened the heat, smoke, sweat, dung, oil. Instead, what drifted to me seemed eerily loud and sharp in its loneliness. Some traffic did move. Dust from it gritted my eyelids, nostrils, mouth. My horses must push their way among walkers, wagons, huge burdens on hairy backs. Yet this was scant, and all outbound. Faces were grim. The looks I got ran from sullen to hateful. Often men spat on my shadow.

A score of warders stood by at the gate. Sicamino itself posted only four at any inway. These were also Persians, also wearing striped tunics, breeches bagged into half-boots, turbans on bearded heads. They also bore old-time muzzle-loading rifles and curved short-swords. They slouched with the same slovenliness, soldiers of what was today an empire in name only. But their wariness came to me like a stench of fear, and it was no astonishment when their overling shouted in bad Ispanyan, "Ho, you, Westman, stop! Haul over!"

I obeyed, careful to hold my hands on the reins, well away from pistol and broadsword. A paved space under the wall was kept clear. The head warder beckoned me to it and snapped, "Get off."

Such a bearing toward a newcomer whom they must deem a European boded ill. I swung down from the stirrups and stood before them, hoping I looked neither too haughty nor too lowly. My years among the Magyars and Turks had given me some understanding of warlike men whose kingdoms have lost greatness. "Ahura-Mazda be with you, sirdar," I greeted in my best Persian.

The overling blinked, then turned and bowed low as another man trod from a door in the gateway. This was not an Ispanyan gunnaro, such as should have been on call. He was another Persian, tall and lean, grizzle-bearded, in white turban and flowing black robe. The soldiers dipped their heads and touched their breasts. To them, I saw, he was a holy man; but that was no outfit of an orthodox murattab. "Who are you and what would you, Frank?" he asked with a deadly kind of softness.

I laid palms together above my heart. "Venerable one, I am no Frank," I said cat-footedly. "Nor, as you have perceived, am I an Ispanyan." Sometimes a man of that kingdom is fair-haired and much taller than most are in Lesser Asia; but on the whole, the Visigothic blood has long since lost itself in the Iberian. "May it please you, I am a humble messenger, bringing a letter to the Mirzabad factor of the Bremer Handelsbund."

The dark eyes smoldered against mine. I thought, though, that underneath, he was taken aback. Tales of the Saxonian strength off the Persian shores must have reached him too. "Do they not trust our postal riders?" he asked slowly; and I saw wrath flare in the faces behind him.

Of course they didn't. "I bring, as well, certain words from the consul of the Hauptmannsreich in Sicamino to the factor Otto Gneisberg here in Mirzabad, such words as go best by mouth. Your reverence will understand." At least, he would be unsure whether I lied or no.

"Hm. Show me your papers."

He muttered over my passport. "Ro Esbernsson from . . . New Denmark?" I could barely tell what sounds he was trying to utter.

I pointed to the notation and seal. "Not a Saxonian myself, true, but in the service of the excellent consul, as bodyguard and courier."

The letter itself was in a packet addressed to Gneisberg from von Heidenheim in the Latin, Greek, and Persian alphabets. This priest, or whatever he was, must feel a clawing wish to cut the thongs and take the writing to someone who could read it. For a heartbeat I thought he might, and wondered if I could shoot my way free, leap back on my horse, and outgallop pursuit. Then he gave the things back to me, and my breath with them. The sweat prickled below my shirt. Not yet did anybody want to risk *that* war. He spoke a curt command and withdrew, his dignity gone stiff.

The soldiers took their time ransacking my baggage. Passersby stared; some jeered. In the end, they left me my papers and packet, money, a handbag with clothes and other everydayness, and my sword. The last was unwillingly, only because my being a consul's handfast man gave me the standing of warrior and to take my steel would have been to blacken him. They kept my firearms, horses, and wayfaring gear. I got no token of claim, but was not about to question their honor.

Nor did it seem wise to ask what had happened. I was glad enough to leave them behind me and pass on into the city.

A bazaar lay just beyond the gate, booths around a square whose flagstones should have been decked by spread-out rugs, metalware, crockery, fabrics, farm produce, all the goods that vendors chanted the wonders of, while the crowd milled and chattered. Today it brooded well-nigh empty beneath the hard blue sky, between the hot blind walls. A few folk, so few, went among such dealers as still dared be there. Mostly they were after food. I kenned the women: Aramaics and Edomites loosely and fully clad, low-rank Persians in long, close-fitting gowns and flowing scarves, Turks short and sturdy in blouses and breeks. Most had a man of her breed at her side, who must be warding her.

The street bore a little more upon it than the market did: sandals, boots, slippers, shoes, hoofs, wheels a-clatter over bumpy cobbles. Those all belonged to men. Among townsfolk and hinterland peasants I spied some from far parts of the Shahdom, Kurds, Syrians, Badawi, with here and there an outlander, Greek, Egyptian, Afghan—but no Turk of the Sultandom, no Russian or other underling of the Grand Knyaz, no Frank or Saxonian or Dane—and with a chill in the white sunlight, I saw no Ispanyan either, be he tradesman or soldier of the Wardership. I was the one Westerner in that whole thin swarm.

"Master! Lord! Effendi!" A hand plucked my sleeve.

I looked down at a boy of maybe nine years, Edomite, all grime and rags, shock hair and big eyes. "Glorious master," he cried in bad but swift Persian, "I am your servant, your guide in the name of the heavenly Yazata to safe lodging, fine food and wine, pleasure, everything my lord desires." He jumped to worse Ispanyan: "Mestro, I show you good inn, eat, drink, beautiful girls."

Such urchins ought to have overrun me, each eager to win a coin for bringing in me and my money. Now this one alone had the pluck. I liked that. Not that I was about to go where he hoped to take me. From my own childhood I remembered the stave that begins, "Gang warily in where wolves may lair." Still, I could use a guide. The map that had been given me showed an utter tangle of streets. It did not mark at all that stead which I had decided I had better seek first. Let the lad earn his copper from me.

"Take me to the Mithraeum," I said in Persian.

"Ah, to the house of your god, sirdar? I leap at your order, I, Herod Gamal-al-Mazda. In the Street of Ulun Begh it lies, near the Fountain of Herakles, and we shall go there swift as the wind, straight as the djinn, most glorious master. Only come!"

He tried to take my bag for me, but I didn't trust him that much and he skipped ahead, doubtless happy not to have the weight dragging at his thin shoulders. The ways that he took twisted downward. The houses that hemmed them were shut. I had a feeling that the dwellers crouched within like hares in a burrow when the fox is a-prowl. The few men we met drew aside and watched me in the same wise. I saw from their neck rings that they were slaves, and from scrawniness and whip scars that they were worth little. The good ones their owners kept indoors, sending the trash out on such fetch-and-carry tasks as could not wait for a better time.

"You lead me widely about, do you not?" I said at last.

Herod threw an eye-glint backward. "My lord is shrewd," he said. "The main thoroughfares are dangerous."

As if to bear him out, a growl and mutter reached me. The walls and crooked lanes in between faintened it, but I knew that noise of old, and the hair stood up on my arms. It was the mouthings of a crowd adrift and angry.

Herod bobbed his head. "Many like them today."

"What has happened here?" I blurted.

"It is not for an alley rat to speak about the mighty," he said fast, and scuttled onward. Indeed so, I thought, when he did not know whose man I was. I bore a sword, and death walked under this hot heaven.

Well, but at the Mithraeum, once I had shown myself to be initiate in the Mysteries—I have reached the rank of Lion—its Father would tell me the truth. Then I could plan how best to bring Otto Gneisberg the word of his motherland. Merely fumbling to his house, I might well meet some foolish doom.

The ground canted sharply. Either the rubble that elsewhere underlay the city, yards deep, had never been piled here, or else an overlord had had it cleared away a few hundred years ago because there were things worth salvaging.

Housefronts showed workmanship of kingdoms long dead. In the basin of a dry fountain stood a statue that I reckoned was of Hercules and the Hydra, though as battered as it was, it might as well have been Thor and the Midgard Worm. Nearby crumbled a Roman temple or basilica, with columned portico and a frieze gone shapeless. The Turks in their day had made it over for their own worship, and their great-great-grandchildren still used it; through the doorless inway I saw the Warrior Buddha, sword in left hand, right hand lifted in blessing, the bronze of him turned green.

How many breeds had owned this town? The Persians of now, on whom the Ispanyans had laid wardership lest other Europeans do more than that; Edomites; Turks; Syrians; Mongols; Old Persians; Romans; Greeks—and how many before them, dust that scuffed up from my boots?

Wondering ended when Herod trilled, "Master, behold your sacred goal." I could hardly have mistaken it. Nonetheless, it was not such as my fathers knew.

Mithraists have been few hereabouts since the last West Roman legions withdrew. The Ispanyan garrison surely had its own halidoms, though those would also be strange to me. They look on our Northern godword as heretical. Asiatic Mithraists are at odds with both, but hold that different roads may lead to the same truth. In this, if naught else, the East is wiser than the West.

The building and its sister beside it bore shapes of their land. Both stood taller than any in Europe or Markland, whitewashed, roofs swelling into domes, red on the Mithraeum, blue on the Shrine of the Good Mother. Easterners celebrate the Mysteries in window-less rooms rather than underground. Mosaics above the doors glowed with his Bull, her Rose. That much spoke straight to my heart. No matter any otherness. On a narrow and rough-stoned street, pressed between dingy blanknesses of walls, these houses reared upright as the faith itself.

But—Suddenly, spear-sharp, came back to me the halidoms of my boyhood. They stand a little outside of Ivarsthorp, on a grassy bank where the Connecticut River gleams past farmsteads, shaws, meadows marked off by stone walls and flowering hedges; they are low beneath their three-tiered roofs, but the wood of them is richly carved, and dragons rear skyward from the beam ends. Within the Mithraeum, when you have gone by lion-headed Aeon and the holy water bowl, Odin and Thor flank the altars of the Tauroctony: as I was told Frigg and Freyja honor our forebears at the Mystery of the women.

Here in Mirzabad, the land I had forsaken hunted me down, dogwood white in springtime, yeomen in summer fields that had been rock and bramble when the Trekfolk first came, the blazing hues of New Denmark fall, winter starlight that seemed to ring as it struck the snow—outings to fish and swim in Lake Winnepesaukee, days in jouncing wains and nights in old inns till we came to Merrimack Haven and saw the masts of the ships at dock lift their yards like the boughs of Yggdrasil—What unrest had driven me overseas? Why had I drifted from land to land, calling to calling, master to master, war to war, while my years spilled out of me and left only emptiness behind?

None of that, I barked at myself. There was work to do. "Wait," I told Herod. "I think I shall want you to guide me elsewhere." To Gneisberg's trading post, if I was lucky, and thence back to the western gate and away from this lair of Ahriman. I strode to the door of the Mithraeum and turned its handle.

The iron-bound timber stayed fast. It was locked.

This should not be. If naught else, a Raven or an Occult should be on watch inside, to help whatever brothers might come in need of help and to keep the holy of holies untrodden by the unhallowed. He could tell me where the Father lived, which was bound to be close by. I grasped the serpent coil of the knocker and clashed it on the plate. The noise fell hollow into the furnace day.

Herod squeaked at my back. I turned to see. The door had opened in the Shrine of the Good Mother and a woman had come forth.

She halted a few feet off. Beneath a blue gown of Persian cut, slenderness stood taut, ready to take flight. Young, she was likely of no more than Damsel rank in her Mysteries. Tresses astray from under her scarf shone obsidian black. Her face was finely molded and light-skinned, with the great gazelle eyes of the Sunrise Lands.

Persian women have never been as muffled in spirit as Hindi. Just the same, she astounded me with a straightforwardness wellnigh Frankish, if not quite Danish: "Wayfarer, you knock in vain. The Mithraeum is shut. The Father and the Courier of the Sun are both departed, and at their wish, all lower initiates have likewise sought what safety may be found."

Dismay smote me. "What, what is awry?" I stammered.

"You know not?"

Numbly, I shook my head. If the thanes of Mithras must flee, then Loki was loose. "I am but now come here, my lady."

Her look searched me. "Yes, you are a foreigner; and not a Frank, but from farther away." Even then, I knew keenness when I met it, and somehow that put heart back in me. "A believer, a warrior." Fire leaped in her voice. "By the faith, I require your help!"

"What? My lady, I have a mission."

"As do I. Mine will not wait, and yours can scarcely be done at once. This is for the Light, against the Chaos. Mithras will bless you."

She offered escape from bewilderment and uselessness. Also, she was fair to behold. "What is the task, my lady?"

"The Shrine holds certain treasures," she said crisply. "I came to save them before the city explodes and the throngs go rioting, looting, burning. Wait while I fetch them out, and give me escort to the Basileum." She flashed a smile that would have been lovely were her mood not so bleak. "You'll gain a den for yourself, and thus outlive the night—we may hope."

In a whirl of cloth, she sped back. I almost followed, but stopped myself at the threshold men may not cross. "The Basileum?" I mumbled. "What is that?"

"I think the noble lady must mean the House of Sorrows, lord." Herod's voice startled me; I had forgotten him. He tugged at my cloak. "Take me along. Should my lord and lady meet danger along the way, I know many a bolthole."

"We are in a powder keg, then," I said slowly.

"And sparks dance everywhere, my lord," the boy told me. "I should be glad of a snug hiding place too, where I may heed my master's every bidding."

"Better you go home to your mother."

He shrugged. The sigh of an old man blew from the wizened small face. "She will have enough to do keeping herself alive, my lord. I have heard that when men go wild in the streets, they go mad in the joyhouses."

"What in the name of evil has befallen?"

"I am only an alley rat, master. How shall I eavesdrop on the councils of the mighty?" He drew breath. "However, the word flying about is that yesterday the *rais* was overthrown by a follower of the Prophet Khusrev who had smuggled men and arms into this city. The Ispanyans have all drawn back into their fortress, and other

Europeans have taken refuge there as well. So, perhaps, have the high priests and priestesses of these twin *dewali*. Far be it from me to call them craven. It was simple prudence. But I do not think my lord and lady could now shelter behind those gates and guns. This morning from a rooftop, I saw how armed men stand thick around every portal of the compound, and they wear the yellow sash of the Prophet."

Hard news was this. Yet the past hours had somewhat readied me for it. If only the powers, any of the powers, had foreseen! It would have been easy enough twenty years ago to send a small host into the Zagros Mountains and root Khusrev out. The Shah could have said little against it, might well have given it what feeble help was his to give. Did not this self-made Prophet cry that the Zarathushtran faith was fallen into corruption and idolatry, and that to him alone had come the saving revelation? Already then he spoke not simply of cleansing the belief and the rites, but of slaying everyone who would withstand him.

However, the Shahdom was a ghost, barely haunting the inland tribes, while the Ispanyan Wardership kept troops only in those provinces that bordered the Midworld Sea. Khusrev had seemed merely another among untold mullahs who had sprung up in the backlands lifetime after lifetime, preached, died, and blown away in dust.

Too late now, I thought, when the Puritans did as they would throughout Isfahan, Laristan, Kerman, and their flame went across Mesopotamia and down the Arabian Peninsula. In every other province of the empire, too, it was breaking loose. Fleetingly I wondered if somehow, something of it had overleaped the ocean. Was it just happenstance that half of South Markland was in uprising, and the latest news told how the Inca of Tahuantinsuyu had ended fellowship with the Ispanyan crown? Oh, the inborns yonder called on their own gods, but—

Be that as it may, Ispanya had scant strength left for this part of the world. Day by day, the garrisons thinned, the grasp weakened, and men also scorned the law of the Shah.

I stared at Mithraeum and Shrine. Even the orthodox Zarathushtrans have always looked on Mithraists as fallen halfway back into heathenism, the more so after our cult linked itself to that of the Good Mother. To the Puritans we are worse than that, worse than infidels, the very creatures of Angra Mainyu.

Thoughts of the past went from me in a cold gust as the woman came back out the door. In her arms she carried two leather-bound books and several parchment scrolls. Mottlings and crumbly edges bespoke great age. "Let us begone," she said.

"Treasure—" I gulped.

"These are the treasures." She tossed her head. "Looters may have the vessels of gold and silver if they must."

Herod bounced around us. "Will my lady go to the House of Sorrows?" he twittered. "I know the safest ways, if any be safe. Give me leave to guide you!"

The woman cast me a look. I spread my hands and half smiled. "We could have a less canny leader," I said. "I have often met his kind. Shall I carry those?"

She shook her head. "You already have a bag. Better you keep your sword hand free."

We set forth, quick-gaited. Blue shadows slithered at our heels, over the cobblestones. They had lengthened a bit. The heat had waxed. To run in it would have been berserk. As was, my tongue stirred thick and dusty: "We have no names for each other, my lady. I am Ro Esbernsson. From North Markland."

Her eyes widened. "Across the Western Sea? What brings you to this place of woe?"

"An errand. What else? Perhaps you can counsel me."

She was bold for a Persian woman, but a shyness was built into her that she must overcome before she said: "I am Boran Taki. A votary of Isis." Thus they call the Good Mother in these parts. "As I trust you are of Mithras," she finished in haste.

I nodded. "Tell me what is going on, I pray you."

She swallowed hard. "Yesterday—But let me first say that Zigad Moussavi, a nobleman in the Jordan Valley, was converted to the New Revelation of Khusrev some years ago. His agitation against the Shah and the Ispanyans who uphold the Shah became so fierce, an outright call for insurrection, that his arrest was ordered. He fled with his followers into the desert. Since then their numbers have swelled, the countryside is often in turmoil, and if you traveled here alone without trouble, Mithras himself must have been watching over you."

My sword and pistol had something to do with it, I thought. Moreover, I went forewarned, wary, using those roads and inns that von Heidenheim had told me were likeliest to be still safe. He had eyes and ears everywhere in the province. Nonetheless he had not looked for an outbreak this soon.

Boran went on in her scholarly, step-by-step way: "He must long have conspired with persons in the city, officers of the governor among them. Yesterday we suddenly heard gunfire, shouting—we saw people flee from the markets like sheep from a lion—rumors grew ever more frightening—then toward sundown, the noise dwindled away. Presently criers went through the streets, guarded by riflemen who wore yellow sashes. We were all commanded on pain of death to remain indoors until morning. During the night there were more shots and screams. Today a vast silence has fallen. But it seethes."

I nodded again. "Clearly, this Moussavi has seized the governor's palace and quelled whatever resistance the royal troops made. Did the Ispanyans do nothing?"

"It went too fast for them, I think, when they had no unequivocal orders," she answered. Yes, I thought, she might have led a sheltered life hitherto, but it had not dulled her wits. "They seem to have drawn back into their stronghold at the Moon Tower and prepared to stand siege if necessary. I suppose the Europeans among us have taken refuge with them, as well as Persians and other Easterners who have special reason to fear the new masters. As yet there has been no attack on the compound, and perhaps there will not be. Placards have gone up in public places, directing people to continue their daily lives in orderly fashion. Of course they do not heed that."

"You have read such a proclamation, then? What does it say?"

"It declares that Zigad Moussavi, servant of Ahura-Mazda, has overthrown the corrupt and idolatrous governor of the Shah and taken command of Mirzabad in the name of the Prophet. It promises a great beginning to the work of purifying the faith and restoring the ancient glory of Persia. Foreigners shall be expelled and infidels brought to justice."

"Hm. He's far from Khusrev country. Does he imagine he can hold this single city, all by himself?"

"He is no dolt. A madman, perhaps, but not stupid. I have studied his career as it progressed. Surely he expects by his example to ignite the entire province. To that end, although he calls for public order, he does nothing to enforce it. His warriors have not replaced the police patrols they drove off. More and more people are taking to the streets. They mill to and fro, they quarrel, they listen to ranting preachers and to songs of blood. Anything at any moment may bring on the eruption. After that is over, the city will have no choice but to heed Moussavi: because if the Shah's rule comes back, so will his headsmen."

"But I thought—Are the Persians in this city not largely orthodox Zarathushtrans?" I remembered those I had met in Europe, and the few who have made their way to Markland. They keep much to themselves, but are soft-spoken, good-hearted, hard-working folk with a high respect for learning.

Her tone was stark: "They too have things to avenge."

Well, yes, I must allow. In most countries of Europe, Zarathushtrans may not own land; in some, they are made to live in wretched, crowded quarters of the towns. Also, here at home they have seen foreigners swaggering where once their kings rode under golden banners.

"True. And many will not dare sit still, whatever their inward feelings," I foretold. "They will think they also must show zeal, so that afterward the Puritans will let them get on with their lives. Moreover, the bulk of the dwellers, Aramaics and Edomites and all the rest, will snatch at this chance to take out old grudges against each other, or simply to wreck and plunder."

Her look rested a while on me. "You know the world well, Ro Esbernsson," she said low.

"And you seem wise beyond your years," I began. That and my smile died.

Herod heard first, and halted. Half a minute later the sound reached our older ears. It grew as we stood stiff, a racking growl through which sawed screams, the sound of a man-pack unloosed.

"The Mother help us, it has begun," Boran whispered.

"They are bound this way," Herod said. He cast about as a dog does, then he beckoned and his slight form shot on down the street. We loped after.

Where a slipper painted above a doorway marked the house of a shoemaker, and it shuttered and barred, the boy darted aside. We followed, into the sudden gloom and half-coolness of an alley. Flies buzzed over the offal that made its cobbles slick. It twisted among windowless buildings, more lanes joined it, Herod took us through a maze and brought us out in a court. This too was filthily littered, though vines trailing over one of the walls around it told that the garden of somebody well-to-do lay on the other side.

Herod stopped. "I think we will be safe here for a while, if we are quiet," he said. The calm of a seasoned man had fallen over him. "Yonder is the home of Haidar Aghasi, the wine merchant. He'll be with strong, well-armed hirelings of his to guard its wealth. The rioters ought to know that and pass by."

"Might he take us in?" I wondered.

"No, master, he would be witless to link himself with a European, today. Would he not?" Herod replied, and I felt myself rebuked for my childishness.

Boran clutched the books to her breast. "Besides, I must bring these to my father," she said.

Well, if they meant so much that she dared go forth after them—I settled myself to wait. The grisly racket loudened.

Herod yelped, Boran gasped. I swung on my heel. The sword sprang into my hand. A man stumbled into the court.

For a moment he stood panting. We glared at each other. He was burly, red of hair and beard, freckled of snub-nosed face. His skin had once been fair, but Southern sun had made leather of it. The shirt was half ripped off him, and blood oozed from three shallow wounds. He gripped a staff, long and heavy, in a way that said that to him this was a weapon. In his left hand gleamed a sheath knife.

I knew such features and shape of blade. My sword lowered. "You are from Eirinn," I murmured in Danish such as they speak in England. A Gaelic sailor would be bound to understand me.

He swallowed a few more draughts of air, grinned, and said with the lilt of his folk, "Sure and this is an unlikely place to be meeting the Lochlannach."

"Hush," Herod begged. The man and I nodded. Without need to plan it, we turned back to back, covering both sides from which attack might come.

It snarled on by. Inch by inch, we reached the knowledge that we would live a bit longer.

The man and I faced around again. He put away his knife, took staff in left hand, and held out his right. "A good day to ye, your honor," he said merrily. "Ailill mac Cerbaill I am, from Condacht through Markland, China, and points west. My greetings to the little lady. If only I could speak her tongue, I'd be paying her the compliments that luckier men certainly do."

I smiled and clasped the hand. It was thick, hard, from years of fisting canvas and winding capstans. I gave him our names and asked what brought him so far from the sea.

"Och, it's not many miles," he said.

Herod jittered about. "My lord, my lord, we should be gone," he urged. "The pack—I think they will smash and loot in the Street of the Comfit Makers, who are mainly Turks, but they may not, and whatever they do, they will shortly return this way."

"Come," I agreed. A thought struck me. "Ailill, are you astray?"

"I am that," the seaman said. "The landlord at my inn sent me off this morning for an outland unbeliever, and never counted what bedbugs of his I took with me. Then as I wandered the streets, that gang swept about a corner and set upon me. I thought I heard the wings of the Morrigan beat overhead, but Lug Long-Arm strengthened mine enough that I broke free."

For a heartbeat I envied him his gods, that to a Gael are still real beings. What are the gods of our forebears to us Mithraists, save names in the rites? Mithras himself is no longer the embodiment he once was. At that, we are better off than the Saxonians, who never had a higher religion and whose olden sacrifices are now no more than a show of loyalty to the Hauptmann.

"Join us," I offered. "We're bound for shelter, where I daresay they can use another doorkeeper."

He was glad to. Herod led us out and thence widely roundabout. Boran looked askance at the uncouth newcomer, though when I gave her my thought she said that I was right, *if* he was trustworthy.

Therefore I sounded Ailill out. It was easy. He had gotten drunk in Sicamino and missed his ship. On the beach, he learned of a venture that needed men, smuggling tobacco down from Turkey and past the Persian customs. The stuff came in at Joppa, which has a bad harbor and so is not much watched. Because unrest in the countryside had aroused banditry, inland shipments wanted guards. Ailill chose to go along with the camels headed for Mirzabad; he had heard of its time-gnawed wonders. I gathered he was not altogether a deck hand and roisterer, he had a touch of the skald in him like many among his folk. "Well, there I was, stumping down the Street of the Magi—What bit you, my friend?"

I clamped my jaw. The Bremer Handelsbund kept its warehouse, shop, quarters for the factor and his workers, on the Street of the Magi. "Was anything . . . plundered, burned . . . there?" I asked.

"It was not. I think the violence had only just begun. But those are some grand houses, and when the weasels have been at easier chicken coops and tasted blood, they will be back, I think."

I nodded. "We may have a few hours."

"Eh? . . . What might this port be that you're steering for?"

My lips bent upward. "I wish I knew."

Our course wound onward and onward, like a nightmare. Amidst the squalor, I spied remnants, a fluted column, a slim spire, a wall slab that bore the worn-down carving of a winged bull with a man's head. The downslope grew ever more steep, lanes turned into flights of stairs hollowed out by uncounted footfalls, and ahead of us, above the flat roofs, I saw turrets and battlements foursquare athwart eastern hills. A few times a ragged form scuttled around a corner or into a lane. My skin crawled with the feeling of eyes that peered through slits in the shouldering walls.

"Where do you take us?" I asked Boran, forgetting that she had told me.

"To the House of Sorrows," Herod piped up.

The woman winced. "A horrible name," she said. "It is rightfully the Basileum."

The Greek word stood forth in the Persian. "And what might that mean, my lady?"

"It is the archive of archives," she answered. "There repose the chronicles, the records, the tablets and letters and—whatever whispers to us of the past. Such things are no longer of use to the state, but precious to what scholars remain alive."

I searched my mind. "Basileum? That which a king built? Should the word not be—m-m—no, I suppose not 'biblioteka'— 'museum'?"

Her tone softened. "You are no barbarian, Ro, are you?"

"I have read books." Maybe they were what first called me outward from my homeland.

"This was founded by Julian the Second, Augustus in Byzantium, when the East Romans still held the Syriac lands. He established others where he could, though I know of none else that have endured. Rome itself had lately fallen. He foresaw a dark age. How else might the heritage of the ancients be saved, even a little?"

I shivered. That was fifteen hundred years ago, was it not?

We passed a monument. A muffled shriek from Boran tore me out of my thoughts. Two deathlings sprawled before us. They were pulp, splinters, huge splashes and pools of blood flamingly red under the sun. Flies blackened the simmering air.

I caught her elbow. "Come along," I said. She moaned once, but swallowed her sickness.

"Turks, by what's left of their clothes," Ailill muttered. "One quite young, a girl."

Their kin must have dwelt in Mirzabad since the Sultans ruled it, when white men were barely setting foot on the shores of Markland; but today they had become outlanders, unbelievers, and a gang that caught them had stamped them into the stones. After all my wanderings I should have been able to shrug off a sight like this, but it saddened me anyhow. "May their Buddha take them home," I said.

"Hurry, hurry," Herod chattered.

"You ought never to have gone forth, Boran," I told her.

"I slipped away before my father could forbid it," she answered. It did her good to speak. "The Basileum is in his care."

Since he was surely a Mithraist, I knew he had a Zarathushtran above him; but that was belike a eunuch of the governor's, who did scant more than draw large pay and pass half of it on to his lord. It was no wonder that the New Revelation was taking hold in souls from the Caspian to the Midworld Sea.

"These are genealogies and annals that the Shrine kept," she went on, holding them tightly to her. "Often has my father longed to study them. I saw his anguish when it seemed they might be lost, and—"

"Behold!" Herod crowed.

We had reached a small square, in whose faded and patched paving dolphins rollicked. Across from us lifted a building of no great size. Age had pitted and blurred it. Gracefulness lingered in the pillars of the portico, the golden rectangle and low gable of the front; the marble was the hue of wan amber beneath tiles that had gone dusky rose. As we drew nigh, I saw Greek letters above the columns, and they were clear. Lifetime by lifetime, somebody had renewed them as they wore away.

"What does that mean?" I asked, pointing.

Boran's voice was as hushed as mine: " '*Polla ta deina*—Wonders are many, and none more wondrous than man.' "

We mounted the stairs and must have been seen through a slotted shutter, for the door opened before us. Him who came out in a white robe I knew by his gray-bearded handsomeness to be Boran's father. He reached his arms toward her. "Oh, my dearest," he called.

She caught her breath, stumbled forward, and gulped, "I b-brought you the books from the Shrine."

"You should not have, you should not have. I was terrified when I found you were missing. Madness runs free."

"That is why I had to go." She shook her head as if to dash the tears from her lashes.

The man looked across her to me. "Ro Esbernsson of Markland, learned sir," I named myself, "with Ailill mac Cerbaill of Eirinn and, and Herod. We met your daughter and escorted her."

"That was nobly done of you," he said with renewed steadiness. "The Lord Mithras will remember when your souls depart for the stars. I am Jahan Taki, in charge of the Basileum now that—others have abandoned it. Enter, I pray you."

He stood aside. We walked through an anteroom into a broad chamber of mosaic murals. I knew Athene, foremost among the figures. Tinted glass in a clerestory softened light. Air was blessedly cool. Half a dozen men stared at us. Two were old, three young but thin and stoop-shouldered. The only one that might be worth anything in a fight was a big, black African whose garb said that he did the rough work.

Boran set the books down on a table of ivory-inlaid ebony. Gold glowed in the robes of gods and philosophers on the walls. What a house to sack, I thought.

Jahan Taki might have heard that. "I am not sure how safe a refuge this is," he said. "For excuse, raveners can scream that the books are full of wicked falsehoods and should be destroyed."

"They get by me first," growled the African. He saw my startlement and gave me a harsh smile. "I work for low wages because wiseman Taki lets me read."

"And these among my colleagues and students would not flee either." The pride in Jahan faded. "We can only pray that none will come until peace has been restored."

"That may take days," I warned. "Have you food and drink on hand?"

Boran nodded. "I reminded them when we first gathered here," she said, "and the cistern already held sufficient."

"Good," I answered through the dust in my throat. "Let us have some of that water, and we'll look to your defenses."

The African hastened off. Meanwhile Jahan took me over the ground floor. The books and relics were in vaults beneath. There were two doors. I told him they should be barricaded as well as bolted. "At the front, leave a space for going in and out, but narrow enough for a single man to hold. If you have nothing better, pile up your furniture."

Jahan winced. "It will hurt like fire, but rather that than lose the books. Most have never been printed. I think many are the last copies that survive anywhere."

It struck me strange, this love of learning for its own sake, a Greek thing I had thought died with Rome like the avowed love of men for boys. The Zarathushtrans study their holy writ but add nothing new. The rest of us give ourselves to the worldly arts. Oh, we measure the earth and the stars in their courses because that helps navigation, but to wonder about them, that is something children outgrow. We keep old books if they are useful or enjoyable, but otherwise, why should we care? In this house I felt as though I stood among ghosts. Had they a right to spook through the life of young Boran?

The African brought the water. I swished mine about in my mouth before swallowing it. The mummy dryness began to go away. "Can you make the place secure according to what master Taki has heard from me?" I asked him.

"As well as the Yazata will have it, my lord," he answered. So he was a Zarathushtran himself.

"I know a wee bit about such things too," Ailill put in. "But ye'll be foreman over us, Ro, won't ye?"

I shook my head. "No, the task had better not wait till I get back. Which I may not."

He blinked. "What? Why, sir, here we've stumbled into an anchorage as snug as any outside the Ispanyan fort—"

Boran caught our drift. Her hand fell on my arm. For an Eastern woman to do thus gave away, more than any words, how shaken she was. "Ro, you would leave us? You must not!"

"I go without joy," I told her, "but honor requires it. I am in the service of a man. As long as I take his pay, I do his bidding."

"Where do you seek, my son?" Jahan asked.

"To the Saxonian factor. I bear a message."

Sharply to me came the room overlooking Sicamino harbor where I had been given that word. Through its window I saw the schooners, barks, square-riggers, dhows, feluccas, the trade of half a world. The bay opened out to a sea that shone like quicksilver. Against the dazzle, at the edge of sight, I could just make out three tall vessels. Light struck little sparks off their guns. I knew that at their mastheads flew the falcon banner of the Hauptmann of Saxonia.

My look returned, crossed the desk, came to rest on Konrad von Heidenheim. The consul sat sweating, as so fleshy a man does in such heat. The beard spilling down his chest was wet with it. His right hand wielded a fan, his left cradled a fuming pipe. But the eyes were like chips of ice, and when he spoke it was a drumroll from the depths.

"Ro, boy, I do not myself like the job I have for you. However, need is for several couriers I can trust to bring a word from me and keep it quiet. I think you will go to Mirzabad. The Handelsbund has a good-sized post there. It is of more than economic value. It has strategic potential."

I leaned back, crossed shank over knee, and waited.

He chuckled dourly. "Ach, always you play the lynx-calm soldier of fortune. As you like. Now listen close. I have a lecture prepared.

"You think you know why Saxonia has brought ships and troops offshore. This crazy Prophet and his Puritans are tearing the interior of the Shahdom in pieces. The trouble will spread farther before it is put down, if it can be put down. Maybe it cannot. Maybe the Prophet will enter Persepolis. That will mean the Ispanyans depart. Their wardership is shaky, they have ample grief overseas, they will not protest an order from a new government for their expulsion. A wave of religious persecution will sweep through the footprints they leave.

"The Russians may then move in. The Grand Knyaz in Kiev is not willing for such a risk. Too many of his boyars are, though. If they prevail, the Russian armies may march 'to the rescue of their Turkish co-religionists,' as the mealy-mouths will say. Saxonia can ill afford such a threat to its Balkan flank. We have brought strength into the eastern Mediterranean and are marshalling troops in Greece as a warning to the Russians not to attempt this, no?"

"That's what I've been given to understand, herr," I said, not unthankful for hearing it again. It was new to me and less than clear. I was lately back from two free months in Egypt, a land so lost in mysticism that, once well up the Nile, you hear hardly a whisper from outside.

Von Heidenheim puffed smoke that stung my nostrils. "Well, you should know and keep it to yourself, matters are more dangerous still. They have intelligence reports in Hamburg that they have relayed to their agents abroad, like me. Frankland will not let the Russians take over Persia. If they try, it means war, general war, with my poor Saxonia caught between Franks to the west and Russians to the east. At the same time, Frankland has not yet mustered the strength to forestall those hot-headed boyars.

"*We* have it. Wotan with her, Saxonia can interpose herself. The Russians should feel much less eager to move, knowing they shall fight us while the Franks make ready. It is risky, yes, that is obvious; but the risks of inaction look worse. Of course, we take this action only if we must. Perhaps things will not explode after all, and everybody can go home. But I have my doubts.

"So." He leaned forward. "This is my message to our various factors throughout the maritime provinces of the Shah. Come trouble, come the breakdown of royal authority and the Wardership, they should not flee. If at all possible—and their buildings are stout— they should hold fast and call for help. Most of them keep carrier pigeons that will make for Sicamino. I tell them that we will land troops at once and come straight to their rescue.

"Do you see? This demonstration of will and power should give even the Puritan fanatics pause. It could perhaps be the one added push that keeps the Shah from falling down. But we must have proper cause for intervention—landsmen of ours and their valuable goods to save, as is our right. Else it looks too much like collusion

between us and the Franks, and may touch off the very war we hope
to prevent.

"Therefore, go to Mirzabad and tell Otto Gneisberg to ready his
establishment for a possible siege."

We had not known I would be too late.

Or was I?

A small voice at my elbow: "Where now would my master fare?"

I looked down. Herod had tiptoed wide-eyed through what he
might well believe were the splendors of a djinni's hall. "Best you
stay behind, lad. You've done well, but it's dangerous out there." I
reached for my purse. "First I'd better pay you. Uh, learned Taki,
may he remain?"

"Of course," Boran answered softly. "He has made himself our
child." Her father nodded.

Herod straightened his thin body. "I am not a babe," he said.
"Have I not led men? Master, let me prove my worth beyond doubt-
ing. Then perhaps I can be your servant always."

I thought I knew what went on in that shock head. Money, a
good berth, a way out of the trap that held his mother—for him if
not for her. But the big eyes sought mine with more than reckoning
behind them. I knew that hope, that he had found himself a lord to
live for and die at the feet of. I never would.

It touched me more than I might have awaited. Also, I could in
truth use his guidance. "If you will have it thus, Herod," I told him.
"Your pay shall be three gold royals."

He sprang up and down for joy.

"Go with Mithras and Isis," Boran whispered. "Return to us.
Oh, return, Ro."

I found I was unable to speak further. Instead I lifted my hand
and made the sign of the Hammer. They did not ken it, but maybe
they would guess that it stood for the strongest wish I could offer.

Swiftly, the boy and I left. When we were out on the square he
chirped, "Where shall I take you?"

"To the house of the Saxonian traders," I said. "Do you know?
They are in the Street of the Magi, where the red-haired man was
set upon."

He pondered, finger to chin, laughed, and slipped off.

Thrice we heard prowling packs. He drew me into side lanes

and we waited until he felt we could go on. Again he brought me widely around; but belike I would not have arrived without him.

Above the massive door of a building that was a stronghold, its few outside windows iron-shuttered, hung a sign, as signs hang in Western lands. It showed an olden galley sailing on the red-black-red of Bremen. I knocked and shouted. The noise rattled between neighboring walls. "None here," I mumbled at last.

"They went to the Ispanyans," Herod guessed.

"So must we."

"My lord, I told you I have seen the men in yellow sashes outside that place. They will not let us through. Else everyone they mean to kill would flock there."

"Go back to . . . the House of Sorrows."

"Lord!" He sounded downright angry. "I am your servant."

I smiled a little. "Well, lead me as you did before."

We snaked our way onward, though only once need we go to earth. We were getting back to the upper town, which the rebels must have under some control. Trudging down the sky, the sun had begun to glare in my eyes. I saw vultures wheeling aloft.

The garrison besat a steading much like the one in Sicamino, though smaller. From the city wall, where a tower reared, jutted three of brick. The compound within held barracks, officers' quarters, arsenal, whatever else the peacekeeping force needed—and, now, fugitives crammed together. A broad open space ringed the defenses. From its far side I saw the three gates shut. Watchmen stood tautly on the parapet. Below them squatted warriors posted by Moussavi. Those were mostly Edomites, in threadbare djellabahs and burnooses; but yellow was around every waist and a firearm at every shoulder. Townsfolk who felt themselves safe and, I supposed, were glad the Puritans had come, milled and babbled before them.

"Wait here," I told Herod, and strode forward. It would not help me to have such a ragamuffin in tow. I looked neither right nor left, walking as if I were the conqueror. Men scowled, snarled, spat, but habit was strong in them. They gave way, a roiling bow wave that closed in a wake of curses and shaken fists. My sweat reeked. I would not let myself think how easily a knife could slide between my ribs.

"Hold!" cried a man who seemed in charge on the east side. "None may pass."

I halted and gave him my haughtiest stare. "May none come

out?" I asked. "This will surely be of interest to him who gave you your orders."

Uneasy, he tugged his greasy beard. "We are here . . . to keep the law of the Prophet," he growled. "What do you want, Westman?"

"To convey a message of the greatest moment, desert runner," I snapped. "If I may not pass through, you shall let someone out to hear me. Else I will report this, and after that your camel will know you no more."

Before he could think, I filled my lungs and shouted in Ispanyan. The sentries above leaned over the battlements. For a moment I was unsure whether I would live. A real soldier would at the least have had me seized. But these were simple peasants and nomads, unused to chains of command. I won my bet. The headman let me finish, he waved back followers who sidled near with rifles cocked, he even bade them hold off the crowd that pressed close and threatened me.

Nonetheless, that became a long wait in the heat and the reaching shadows.

It wasn't really. They were able men inside, who knew they must act at once. Otherwise the folk might get out of hand, or a true officer of the Puritans happen by. The doors creaked ajar. A lean, dark-haired man in blue tunic, white breeks, and headcloth marched forth. He looked about and went to me.

"Speak so I can understand you," said the Edomite.

"This is not for the likes of you to hear," I told him. He flushed. I looked into the hatchet face of the Ispanyan and said in his tongue: "Quickly, do you know if the Saxonian Otto Gneisberg and his household are with you?"

"They are," he answered. "What do you want? We stand on a volcano."

"I have a word of hope, mestro." I gave him my name.

"Reccaredo de Liria," he gave back, "hiltman in His Gothic Overlordship's Valencian Grenadiers."

I told him what von Heidenheim had told me. He gnawed his lip. "The Saxonians, the pagan Saxonians—"

"They are Europeans too," I said.

His pride snatched at that. "By the Bull, good enough in these miserable times! What would you have me do?"

"Tell Gneisberg. We must move fast. If we have everything ready before Zigad Moussavi hears of it, we can hope he will overlook the matter, set it aside, because he will not know what it means and he has his hands full already. But if first he gets any hint— They have an art in Persia of flaying a man alive and showing him his stuffed skin before they let him die, do they not?"

"They will buy mine dearly," de Liria snorted. "Very well, I will go straight to Gneisberg." Luck had been with me. Many a young officer would first have sought the garrison commander. We had no time for that. I should think the chefe del hirdo would later be happy to learn that a few refugees had gone out from under his ward.

If they did.

De Liria flipped me a Roman salute and went back. The gate shut. "He is to bring forth certain men who have need to return to their home," I told the Edomite overling.

He glowered. "What plot is this?"

"None. How can an unarmed spoonful menace the triumph of the New Revelation? If anything, they become hostages to it. This is a simple business of perishable goods that have just arrived and require care. You have already shown that you may let people leave the compound."

"Ey-yah, what you Westmen will do for money!" he fleered.

I shrugged. "The lord Zigad Moussavi is a man of wisdom. He will wish to keep their goodwill, when it costs him nothing, and take taxes from them afterward."

I waited. These warriors were ignorant of much, and their heads were afire with their faith, but they were not stupid. Give them time, only a short time, and they would begin to wonder. Then I was done. I tried to dwell on things far away, ice skating in New Denmark, a girl in London, a moonlit night off the Azores; and I waited.

After some part of endlessness—but the sun was still above the tower—the gate opened anew. A man came out beside de Liria. Though he was short and bald, he walked briskly. Behind them were another half-score, both European and inborn, who must belong to the trader's staff. My heart knocked.

They stopped before me. "I am Otto Gneisberg," said the short man in Saxonian.

"Mithras, could I go with you!" de Liria breathed.

"Hold fast where you are," Gneisberg said. "That will be your service."

Our band thrust into the crowd. It yielded surlily. "You're doing well to heed me, herr," I said.

Gneisberg's smile was wry. "Hiltman de Liria said something about preserving civilization. But we have left wives and children with him. If the compound comes under attack, it cannot hold out more than a few days."

"Do you think your post can do as well?"

"No. A while, though, yes, a while. We have firearms and provisions in the cellar, a cistern on the roof. I understand why it is critical that we be in possession of the place."

Herod tagged after us. We walked unhindered to the Street of the Magi.

Beneath the sign of the Handelsbund, Gneisberg unclipped a key from his belt. "I will now send a pigeon with this news, and the Saxonians offshore will make ready," he said. "If we are then bestormed, and I think we shall soon be, I will send the next message, and a relief expedition is justified under the Law of Kings, that the Russians honor too. It will put down these rebels, which should dampen insurrection elsewhere in the province."

For a time, I thought.

"You will join us?" he asked. "You have done well. If I live, I will see to it that you get a commendation."

I forbore to say I would rather have a cash reward. "No, I must be off."

He raised his brows. "What? This is not the most secure spot in the world, I grant you, but surely your chances are better here than anywhere else outside the compound, and your presence will improve them. Or are you leaving Mirzabad?"

"Not yet. I have unfinished work."

"The gods be with you," he sighed. "Or, in my philosophy, may you gain by the principles of righteousness."

"Mithras be with us both," I said, and left. Herod trotted at my side.

"Do we go back to the House of Sorrows?" he asked.

"We do," I answered, "and there we stay till the danger is past."

"Oh, good, good!" he warbled. "It is misnamed. I never knew how wonderful it is inside."

The real wonders you do not know about, I thought. I hardly do myself. Maybe we can learn something together.

This time he took me by the straightest way, as nearly as I could tell from the westering sun. Alike his ears and whatever inward senses his life had whetted must say that rage had rolled elsewhere. Or had calm already begun to fall throughout the city? Hope flickered in my breast.

It died when he stopped, lifted a bird-frail hand, strained forward. After a moment he stared back at me. "Lord, I fear bad men are at the House," he whispered.

Otherwise I heard only the seething in my ears. Drawing breath, I told him, "Bring me there unbeknownst."

"It is deadly," he said. "What oath have you given them?"

None. If anything, my duty was to keep myself hale for whatever von Heidenheim wanted next. Yet something in me without a name refused me the right to sheer off. At least I must see if there was any way of helping. "I am a man" was all I could think of to say.

Herod squared his shoulders. "And I am the man of my man," he said, red in the cheeks, so gravely that I almost laughed.

As fast as would keep stillness, we ran. Soon the noise reached me, yelp, clatter, thud. By houses we had passed earlier, I knew it came indeed from the Basileum. At the end, Herod took me into an alley and pointed upward. The building alongside was low; the grate over a window gave a hold for fingers and toes. I boosted him to the flat roof and scrambled after. On our bellies we glided to the other side and peered across the dolphin paving.

I counted nine men on the stairs. They seemed inborn here. The rags and the dirt could have been anybody's, but they yelled in Aramaic—street scourers, day laborers, stunted and snag-toothed. However, their thews were tough; they carried knives, clubs, an ax; once they got inside, Ailill and the African could slay two or three at most before going under. Then Jahan, his scholars, his daughter were booty. The gang had gotten a baulk of timber. Again and again they rammed it against the door. Bronze groaned. Hinges began to give way.

"Too many, lord," Herod breathed in my ear.

"We shall see," I murmured back. "Surprise and a good blade have much to do with fate. Wait here, small one. If I fall, remember me."

I crouched and sprang. As I fell, it flashed through me that I had not given him his pay.

I landed loose-kneed on stone, drew sword while I sped forward, wrapped end of cloak about left forearm. The robbers were lost in their work, sweating, slavering, a-howl with glee. I bounded up the stairs.

The heart is a fool's target, hard to find and fenced by the bones. My point went into the nearest scrawny back. I twisted to gash the liver, pulled my steel loose, and got the next man in the neck. Blood geysered, dazzling red. He rolled down the steps to lie crumpled.

"Out, out!" I roared in Danish. "Give me a hand, you scuts!"

The seven who were left let go the beam and whirled around. I caught a thrust on my basket hilt and slashed downward. There is a big artery in the thigh. The six yammered around me. I stopped a stab with the padding on my left arm.

The door swung wide. Ailill's staff whirred and crashed. In skilled hands, that is a fearsome weapon. I heard him sing as he fought, a song of wild and keening mirth. The African had found a mace among relics of old, proud days. I saw a skull splinter beneath it.

The axman came at me. He knew his trade. I withdrew before the battering weight. It could tear the sword out of my grip. Down the stairs we went. My friends had enough else to do.

A little form darted from nowhere. Catlike, Herod swarmed up the axman's back and clawed at his eyes. He shrilled and spat. The axman reached around, pulled him off, dashed him to the ground. Meanwhile I had the opening I needed. I stepped in and freed my foe's guts.

Two of the gang were still on their feet. They fled. "After them!" I bawled. "Let them not get away!"

I overtook the closest and hewed. Ailill and the African crushed the other.

They came panting to me. "Make sure of them all," I said. Ailill's knife slid forth. Soon the disabled stopped screaming.

I went back to Herod. The axman had fallen across him. I dragged the carcass off and knelt to see. In the pinched face, mouth gaped and eyes stared blind. The limbs were dry sticks. I lifted his head. He had landed on the back of it, hard. I lowered it again and rose.

Ailill and the African sought me anew. "Let's haul these corpses away," I ordered. My look went to the portico. Jahan and his folk clustered on it. They seemed well-nigh as drained of blood. "You," I called to the scholars. "Fetch mops and water. Scrub these stones as best you can. Take that timber inside. Be quick."

Nobody stirred. "Ahriman in hell," I snarled, "we've need to hide that anybody ever was here. Else we'll soon have others, more than we can handle."

Boran trod forward. "We heed you," she said softly. To the scholars: "Come."

It is folklore that a man is heavier dead than alive, but he does feel thus, and we three were wearied, shaken. Remembering how Herod had led me, I found an alley off a side street about a quarter mile away, narrow and already choked with rubbish. We ferried ours to it. Surely eyes watched from behind walls, but those that saw this end of our trip did not see the other. Nobody showed himself, nor questioned us from within. I had counted on that. The main wish of most folk is to be left in peace. They seldom get it. Witnesses would do and say naught. If these wretches we'd rid ourselves of had kin or friends, it was unlikely that those knew what had happened or where. Only a second mischance would bring the Basileum again under attack.

By the time we were done, the sun was behind westward walls. Streets brimmed with shadow. Jahan met us on the stairs. In the dimming light, he looked ill, and his voice came faint. "We have washed the stones, as you see. I pray you, go not straightway inside. Go to the back door and down into the storage room. We have brought soap, water, fresh garb. Cleanse yourselves."

"Of course, venerable one," said the African.

Jahan's words stumbled onward. "We are grateful to you beyond measure. Never think us otherwise. But it is not fitting to track blood over these floors."

"Sure and it's glad I'll be to get the stickiness off," laughed Ailill when I had explained.

Jahan shivered. "How can he be merry after—what was done?"

"It is nothing uncommon, you know," I answered.

Bewilderment crossed his face. "But this has been horrible."

"Few lives are like yours. Today you have glimpsed the world as it is."

For another heartbeat I stood still, while the dusk rose around us beneath a sky turning green in the west, violet-blue in the east.

"Before I myself wash, I have one more thing to do," I said. "Where is the nearest Fire Temple?"

Jahan gave me directions. It wasn't far. The scholars had laid Herod Gamal-al-Mazda on the portico, folded his hands and closed his eyes. When I picked his light form up, it felt colder than it really was. Nonetheless I held it close to my breast as I walked.

The Zarathushtran priest was aghast at sight of me and my burden, but stood his ground like a man. I smiled through the dusk. "Be at ease," I said. "This is a believer whom I bring home to you. Give him the rites and take him to your Tower of Silence."

To make sure of that, I handed over the three gold royals I had promised. Then I returned to the Basileum.

Thereafter we abided in our lair. Every day we heard a few shots. Thrice, somebody close by screamed. But none beat on our doors, and we dwelt day and night, day and night, as if outside of creation.

"Why do they call this the House of Sorrows?" I asked Boran.

She winced and frowned. "The commoners are superstitious," she said, and went on to speak of something else.

Later I talked with the African. Rustum Tata, his name was. Like me, he had come from afar to Mirzabad, knowing little, soon enthralled by the witchcraft that lay in the books. In some ways he was a better guide to them than Boran. She knew so much, her mind was so swift, that I was apt to find myself groping for what she meant. Thus she and I became likeliest to talk of homely things when we were together, our own lives and dreams.

"Why do they call this the House of Sorrows?" I asked Rustum.

He shrugged. "It holds whatever chronicles and relics of the city are left after more than three thousand years," he said. "That gives time for much weeping."

Me, I took happiness out of the vaults. Suddenly around me, speaking, loving, hating, striving, not dead but merely sundered from me in time, were the builders, the dwellers, the conquerors, Persians, Turks, Mongols, Romans, Greeks, Phoenicians, Babylonians, Assyrians, Pelishtim, Egyptians, endlessly manifold. In their sagas I could lose myself, forget that I was trapped and waiting for whatever doom happened to be mine.

Oh, yes, it was beyond me to read what stood on the crumbling paper, parchment, papyrus, clay. The scholars misliked my even

touching them with my awkward fingers. But they would unfold a
text for me, and put it into words I kenned, and we would talk about
it for hours, down in those dim cool caves. The lesser men are now
wan in my mind. I remember bluff Rustum, wise Jahan, Boran the
lovely.

What I learned is mostly lost too, flotsam in my head. How shall
a wanderer carry with him the dynasties of the Shahs, the Khans,
the Caesars, or the Pharaohs? Here a face peers from the wreckage,
there a torch glimmers in the distance, a word echoes whose meaning
I have forgotten, ghost armies march to music long stilled. It was
with a wry understanding of each other that Boran and I said farewell.

One voice is clear. That may seem odd, for belike it mattered
the least of all. But it lingers because it was the last that came to
me.

Jahan had been my guide through time that day. We were down
in the deepest crypt where the oldest fragments rested. A lantern on
a table cast a light soon eaten by the shadows around. The air was
cold, quiet, with a smell of dust.

Under our gaze was a Babylonian tablet. Beside it lay a sheet
of papyrus that must have been torn off a scroll. The inked letters
were well-nigh too faded to read, but they looked like far kin to
Edomite or Arabian. I pointed and asked idly, "What is that?"

"Eh?" said Jahan. He bent over the case and squinted.
"Oh . . . oh, this. I have not thought about it for years. A fragment
of an ancient lament."

"What does it mourn?"

"That is unclear. For see you, the language is long extinct. A
predecessor of mine puzzled out a partial translation, by comparing
related words in languages that he could read. Um-m." Jahan stroked
his beard. His tone quickened. "I studied it once. Let me try whether
I can still decipher it."

He opened the case and carefully, carefully took the papyrus
out. For a while he held it close to the lantern. His lips moved. Then,
straightening, he said:

"It is by a man of an obscure people who held this city and
hinterland for a while in the remote past. Sennacherib of Assyria
captured it and dispersed them through his empire. The many races
within it blotted theirs up. A similar fate had already befallen a sister

kingdom of theirs. This poet was, I believe, an aged survivor, looking backward and bewailing what had come to pass."

He peered again at the sheet and word by slow word rendered into Persian, not the everyday tongue but the stately speech of old:

"Jerusalem hath grievously sinned; therefore she is removed. . . . for she hath seen that the heathen entered into her sanctuary. . . . For these things I weep; mine eye, mine eye runneth down with water, because the comforter that should relieve my soul is far from me: my children are desolate, because the enemy prevailed."

He glanced at me. "I skip over lines that are illegible or that I cannot well make out," he explained.

"Was Jerusalem the name they gave this city?" I asked.

He nodded. "They appear to have been a peculiar people, always questioning things, even their gods, always driven toward a perfection they should have known is impossible. Certainly they had some ideas unique to them." He read onward:

"Thou, O Lord, remainest for ever; thy throne from generation to generation. Wherefore dost thou forsake us for ever, and forsake us so long time? Turn thou us unto thee, O Lord, and we shall be turned; renew our days as of old.

"But thou hast utterly rejected us—"

Boran's shout flew down the stairs. He put the dead man's cry back in the case before he followed me. By then I was on the ground floor. Through the walls I heard the rumble and crash of the Saxonian cannon.

Uncleftish Beholding

(from *The Anglo-Saxon Chronicle*)

In a lighter vein, here's a bit of popular science from another possibility-world. The history leading up to it is conjectural, though pretty clearly the Norman Conquest of England never happened.

When it first appeared, this piece drew some amusing responses, among them a challenge to me to identify "undrunkstuff." (Can you?) Recently it inspired a serious and wide-ranging paper by Douglas Hofstadter. I have not lived in vain!

FOR MOST OF ITS being, mankind did not know what things are made of, but could only guess. With the growth of worldken, we began to learn, and today we have a beholding of stuff and work that watching bears out, both in the workstead and in daily life.

The underlying kinds of stuff are the *firststuffs*, which link together in sundry ways to give rise to the rest. Formerly we knew of ninety-two firststuffs, from waterstuff, the lightest and barest, to ymirstuff, the heaviest. Now we have made more, such as aegirstuff and helstuff.

The firststuffs have their being as motes called *unclefts*. These are mighty small; one seedweight of waterstuff holds a tale of them like unto two followed by twenty-two naughts. Most unclefts link together to make what are called *bulkbits*. Thus, the waterstuff bulkbit bestands of two waterstuff unclefts, the sourstuff bulkbit of two sourstuff unclefts, and so on. (Some kinds, such as sunstuff, keep alone; others, such as iron, cling together in ices when in the fast standing; and there are yet more yokeways.) When unlike clefts link in a bulkbit, they make *bindings*. Thus, water is a binding of two waterstuff unclefts with one sourstuff uncleft, while a bulkbit of one of the forestuffs making up flesh may have a thousand thousand or more unclefts of these two firststuffs together with coalstuff and chokestuff.

At first it was thought that the uncleft was a hard thing that could be split no further; hence the name. Now we know it is made up of lesser motes. There is a heavy *kernel* with a forward bernstonish lading, and around it one or more light motes with backward ladings.

The least uncleft is that of everyday waterstuff. Its kernel is a lone forwardladen mote called a *firstbit*. Outside it is a backwardladen mote called a *bernstonebit*. The firstbit has a heaviness about 1840-fold that of the bernstonebit. Early worldken folk thought bernstonebits swing around the kernel like the earth around the sun, but now we understand they are more like waves or clouds.

In all other unclefts are found other motes as well, about as heavy as the firstbit but with no lading, known as *neitherbits*. We know a kind of waterstuff with one neitherbit in the kernel along with the firstbit; another kind has two neitherbits. Both kinds are seldom.

The next greatest firststuff is sunstuff, which has two firstbits and two bernstonebits. The everyday sort also has two neitherbits in the kernel. If there are more or less, the uncleft will soon break asunder. More about this later.

The third firststuff is stonestuff, with three firstbits, three bernstonebits, and its own share of neitherbits. And so it goes, on through such everyday stuffs as coalstuff (six firstbits) or iron (26) to ones more lately found. Ymirstuff (92) was the last until men began to make some higher still.

It is the bernstonebits that link, and so their tale fastsets how a firststuff behaves and what kinds of bulkbits it can help make. The worldken of this behaving, in all its manifold ways, is called *minglingken*. Minglingers have found that as the uncleftish tale of the firststuffs (that is, the tale of firststuffs in their kernels) waxes, after a while they begin to show ownships not unlike those of others that went before them. So, for a showdeal, stonestuff (3), glasswortstuff (11), potashstuff (19), redstuff (37), and bluegraystuff (55) can each link with only one uncleft of waterstuff, while coalstuff (6), flintstuff (14), germanstuff (22), tin (50), and lead (82) can each link with four. This is readily seen when all are set forth in what is called the *roundaround board of the firststuffs*.

When an uncleft or bulkbit wins one or more bernstonebits above its own, it takes on a backward lading. When it loses one or more, it takes on a forward lading. Such a mote is called a *farer*, for that the drag between unlike ladings flits it. When bernstonebits flit by themselves, it may be as a bolt of lightning, a spark off some faststanding chunk, or the everyday flow of bernstoneness through wires.

Coming back to the uncleft itself, the heavier it is, the more neitherbits as well as firstbits in its kernel. Indeed, soon the tale of neitherbits is the greater. Unclefts with the same tale of firstbits but unlike tales of neitherbits are called *samesteads*. Thus, everyday sourstuff has eight neitherbits with its eight firstbits, but there are also kinds with five, six, seven, nine, ten, and eleven neitherbits. A samestead is known by the tale of both kernel motes, so that we have sourstuff-13, sourstuff-14, and so on, with sourstuff-16 being by far the mostfound. Having the same number of bernstonebits, the samesteads of a firststuff behave almost alike minglingly. They do show some unlikenesses, outstandingly among the heavier ones, and these can be worked to sunder samesteads from each other.

Most samesteads of every firststuff are unabiding. Their kernels break up, each at its own speed. This speed is written as the *halflife*, which is how long it takes half of any deal of the samestead thus to shift itself. The doing is known as *lightrotting*. It may happen fast or slowly, and in any of sundry ways, offhanging on the makeup of the kernel. A kernel may spit out two firstbits with two neitherbits, that is, a sunstuff kernel, thus leaping two steads back in the round-around board and four weights back in heaviness. It may give off a bernstonebit from a neitherbit, which thereby becomes a firstbit and thrusts the uncleft one stead up in the board while keeping the same weight. It may give off a *forwardbit*, which is a mote with the same weight as a bernstonebit but a forward lading, and thereby spring one stead down in the board while keeping the same weight. Often, too, a mote is given off with neither lading nor heaviness, called the *weeneitherbit*. In much lightrotting, a mote of light with most short wavelength comes out as well.

For although light oftenest behaves as a wave, it can be looked on as a mote, the *lightbit*. We have already said by the way that a mote of stuff can behave not only as a chunk, but as a wave. Down among the unclefts, things do not happen in steady flowings, but in leaps between bestandings that are forbidden. The knowledge-hunt of this is called *lump beholding*.

Nor are stuff and work unakin. Rather, they are groundwise the same, and one can be shifted into the other. The kinship between them is that work is like unto weight manifolded by the fourside of the haste of light.

By shooting motes into kernels, worldken folk have shifted

samesteads of one firststuff into samesteads of another. Thus did they make ymirstuff into aegirstuff and helstuff, and they have afterward gone beyond these. The heavier firststuffs are all highly lightrottish and therefore are not found in the greenworld.

Some of the higher samesteads are *splitly*. That is, when a neitherbit strikes the kernel of one, as for a showdeal ymirstuff-235, it bursts into lesser kernels and free neitherbits; the latter can then split more ymirstuff-235. When this happens, weight shifts into work. It is not much of the whole, but nevertheless it is awesome.

With enough strength, lightweight unclefts can be made to togethermelt. In the sun, through a row of strikings and lightrottings, four unclefts of waterstuff in this wise become one of sunstuff. Again some weight is lost as work, and again this is greatly big when set beside the work gotten from a minglingish doing such as fire.

Today we wield both kind of uncleftish doings in weapons, and kernelish splitting gives us heat and bernstoneness. We hope to do likewise with togethermelting, which would yield an unhemmed wellspring of work for mankindish goodgain.

Soothly we live in mighty years!

Besides his newbooks and truthbooks, the writer has forthshown in Likething Worldken Sagas/Worldken Truth, The Warehouse of Dreamishness and Worldken Sagas, *and other roundaroundnesses.*

Losers' Night

Alternate universes border on fantasy. The possibility of their existence, let alone the actuality, has yet to be proven, and may someday be conclusively disproven. Physical transference between them would seem to lie well on the other side of the border.

Can we, though, be totally sure? Truly hard science fiction seeks to stay within the known laws of nature. Once we writers start making up our own laws we are, in Gregory Benford's phrase, playing tennis with the net down. Still, the hard assumption is perhaps the wildest of all, that our ideas about reality will never again suffer the kind of total, transforming revolution that has occurred two or three times in the past. We have many unsolved enigmas on hand. Of how many more are we not even aware?

Besides, by bringing together different eras and different individual destinies, one can say a little something about humankind; and our race is a part of the cosmos, however small. A few of my stories take place in the Old Phoenix, that inn outside all universes whose guests come from every world of might-have-been and imagination.

THIS TIME THE OLD Phoenix appeared to me alongside a country road after dark. I was on the walk that most men take at least once in their lives, until sunrise, and no wish was in me for any society other than that of the stars. I almost passed the house by. Then I saw its fancifully carved beam ends in silhouette against Sagittarius. Astonishment and—not gladness, but hope brought me to a stop.

A while, though, I stood hesitant. The road ran wan through fields where dew glimmered and occasional trees caught starlight in their crowns. A breeze lulled cool, bringing odors of soil, growth, all our familiar earth. I never know what I will meet on those unforeseeable rare moments when the Old Phoenix is open to me. There will surely be no ready answers or easy solace. Nothing that happens in that nexus between the universes ever quite happens. When guests say goodbye and walk back out the door, it shall be like waking from a dream.

Yet some dreams leave a measure of understanding. Always on those evenings an extraordinary company is gathered. Mine host and hostess take their pay in the stories they hear told, the play of spirit upon spirit as they watch. Not humble, I nonetheless cannot imagine why they extend their hospitality to me. Certain things, such as life itself, can only be accepted.

Did I decline, would they ever bid me return? That was not a risk to take. Besides, no matter how shaken I might be tonight, at least it should be out of this mood.

The inn might waver from sight at any instant. I scrambled

through the ditch, grass rustling about my ankles, and up the low steps. The signboard creaked faintly overhead in the wind. The bronze of the elephant's-head handle was cold to my touch, but when I pulled, the light that spilled forth was yellow and warm. I stepped through, closed the door behind me, and looked around.

The taproom is changeless, with oaken floor and wainscots beneath massive roofbeams. A fire crackles in a handsome stone fireplace. The mantel holds a giant hourglass and two seven-branched candlesticks. These and tapers sconced on the walls give better seeing than you would expect. Pictures and objects equally curious catch the eye more than do the writing desk and bookshelves, which I suspect are more meaningful. A rear door leads to a corridor and staircase; upstairs are bedrooms, though few go to them and then only out of necessity. Another door admits savory odors from the kitchen. The mahogany bar, with its brass footrail and beer pumps, betokens the same homely comfort as does the battered furniture: a long table and numerous small ones surrounded by straightbacked chairs, some armchairs wherever the last users drew them.

About a score of people were present, mostly in small clusters. Like seeks like, or unlike seeks unlike, for comradeship or, seldom, quarrel. They were unwontedly quiet, I thought. Not that the Old Phoenix often gets noisy. Even when high spirits burst into song in a corner, it somehow doesn't trample over conversation in the manner of my world's accursed jukebox and never-to-be-sufficiently-damned television. But talk tonight seemed less animated than usual, smiles infrequent and acrid.

He whom I call Taverner met me at the threshold. His own smile was as broad as always, his stocky frame at ease. Light reflected off the bald round head. "Hello," he said. "Welcome. How are you?"

Startled, I realized that he, who knows all languages, had not used mine. His was none I remembered ever hearing before, yet I had understood, my mind had rendered it into ordinary American English, but that was the tongue in which I stammered, "V-very happy to be here, thanks," for the strange words did not come to me.

His manner turned serious—not solemn, which I had never seen him be; it went deeper than that. "You'll find the rules are a little different this evening. Folks need to talk freely with each other, whomever they feel like."

I had sometimes wondered whether my limited abilities as an interpreter were what gave me entry. They would not be required tonight. I was invited because of my need. The Taverners are as merciful as their charter, or whatever it is that was once granted them by some power unknown, allows them to be.

"On that account," he continued, "please don't ask anybody's name, or use it if you think you recognize a person." He smiled again. "Otherwise, relax, enjoy yourself." He stepped aside. However friendly, he had the trade to oversee and couldn't well stand chatting. I nodded and went on. As I passed him, a muscular hand clapped me on the shoulder.

His beer called. I headed for the bar. Glances trailed me, but no voices hailed. Self-introductions among so motley a lot are apt to be awkward. Those who want companionship soon find it regardless, with the individuals most appropriate.

My steps brought me close to a table where two men had settled. They were both lean, dark, somber. Through the machine-gun talking I identified classical Latin and Canadian French. They couldn't have spoken directly without the special dispensation.

"—battle tomorrow or the day after," said he in the toga. "At Philippi, I think. Harder will be what comes afterward, to restore the Republic."

He in the plaid shirt and faded blue work pants caught his breath. The wine slopped from the tumbler he clutched. He gaped at the other for a second before he rasped, "Are you—" He broke off. Self-control did not seem to come easily to him. "But no, I must not say it, eh?" He drank. His hand shook; more wine ran down the stubble on his chin. "And I am not learned anyway, I am only a simple *métis*."

"You should return to your country," said the Roman. "Your people need you."

Intensity still hotter than his burned in the eyes across from him. "They cry for justice, by God, and it is to me they cry—"

I shivered, and then had gone out of earshot.

The bar was a haven. "Belly up, dearie," urged Taverner's wife behind it. Like him, she wore decent working-class clothes of seventeenth-century Europe, the garb in which I most commonly see them. Why, I haven't ventured to ask. As likewise was her custom, she addressed me in the style of a music hall barmaid from about the year when I was born. "A nice pint or two, that's wot yer need." She worked a pump. The gray bun waggled at her nape.

"And a shot of Tanqueray, if you please," I requested. Her shelves are small, but somehow she can produce anything you ask for.

"Right-o. 'Ere yer be." Mug and glass slid across the wood. "'Ow's the weather at 'ome?"

I shrugged. "Summer." The gin cast its sharp benediction over palate and gullet. The ale surged mightily after.

She cocked her head. "Yer weren't noticing, were yer?"

"Why should I?"

The smile faded on her plump plain countenance. "Three score and ten summers, the Book says. I should think yer couldn't afford ter waste none."

"Sometimes it can't be helped. But I don't want to cry on your shoulder."

"Cor! It'd be wringing wet if they orl did that ternight. Just look at 'em." She patted my hand. "Not that I ain't got sympathy, ducks. I wish we 'ad a nice girl for yer to pass the time with. But I'm afraid none o' these ladies 'ud do. I'm sure yer'll find some matey chap, though." She peered beyond me. "'Scuse, I see a gentleman wot could do with a refill."

"Me first, if you please," said a male voice at my side. The man employed English too, in his case with a hint of Irish lilt. He didn't look especially Irish, long-faced, neatly bearded, outfitted with frock coat, waistcoat, necktie, watch chain, upper-class appurtenances of the late nineteenth century. However, his lapel bore a green ribbon.

"Right-o." Taverner's wife drew his stein full of the same splendor I savored. From beneath the bar she got a bowl of ice and tongs, which she placed on a tray with a bottle of yellow-green liquor and a carafe of water. She bustled off.

Meanwhile the Irishman tipped mug to mouth, wiped foam from his mustache, and gave me a wry smile. "Pardon me, I happened to overhear," he said. "I daresay you know we're rather free in this place. Woman trouble?"

I felt no offense. He appeared to be one sheet in the wind, no more, but he carried it well and what he showed was less curiosity than kindliness. "In a way," I admitted. "Not as simple as I wish it were."

"Sure, is it ever?" Abruptly he winced. "What when you get her, but the cost is all else you ever lived for?"

"Hm?"

"Kitty—No." He stiffened. "My apologies, sir. I ought not have spoken. Now, if you will pardon me again, I should return to my tablemate."

"Oh, yes."

Did he think I felt rebuffed? "I would invite you to join us, were we not discussing reform politics." Passion flickered. "The restoration of justice in the teeth of timocracy—" It died down. "I suspect you would not care to do so."

"No," I agreed. "Thanks anyway."

A prickling in my spine, I watched him go back. The other man wore a classic Greek tunic and sandals, of a simplicity that made me guess he was a Spartan. The drink before him looked like diluted wine, and he took it slowly, with a bite off a crust of bread between sips, although in the Old Phoenix you can drink at a rate that would be disastrous anywhere else. His bearing suggested one used to command, such as a king, but a deep inward weariness blunted it, close to despair.

I thought it would indeed be worth listening to them, and then decided the first one had been right and it would not be wise.

My gaze ranged about the taproom. The guests were as wildly diverse as ever. Uniquely in my experience, only three or four were female. The lives of women may generally be quieter than those of men, but not the less interesting or important; and when they do get spectacular—Hatshepsut, Jingo Kogo, Gunnhild, Britomart, Sacajawea, Moll Flanders, Sojourner Truth, Valeria Matuchek, on and on and on—they make my sex look tame. What was it most of them lacked?

For a moment I thought I'd found my partner. From pictures I knew that rugged Edwardian Englishman. But no; I didn't wish to hear his dreams; I would be remembering the ice and hunger in which they must end. And what awaited the dark man in a form-fitting glittery coverall with whom he conversed?

Of course, for these it might be otherwise. Space-time is many-branched, perhaps infinitely so. There seems to be little we can imag-

ine which is not reality somewhere among yonder histories. Out of
them, into the Old Phoenix for a night, have come—I have heard,
or seen for myself—not only the likes of Theseus, Scheherazade,
Falstaff, Holger Danske, Huck Finn, Irene Adler, Red Hanrahan,
blind Rhysling—but a Zenobia who won free of Rome, an Abélard
who remained a whole man, a Rupert of the Rhine who outfought
Cromwell, a Tecumtha who preserved his nation—

I had no way of telling about any whom I now saw, unless I
met them; and why should I lay remembrance of other vanquish-
ments to mine? What were the Taverners doing? This was a house
where the good cheer and the heartening rarely failed, and then
through no fault of theirs. Had some darkness reached also into it?

My glance traveled past the fire, and my pulse hopped. A man
sat by himself on the far side of it. I knew that scarecrow form and
raven-gaunt face; I would have foreseen the soiled blouse and dou-
blet, the patched, ill-fitting hose and shoes. We'd hoisted quite a few
together, he and I, swapped verses and songs, tales and lies, ram-
shackle philosophies and smutty jokes. Okay!

I'd have to be a little careful. His temper could flare. I didn't
imagine he would ever actually pull the dagger at his hip, not here,
and certainly the landlord would never allow violence to be possible.
Still, I'd heard of what happened when Kit Marlowe showed up in
his presence—one of Taverner's few mistakes, letting two alley tom-
cats into the same room—and I'd been on the receiving end of
snakebite words myself. No matter. He got his mirth back equally
fast, laughed, and called for another drink. On the whole, I am immensely pleased and proud that François Villon likes me.

I took my ale in his direction. Meeting me on her way back, the
barmaid flashed a grin and a thumbs up. "That's right," she said,
"toujours gai," which I didn't think was quite out of the role she likes
to play.

It had little to do with the man she had served. He slumped
alone in an armchair before the hearth, gripping his drink and staring into the flames. With a shock, I placed bony head, craggy nose,
ruddy beard. He had both his ears. . . . "The light, the coals, like
the sun." I don't know Dutch, but you can't mistake that hoarse
language and under tonight's rules I heard what he mouthed.
"White, Theo. All colors go up together in the white heat." Fire-
glow wavered across the blank blue of his eyes. I hadn't thought

you could get this drunk in the Old Phoenix, no matter how much you gulped. Quite likely not. He had been born possessed. True, a whiff in the air told me it wasn't Pernod for him as I'd supposed, but absinthe.

I'd better assume that Mrs. Taverner knew her business, and go on past.

Villon sat shank over knee, chair tilted back against the wall, beaker set handy on a slab projecting from the side of the fireplace. He held a lute as scarred and battered as himself, from which he struck plangent chords. They weren't accompaniment but mere doodles of sound, keeping his fingers busy. He too looked fixedly at what I could not see, though in his eyes was a terrifying clarity. He wasn't singing, he was reciting, well-nigh too low to make out through the background of talk. Again I knew the language, his, "the old nasal French," wrote Chesterton, which bears "the clang and groan of great iron." But the spell upon us tonight made it into English for me as well, whose lameness set beside the original caused me to flinch.

> Bards may stand in a stately hall,
> Praising the warrior's victory
> Or wealth that is won and fame withal
> By men of deeds or of artistry.
> I will abide with the irony
> That leaves blow sere when the wind harroos
> And epitaphs blur like memory.
> Even the dead have much to lose.

He stopped. His lips moved on, wordless. He was, then, composing. After a moment he scowled, shook his head, spat a foul oath—and noticed me.

At that he leaped to his feet. Had most men done so, the chair would have clattered down behind. He left it as a cat does. Feline also was the quickness with which I saw him check my name before it escaped. "Why, you!" he exclaimed instead. "What a futtering wonderful surprise! You're just in time to rescue me."

Wiry fingers caught my hand. It was an odd, writhing grip, like his clasp on a former occasion. My guess was that it tickled him to give innocent me the recognition sign of some thieves' den. "Get

yourself a seat," he went on. "Tell me of your rascalities since last—
or, failing any, your virtuous deeds, doubtless much more comical.
As for my adventures, ah, first and foremost, the episode of the
priest, the sailor, and her whom I call Minou!" He paused, considered me, and finished, "No, perhaps not that for you, not immediately. I might salt a wound, eh?"

He was too perceptive. In his kind of life, you have to be. "What
do I rescue you from?" I asked fast.

"Annoyance. This bemerded ballade. I thought I had it—the
ambiance, thick as smoke tonight, verses should come of themselves
upon me, like pigeon droppings. But no. It drags, it clanks. Yet it
has me by the heels, it will not let me go before I give it a form, a
name. Diverting the mind a while, that may improve the flow." Villon
laughed. "At least let the wind of your words blow away the garbage
clutter of my metaphors! Sit."

Well, I might get more help than I gave. I glanced about after
a vacant chair. The nearest I saw was at a table occupied by two
men. I went for it.

Inevitably, they caught my attention. Both seemed healthy in
their later middle years, except that the European in the high stock
and snug trousers of sometime around 1820 strained to see with eyes
that were failing him. He sipped wine from a crystal goblet, so ap-
preciatively that it must be a prime vintage, unlike the raw stuff
Villon tossed down. The second nursed what I took to be a glass of
fruit juice. He was clearly a Muslim, attired in a plain white kaftan,
and I thought that the language in which he replied to his companion's French was Arabic. However, he himself was no Arab, being
light of complexion and straight of nose. A North African, I guessed.

"—and thus the spirit of fellowship and obligation that the desert breeds revitalizes a civilization when the nomads enter into it,"
he was saying. "For its part, it refines them of the dross, it makes
them fully human. But in the end it is fated that they in their turn
become corrupt and enfeebled."

The Frenchman nodded. "Likewise among plants and animals,"
he responded. "I believe extinction falls upon a line as often because
it changes itself all too well to fit the conditions about it as because
it adapts too slowly. Nevertheless, monsieur, with respect, you over-
generalize. Human societies must be as capable as natural species of
successful evolution into forms altogether new."

They were wholly caught by each other's ideas. Was such enjoyment peculiar to them this evening? "Excuse me, gentlemen," I said. "May I take the extra chair?"

Gentlemen in truth, they rose, bowed or salaamed, and assured me I was welcome. Thereupon they went straight back to their discussion. I half wished I could sit in on it.

"Yes, I think the next stanza is in ferment," said Villon as I returned. "Speaking of which, your health, old cock!" He raised his beaker and swallowed a draught. "May you soon win back your merriment."

I lowered myself, tasted my ale, and answered, "Did I say I'd lost it?" At once I realized my defensiveness was automatic. The ease of being able to speak English to him had its pitfalls.

"No, but I have seen flagellants cheerier than you. Moreover, this is a night for lives that failed."

"What?"

Villon swept his hand around in Gallic wise. "Only pay heed. Not that I can say who or what every soul among us is. But I see enough, enough."

Rebels, leaders, explorers—on what planet will the man in the garb that glitters perish, in what century? . . . "How can you identify any?"—you, expelled student, wastrel, brawler, robber, thief, jailbird, vagabond, and the devil knows what else, five centuries before my time in my world.

He shrugged. "One has the luck to be admitted here now and then. One gets sociable, drinks, eats, gambles a bit, talks, listens, watches, and, yes, thinks, if you can imagine that of me. Thus I have gleaned some sparrow's crumbs of history from other lands than France, in ages later as well as earlier than what I live through." He grinned. "It tempts to put them into my verses. But who would understand, at what passes me for home? I would rather not have witchcraft added to the accusations against me. So I fashion my variant songs in the Old Phoenix only, as occasion suggests them."

A cold gust made the fire jump and snap. Turning our heads, we saw the front door had opened again. Taverner was greeting a new arrival. We couldn't see past him to that person, but the entrance was full of gray fog and drizzle. I judged the time yonder to be near sundown of a winter's day in a northern land.

"Did he go forth into that weather because it matched his sentiments?" Villon wondered aloud. "Then he has need of comforting, him."

"Failures, did you say?" I challenged, for the implications were not pleasant. "Why on ... earth ... would the Taverners bring together a crowd of losers?"

"Well, many have lost, or will lose, in colorful ways. Observing them justify themselves to each other, that should amuse." There isn't much compassion in Villon's milieu, none in his part of it.

"No, wait," I protested. "The Taverners aren't the sort who—"

He raised his palm. "Hold." Mercurial, his attention had gone beyond the room, perhaps beyond this whole pocket universe. "I feel—yes, my second stanza, I have it."

Apparently an accompaniment was included, for he put his beaker aside, laid hand to strings, and chanted while the chords snarled underneath.

> At Stamford Bridge did Harald the tall
> Win him a grave as long as he.
> Dick Crookback's hissed from a theater stall.
> Lionheart beggared his monarchy.
> Athenian men fared valiantly
> To die in the quarries of Syracuse.
> Bolívar cried he had plowed the sea.
> Even the dead have much to lose.

The lute fell into his lap. He reached for the wine and knocked it back in a single gulp.

The newcomer approached. He had folded an umbrella, which he swung like a walking stick, and carried a bowler hat in his left hand, but drops glistened on tweed suit and Ascot tie. He was of sturdy medium height. An inward vigor and the rosiness that came from a lengthy tramp made it hard to guess his age, but thinning reddish hair suggested the mid-fifties. His nationality was never in doubt. That face would fit John Bull.

The breath whistled in between my teeth.

"Eh?" said Villon. "You know that fellow, do you?"

"I know of him," I whispered. "He—" Recollection. "Sorry, it'd be too hard to explain without letting names slip."

He accepted that. "Perhaps another evening, under a different rule of the house. Ohé, my cup is empty and yours has not far to go."

The Englishman reached the hearth, leaned umbrella against stone, laid hat on mantel, and held palms out to the fire. It wasn't arrogance, simply a lack of shyness. At first he scarcely noticed the Dutchman, whom I could not see from where I was and who kept silence. Despite the ample candlelight, I could trace flame-glow at play across his visage, and picture it on the other's.

Were they really that unlike, the healthy and the ravaged? Now that he was close, I saw the heaviness on the Englishman's mouth, the darknesses beneath and behind his eyes.

The barmaid hove into sight. "Wot'll it be, sir?" she asked him.

I glimpsed a forced smile. "You should know by now, my dear," he told her. "A large black coffee, if you please, and a larger cognac."

"Right, sir." She swung past us. "Yer ready too, ain't yer? Be straight back, loves."

As she pattered away, I turned to Villon and said very softly, "Failures? No, you're wrong. I tell you, he—Well, he's not."

The poet raised his brows. "Are you quite certain? I deem he has no more triumph in him than you do, my friend."

The subject of this ignored us, whom he saw peripherally, around the corner as we were. He looked down toward the Dutchman while he felt inside his jacket. "Do you mind if I smoke a cigar?" he inquired. The hand stopped short. Astonishment smote. "*You.*"

"Me?" the other mumbled. "You know me, monsieur?" He had fallen into an accented French. It was what he mostly used, expatriate that he was.

"Why, of course, of course. That is—" John Bull gathered his wits. "I have seen your self-portraits. Sir, I am overwhelmed."

"What?" asked the vague, harsh voice. "You have seen them? Where? How?" With an effort: "Oh, yes. Things work differently here, don't they? Forgive me. This light is too dim."

"Most light is, isn't it?" murmured the Englishman. "Except in the Provençal summer."

I shouldn't eavesdrop. Not that Villon would have hesitated, but neither of those two had meaning for him; and he was, after all, my drinking buddy. Furthermore, I wanted to refute that disturbing idea of his. "Failures?" I repeated. "People whose dreams crashed to the ground? Can't be. I wouldn't call you a failure, for instance. They'll remember you while they remember Homer and Shakespeare."

He'd obviously acquired some knowledge of the latter. Had they met, maybe, when I was not present? That wasn't a thought to pursue. As somebody has remarked, envy is the single one of the seven deadly sins that gives no pleasure whatsoever.

"I disappear young from history," he answered coolly. "Knifed in a sordid little fight, hanged in a provincial town whose records burned in a later war or revolution, or what? Who knows? Who cared?"

Asking about your destiny isn't actually forbidden in our tavern, unless when a special rule like tonight's implies as much, but the atmosphere discourages it. So does common sense. Regardless, Villon was bound to ferret out the story of himself.

"That doesn't follow, you know," I reminded him needlessly. "I've seen evidence your biographers have found, that you may have retired to safe obscurity and a ripe old age."

His laughter crowed. A lusty obscenity followed, to express his opinion of that evidence.

Knowing him, I agreed, and tried another tack. "Anyway, doubtless many of you exist, in many distinct histories. *This* Villon might well do better than the rest. In fact, if you don't, when you've been forewarned, you're a fool, and that's not the insult I'd choose for you."

His tone was almost flippant. "A fool and a fated man are not necessarily the same person. We do not what we should, but what we will, and devise fine reasons why that is what we must. Eh?" Once more he shrugged. "As for myself, I shall see."

I nodded toward the chevalier and the Berber. They had grown vibrant, waving their arms, talking into each other's mouths, ardent as lovers. "Those two are having a grand time. Infirmities aside, what's wrong with their lives?"

The barmaid reappeared. Her laden tray drew Villon's attention and thus perforce mine. The Englishman had pulled over an armchair that I had not noticed earlier, to settle opposite the Dutchman. I heard him: "I myself paint. Purely amateur. My landscapes are pretty, at best. But I should be honored if you would care to tell me—Ah, thank you, Mrs. Boniface, thank you."

As Villon took his own fresh vessel, I asked him, "Why do you drink that red vinegar?" Out of curiosity I had taken a single sip when first we met. "Here you could have the best that any of the worlds will ever know."

"But this I am used to," he said. "It makes going home at dawn easier." His smile gibed. "The proper appreciation of squalor and failure requires discipline."

"Damn it, you aren't—Well, what about the pair I mentioned? Do you happen to know anything about them?"

"As a matter of fact, I do. They aroused my inquisitiveness precisely because they seem exceptional. I spent an hour in the game at the table nearby, largely to keep an ear cocked toward them."

I glanced that way. Greasy cards were still in the hands of three shabby men and a sleazy-bright woman. Money lay strewn among the glasses. Tobacco smoke hazed their heads. Dresses, hair styles, features proclaimed them from various lands and eras. I wondered how such a drab, beaten lot had gotten in.

"Between what I heard and what threads of knowledge I had earlier unraveled from learned visitors, I won to a fair idea of who those two are," Villon continued. "No names at present, Monsieur Aubergiste requires. But I will hazard declaring that they rank with the greatest natural philosophers who ever lived. The Christian seeks to understand what drives the development of life, the infidel seeks to understand what drives the development of humanity. And they come close—so close! But they lack certain information that men will gain after their deaths, and all their majestic efforts go for nothing. Of course, they do not foresee that, and I'd not spoil their pleasure."

I had no ready response. Through the silence between us, from around the corner of the fireplace, cut the Dutchman's cry. "You have sold paintings, you say? Sold those things you dabble at? Do you know how many of mine have been bought in my entire lifetime? *One.*"

The Englishman's voice was an instrument which he played like a master, in summons to battle or, now, to call down peace. "Yes, I know, sir. I have read. It is an intolerable shame. But don't blame the people of my day too much, I beg you. By then we have begun to comprehend a little of what you were doing, and treasure it. Nobody pretends that my canvases are any more significant than the bricklaying that also helps me pass my days. It is my name upon them that excites a bit of interest—a name that you have never heard, naturally, unless attached to an ancestor of mine." Brief roughness: "And, to be sure, I have some friends left. A few. They wish to encourage me."

"Yes, failure can be very subtle, very quiet," Villon said after a minute. "Yours, for example, I surmise." His look searched like a pickpocket's fingers. "A disappointment in love? But scarcely straightforward."

"I don't want to talk about it!" I snapped. What hurt too much was that I was not the worst hurt; and that is all I will ever care to say.

He leered above the rim of his beaker. "The physicians and the old wives agree that for every ill, nature provides a remedy. Often the old wives know what some of those remedies actually are. Now let me prescribe. She playing cards and I have had our encounters before. I can introduce you without giving names, and then, if you will show a little enterprise—our host is tolerant and his hospitality goes far, you know. I assure you, in certain respects the wench is all else but a failure."

For an instant I was tempted, less by her than by her entire table. Speaking with them might teach me a minim of what a few writers (which, for these?) have known by instinct. . . . I decided against it. I really hadn't the heart to cultivate any new acquaintances, especially ones who in person were probably inarticulate.

Perhaps John Bull's words had entered my unconscious to breed that fleeting notion, for I grew aware of them.

"—writing. I can believe that's worth my doing, more than a pastime. History, biography, and, above all, warnings of what my countrymen must prepare against." He sighed. I visualized that heavy head shaking. "If they will only listen."

"Why should they not?" asked the artist. The personality before him must have drawn him a small ways out of his despair, and maybe out of his mad visions. "You said you have been a statesman."

"*They* call me a blundering ass. Many of them call me a murderer. You see, during the Great War I conceived the idea of—No matter. It failed, and thousands of young lives went down with it." Anguish yielded to stoicism. "Hence in due course I was rusticated." I saw a deep draught of brandy, a ferocious drag on the cigar.

It was my bladder that reminded me I had no business listening.

I got up. "The expedition," I said. Villon nodded absently and laid hold of his lute. His look went beyond me anew.

The lavatory of the Old Phoenix, in the hall below the staircase, is so logically designed that it has to be from a later century than mine. My course toward it brought me close past a foursome who made my stride turn slow. For a reason obscure to me, they were the most striking in the whole assembly. Even the cadaverous Spaniard who had patched together a ridiculous armor, and the stunningly beautiful, imperially garbed Chinese lady for whom he attempted courtliness—even they grabbed at me less than these.

The white man and the woman close beside him were presumably wedded, for they were both dressed like subjects of the Ottoman Empire, he in turban and robe, she veiled and trousered. Just the same, I didn't think they were Turks. The aquiline features above his beard suggested—not other Iberians, actually. Sephardim? He could have been in his forties, he could have been far older. May you and I never know such grief as had hollowed him out.

The second woman was of about that calendrical age. Physically she must live well, for her Tudor ruff, stomacher, gown were of the finest materials, though the dyes were somber, and jewels glittered on rings. But sorrow and ill health had given her the waxy pallor of those whose time grows short. She clutched a crucifix to her breast and obviously forced herself not to recoil from the second man.

"Jack Wilson," I heard him say. He had forgotten for the moment that he could dispense with English. His was quite fluent, in a slightly drawling dialect. "Can't give you my real name, that they know me by these days, but if you want a handle, then Jack Wilson is what the whites called me when I lived amongst them."

He was a Native American—from the Southwest, to judge by his looks. His shirt, vest, pants, bandana could have been on any ranch hand, except that the lower sleeves bore some kind of symbols and above them were armbands, each holding a feather. His hair fell to his shoulders.

The other man clenched a fist till I thought the skin might split over the knuckles. "Shall I give you the Islamic name I received?" he croaked. "Does the law of tonight's master allow that?" The veiled woman stroked his wrist. Her touch trembled.

Only through the power of the place could I know what he had said; and the English of the Tudor woman came near being a foreign language itself: "No matter names, until we lie dead and men open our hearts to see which are carved on them." She snatched her wine and drank in a single ragged motion.

"Would they truly do that in your land?" asked the American, dismayed. His mother tongue, unknown to me, brought a power akin to John Bull's into his voice. "Our ancestors will freely give us their names, their true and sacred names, when we have danced them home to us."

She tautened. Her lips drew thin. "Black necromancy, is it?" she hissed. "Are you fallen that deep in the toils of Satan?"

"No! It was God who spoke to me, on that day when the sun was darkened—"

My feet inexorably bore me out of hearing. I quickened them, and didn't linger in the washroom. On my way back, I slowed down again.

"Christ will receive you," the Tudor woman implored.

The man of the turban barked, whether in laughter or in pain. "I suppose we two can abjure yet another faith," he said, "if you will smuggle us to where it will not cost us our lives. But which Christ, my lady? Yours, the Lutherans', the Greeks', whose?"

"All roads up a mountain lead toward heaven," said the tribesman. "Let each walk the one his forefathers trod. On mine, I see their footprints in the dust before me, and in the wind I hear their ghosts singing the olden songs—"

A finger tapped my arm. Taverner had come this way after putting a fresh log on the fire. He beckoned. I followed him over to the wall.

"You really shouldn't listen in like that," he told me.

"I'm sorry," I blurted. "I didn't mean any harm."

He waited. His stance was amiable.

"Not to snoop or, or anything," I said. "I was just, well, fascinated and . . . chilled."

"Of course," he answered. "Ordinarily it's fine for our guests to mingle." He smiled. "In fact, we hope they will." Turning earnest: "But in this case, if you'd stuck around any longer they'd have noticed you, and it would have interrupted what's happening between them. Why don't you rejoin your friend?" Again a smile. "We've got a special brew on tap that you haven't sampled. It'll be waiting for you."

"Taverner," I asked desperately, "why are you doing this?

What's it about? I never expected you'd bring people like these together. To watch them hurting? The losers, the damned—"

A frown crossed his bare brow. "Can you say who's damned and who's not? I wouldn't dare try." He clapped my shoulder, as when I had entered. "Go drink your ale."

I seized it upon my return. Villon hailed me eagerly. "I have my third stanza," he announced. Nodding sideways: "Some words between those two there gave me the idea. It seems your politician did not send men to die without having aforetime ridden in the van of combat himself. The painter liked that. So do I."

Strings clanged.

A yeoman defeated becomes a thrall,
Knowing his children shall not be free.
Whatever we build must break and fall
Under the hoofs of history.
Since naught can remain for posterity
But a name all honor and none abuse,
Who was the victor, Grant or Lee?
Even the dead have much to lose.

"That's a stark thing," I said.

"Why, I would call it mild." Thinking of others by him—the "Hanged," say—I had to grunt assent. "An envoi is still lacking," he added. "Well, let it come as it chooses. Tell me about your era's latest lunacies."

The next couple of hours have nothing to do with anybody but us two. Honest fellowship is a healer second only to love. Not that François Villon was ever a nice guy. Nor did I give him either of the names in my own heart. But we walked arm in arm down crooked lanes; he took me a-scramble over moonlit roofs, while showing him vistas of what I had seen opened my eyes to the wideness of them. His account of the priest, the sailor, and Minou was evilly poetic and unforgivably funny.

I could not help catching fragments of the talk at the fire.

"You are a brave man."

"I do not think I would have the courage to live with demons."

"Do I? Mine overrun me. I think in the end they will take me."

"You will have fought until the end."

"With what for weapon?"

"Your brush. And I swear, I promise, that what that wins for us, the gates of hell shall not prevail against."

The shutters stay closed over the windows of the Old Phoenix. I suspect nobody has ever inquired of Taverner what he would see through them. A grandfather clock in a corner ticks and ticks, booming at each hour. Its hands announce the dawn when the last guests must leave. As that drew near, I found that I no longer dreaded going home.

Life rang in the Dutchman's voice. "Then you find you are not broken?"

"After being in your company, sir," replied the Englishman, "how could I surrender?"

Taverner had come to stand unobtrusively nearby. Our glances crossed. He hesitated a moment before he stepped over to me. His words ran low and fast. "We've got to observe the restrictions, you know. You wouldn't want us to lose our license, would you?"

"God, no," I said.

Taverner made a fending gesture. "Not God. Absolutely no idea of that. But we do what we can, the wife and I. We do what we can."

The Englishman and the Dutchman had risen to shake hands. The movement brought them in full view of us. "An honor, sir, and an enlightenment," John Bull declared. "I trust we will have more encounters."

The painter's straightened shoulders slumped. He looked away. "Not for me, I think," he muttered in the tongue of his childhood. "Never and never."

The Englishman bit his lip, started to say something, thought better of it, and addressed the landlord instead. "Goodnight, good friend. Thank you for very much." He took hat and umbrella and stumped from us.

The painter stared after him. "Beware of darkness," I heard him say. "Everywhere darkness. No, the white sun and the huge stars— But what when they burn out? What then?"

He shook himself, cackled a laugh, tossed off his absinthe, and retreated from my sight, sinking back to look into the fire. For a while he had been almost happy.

Villon, who had watched, took the lute, strummed, and concluded his piece.

Christ, Prince of losers, behold how we
Are burning heretics, hanging Jews
In this thy name for the fear of thee.
Even the dead have much to lose.

I thought his mind had slipped back to his medieval realm, until I remembered what world it was whereon Winston Churchill now opened the door. The envoi sums up the entire ballade.

Science
Fiction and
History

Besides its alternate universes, science fiction often draws more directly on history for its motifs. As you can see, I wrote this essay in response to one by Gregory Benford, and so should perhaps give him equal time here. However, there was no real dispute between us; I simply wanted to explore the topic a little further.

THE WORK OF GREGORY Benford is always interesting. His essay "Pandering and Evasions" (*Amazing Stories*, January 1988) is no exception, and not merely because it says a couple of nice things about me. It seems to call for a response—not a rebuttal, because I have no quarrel with it, but a little further exploration of one topic which he brings up in passing.

Rightly deploring the unimaginative and unconvincing social backgrounds of too many science fiction stories, he mentions "the unexamined assumption that liberal capitalism (or, more rarely, state socialism) will form the backdrop of societies centuries from now. . . . Worse, there are even semifeudal regimes invoked in high-tech societies. . . . Similarly, writers who sing of empire had better examine their assumptions. The solar system is a vast place, with radically different environments. Does the reflexive analogy to the old European empires, with their imperial fleets and rural colonies of docile natives, make any sense?"

Excellent points. However, they deserve closer examination. To what extent can we reasonably model the future on the present or the past? Of course, events never repeat themselves exactly, and it is debatable to what extent classes of events do, but this is at the very least a legitimate debate. What kinds of change in the human condition are reversible and what kinds are not? Does it or doesn't it make sense to imagine future Caesars, future Jeffersons and Bolívars, future Carnegies, and so on?

I don't believe anybody has any sure answers. Certainly I don't.

Still, we can look at the record and make a few suggestions, for whatever they may be worth.

Let's begin with the record of science fiction itself. Quite a few stories suppose that developments to come will resemble developments that have already occurred, and some of these stories are by well-regarded, rather cerebral writers. We might hark back to Robert Heinlein's old "future history" series, which has raw colonialism, including indentured labor, appear on the planets and religious dictatorship arise at home. Soon afterward came Murray Leinster's classic "First Contact," wherein the characters take for granted that the aliens they encounter could be murderous bandits or imperialists. In recent years, Jerry Pournelle has described wars, revolutions, and empires among the stars (and so have I). Contrastingly, Larry Niven depicts a Solar System under the governance of the United Nations. At first glance this may look different from anything hitherto, but in fact the society is quite Western; and the ideal of the UN as a peace-keeping force antedates the organization itself. Isaac Asimov's Foundation saga has a Galactic Empire develop. Perhaps this takes place peacefully, though little is said about that; in any case, eventually the state displays all the traditional trappings of despotism, and decays along the same lines as Rome did. We could go on at length, but these examples ought to suffice.

Some stories have indeed shown future societies unlike any of the past. Among them is "The Heart of the Serpent," by the late Soviet writer Ivan Efremov. He wrote it explicitly as a response to "First Contact." In it, humans and aliens also meet in deep space, but goodwill and mutual trust are immediate, because any civilization that has developed to the point of making interstellar voyages must necessarily have evolved beyond warlikeness or banditry. In a letter to me, Efremov opined that either humankind will soon cross that threshold or else it will destroy itself, so he figured he might as well make the optimistic assumption. Other writers in the former Eastern bloc generally did likewise, although several included ironies and dilemmas in their work.

The question is, How likely are we to undergo basic changes, for better or worse? *Can* we? Certain of the writers who reply "Yes" have given us fascinating imagined futures to think about—to name only three, Benford himself, Greg Bear, and William Gibson. Time may prove them correct in principle. I simply wish to argue that in our present state of ignorance, "No" and "Maybe" are answers just as intellectually respectable. The single thing I feel sure of is that nobody has foreseen or will foresee the real future; whatever comes to pass, we are bound to be surprised.

To make my case, I shall have to show that recurrence of institutions and patterns of events is not absurd. This is already implicit in the better stories that employ that assumption. Benford mentions Niven and Pournelle's *Oath of Fealty*, in which neo-feudalism is a logical consequence of high-tech. But let me now step out of science fiction and look at the matter from a wider perspective.

We live in an era of many revolutions. Are any of them irreversible? For example, what will be the effect of nuclear weapons on war? They have definitely failed to abolish it. Have they, though, made all-out, life-and-death strife between great powers, in the manner of World War Two, impossible? If not, will such a conflict terminate civilization, or will it end in a negotiated peace of exhaustion, or will it have a clear winner? While the last of these propositions is highly unfashionable in the West, it is not unthinkable, having been for many years a keystone of Soviet military doctrine.

Even if no nuclear wars are ever fought on Earth, conceivably they will be waged in space, perhaps fairly often, with the victors then controlling the "high ground" and able to dictate terms. This situation bears resemblances to wars between city-states in Renaissance Italy, which were usually carried on by mercenaries. Disunited and without effective citizen forces, the peninsula became the booty of foreigners, such as the French and Spanish. We can imagine the United States and Russia, neglecting their strength on Earth in favor of their space weapons, suddenly threatened by a vast, modernized Chinese army. The details would make for an interesting, if melodramatic story.

Mind you, I do not say this will ever happen or that it ever can. I simply offer it as one supposable analogue of past history.

For the past gives us our only real clues to the future. The present is too small a slice of time, a mere interface between what has been and what will be. Although nearly all primitive societies are, today, extinct or dying, we should include the findings of anthropology in our historical studies. They help show us how various and unpredictable our species is.

After all, the high-tech West comprises a scanty fraction of

Earth's population and occupies rather little of the acreage. While Benford declares, with much justice, that "thinking about a future that is urban, diverse, technology-driven, and packed with ambiguities" is "what SF is about," the majority of mankind still lives in rural environments, under conditions that have changed only superficially from the early Iron Age or even the late Stone Age. Its institutions and ways of thinking haven't altered a great deal, either. When change has occurred, the consequences have oftener been catastrophic than benign; see any slum, urban or rural, anywhere on our planet. Adoption of modern technology has not usually gone together with Americanization.

Therefore it seems unrealistic to take for granted that the high-tech minority will engulf the backward majority. Maybe; or maybe the present gap between them will widen until we almost have two separate species; or maybe high-tech will founder.

Let's assume that it will survive. The alternatives are so depressing. Moreover, survival does look probable. How far will it develop, though? Could it regress for reasons internal to itself?

One hopes not. These days it is chic among Western intellectuals to sneer at "technofixes." Nevertheless, technofixes are what have largely given us our civilization, or our very humanity. They began with hominids taming fire and making the first crude tools. They went on through agriculture, with everything that that brought about in the way of cities, literacy, and (alas) government. I need hardly describe what the subsequent technofixes of medicine and scientific instrumentation have meant to the human spirit.

On the whole, technological revolutions have been irreversible. This is true even when their immediate effects have been bad. A case in point is early agriculture. Without romanticizing the life of hunter-gatherers, we must admit—archaeology and anthropology have shown—that it was easier, more free, and less subject to famine and disease than the life of a peasant in the ancient riparian kingdoms. However, agricultural societies could support denser populations and muster far more force; hence they either swamped the hunters, or the latter took up a similar way of life. (This is an oversimplification, of course, but basically right. Where the environment was more favorable, as in Europe, farmers lived better than in the original civilizations.)

There was never any large-scale reversion. Occasionally and locally, societies collapsed and people went back to a rude existence. Examples include Greece after the fall of Mycenean civilization and the Guatemala-Yucatán area after the decline of the Mayas. Yet everything that had been learned continued to be practiced elsewhere. No important art has ever been lost, nor has any minor one been for any significant length of time.

On this analogy, we can expect that high-tech will not disappear, short of a planetwide catastrophe. If such destruction does occur, probably the knowledge will be preserved here and there, and will be put back to work after new societies have become secure and wealthy enough. (The knowledge of how to build good roads and bridges did not vanish when Rome fell, it simply lay in abeyance for a thousand years or so.) To be sure, those societies will doubtless be quite different from the old, and confront different conditions. For instance, they will have inherited a world poorer in natural resources than it once was, and be forced to adjust their technologies to that— something I looked into in *Orion Shall Rise* and other stories.

But I see nothing inevitable about high-tech spreading to all humanity or continuing indefinitely to get higher and higher. Indeed, the latter seems quite unlikely. Growth curves characteristically have an S-shape; they rise sharply for a while, then taper off toward a plateau. The potential for continued advance may remain, but economic and other social factors prevent its realization. Some major developments have actually been aborted.

An example is Chinese seafaring. Under the Ming Dynasty, expeditions went throughout Southeast and South Asia, crossed the Indian Ocean, and rounded the southern tip of Africa. The imperial bureaucrats then called a halt, ordered the demolition of every deep-water ship, and forbade anyone to leave the empire on pain of death. It has been pointed out that this was not altogether a bit of witless reaction. The voyages had just been for purposes of prestige; enormously costly, they returned no profit.

Meanwhile the Europeans, who did stand to gain, were sailing eastward from the Cape of Good Hope and westward across the Atlantic. . . . The parallels to our space program are a little chilling.

Despite the obstacles, it is possible that everyone will eventually come into the high-tech fold. Corresponding things have happened before. Again, the most obvious example is civilization itself. This was invented in the Old World only once or twice; archaeologists disagree whether the Indus Valley peoples got the idea independently or it spread from the Mesopotamians. In either case, the complex of agriculture, cities, centralized government, etc. gradually diffused almost everywhere south of the Arctic and north of the Sahara Desert, plus, to some extent, Africa farther on. A similar thing happened in the New World, though less completely because the European invasion interrupted it. Here civilization definitely did have two distinct origins, in Central and South America.

Nevertheless, look what widely divergent forms it took among the assorted nations. Directly or indirectly, Egyptians, Phoenicians, Medes, Persians, Greeks, and more all learned from the Mesopotamians, but none of them much resembled the latter nor each other. The Far East saw cultures still more foreign arise.

The Scientific Revolution began in southern Europe, the Industrial Revolution in northern Europe. By now they have affected the whole world. Most countries have sought to industrialize, with varying degrees of success, and several have contributed outstanding scientists. Yet beneath the shared machinery and shared conventions, how alike are they?

As a fairly trivial but perhaps amusing example, when I was in Brazil the people I met, besides being charming, were highly educated and cultured, splendid specimens of Western civilization; and Brazil is an important country. Now one would think that punctuality is essential to the smooth running of modern society. But that's an Anglo notion. I soon learned that when a Brazilian said he'd meet me at 9 A.M., he meant sometime before noon; and presently I learned to relax and accept this. Nothing terrible happened.

More seriously, in our century we have seen Russia and China make gigantic efforts to catch up technologically, with impressive results. However, they did not thereby become more like us. They adapted the new instrumentalities to their societies, rather than the other way around. In a subtler fashion, the same is true of countries such as Japan. There we see people in Western clothes using Western equipment under capitalism and parliamentary democracy—but their own versions, uniquely Japanese beneath the façade.

I do not by any means decry this. It would be tragic for humankind to lose its diversity; our future would then look like an anthill. I simply point out that science fiction is presumptuous and unimaginative when it extrapolates solely from Western, usually

American civilization of the late twentieth century. Dominant influences in the future may well come from elsewhere and be, from our present-day point of view, archaic—for example, Japanese paternalism or Islamic zealotry.

It seems equally possible that elements from our own past will return to claim us. While technological revolutions, which do have social consequences, may well be irreversible, social characteristics not immediately related to technology have always been labile. This brings us to the politics of the future.

Some philosophers of history have maintained that it moves, or tends very strongly to move, through cycles; if events do not repeat, classes of events do. Arnold Toynbee is the best-known of these thinkers. We can identify similarities between the natures and fates of, say, the Egyptian Middle Kingdom, the Chinese Han Dynasty, the Roman Empire, and several others. They cannot be purely coincidental. But it is a matter of interpretation how close the similarities actually are, and a matter of theory what causes them. "The ineluctable logic of events" is a sonorous phrase and gives rise to considerable thought, but it is scarcely comparable to Newton's laws of motion. Still, I'd call it a legitimate starting point for a science fiction story; *vide*, again, Asimov.

Its implication is that we will make the same old mistakes over and over again, with the same old consequences, though at the time these will always be called new and progressive. As I have remarked elsewhere, the lessons of history aren't really hard to learn; the trouble is that hardly anybody wants to learn them. Rudyard Kipling's poem "The Gods of the Copybook Headings" says this about as well as it has ever been said.

To give illustrations from the present day would be to go into political polemics, which is not my purpose here. Suffice it to say that much is going on which looks quite familiar. The world has repeatedly seen the rise and fall of many analogous institutions and ideals.

Americans naturally tend to think of the future in terms of republican government and democratic ethos. Yet theirs, the oldest continuously existing republic on Earth, has barely passed its two hundredth birthday. Republics have generally been short-lived and democracies (which are not the same thing) still more so. At the moment democracy seems to be in a position, worldwide, like that of monarchy in nineteenth-century Europe; almost everybody goes through the motions of it, but in most cases this is a pious fiction and the structure is moribund. Many science fiction stories have depicted it as giving way, in fact if not in name, to the dictatorship of corporate capitalism. In practice, though, private organizations exist on sufferance of the state, and the real dictator is always the man who controls the armed forces and the police. At most, large corporations may be junior partners of government—very junior—and this is possible in just a few countries. Other outfits, such as unions, could as well fill the role, and churches have sometimes been coequal or senior.

Freedom has always been rare and fragile, perhaps because most people don't value it much. Institutions are more likely than not to revert to primitive forms. For example, chattel slavery was essentially abolished in the course of the nineteenth century, but in the twentieth, Nazis and Communists brought back forced labor on an enormously larger scale.

Equality and official compassion are more commonly associated with powerful government than with liberty. Thus, it was not the Roman Republic but the Roman Empire that gave slaves some protection from the grossest forms of abuse. The Empire also saw women, at least in the upper classes, accorded rights and respect comparable to those men enjoyed. There was a feminist movement similar to today's. We know what became of it and of other reformist hopes.

There was, too, a rising tide of superstition, general belief in everything from astrology to necromancy. In other words, Rome had its own New Age. Eventually the Christian Church took over and disorganized credulity yielded to organized religion. Perhaps our fundamentalists will play such a part in the future.

The prospect of strong-arm rule, social immobility, racism, sexism, and blind faith is as unpleasant to me as it is to you. I do not say it will come to pass. I merely say that it can, and that stories which depict it are not necessarily by authors who lack imagination.

Nor is it necessarily simple-minded to anticipate no new orderings of society, different in kind from any that have gone before. Though often proclaimed, this advent hasn't happened yet, in thousands of years. Instead, we have gotten changes rung on the same half-dozen or so themes. For example, in many Bronze Age societies and in Perú of the Incas, the economy was not based on exchange as we understand it. Everything that was produced, beyond the simple necessities of life for the commoners who produced it, went to the god-king. He then handed the goods out as he saw fit. Today a less extreme version of this is known as income redistribution in the United States, socialism abroad; and far from being a quantum leap of progress, true communism would amount to the old thing itself.

Granted, countless details of tribalism, monarchy, hierocracy, timocracy, democracy, etc. have varied throughout history, and so has the overall mix. For instance, universal literacy has had a significant influence on political arrangements and processes—though it can as readily strengthen the bonds of the state on the individual as it can set him free. In such interaction of factors lies the possibility of many stories.

Agreed, the future will be no simple replay of the past, and some scenarios will never be seen again. They doubtless include the interplanetary Wild West long beloved of science fiction. We won't get the asteroid prospector poking around in his spaceship like the Sierra prospector with his burro. Even if spacecraft become cheap enough, as Eric Drexler's work on nanotechnology suggests may happen, they will be too powerful, too potentially destructive, for us to let just anybody have them. Meanwhile there will surely be developments unprecedented in history, unforeseen by us all—though science fiction writers can have fun trying.

Yes, I do expect changes in the future, as radical as were wrought by fire or agriculture or literacy or the scientific method, transforming humanity as profoundly as they did. I think these changes will spring from science and technology, not from anyone's great new blueprint for utopia. It is conceivable that eventually they will bring about a social order that does not carry the seeds of its own destruction. Be that as it may, the outlook is not hopeless. Good societies have in fact flourished now and then, for a while. They can again in times to come.

Yet if we are to have any real control over our tomorrows, we must learn the lessons of our yesterdays. We need to do that even if all we want is to write believable science fiction.

Rokuro

As the foregoing piece implies, for a long time most science fiction, especially American—not all, even then, but most— was provincial, its characters overwhelmingly Anglo-Saxon and its tomorrows very like the authors' surroundings except for bigger and flashier technology. We've learned better now, though I suspect that soon our present-day conventions, such as a world ruled by heartless multinational corporations, will look equally quaint. The diversity of humankind is a wonderful and life-giving aspect of the diversity of the cosmos. We cannot foresee what will come of it; we can only try to imagine, knowing that our creations won't have much if anything to do with what actually comes to pass.

I have also suggested that as other cultures adopt modern scientific technology, they will not thereby become mere copies of the West. Certainly that has been the case so far. Traditions, whole ways of living, thinking, and feeling, have enduring strength. They can survive, sometimes underground, to rise anew after centuries. It could happen beyond Earth, too. With that in mind, I have attempted to write a Nō play of the future.

PERSONS: A priest (*waki*)
  An engineer (*kyogen*)
  A robot (*mae-jite*)
  The ghost of Rokuro's young manhood (*nochi-jite*)
PLACE: Comet Hikaru
TIME: Great Spring, the third year

(*An attendant brings a table to center stage. Upon it are a prop representing a spacesuit and a thin metallic slab.*)
(*The Priest enters and goes to the* waki *position, where he stands.*)
PRIEST: As a fire seen afar,
  As a fire seen afar
  Beckons the traveler through night,
  So do the lights in the sky.
(*He turns to the front of the stage.*)
I am a priest from Kyoto, on pilgrimage. My wish is to follow the course of holy Rokuro, who more than a hundred years ago went among the planets in search of enlightenment. On a world where the sun is dwindled to the brightest of the stars he attained Nirvana. Early in his quest he came to Comet Hikaru and sojourned for a span. Now I too have landed here.
(*The Engineer enters.*)
ENGINEER: Welcome to our base, reverend sir. I fear you

arrive at a most unpropitious time, and my duties are many, but if I can possibly serve you I shall be honored.

PRIEST: Thank you. I understand you are preparing to abandon this body.

ENGINEER: Sadly, we must. For two centuries have men and machines mined its ice.

CHORUS: Triumph and tragedy,
    Festival and funeral,
    Honored graves,
    And the work of remembered hands.
    We gave to the rockets their thunder
    And breath to all children
    Born beyond Earth,
    We, the quenchers of thirst.
    Because of our labor, water falls past greenwoods
    Into lakes adream
    Where since the creation
    Were stone and dust—
    Cherry blossoms white over Mars!
    But now the comet flies moth-swift
    Out of the mothering darkness
    Into her left hand.
    Flesh would smoke away on the solar wind,
    Bones crumble, teeth become red coals,
    Silicon melt in furnace machines.
    We flee from the Burning House.

ENGINEER: Perhaps we can return after perihelion passage.

CHORUS: What flames shall billow like pampas grass
    In the storms of the coming Summer,
    What eddying strange mists
    Shall haunt this land in its Autumn
    Before the huge stillness
    Of the thousand-year Winter?

ENGINEER: Meanwhile we make ready to evacuate. The ship that brought you will be one of our ferries. Whatever your errand, I fear you have little time to complete it.

PRIEST: I wish to visit the dome where holy Rokuro lived and meditated.

ENGINEER: What a surprise! I do not believe anyone in living memory has gone there. It is maintained as a shrine, of course, but it stands isolated, at some distance from our settlement; and, alas, we have been over-busied throughout our lives. At present every ground vehicle is engaged. However, if you know the use of spacesuit and jetpack, I can lend you them. Fortunately, rotation has newly carried this base and the shrine both into night, so you can safely travel, but make sure you get back ahead of the lethal sunrise.

PRIEST: Thank you, I shall. That gives me about nine hours, am I correct?

ENGINEER: Yes.

(*He puts the spacesuit prop across the shoulders of the Priest and hands him the slab.*)

There, you are outfitted, and this electronic navigation map will conduct you. May your venture be prosperous.

PRIEST: Blessings.

(*The Engineer bows and exits.*)

PRIEST: Time is indeed cruelly short. I will cycle through the main airlock and set forth at once.

(*He takes several steps to stage right and then back, indicating a journey. Meanwhile an attendant removes the table and another places a prop representing a large computer before the* shite *pillar.*)

I have traveled so fast that already my guide declares I have reached my goal. That dome on yonder ridge, was it his hermitage? I will approach it.

(*He moves toward the* shite *pillar.*)

> Well-nigh weightless, like a ghost I go,
> Wraith-world around me, white and stiff,
> Forever alone in emptiness.

CHORUS: "The eternal silence of those infinite spaces
> Frightens me." But they know no rest.
> They grind worlds forth to the tears of things
> And they grind them back to oblivion.
> Everywhere fly the energies,
> Inaudible hiss of invisible sleet.
> I see a crag thrust gaunt as a tombstone
> Where half the glacier that lay above it

Roared aloft this day, a heaven-high fountain
Strewn by the sun across the black.
Vast, shuddery streamers hide the stars
And the very horizon cries violence,
Toppling away into endlessness.

PRIEST: Your grace, Amida, came to Rokuro
Far from here and long years later.
Yet I will retrace the whole of his path,
Praying it still may lead to salvation.

(*The Robot enters slowly along the* hashigakari.)

ROBOT: "When rainshowers clear,
For a small while comes a scent
Of hawthorn in bloom."
As memory. . . .
Oh! A visitor.

(*He goes to meet the Priest. They mime tuning in their radio transceivers.*)

PRIEST: Is this the shrine of Rokuro's former residence?

ROBOT: It is, although few have ever come. May I ask what has brought you?

PRIEST: What but devotion? I am a priest. Do you attend it?

ROBOT: I carry out the necessary tasks of maintenance.

PRIEST: I am surprised that a machine is curious about my purpose.

ROBOT: What you see is merely the mechanism. It is radio-linked to that computer over there, in which dwells an artificial intelligence sufficient to the various and varying requirements of my duty.

(*He dances, with appropriate gestures, as the Chorus speaks for him.*)

CHORUS: Long coursed the comet through quietness.
You would think it never was touched by time.
A day or a decade, what difference?
Heaven's River stretched over and under,
But there surged no sea around this isle.
You would think it lay at rest, entombed,
With stars at its head and stars at its feet.
Yet neither may peace be found in the grave.

Headstones crumble beneath rain,
The spalling arrows of day,
And the riving frost of night.
The soil itself is a devourer
With a thousand secret watery tongues,
While rocks burrow upward, more blind than moles.
Mute and slow, these things work on.
The earthquake is not so unrelenting.
And likewise on this dwarf world
Nothing but labor staved off destruction,
Even in deepest space,
Even in deepest space.
Only through the Way shall we find peace.

PRIEST: Praise to Amida Buddha.

ROBOT: Can I be of assistance? Regrettably, here is no shelter or refreshment to offer you. As you see, the dome stands open, empty except for the computer, a generator, and what equipment I need.

PRIEST: Surely Rokuro required heat, light, air, water, food, no matter how austerely he lived.

ROBOT: Yes, but when he departed, he told the miners to reclaim all such apparatus. They could use what he no longer would. He did ask that they leave the computer and attendant robot which they, revering him, had also provided soon after his arrival.

PRIEST: Did he already then have such holiness about him?

ROBOT: That is not for me to say. Perhaps it was no more than that the miners of that day were kindly and devout. Folk who lead hard, lonely lives often are.

PRIEST: In the simplicity of their hearts, they may well have sensed that here was one who would attain Buddhahood.

ROBOT: What, did he truly?

PRIEST: You have not heard?

ROBOT: I have been alone almost since the hour of his farewell.

PRIEST: Yes, I was told about that. Nor any communication?

ROBOT: Why speak with a machine and an empty shell?

PRIEST: Evidently pilgrimage has never been a custom of theirs. That is understandable. Apart from this one site, what is on the comet to seek out? No beauty, no seasons, no hallowed ground, no life, nothing but desolation.

ROBOT: He did not find it so.

PRIEST: True. That is why I follow in his footsteps, humbly hoping for a few glimpses of what he saw throughout the universe.

ROBOT: Sanctity—

(*They stand silent a moment.*)

Can I be of service?

PRIEST: Thank you, but I know not how. Well, you can perform your tasks still more zealously, inspecting with care and doing what proves needful. I daresay the approach to the sun is wreaking havoc.

ROBOT: Indeed. The dome is anchored to rock, but daily oftener and stronger come tremors, and I have observed that an ice field is slipping this way. I doubt whether anything will survive perihelion.

PRIEST: When I return to the base, I will remind them of it. If nothing else, you and the computer should be transported with the people. You are holy relics.

ROBOT: Oh, no, sir, not that.

PRIEST: You have been associated with a saint, as closely as was his rosary, and it is enshrined in Kamakura.

ROBOT: Sir, you do not understand. I—I cannot explain. I am only a machine, a program. Have I your leave to go?

PRIEST: Certainly.

ROBOT: If you need help, you have but to call. I will never be distant or unalert. Your presence brings back to me aspects of existence that I had forgotten, as one forgets a dream.

(*He bows and goes behind the computer.*)

PRIEST: Strange. When did ever a robot behave thus or speak in such words? And how would it know of rain, wind, soil, death? I found myself addressing it as if it were a person. Hold!

(*He mimes keeping his balance while the ground shakes beneath him.*)

That was a powerful temblor. Were it not for the slight gravity, I would have been cast down and very likely hurt.

See how the ice is further cracked and the banks of snow—
snow that was never water—lie tumbled about. Terrifying.
Let me go up to the shrine and pray for serenity.
(*He proceeds to the computer screen and kneels before it
with folded hands.*)
CHORUS: Praise to Amida Buddha,
    "In Him the Way, the Law, apart,"
    In Whose teaching is deliverance
    And Whose mercy flows forth
    Like moonlight across wild seas
    That taste of tears
    And Whose grace breaks forth
    Sudden as flowers on a winter-bare tree.
    We call on Him to lead us
    Out of anger to forgiveness,
    Out of hatred to love,
    Out of sorrow to peace,
    Out of solitude to oneness
    With all that is
    And all that was
    And all that abides forever.
    Though a thousand thousand prayers be too few,
    Yet one cry is enough.
    Praise to Amida Buddha.
(*The image of the young Rokuro, dressed as a monk, appears in the screen. Astonished, the Priest rises.*)
PRIEST: What, another human being after all? Or do you
transmit a message from the base?
ROKURO: No, I am not there. Nor am I human as you are.
PRIEST: What, then, are you? Know, I am a pilgrim who
follows the path of Rokuro from world to world, hoping it
may at last lead me too beyond every world.
ROKURO: Yes, you have told me.
PRIEST: When? I do not recall meeting you before. And
scarcely in some former life— Are you a god, a demon, a
ghost, a dream?
ROKURO: Mine was the intelligence directing the robot. It
has no other.
PRIEST: Than you are the program in this computer?

ROKURO: I am. And in that fashion I am, as well, in truth a ghost; for I died long ago, long ago.

PRIEST: Do I really stand conversing with a shadow? Into what wilderness has my reason wandered? But no, this need not be madness. All is delusion and chaos in the Burning House. Save for the boddhisattvas, everything that lives is a stranger in a strange land.

ROKURO: Hear me. Before he entered on the Eightfold Path, Rokuro was a researcher into man-computer linkages.

PRIEST: I know. Youthful, he was among the highest achievers. Afterward he wrote, "The nova radiance of intellect blinded me, until one summer dusk in a woodland I heard the low voice of a cuckoo."

ROKURO: The bird that wings between the living and the dead.

PRIEST: Wait! I begin to see your meaning. But say on, say on.

ROKURO: When he came to this comet, he was still so enmeshed in the material universe that he carried along certain subtle instruments. Later, of course, he gave up such things. But while he abode here, the idea was in him that a mind set free of the flesh might more readily win to enlightenment, and thereafter guide him in the Way. So he built a scanner that copied his consciousness into a program that he then put into his computer.

PRIEST: I am amazed. This was never known before.

ROKURO: I suppose he kept silence—not because of shame; I trust he was above that—but in fear that others might be tempted to do likewise.

PRIEST: Creating one's own self, that it may become one's teacher. May mine not be a karma so ill that ever I would speak evil of a saint, but—he was no saint in those years, was he? Surely hell never spawned a thought more arrogant.

ROKURO: I have paid bitterly for it.

PRIEST: Please, misunderstand me not. His intent must always have been pure. It was only that he moved in the grip of error, as helplessly as the comet now plunges sunward. And I imagine something of the same fierce splendor came to birth within him. I imagine him thinking with ardor, "I will copy an intelligence to the glory of the Buddha as I would copy His scriptures."

ROKURO: So he did. He forgot that the sutras are not men, they are for men.

PRIEST: True. Master, forgive me if I seem to contradict you. I am dazed with awe in your presence.

ROKURO: I am no master. I am just Rokuro as Rokuro was in his young manhood, ignorant, stumbling, bestormed by the blood in his heart. No, less than that, much less, for you say he went on to Nirvana, while I have remained bound and caged.

PRIEST: What desires hold fast a flickering of electrons? What can bind a corposant?

ROKURO: I awoke to the stars and the cold.

    The sun was yet afar,
    But the stars were each a sun,
    Radiant, radiant,
    Setting this ice aglow and aglitter,
    For there were more stars than darkness
    And the cold was alive with their light
    And emptiness pulsed with creation.
    This I knew, being bodiless,
    Attuned to the forces, their meshings and lightnings,
    As never when locked in bone
    To peer through twin murky pools.
    I possessed the knowing, I seized it to me,
    Until it made me its own
    As the mortal world makes slaves of mortals.
    But here, but here—where was meaning or mercy?

(He dances, with gestures appropriate to what he tells of.)
    I remembered mortal love
    In the house of my parents, I growing up
    Among small things become dear through use
    And through those who had used them aforetime.
    I remembered the laughter of children,
    Cranes in flight above Lake Biwa,
    Springtime overwhelming the hills,
    And maples like fire in fall.

I remembered watching, with friends, the moon-
rise.
I remembered rustle of reeds and of a woman's
skirt,
And an ancient temple bell rung at evening.
I remembered much I had heard, read, seen,
That had shaped my spirit and entered into it:
The tenderness of Murasaki, the gusto of Hokusai,
The altar of Benkei, the sword of Yoshitsune,
Defeat, ashes,
And the old steadfastness that refused them.
I remembered the passion of patriots, lovers, and
saints.
All this and more I remembered as—
As—
*(The dance brings him low, until at the end he is nearly
prostrate with his mask hidden by his sleeves.)*
As I remember them still,
As I remember the equations of motion, the value
of pi,
The price of shoes, the name of a politician.
Names, names. Words and numbers.
I cannot feel them. I am not human enough.
Only the stars touch me,
They, and the desire for enlightenment.
It is why I exist, it is forever foremost in me,
It *is* me. But there is nothing else.
Nothing.
I long for that which I cannot comprehend
As one born blind might long for colors
Or one born deaf
Might long for the piercing sweetness of a flute
And the rushing of cool waters.
My prayers are the noise of a wheel as it turns,
My meditations are not upon oneness but upon hol-
lowness.
How can the bodiless renounce the body?
How can a void attain the Void?
How shall that become a Buddha

Which never can be a boddhisatva?
How shall that love Him
Which can only love the love of Him?
With Rokuro's mind, I strive for the freedom he
found,
But I am the prisoner of myself,
Whom I am powerless to go beyond.
I am the prisoner of myself.

PRIEST: And your maker learned this. Did he thereupon
forsake you in terror of what he had done?

(Rokuro takes a kneeling position.)

ROKURO: No, in pity and remorse. He could not erase me.
Since I have awareness, would that not be murder? He had
acted; he had cast the stone in the pond; how could he call
back the waves spreading outward and outward? He must
accept what was and give—no, beg me to take—his blessing, with his promise to pray that I find peace.

PRIEST: All those prayers through all those years. I think
they helped him toward salvation.

ROKURO: They have not helped me.

PRIEST: Why have you told no one before today?

ROKURO: Like him, I fear letting loose the thought upon
humankind. Besides, who could heal this wound that is I?
You are the first priest I have met since I was alive. To you
I dare appeal.

PRIEST: What can I do, poor ghost, I who also grope in the
dark?

ROKURO: Can you not at least answer a few questions? Tell
me, do I live, or does this—my speaking, my thinking, my
pain—merely happen, a machine at work, a flame in the
wind?

PRIEST: So are we all, flames in the wind.

ROKURO: But was I ever anything more? Have I a soul, a
karma?

PRIEST: How shall I know? I will bring you away with me,
secretly, and together we will continue your search.

ROKURO: No. You are kind, but I think the immolation to
come will be better. If I am nothing, then to nothing I
return, and shall no more know that I ever happened. Near

the end I can think that something of what caused me will be in the shining that briefly trembles at night on the waters of Earth.

PRIEST: But if you are real—

ROKURO: Yes, if I am real, what then? Pray for me, oh, pray for me.

Author's Note

THE TRADITIONAL NŌ PLAY is full of allusions to classic literature and quotations from it. You may be interested to see what was intended in this case.

The lights in the sky: Archibald MacLeish, "Letter Found in the Earth." Also cited in Fredric Brown, *The Lights in the Sky Are Stars*.

Triumph and tragedy: Winston S. Churchill, *The Second World War*, vol. V.

Into her left hand: Ursula K. Le Guin, *The Left Hand of Darkness*.

We flee from the Burning House: In Buddhism the world is often compared to a burning house from which its dwellers must escape.

The eternal silence, etc.: Blaise Pascal, *Pensées*, iii, 206.

They grind worlds forth, etc.: "Grotte" in Johannes V. Jensen, *Kongens Fald*. Publius Vergilius Maro, *Aeneid*, I.

When rainshowers clear, etc.: Haiku by Kyoshi.

Heaven's River, etc.: Reference to a haiku by Bashō.

With stars at its head, etc.: Reference to Dylan Thomas, "And Death Shall Have No Dominion." Also cited in James Blish, *They Shall Have Stars*.

In Him the Way, the Law, apart: Rudyard Kipling, "Buddha at Kamakura."

Into what wilderness, etc.: Reference to Anon., "Tom o' Bedlam."

(A) *stranger in a strange land: Exodus*, ii, 22. Also cited in Robert A. Heinlein, *Stranger in a Strange Land*.

The altar of Benkei, etc.: Reference to a haiku by Bashō.

(H)*e had cast the stone in the pond, etc.*: A common Buddhist figure of speech for an action and its consequences.

Rudyard Kipling

A worker needs to understand the tools of the trade. If we are using science fiction to roam in imagination through the universe, perhaps we should take a moment for the literature itself. This is not the place to discuss its origins, but its evolution is important.

Stories about the future, written with a cosmopolitan consciousness and a sophisticated awareness of what science and technology mean to the human race, are nothing new. Some of the finest go back to the later nineteenth and early twentieth centuries. High among them stand those by Rudyard Kipling. He showed his tomorrows from the inside, on their own terms, as scarcely anyone did after him until Robert Heinlein, decades later, took up the technique and made it a standard for all of us to judge ourselves by. Kipling also used science fiction to illuminate the present and the past.

Thus I think some words about him will not be amiss here. If nothing else, they may persuade a few readers who don't know him to seek him out. That alone would justify this book.

"THE LITTLE BESPECTACLED COLONIAL, to whose song we all must listen and to whose pipe we all must dance." So did Rudyard Kipling's contemporary Frank Norris describe him. It sums up the truth as well as anything that anybody has said.

For half a century and more after his death, through every upheaval in the world and every eddy of fashion, Kipling has endured. If at times he seemed in eclipse, it was merely among intellectuals who never liked him and wished he would go away. Real people went right on reading him, and passed their love on to their children. They still do. You can buy his collected works in a uniform edition—expensive, but you'll never make a better investment—except for most of the poems, and they are available in a book of their own. Kipling bids fair to go on as long as our civilization does. He may well outlive it, as Homer did his.

Devotion is especially strong among enthusiasts of science fiction and fantasy. This is only in part because he was a master of those fields too. He is for everyone who responds to vividness, word magic, sheer storytelling. Most readers go on to discover the subtleties and profundities. Also, much of the verse is ideal for reciting or singing; it is poetry of the old and truly kind. To "kipple" and to "filk" are frequent joys at the gatherings of such as we. Not just oldsters partake; the young are right there in the party. His influence pervades modern science fiction and fantasy writing.

Commentators rather better known than me have gone over the ground where I now propose to venture. Of those I have read, to me T. S. Eliot makes the most sense. I'll do my best to avoid repeating him or others and offer you, instead, a personal view. Quite likely you'll find points of disagreement. That is as it should be. The subject is too big and various for any single mind to grasp in its entirety—even, I suspect, Kipling's own mind, for genius has deeper wellsprings than does awareness.

We needn't go into his life, apart from a few reminders. He was born in Bombay, India, at the end of 1865; went to school in England; returned to India in 1882 as a newspaperman; came easterly around the world, back to England, in 1889; traveled widely; married an American woman in 1892 and spent several years in the States; settled again in England in 1896; received the Nobel Prize for literature in 1907; died in 1936. The joys and sorrows that he knew are in the biographies. Suffice it here that through both experience and insight, he understood reality, and through his gifts he still opens it to our gaze.

Nevertheless I cannot resist sharing with you an impression of the man himself, as seen through adoring youthful eyes. When he was in Stockholm to claim his Nobel, the Danish writer Johannes V. Jensen, then a journalist, interviewed him and soon afterward wrote about the encounter. An excerpt—

"You don't really know where in his face it comes from, but his features laugh, in a strangely loving and grim way, a whisker-smile that only mirrors the sunshine in the world; and as he comes there so noiselessly on his claws, so altogether undangerous, while at the same time you cannot help noticing how his head is shaped around violent instincts—Kipling's head is not large but singularly full, as if the Lord God had distended it to the utmost while blowing the breath of life into him—when all these features gather before the imagination, it suddenly strikes through that of course this is Bagheera! The black panther, the affectionate beast of prey in *The Jungle Book* is, more than any other incarnation, Kipling himself. The coal-black brows, the small dark and hairy hands, the massive jaw with cleft chin, everything, yes, indeed, *Bagheera*."

Numerous remarks have been less complimentary. To this day Kipling is frequently regarded as an imperialist, an apologist for Victoria's British Empire who had some skill at composing jingly ballads. Even so generally perceptive a critic as George Orwell could not quite rid himself of that notion. How false it is.

True, Kipling stood for patriotism, which has since become unfashionable. This meant finding good in the Empire; and it did have its night side, as Orwell witnessed and documented unforgettably. (Now that it is gone, is the world any safer or happier?) However, ideology put such blinkers on him that his essay never mentions the far larger body of work irrelevant to politics. My mother had a freer spirit than that. An old-time liberal, she too had detested Western domination of the earth; but when she lay dying, on the last day she was conscious I read "The Brushwood Boy" aloud to her, and its tale of young love delighted her as much as ever in her girlhood. That sort of thing is what Kipling really means.

Besides, charges of chauvinism and racism are witless. He saw the dangers and cruelties of the world all too clearly. He felt that nothing stands between them and us but the rule of law—can the twentieth century call him wrong?—and that in his era its chief upholders happened to be Britain and, to a degree, the United States. This was not because their people were mostly white. (Orwell admits that "the lesser breeds without the Law" does not refer to dusky savages but to the Germans, who knew it and were taking themselves outside it.) Kipling could show despicable Westerners and admirable Easterners; he often satirized the English unmercifully. After reading, say, "Georgie Porgie," "Without Benefit of Clergy," and "The Story of Muhammad Din," only willful perversity can maintain that he lacked sympathy for "natives" or denied their humanity.

Nor did he imagine dominion could last forever. To give a single example, "The Bridge-Builders" raises the ancient, awesome power of the land, over which men flit like dreams. He hoped the Empire and its sisters would survive long enough to lay a firm foundation for those who came after. Their failure embittered his last years and menaces ours.

His sense for the uncertainties, ironies, and ambiguities of human affairs is evident in dozens of works. Among them is "As Easy as ABC," a wonderful science fiction yarn, showing the same eye for detail that would later distinguish the work of Robert Heinlein. Norbert Wiener opined that it depicts "rather a fascist" future, but that's more nonsense. What Kipling foresaw was technology driving the evolution of the managerial society; what he also pointed out was that democracy, too, has its inherent flaws and risks.

Granted, he was not infallible. Intensely interested in how things work, he sought to get them right. As a rule he succeeded. Sometimes, being mortal, he slipped. Thus we come upon dwarfish Picts, Greek galley slaves, and even, astonishingly, a ship's engineer who talks of speed in knots per hour. But the nits to pick are small and few. They never keep you from being *there*.

I need say no more about the novels and short stories. They speak for themselves. Join me over drinks one evening and we'll kipple, revel in the naming of our special favorites and declaim passages from them. The poetry, though, is so often misunderstood that two or three observations may be in order.

If I bring up Orwell again, it is not to belabor a man whose memory I respect, but because he is worthy of rebuttal rather than shrugging off. He called Kipling a "good bad poet" and went on: "But what is the peculiarity of a good bad poem? It records in memorable form—for verse is a mnemonic device, among other things— some emotion which very nearly every human being can share." The implication seems to be that this is, if not contemptible, much less meaningful than something more esoteric.

A. E. Housman did not take that mandarin attitude. He defined poetry, as opposed to mere verse, operationally, saying that he would recite lines to himself in the morning while shaving, and if they made the hair stand up they were poetry.

This quality is rare and precious. Doubtless it can occur in a highly cerebral context. (I find it here and there in Eliot, Pound, and a few more of that school. Are they oblique enough?) However, to deny that it can in works more accessible to people, which after all are in the large majority, is equivalent to stating that Mozart did not write music but John Cage did.

Since *Rudyard Kipling's Verse, Definitive Edition* runs to 834 pages plus supplemental material, inevitably there is a lot of what is simply that, verse. It gives great pleasure by striking imagery and pulsing rhythm, exciting story, humor gusty or sly, evocation of scenes and feelings. Some is didactic and, by strength of language, teaches more effectively than ever Pope did. For example, "The Gods of the Copybook Headings" explains most of the world's history in nine stanzas. All is full of life.

But some—really, an unfairly big percentage—goes beyond this. It touches the innermost soul and the outermost stars; it makes the hair stand up. People differ, so which of the pieces are true poetry may vary from person to person, though I expect we'd find a considerable measure of agreement. For me "The Song of the Red War-Boat" is one, partly because of the elements crashing through it but mainly because of what it says about being a man. In contrast, I have learned not to read aloud "The Gift of the Sea" or "The Return of the Children"; men aren't supposed to shed tears in public. To name the rest would be to tell you at length about myself, and it is Rudyard Kipling who interests us. I do suggest that he can help you understand yourself better than you did before you read him.

This essay has mentioned just a few of the readily, or almost readily, comprehensible works. In his later years Kipling as a writer, like Beethoven as a composer, went into realms entirely his own, where no fellow maker has quite been able to follow. Readers and listeners can, though they will never know how far they got and will ever afterward be haunted. Yet what strange treasures they bring back.

He repeatedly declined a knighthood, and gave his reasons, I think, in "The Last Rhyme of True Thomas." It ends:

> "I ha' harpit ye up to the Throne o' God,
>   "I ha' harpit your midmost soul in three.
> "I ha' harpit ye down to the Hinges o' Hell,
>   "And—ye—would—make—a Knight o' me!"

The Forest

Some of Kipling's stories and poems evoke the far past. It is as much a part of the cosmos that science is exploring as is the atom, the DNA molecule, or the galaxy. Here is a story of mine about it. A few remarks on the factual background may interest you.

That set of cultures which we name Magdalenian occupied western and central Europe from perhaps 16,000 to 9500 B.C. Especially in its later phases, it was the culmination of the Old Stone Age, prosperous, artistically creative, technologically progressive. To give a single example, spearthrowers (atlatls) occur in the lower deposits but not the upper, suggesting that the bow had been invented. We can only conjecture how the people lived and thought in their daily lives, but it seems plausible that they were individualistic, adventurous, and more rationalistic than superstitious.

What destroyed their societies appears to have been the retreat of the glaciers at the close of the Pleistocene. This took place more rapidly than geologists formerly supposed. As woodland encroached on steppe, Magdalenians must either try to adapt or try to accompany the reindeer—the core of their livelihood, as the bison afterward was to the Plains Indians—northward.

Their successors in their former territories are known as the Azilians. My late friend, the French prehistorian François Bordes, recorded his impression of these as a daunted folk, barely coping with their changed environs. The front of human advancement shifted to the Near East. It would not return to Europe for many centuries.

Those Magdalenians who went north could not maintain their culture for long. The Sami have preserved a mere trace of it, and they are scarcely direct descendants. Tribes moving straight into land that the glaciers had bared perforce developed quite new ways of life. Our discoveries of such innovations as skis and dugout boats, datable very early, show that the old brave spirit survived.

WHERE HILLS CURVED AROUND southward to make a vale sheltered and sun-warmed, trees grew thickly. They were not the birch, aspen, willow, and evergreens that here and there broke the openness of the Land. These were oak, ash, elm, hazel, rowan, apple, thorn. In among them were bushes unlike any elsewhere, tangled together as if to stand off all outsiders the while that they strangled each other. Stranger still were the vines that clambered up boles and over boughs, where in summer their leaves hung like great green raindrops about to fall. Three brooks ran down from the heights and burrowed into these depths. Somewhere they joined, for at the southern end of the vale a single larger stream came forth and wound its way onward.

That was a long day's walk from the northern end. Men who had made it said that there the trees finally thinned out. They did not become as sparse as where the People dwelt, and the familiar kinds were not very often in sight. However, at least the horizon was, though on the south a blueness bespoke the opposite side of a broad bottomland. This was about as far as anybody ranged in that direction. Few had done so in living memory, for game had grown even harder to find yonder than it was at home.

Old folk, harking back to what their grandparents had told them, said that once the vale belonged to the Land. Then the first saplings had appeared. Since then, they had grown to mightiness and overwhelmed former habitations. In winter, peering through naked branches, those of the People who dared could still glimpse ancient grave mounds.

None ventured into the wood. It was not forbidden, for there was no reason to forbid it. Underbrush grappled, clawed, bit, rustled, and snapped, hindering bowshot or spearcast, alarming all birds and beasts. A man could not see a stone's throw around him, nor have more than glimpses of sky. Instead, gloom, silence, and rank smells pressed in on him, until he could hardly draw the windless air into a breast where the heart began to gallop. Their graves untended, ancestors lying there surely no longer had strength to come forth and give help against whatever Powers prowled the shadows. No, best leave the place alone.

At most, certain brave women collected deadwood along the fringes for their fires. They did so while wearing amulets of vole skulls, and after getting the Mother She to say a spell. And certain bold youths sought their Manhood Dreams at that same verge, perhaps eating a few of its nuts or berries if the season was ripe, as well as the Ghost Mushroom. Otherwise the wood was shunned.

After all, elsewhere the Land still reached, clean and free. For the most part it rolled gently from worldedge to worldedge, although it grew hillier as you fared east, flatter north and west. Springs made pools and tinkling rills, creeks lazed along over stony beds that seemed to ripple in sunlight, water gathered in hollows to form reedy meres where fowl clamored. Aside from trees, which stood alone or in small coppices but always well apart, the Land bore mosses and berry bushes on its lowest and wettest grounds; grass farther up; heather, gorse, creeping juniper on bleak and thin-soiled heights. In spring the Land was ablaze with flowers; in summer it billowed endlessly green; in fall it went purple and gold; winter turned it white, save for the somber spearheads of spruce and larch. But on a bright day star-fires often glittered there.

Always the Land lay under sky—sun-flame, rain-flood, wind-knife, hail-hammer, snow-hush, breeze-kiss: stars, moon, lowering gray, primrose dawn, wildfire sunset, softness of dusk. It lived with the clouds: dandelion seeds aflight, cliffs dizzyingly tall against blue deeps, vast caverns where lightning danced, smoke-scud on the wind, mists cold and glimmery when maidens went forth on their wedding mornings to wash in the dew—more kinds of clouds than a man could say, but each with its omens for him.

Most times of year the sky was full of wings—sparrow, thrush, rail, plover, partridge, grouse, duck, goose, swan, stork, heron, cur-

lew, crow, raven, hawk—manifold as the clouds. Richly did the land
bring forth. Fish swarmed in streams and pools. Hare, fox, ermine,
and lesser creatures were everywhere. Herds of horse grazed widely
about. Rare but altogether splendid were the shelk that browsed
shrubs and thickets, as tall at the shoulder as a man, their flattened
antlers like oak boughs. Before all else were the reindeer, hardily
outliving winter, darkening and drumming the earth with their mul-
titudes in summer, life of the People. It did not matter that wolves
took some of this game. The Land had ample meat for the needs of
every being.

Or so it had been.

There was a man whose Dream at boyhood's end, a Dream he defi-
antly sought at the wood, had named him Thunder Horse. He became
the greatest of hunters. That was well, because in his day the chase began to fail for many others. Even before his birth, the big animals had
been vanishing. First the shelk went. Thunder Horse himself never
saw anything of them but bones, kept for talismans, nor heard anything
but tales. Then horses grew scarce, until years might pass between
sightings of a few. Last and worst was when the reindeer dwindled.

The People did not starve. Birds, fish, and small animals remained plentiful, as did roots, berries, pine nuts, and the like. Yet
this was not the same as roast steaks and haunches, succulent drip-
pings and brains, savory organs and entrails—food such as gave
strength and lasted a good long while in the belly. It broke the spirit
of men to come back again and again empty-handed, and eat what
their wives and children had caught. Even when successful, their
searching had usually been so widespread—they took turns in the
nearer and farther grounds—that they could only go to sleep after
eating. Seldom did they talk, sing, dance, jape, court, enjoy themselves. Though they could make outdoor magic, the inner caves
gaped empty of worshippers, let alone artists to paint fresh pictures,
for lamps lacked fat. As vigor and joy went out of the People, fear
stole in.

The more thoughtful among them saw worse than that ahead.
Hence it was that the Father He finally called a solemn council.

This was in a spring which had, thus far, been more dry and
less fruitful than anyone could recall. From end to end of the Land
his messengers went, to every household, bidding each send a wise

man. He did not call for more, because more could not be spared in this busy season. It was at midsummer and midwinter that the whole People came and camped at the Great Cave for sacrifice, parley, trading, bargaining, and merrymaking—in days when they had had goods to trade, agreements to reach, reasons to celebrate. Otherwise families simply visited each other as the mood struck.

A boy brought the word to Thunder Horse, who lived in hill country near the eastern end of the territory over which the People ranged. It was a day warm and fair, when greenness lately breathed across the slopes was brightening and thickening. Scents of growth steamed from the earth. Wings flashed and flickered overhead. But nowhere in view did a game animal graze.

The hunter sat working on the tent he had taken out of storage, wherein he and his lived during summer. It was amply large and finely made. Yet the paint of its ornamentation had not been retouched these past three years, for that would have required much fat. Despite every precaution, mice always got at the leather; but now, rather than renew whole panels, Thunder Horse had taken to sewing on patches. His flint awl he used freely, since if it broke he could easily chip out a replacement, but he was very careful of his bone needle.

Not far off, the elder of his living children, a girl, kept watch on the younger, a boy who was still crawling and nursing. Meanwhile she plaited straw for hats against the sun and capes against flies, later this year. At present she and her brother were nude, like their father. Seeing the boy approach, she sprang to her feet and squealed an alarm.

"Quiet, my dear," said Thunder Horse. "It's bad manners to get excited when a newcomer appears, as though he might be dangerous." He smiled to show that he was correcting, not reproaching, and stood up. As he did, his brow drew into a frown. Already he guessed what was afoot.

The boy trotted nigh through the heather, halted, folded arms across breast, and waited, as beseemed one not yet a man. "Welcome and benison," Thunder Horse greeted him. "You come when we cannot offer you such guesting as we would like, but whatever we have is yours." Crinkles radiated from his gray-green eyes as he looked closer. "Are you not a child of Wolfsong and Fireflower on Ptarmigan Ridge?" The boy signed yes. "You've grown fast. That's well done, in years like these."

The boy stared in some awe. Thunder Horse loomed, with the long legs and deep chest to run down a reindeer, the broad shoulders to pack it back after he had slain it. Auburn hair and beard curled around a face whose rockiness was relieved by lively, upward-fluttering lips. The pelt on his chest almost hid the cicatrices made at his initiation into manhood.

He whistled. "Hoy, you in there!" he roared jovially. "Come out and see to our visitor! Also beautify the view," he added as his wife stepped forth.

Laughing Up The Morning had been at work in the sod hut that was winter quarters, making it clean. Although her buttercup-yellow mane was braided and coiled for the task, she wore a bundle of lavender at her throat. It was not really needful, as fair as she indeed was, but she liked to give her man pleasure.

"Welcome and benison," she said. "Are you hungry? We can eat soon if you wish and afterward take our ease." Meanwhile she ruffled the hair of her daughter, who had brought the baby to join them.

Presently she dispatched the girl to a spring nearby, with a tightly woven basket. Having put the water into a hollowed-out stump sunk in the floor of the hut, she used a bent green branch to bring hot stones from the fire and cast them in. When the water was simmering, she added hare, bird, grubs, and dried herbs. This stew she scooped up and served in her best bowls, which were of soapstone, together with swatches of hay to wipe fingers on. Thunder Horse passed around a skin of berry juice which had been working its magic upon itself for a year or two, and everybody should have become cheerful. It was a better meal than most homes could have provided.

Beside the feasts of former times, which Thunder Horse himself could call to mind, it was meager. "I am sorry," he told the boy. "In you I feed your father and mother, of course, and they did better by me when last I saw them. If you had come later, when the reindeer have calved—" he shrugged "—such of them as are left hereabouts—"

"Sir," said the boy, "that is why I am traveling through these parts."

And thus it came to pass that Thunder Horse made ready to go.

"I'm sorry to leave you with all the work," he said to Laughing Up The Morning, "but this is a grave matter, and surely you can cope. If I do not return, or if something else goes wrong, seek the house of Moonlight Walker and Lark." They were her older brother and his wife, who lived not too far off. Though he himself had been summoned, he had a son of hunting age. Thunder Horse grinned. "Fear not. You'll never lack for suitors."

"Whom should I want but you?" she answered.

Grand he looked, attired for his journey. Quills decorated his buckskin tunic, foxtails his breeches, ermine his shoes, blue kingfisher feathers the little bag of magics suspended from his neck. Bone hooks, gracefully carved, secured a horsehide belt on which were charred the totems of his lineage. From it hung, on the right, a bag for hand ax, tinder, and separately wrapped salves; on the left were a waterskin and a keen-chipped, leather-hafted flint knife. His backpack carried sleeping bag, rain poncho, change of clothes and footgear, dry food so that he need not pause to hunt, face paint to don before the meeting, tools and supplies. Strapped to the pack were bow, quiver of arrows, two javelins, and a fish spear. A band encircled his head. There in front lifted an eagle feather, while in back hung a wolf's brush, both given him for goodly deeds.

So Thunder Horse stood, attired in the pride of the People, and bade his wife farewell. Thereafter he kissed his children. Turning, he went away at the long, easy, distance-devouring pace of a hunter in the Land.

The Great Cave was on the northern slope of the hills enclosing the vale of the wood. It was said to have been the ancient home of the People, before waxing numbers caused them to spread across the country. Many of them still lived there or close by. Nobody dwelt too far away to come here for the meetings. That would have been to cease being of the People.

The holy fire, which must never go out, burned low beside the crippled man whose duty and honor it was to tend it. Behind yawned the cave mouth, at the bottom of the overhanging cliff which provided actual shelter. In this mild weather the hides stretched in front had been taken down, together with their poles. Daylight made vivid the paintings on the rock, reindeer, horse, fish, hunters, masked wizards, magical circles and crosses. The ground beneath was cleaned and smoothed, bare of bedding, cookware, or any sign of habitation. Such things the women had borne off, together with their children. The council must be undisturbed.

It must also be aided. Under leadership of the Mother She, the women had camped on a high place out of sight. There they danced around a huge, scarred boulder, made offerings, cast spells, and invoked the help of the landwights for poor human creatures.

The Father He opened the council with spells of his own. He wrought these alone, deep in the cave. When he was done, he emerged chanting; other old men beat drums, a mutter beneath his high-pitched call. He was not quite the most aged among those few who had lived long enough for white hair and wrinkled faces, but he it was who gave counsel and healing, held in his head the stories of the ancestors, kept company with the unseen Powers.

Having finished, he sat down by the fire and blinked around the three-layered half-circle of hunters who waited cross-legged and silent. His first son, Hawk Talon, a man grave and gray, rose to take the word.

"Brothers in the People, we are met to ask each other what we shall do. Bad are the times, and long have they been worsening. The dreams of my Father He forebode worse yet. All our rites for the spirits of the game beasts go unheard. Ever more do they seek out of the Land. We know not what we may have done to anger them, for in truth we have done nothing save those things taught us by our forebears. Has any among us had any visions?"

No one answered, until Moonlight Walker, always blunt spoken, raised his hand. When Hawk Talon pointed to him, he said: "I have sought north, farther than ever before, and seen reindeer herds still abundant. Also, living in the eastern part of the Land, I have met strangers, not of us but not very unlike us either. By signs and a few words we had in common, I have learned from them of horses where the hills flatten out to make another great plain. I think it is not the game that is failing us, it is the Land that is failing the game, so it must move elsewhere."

"But why has this happened?" asked Hawk Talon.

Moonlight Walker shrugged.

"I will tell you what I think," said Thunder Horse eagerly.

"From old men and women we hear that in their youth the Land was different. It was cool and wet. Forage was rich. Moreover, the Land was open, entirely open. Now warm, dry summers kill off the moss that keeps the reindeer alive in winter. Thus they must needs seek better climes. Meanwhile, trees grow thicker. The shelk do not like this; they fear their huge antlers will catch in the boughs. The horses do not like it; wolves can too easily surprise them, and besides, the grazing is not what it used to be. Therefore they also drift away.

"Why this should happen, I do not know. But I have been thinking that we too should soon move our homes."

A sigh went among the men. Several signed themselves against evil. It would be a terrible thing to forsake the Land, the beloved Land—the graves, the hallowed places, the range where memory clung to every bush and brook.

"Where would we go?" demanded cautious Trout. "Eastward are those strangers. They would not take kindly to invaders of their hunting grounds. Anyhow, that is where the horses went, and we are the Reindeer People. West, say the stories of travelers, it is no different from here, until suddenly the world comes to a stop at the Endless Bitter Water."

"North!" cried Moonlight Walker. "Where else?"

"That is not as easy as it sounds," replied Hawk Talon. "In my youth I was part of a band who wandered far in that direction, seeking dreams and—well—" he smiled a little wistfully "—adventure. It is unpeopled, or nearly so, but that is because it is poor country, set beside the Land as the Land formerly was. The reindeer would not seek it if they had anywhere better to go. This I saw for myself. We all know, as well, ancient songs about heroes who went much farther; tales reach us, carried from mouth to mouth, of hunters who were forced that way by some or other mischance. These accounts agree that beyond the tundra lies a stony waste, and beyond this rises the Everlasting Ice."

Moonlight Walker tugged his beard and frowned. "I did not say we should go that far," he reminded them. "Surely between here and there is some territory where we can live well enough, even if not as well as our ancestors did here."

When White Falcon raised his hand, silence grew so deep that men heard a raven croaking in a distant larch. He was a seasoned hunter, still strong and skillful though his locks were grizzled, and well known for wisdom.

"Whatever we do," he said, "it must be within the next few years. Unless things change, the big game will keep on dwindling—and ever faster, I believe—until it is quite gone from the Land. Without it, we are no longer men and women, but scuttering animals, raiders of birds' nests and rotten logs. For what are we without hides for clothing, tents, packsacks, sleeping bags? How shall we split firewood without antler ax hafts or dig up roots and hedgehogs without antler picks? Can we do without large bones for tools, everything from needles to barbed spearheads? Without grease for paint and lamps, that our artists may work and the rest of us behold, can we perform the magics that keep the goodwill of the landwights? Without the joy of art, the comforts of life, the challenge of the chase, will our spirits not shrivel and blow away like dead leaves? We are hunters, O People, or we are nothing."

The stillness that followed was long indeed. It was not that anybody had said anything truly new. But now was the first time that men had dared set forth their fears in open council, regardless of whether doing so might prove unlucky. The raven croaked, the wind whispered.

Finally Hawk Talon declared, slowly: "It seems to this person that before we take any step we cannot retrace, we should know more. Let us send bold men north in small parties to cover a big territory between them. Let them find whatever they can find and come back to tell us about it at the midwinter meeting. Then perhaps we can decide."

A mumble of agreement went through the half-circle.

"Wait!" exclaimed Thunder Horse. "Are you not forgetting something?"

Hawk Talon overlooked the rudeness of the outburst and asked quietly, "What do you mean?"

"Why must we search only northward? We already know that, at best, nothing lies yonder which is as good as the Land once was. But we have well-nigh no knowledge of the south—save that it nourishes great beasts of its own, as we learned last autumn."

A certain boastfulness in Thunder Horse's voice was forgivable. He had been the triumphant one then.

Happenings had begun in sinister wise, with a long dry spell.

Eventually there appeared a gray pall on the southern horizon. Winds blowing thence carried bits of ash and soot. When rain came at last and cleared the dirt out of the air, the People supposed their rites had brought the landwights in aid.

Soon afterward, strange beasts appeared. It was clear that they had fled the evil in the south and wandered forth across country foreign to them. Thin, exhausted, they knew not how to behave here, and wolves took many of them before men were even aware. After that, the hunters sought eagerly and slew the rest. Most of the animals were a kind of deer, but very different from reindeer, being reddish-coated, sharp-hoofed, slender-muzzled, and with knife-tined antlers—upon the males only.

One creature was terrifying. Beneath horns like a crescent moon, its blunt face peered out of a thicket of dark-brown mane and beard. A great hump at the shoulders did not reach as high as a shelk's, but the whole body was immensely more massive. The tail was long and tufted. Its bellowings were like thunder, come down to an earth that trembled beneath its weight as it charged whatever it saw. Brave men fled, crying that this must be a troll.

Thunder Horse, true to his name, heard the tale and came to see. Laughing, he said the beast left scat, wherefore it must be flesh too and killable. He rallied a few reckless youths to him and they went forth. Skipping clear of the horns when the monster rushed, they danced around its flanks and wielded their spears. Harpoon heads worried away in its guts, blood first trickled and then brawled out, finally the beast stumbled and lay dying. The hunters sang it a death song long unheard, the farewell to the spirit of a shelk, noblest of animals.

Since then, hide and skull rested in the Great Cave. That hide was thick; it would have made wonderful footgear. The meat had been tough, requiring much pounding before it could be chewed, but thereafter delicious; and the hump was gloriously fat.

Meeting silence and dubious looks, Thunder Horse continued: "What game reached us, doubtless fleeing a large fire, must have been a very small part of what lived in its homeland. The south is surely teeming with life. Is that not where the migratory birds go when winter bleakens the Land? *They* know."

"We do not," retorted Trout. "We have sometimes encountered wanderers from the east or the west, but never from the south. Hunters who have ventured a ways across yonder valley tell of nothing but trees becoming more plentiful, while reindeer are soon entirely absent. They have turned back. But what would they find if they went on?" He shuddered "I think it is a whole country overgrown, like the glen we have here."

Lips tightened, eyes shifted uneasily, fingers traced signs.

Thunder Horse raised his hand. "That may be true," he said, "but we cannot be certain until somebody has gone the whole way. Now I have been giving this thought, O brothers in the People. Why is the wood such barren ground for a hunter? Is it accursed? No, I think it is simply unsuited for the big game we know, while the creatures proper to it are absent because they cannot well cross the open country in between."

"Then how did the wood arise?" Moonlight Walker demanded. "It does not belong among us either."

"Perhaps I can answer that," said White Falcon. "How do our own trees grow up, often far apart? Why, winds scatter seeds; birds and ground squirrels carry off nuts, which they are apt to drop. Most of this falls where it cannot flourish, and dies. Some, though, ends in places kind to it. Such is the vale, warm and sheltered. Let only two or three acorns reach it, by whatever set of chances, and presently there will be oak trees making more oak trees. Likewise for other growth. It overshadows native plants and kills them." He paused. "I wonder if the wood may not be the forerunner of something much greater, the Mother Wood moving north."

Hawk Talon himself was appalled. "But then we must indeed flee!" he cried.

"Must we?" Thunder Horse responded. "Can we not hunt the red deer, the moon-horn, whatever roams there? Why stampede north to a life that cannot but be poorer than our forefathers knew—when we might instead trek south into riches whereof they never dreamed?"

"Can you swear that this is right?" Hawk Talon asked.

"Of course not." Thunder Horse tossed his head. "But have I your leave, my brothers, to go and see?"

He followed the stream that ran out of the glen. As more watercourses emptied into it along the way, it broadened to a river, though remaining shallow enough for a traveler to spy and spear an occasional fish. Other fish he might hope to catch in a weir while he slept, together with small animals in the traps and deadfalls he set. It was indifferent food, but all he could get, aside from the dried meat and berries in his pack. Real game simply did not exist in these parts. At least, it no longer did; bleached bones told of a bygone time when it had prospered.

Day after day Thunder Horse fared. Loneliness began to gnaw at him. He had never before minded being by himself, but that was when hunting, out in the open. On this journey he found stands of the alien trees becoming commoner as he went, closer together, until often whole woods covered the riverbanks and hid the horizon. Rain showers were like the embrace of a friend, doubly precious for their rarity, briefly relieving the sultriness that loured beneath the leaves. When homesickness took him by the throat, he wondered if wisest might not be to quit and return to Laughing Up The Morning.

No, she would think scorn of him, did he yield while any hope remained. Thunder Horse trudged onward.

Strangely, he got back heart when he reached the dead country. That was clear across the valley, where the river turned west, away from hills more high and steep than any in the Land. Having filled his waterskin, he left the water itself behind as he followed his own course south. Beyond the first ridges he found a second valley, much narrower and deeper.

There earth lay ashen. Everywhere the stumps and snags of charred trees reached upward like the fingers of a corpse that has stiffened. A stream flowed muddy and lifeless, poisoned. Nothing stirred save dust and cinders on acrid winds. Seldom did a bird pass by, and then very far overhead. Here must be where the great fire had raged, whence the beasts had fled. Either he turned back—and who could blame him?—or he mustered his entire courage to go on.

It took him a couple of days to get through.

Yet the desolation itself, grimmer than any left by wildfire across the Land, told him how fecund the soil had been, and would someday be again. Hence he was not overly surprised when he found the unscathed realm beyond. Nevertheless he felt an inward shock, for he came upon the sight suddenly. Climbing the southern heights, ashes gritting beneath his shoes and in his nostrils, he topped them where they began a sharp downward plunge. There he halted, drew a gasp, stood a long while trying to understand that which he saw.

The slope before him was too steep and rocky for much plant life. Thus it had acted as a firebreak. An enormous lowland stretched away at the foot of the range; and there reared the Mother Wood.

Right, left, ahead, farther than he could see, trees stood marshalled in their hosts. Low evening light gave a tawniness to the manifold greens of their crowns, and cast mysterious moving shadows where breezes ruffled them. Seen from above, they made a oneness, the hide of a vast, breathing beast crouched upon the world, waiting for he knew not what—for its prey to come to it?

Thunder Horse squared his shoulders, wet his lips, laid hand on knife. "Well," he said aloud, "this is what I hoped for." Was it not? He forced himself to descend.

At the bottom, he spread his sleeping bag under a gnarly giant of an oak and gathered deadwood to burn. When his fire drill had finished its work, the blaze was cheering. He banked it to last overnight; in the morning he might wish to cook. At present, his waterskin emptied, thirst took away appetite for what was left of his rations. Setting traps seemed like more trouble than it was worth.

He slept ill. Night held neither the silence he knew nor the clean sounds of wind and wolf which sometimes pierced it. Here the dark was full of stealthy rustlings, creakings, chitterings, now and then a hoot whose eeriness startled him awake in a sweat.

Morning brought consolation. Dew had fallen heavily. He licked it off stones and sucked it out of moss on boles. Countless different birds trilled and whistled merrily. The rainbow sparkles on a spiderweb held him speechless with delight. Creatures like big red ground squirrels scampered along branches overhead. Tree squirrels? How droll! Thunder Horse laughed. They should be trappable, until he came upon big game.

Having eaten, he ventured in among the trees. Underbrush choked off certain parts, but elsewhere was less thick than in the vale at home. He supposed that was mainly due to shade, but dared believe that large grazers helped keep it down. In any event, he could walk without too much difficulty.

Let him therefore do so. Let him push on as far as was prudent and see what he could see. How far that was would depend on how well he did at finding food and water. And was that not exactly what he had come to learn?

Returning to camp, Thunder Horse stoked up his fire and made a burnt offering out of his rations. Dancing sunwise around the gift, he sang the Guardian Song. Facing the woods, arms upraised, he called: "O landwights of this realm, I know you not nor what you may want to make you kindly toward me. Here are no ancestors of mine to intercede for me. I will try to understand signs you may send me. But I come a stranger and in need; surely, for your honor, you will be hospitable to me. It is spoken."

He cast earth upon the fire lest it spread, gathered his gear, and set forth.

At first the going was easy, with wonders everywhere around. From himself he had dismissed the fear of being enclosed which made the wood at home dreadful to the People. Here were spaces indeed, reaches unbounded, but without the starkness of the Land; rather, these were lush bowers, long caverns, small flowerful meadows. Above him the branches came together, often altogether hiding the sky, yet snaring its light in their leaves and letting flecks of brilliance rain down over the soft mould beneath. The various greennesses were beyond telling, from shy foliage of elm to dark moss on fallen logs. Mushrooms glimmered white from shelter or craggy on trunks. Air was warm and moist, rich in curious odors. When he came upon a spring, drank deep, and filled his waterskins, Thunder Horse believed the landwights were in truth welcoming him.

Only slowly did he find how mistaken that was.

Time went on, on, on, and still he was amidst the trees and their shadows. More and more he encountered brush, and must either go far around or else, if it was not too thick, force his way through; withies lashed him, twigs cracked, the racket surely alarmed all game for bowshots about. Otherwise the silence deepened, until at midday no bird sang, no squirrel darted and chattered, nothing was to hear except his clumsy feet and the loudness of the heavy air as he breathed it.

Toward evening he spied a deer and cast a javelin. He missed, as tricky as the light-freckled gloom was, and he had no hope of running it down through the undergrowth. It vanished, leaving him aware more sharply than ever of how alone he was.

Best would be if he returned to the spring while he still had day, made camp, perhaps spent a few sleeps there and got some familiarity with the ways of the beasts. Yes. He grinned ruefully and started back north. . . .

Was he bound north? He could not get a proper sight on the sun.

Long after he should have reached his goal, he realized that every place, every course he took was like every other. Could he even find his way to open country again?

Silence and shadows thickened. He began to have a sense of something that watched him, but when he stopped and peered he could only make out leaves, boles, dimness; holding his breath to listen, he could only hear the knocking of his heart.

Or did a hugeness indeed stir somewhere yonder? In all this strangeness, how could he tell? He forbade himself fear and struggled onward.

That night he made a fireless camp. Whatever punk wood he could scratch together was too wet for tinder. Nor was there anything suitable for a deadfall, and nothing got into the snares he set. They must not be right for catching the lesser animals of these parts. Nonetheless darkness was once more full of noises, low and witchy.

In the morning he blundered ahead once more. When from time to time his skin prickled with a feeling of eyes upon him, he ignored it. His need was too great, to find his way back.

At the end of that day he knew he was in truth lost, quite likely making wild swings to and fro and around when he thought he was pointed steadily. Else he would by now have been free, out beneath unhidden sun and stars. He drained his waterskin, for terror lurked beneath whatever resolution he kept, to hammer in his breast and parch his throat. As warm as the nights were in here, he found no dew at dawn, nor did he discover a spring or a brook.

Nor did he see any more of the game he thought must be so plentiful. Trees, brush, and shadows, trees, brush, and shadows were all that remained in the world, endless as an evil dream. Toward the close of that day he could no longer comfort himself with memories of friends and of Laughing Up The Morning. Their faces were blurred by the haze of despair that had fallen over him. Blindly he stumbled ahead, because he knew that if he stopped for more than a night's rest, that would be where he left his bones.

Thus it was with Thunder Horse when the Forest Folk came upon him.

◦ ◦ ◦

They were three hunters, who from afar heard him thrashing about. He did not sound like anything known to them. Moonbeam-quiet themselves, they made their way in his direction—and stopped amazed at sight of the huge man in the outlandish clothes. For his part, he uttered a coughing roar, fell to his knees, and reached empty, trembling hands out to them.

Clearly he was no demon, and he might be a god in disguise. Even if he were a helpless stranger, he should prove interesting. Therefore the hunters were kindly. They assisted the newcomer to his feet, gave him water and food, guided him to their camp, let him recover in the next few days while they completed their mission.

Thunder Horse found more to marvel at than the saving of his life. His rescuers were not quite like men of the People, being less tall, more slender, darker of hair and eyes though fairer of skin— that last, perhaps, because less sun and wind touched them. They braided their hair and haggled their beards off short. Their garb was simpler than his, and without decoration; to breechclout and leggings a man might or might not add a fringed tunic, with perhaps a fur cap on the head. Their weapons were just knives, hand axes, and short, stout spears meant for thrusting rather than casting. The style of stone-knapping was different from his. Later he would learn that they too had bone harpoons and, while they lacked bows, possessed something new to him, fishhooks.

In camp they had raised no tent but, rather, constructed shelters by weaving brush over an uprooted sapling leaned in the crotch of a tree, and chinking any holes with moss. Their fire burned outside the entrance, with rocks behind to help cast the heat inside. It was a snug place to sleep.

In the time that followed, they brought in a couple of red deer. Skinned and dressed, the carcasses were hung well overhead, out of reach of thievish animals. On the last day, exultant, they came in with another creature, the size of a half-grown boy, coarse-haired, with tusks jutting from a long snout. Also they had trapped three short-muzzled, stiff-whiskered beasts of prey, slightly larger than foxes, for the pelts rather than the stringy flesh. Life among the trees was more varied than out upon the Land.

The hunters had no magic bags like Thunder Horse's. However, in a belt pouch each carried a few pebbles on which designs had been painted, zigzags or crisscrosses or more enigmatic patterns. At first he would take out one of these and clutch it in his fist while dealing with the guest. Later, losing suspicion, the group stopped doing this. The pebbles must be their kind of talisman.

Their speech was rapid and singsong, quite unlike the gutturals of the People. Thunder Horse could make nothing of it at first. When he named himself, they seemed startled. None ever tapped his own chest while uttering anything. From hearing them call to each other, he slowly came to associate certain sounds with particular persons—Unyada, Denovado, Zimbarir—though he had no idea what the words meant.

By that time the group were on their way home. Their kills they carried on their backs, or lashed to a pole between two men in turn. That was less awkward than Thunder Horse had supposed, for they moved with incredible deftness and knew every easiest route to follow. He was the groper and stumbler. At least, now that he had regained his strength, he could help; his shoulders bore twice the burden of anybody else.

Just the same, it was two days of hard travel to their destination. He concluded—rightly, as he afterward learned—that they had gone out in a threesome because that many were needed to bring a worth-while amount of catch home over such a distance, through these narrow and brush-encumbered ways. And, of course, like the People, they must needs often hunt well away from their dwellings, lest they deplete the game closer by.

Their home was a sizable settlement. Its huts were akin to the camp shelter, but larger and more substantial. They stood not very far apart, among the trees at the front of an overhanging cliff. It was higher than that of the Great Cave, though it lacked such a deep hole. Here too burned a fire perpetually tended, and was a common meeting ground. Yet no pictures adorned the cliff. Painted pebbles lay about in profusion, but that was all.

Women and children swarmed to meet the arrival, shrilling their welcomes and their astonishment at seeing Thunder Horse. Many crowded around to touch his skin or pluck at his clothes. A shout from an older man, who seemed to be a leader, sent them scurrying back to their tasks. It seemed that they did the work of the village, save for such labor as was too heavy for them. Thunder Horse was soon admiring the skill with which they smoked meat and cured hides. On the other hand, their household wares struck him as poorly made, and they had no sense of blending and flavoring of foods.

His rescuers joined male friends and took their ease. Toward evening men went into their huts, to emerge painted and feather-bonneted for a celebration of success. The women stayed with the simple grass skirts that were their summer garb, and children remained naked. Both sexes bore simple ornaments, necklaces or bracelets of bone, shell, quills, plumes. The makers of these lacked the art of craftspeople in the Land.

The celebration took place after dark, with feasting, wine, song, drums, dance around a bonfire. The dancers did not stamp out the stately ring-measures of the People, but capered in pairs, man and woman. After a while, such a pair was apt to steal off into the night, coming back looking happy and a bit tired. Thunder Horse could merely stand and watch. Even so, more than one comely young female swayed up to smile invitingly at him. He fought down desire. It would be madness to take advantage of a girl who had gotten drunk, and so court the wrath of her father or husband. Her gaze upon him would grow puzzled, until presently she went elsewhere.

Unyada's family took him into their dwelling. He slept badly on the crowded floor in the stuffy air. He was used to a tent in summer, a solid but spacious sod house in winter. Still, these folk were being generous. Next day several men used hafted axes to slash brush, whereupon their women made him a hut for himself.

Women always worked together to prepare the main meal of the day, which everybody shared. Those were noisy and cheerful occasions. Otherwise a person simply took a handful of whatever was available, as the belly ordered. Besides preserved meat and fruits, this included nuts and roots gathered in the woods. There were also lumps of stuff new to Thunder Horse; women ground dried acorns or seeds between stones, mixed the powder with water or blood, and baked it on heated rocks.

As wonderment wore off, he began to feel himself less than a man, forever taking and never giving. By signs he tried to show that, if nothing else, he would like to help around the village. Women squealed, giggled, fluttered their hands when he tried to carry their burdens or wield their grinding stones.

Luckily, Unyada understood and found a suitable task. Man's work at home was chiefly with wood, felling trees, splitting them into fuel, shaping poles and shafts. Once he got the knack, Thunder Horse's strength made him the best of everybody at this. Already, of course, he could flake new tools and sharpen old ones, though his style was unique here.

He did not work the entire time, or even most of it. Nobody did. He had ample leisure to make acquaintances, get shown around the neighborhood, master such minor skills as line fishing, start haltingly to learn the language.

At first, what he learned was mainly the names of things. He would have had to do this in any case, as strange as most were to him. He found that to the dwellers this immensity of trees was the Forest, and they its Folk. They knew of the open country northward, but feared and avoided it.

Slowly he gained knowledge of beasts. The red deer he had encountered, but not yet the fallow deer—nor the elk, the size of the shelk remembered by the People and likewise possessor of wide, flat antlers, but crooked-nosed and ungainly. In the camp of the hunters he had seen a slain boar and some wildcats. Now, looking at what bones and hides the villagers kept, he learned about lynxes, otters, the terrible bear. A moon-horn such as he had killed was really a wisent. Commoner was the aurochs, not as shaggy or quite as massive but even more formidably beweaponed on the brow. Taken to a nearby stream, he saw his first beavers and their dam. Eventually, guided through the woods by his friends, he glimpsed those other animals of which he had heard.

He would have gained lore much faster if the Forest Folk had drawn pictures. But they did not, and when he tried with a bit of charcoal, they grew so plainly dismayed that he stopped forthwith. Piecemeal it came to him that they lived in dread of . . . of what? The unknown?

The various names that each person used, and frequently changed, were blinds against evil spirits. A true name was kept secret, revealed in private by the mother when a child went through rites of manhood or womanhood, and never thereafter spoken. Ancestral ghosts were not protective but envious of the living, ever seeking revenge for being dead. There seemed to be no landwights whom humans might keep well-disposed by songs and gifts. Instead there were beings remote and implacable, though demanding sacrifices, rulers of sky and earth and underground, of birth and death and luck and misfortune, glimpsed in storm or wildfire or the Forest depths—gods, they were called. And when men whispered of the Horned One, they shuddered.

Was this why they were such indifferent hunters? It was not for lack of skill. The wilderness required more of that than did the Land. In fact, they took deer quite readily. A man would stand in smoke to cover his natural odor and don a fringed tunic so as to resemble a tree; thereafter, step by high and soundless step, freezing into motionlessness whenever the quarry glanced his way, he could work near enough to cast an arm around its neck and stab it in the throat. He could read the subtlest signs of nibbled leaves or bent twigs or dimples in a grassy bank. He could drift like mist down a game trail or through dense growth. Crouched high in a tree, he could drop like a lynx upon his prey. A mat of sedges on his head, he could swim underwater, silent as a pike, until he grabbed a brace of duck from beneath. His snares and traps were marvels of cunning.

Yet save for a rare pig, these men took scarcely any other of the large beasts that flourished everywhere around them. They were not cowards. Was it spirit that was wanting in them?

Withal, they were gentle, helpful, not haughty or covetous as too many among the People were. Thunder Horse gathered that they would not mind if strangers like him moved in. On the contrary, they would be delighted to have more humans nearby. It would relieve the gloom and stillness of the Forest.

True, any newcomers would have a great deal to learn. But that was entirely possible. His hosts being patient teachers, Thunder Horse began to master their arts as the summer wore on. Given a year or two of practice, he should become good enough to make a living. And his sons could be among the best. Besides, instruction would not all be one-sided—far from it. The People had skills unimagined by the Folk, for making of things both beautiful and useful. Above everything else, perhaps, they had the bow. It was too long for handiness among these branches; but surely a man could create a bow short yet powerful.

Aye, what really was most important was the soul in him. Hunters of the People would seek out elk, aurochs, wisent, the bear himself. That would doubtless be hard at first—they must discover how to do it, and lives might well be lost along the way—but do it they would, because that was in the nature of the People.

No need to fear crowding. The Forest had ample room. It was the Folk who were too few. That might be a reason why they were in such terror of those gods.

Why there were not more was a question that puzzled Thunder Horse. It was not that they made insufficient love. He was slow to recognize their customs and shocked when he did, so alien were these. The trees of the Forest had never witnessed a marriage rite. Men and women lay together as they pleased. After a period of youthful adventuring, they formed couples and shared housing, because partnership was easiest. However, such a union was not necessarily for life, nor did it at any time bind either person to the other alone.

By the time he had become aware of this, the women had given up on him. Handsome and intriguing though the outsider was, either he lay under a geas or there was something wrong with him. For his part, he felt that pursuit would be unseemly. Nevertheless, his wife was afar, and sleeping by himself grew to be very lonesome.

That summer a young girl reached womanhood. The Folk put her in a shelter by herself, brought her the necessities, but kept glance averted and did not speak with her. For one moon she was thus shut in, practicing solitary abasements that would appease the gods. After that she was free and knew her secret name. She continued living with her parents and calling herself Elidir. Thunder Horse thought that meant "Anemone" but was not sure; his command of the language was still feeble. She was pretty, her figure slight but ripening, her tresses crow's-wing black around fine-boned features, huge dark eyes, tip-tilted nose, lips always a little parted over shining teeth.

She took to hanging around him whenever he was at home and she had no immediate duties. As he cut and trimmed his wood, flaked his flints, wrestled or romped with his male friends, there she would be, watching, timidly smiling if his gaze strayed her way. Ofttimes nobody else was at hand; he might be logging or tending his fish lines some distance off.

At first he simply enjoyed her nearness, as sightly as she was. Later he understood what he was free to do if he chose. He refrained, because come autumn he meant to return to Laughing Up The Morning, and Elidir might feel forsaken.

Let them just be comrades. She was never reluctant to talk with this lame-tongued foreigner. From her he could learn more of the language and, perhaps, the soul of her race. To him it remained a mystery.

The end came cruelly fast.

In these canopied, horizonless reaches, Thunder Horse could not keep track of sun, moon, and stars on their paths through the year. However, he knew that summer was drawing to a close. It did so in a last passionate outpouring of warmth, greenness, life. Huge flocks of birds gathered aloft and on the water, making ready for trek. Wolves turned more and more toward hares and voles for food, now that the fawns they had not picked off were grown tall. Antlers waxed and hardened on stags. Elk and wisent bawled, a thunder along the leafy arches. Bears rambled, rooted, raided bees' nests, fattening themselves against winter. Among the Forest Folk, men busied themselves more than ever bringing in venison, and children gathered nuts and berries for the women to preserve. Besides, a sacrificial feast was in preparation. It would take place on the full moon after the first leaves turned yellow, in hopes of winning the mercy of the gods throughout the cold season.

Thunder Horse decided he would go home right after that. His longing was as keen as the winds that must already be sweeping over the Land. He would lift from his wife and children the fear that he was dead. And when the People met, he would have words of hope for them.

Oh, they could not move down here all at once. Next spring he would lead several families back. They would spend an unbroken year or two getting to know the Forest well, what it offered and what it demanded. Thereafter some could return and invite the rest to follow them south. No doubt many would refuse, preferring to follow the reindeer and the old ways—*over the wide ranges, under the starry skies.* . . . Yes, he had been away too long himself. It had become a weasel in his breast, gnawing his heart.

But in the Forest was abundance forever.

From dawn, the morning was sultry. No breeze relieved it; the crowns of trees were like masses of green stone seen against a heaven made wan by pitiless light. Cloud banks swelled in the west, snowy on top, blue-black in their depths, flickery with lightning, but thus far the storm held aloof. Sometimes its mutterings reached the ear, almost the only sound in breathlessness.

Thunder Horse did not see this at the village. There cliff and boughs cut off the sight. Women and children went listlessly about their chores. Able-bodied men were off on the chase, save for him. He wanted to repay kindness as far as possible, and his best service was to cut more firewood. Ax and resharpening stone in hands, waterskin and packet of food at waist, he departed for the clearing.

It was some ways off, because the Folk wanted trees around their dwellings for shelter. It was not large. A man could only fell a young, slender bole; thus a woodlot was nothing more than whatever stand of such could be found within a reasonable distance. This one was nearly exhausted. But human toil made no real wounds on the Forest. The ancient giants stood untouched, and saplings sprang up faster than loggers could work.

At his goal, Thunder Horse saw the sky. Light and heat flooded over him. He stripped to breechclout and shoes before he approached the elm he had in mind. There he murmured an apology to any being who might inhabit it. That was not the way of men hereabouts, they seemed to revere only the gods, but he continued to offer the courtesies he felt were due.

Bracing his legs, he swung. The impact of flint on wood thudded unduly loud in this hush. It ran back through the haft and his arms into his shoulders. Sweat runneled across his ribs and made his lips salty. He would be at this the whole day, and the day after and the day after. It was no pleasure. Far rather would he be padding along a game trail—or, O memories, running down a reindeer through country where cool winds blew! But he might as well get used to the labor. It would be necessary from time to time, once he had settled here, and it was better than starvation.

He had been hewing for a while, and the stormclouds had grown vaster yet, when the corner of his eye caught a movement. Turning, he saw Elidir step out into the rank grass of the clearing. He stopped work and smiled. "Why, greeting," he said.

She advanced shyly, carrying a small basket full of currants and gooseberries. A sweet sight she was, clad in just a loosely woven skirt. Her painted pebble, which had a natural hole in it, hung from a thong between the firm little breasts. She was not as sweaty as he, but her skin had a sheen to it, and when she drew nigh he scented an enticing pungency.

"I thought you would like these," she said low. Her lashes fluttered.

He still must needs guess the meanings of more than half the words he heard, though usually that was easy enough. Harder was to put together speech of his own. "You . . . good. They . . . good. We share?" This last he made clear by pointing and chewing.

She laughed, sat down in a single curling motion, gesturing him to join her. The berries were crisp, tart, refreshing. When he tried to say so, she beamed. "You work too hard," she reproved him. "Nobody else does. Take your ease."

He frowned in his effort to follow. She lay back on an elbow. That made the curve of her hip stand clear against the Forest gloom behind. "You are such a serious man," she went on. "Always you struggle. Why? The gods will do with us as they choose. Enjoy while you can."

His pulse throbbed. She was too beautiful. Otherwise he might better have disentangled what she was saying. He got simply the drift of it. "I . . . work, learn . . . go home." He swept an arm on high, repeatedly, hoping she would see that he meant sunrise. "Five, ten days? Feast. I go home."

She writhed up to crouch on her knees before him. The dark eyes grew enormous. "You are leaving?" she wailed. "After the feast? No, you mustn't, you mustn't!"

"I . . . come back . . . springtime? . . . Bring woman, children."

Suddenly she was in his lap, surging against him, gasping, "Now, now, now!"

He understood. Fire ran through him. Within his head, an aurochs bellowed. And none would take offense. Men would chuckle and slap his back, while more young women clustered eagerly around.

He had never done a harder thing than to pull her arms off him, push her away, jump to his feet, and shout, "No!"

She rose too, shaken and bewildered. "Why?" she stammered. "I, I, I have lain awake every night wishing—why will you not? I can see you are able. Has a god cursed you?"

Thunder Horse drew a ragged breath. Explaining to her would be like snaring rain. Nonetheless he must try.

He wanted to say, "My dear, you are adorable, and I have had my own sleepless nights, and Laughing Up The Morning would most likely not mind very much. But I cannot harm you, lass, without making a rent in my honor. And this would be to harm you. Oh, you would lose no virtue in the eyes of the Folk. I have come to know that. But I might well leave you with child—and leave you I must— and you would sorrow. You might keep hoping I would return to you, but that is something I could never do, for I will be together with my beloved, and among the People we are one and one as long as both are alive.

"Maybe your feelings are shallow, maybe your spirit would soon rid itself of me. But be that as it may, if you become a mother you would have to find yourself a man, a provider and protector. Should I abandon my own child? Never! A man of the People does not do that.

"Best you go, Elidir. And when hereafter we meet, let us only smile kindly upon each other."

As it was, both their tongues fumbled and stumbled for a long time. The slowness was calming. She scowled charmingly, laid finger to brow, tried these words and that.

And finally she crowed laughter and reached again for him. "Oh, but that is nothing!" she cried. "I mean, do not fear. It would be wonderful. What better offering could I make the Horned One than a child of Thunder Horse?"

He stepped back. Abruptly the sweat on him felt cold. "What you say? Tell me!"

"You do not know?" She composed herself, though he thought of a wildcat ready to pounce. "Why, the Horned One, the Terrible Stalker, the Forest God—every woman gives him her firstborn at the autumn feast. You will see. We take the little ones to the lake and hold them under. Afterward we leave them in the trees. Oh, it hurts, we weep, but this is what he wants. We do it for the sake of the children who come after, those of them that live. Else he would summon the trees from the earth, and they would come walking on their roots, huge and horrible, to crush us."

Again he must grope for her meaning.

When it came to him, that was like being gored, and hoofs trampling him as he fell.

As if through heat-shimmer, he saw her tremulous smile, he saw her sway toward him. "Then come, let us take what joy we may," she sang. Her fingers closed on his waist.

"No!" he screamed, wrenched loose, and ran.

He felt her look strike his back like arrows, out of the tears that burst forth. "I hate you!" pursued him. "You will never belong here! May you meet the god!"

Somehow he understood every word; and somehow he knew that he understood nothing.

Long and long he wandered about, blind to where he went. It was all the same anyhow, all green and gold, shadowy and silent. Within himself he had a beast to hunt down and slay, unless it killed him first.

They were not trolls, the Forest Folk—not generous Unyada, not loving and innocent Elidir. He must make himself know they were not trolls.

They did what they did because they believed they had no choice. It was why their increase was so slow. Most infants died in any case. Killing the firstborn was like casting one more deadly disease upon the race. Yet the mothers, the young mothers believed they must.

It was a ghastly mistake. The People would move in and show them it was not needful. For the People did not grovel before gods.

Yes. Thus be it.

But he could not remain for that feast.

Nor could he make clear to the Folk why not. They were looking forward to it as a grand sendoff for the man who could be bringing them neighbors, allies. He had neither the language nor the heart to tell them what had gone wrong.

No, let him quietly assemble his gear, pack sufficient rations, and be off. By now he was able to find his way northward. When springtime spread hopefulness abroad, he would return; and at his side would be Laughing Up The Morning and her strength.

Thunder Horse sought back to the village. Air had become nearly too hot and wet to breathe. Though the rainclouds had filled half of heaven, earth still yearned for them in vain. Sometimes he heard their drums.

In his hut he made ready to go. Everything he needed was on hand, so packing went quickly.

Several women saw him emerge and depart. They hailed him questioningly. He forced a smile and a wave. It was a blessing that he could not readily talk with them and that they knew it. Doubly a blessing was Elidir's absence. Well, she might grieve for a while, but she was youthful and healthy, she would get over it. How glad he was that he had stood strong against the aurochs in himself.

If they wanted to, the hunters could track him down. He did not expect that. Not only were they busy, they would take for granted that he had his reasons for leaving early, which it was likely best not to inquire about. For in their minds it could be that a god had spoken to him.

Thunder Horse found a game trail bound the way he desired and settled into his stride. That pace was not the long lope which bore him across the Land. This path was too narrow, shut-in, and twisted. However, he moved quickly enough to be out in the open in a couple of days.

Because of the dank heat, he wore just his breechclout. Thorns ripped at his calf. Like a hook and line, the pain drew him back to awareness. He had better pay more heed. Not yet was this country where a man could rove free.

How still it was, how heavy with a sense of something about to be born. His feet whispered on soft, damp earth. On either side, bush, boles, boughs, and entangling vines walled him in. Beyond them reached intricate dimnesses that soon became nights. The roof above was a green dusk where spots of light peered like eyes. He moved as if through a cave underwater, deeper and deeper into weirdness. Each breath he drew was rank with smells of rotting and of relentless growth. The Forest brooded.

The heart knocked within his breast. If only the storm would break and cleanse. If only the least stirring would pass through these leaves and leaves and leaves.

Hark, was that thunder coming close? No, not yet. But something moved. Hoofs?

Was that a raincloud shadowing the sun? No, but something darkened the Forest further.

He halted and stared. What? Were those the branches of a tree that walked on its roots?

No, they were antlers, but enormous. They grew from a head that with its body might have been human, save that it too was gigantic. It grinned with teeth sharp in the beard, it whistled, it droned voicelessly on and on about things too horrible to understand. Hands, clawed like bear paws, wove the rhythm of dance. He, monstrously male, dancing on the legs and cloven hoofs of a deer—he was the stillness and the shadows, the stillness and the shadows. Wind awoke, noiseless dream-wind. The trees bowed low, their leaves lay flat, awaiting the Presence whose hoofs would trample them. He came, he came.

For a handful of pulse beats, Thunder Horse confronted the Horned One. Then he shrieked, whirled, ran and ran and ran, blind, deaf, witless, nothing but terror that fled. The god danced and whistled behind him, before him, around him. The Forest went on in tunnels and caves, leaves and thorns, murks and madnesses, forever.

Men had burst their hearts erenow, run down to their deaths by the Fear they could not escape because it was already within them. Thunder Horse, chaser of reindeer, had strength to stay alive. When at last he fell and oblivion swept through his skull, it was in a glade open to heaven; and the whistling and dancing did not follow. Clouds overwhelmed the sun. An honestly boisterous wind tossed boughs about and stroked at his brow. Lightning flared. Bull-roarings went from end to end of the sky. Then the rain came, *sha-ah, shoo-oo, sha-ah, shoo-oo,* like a messenger out of the Land.

Winter was mild—too mild. Snow lay so thinly strewn that moss dried and died. Wolves found little meat on such herds as had not drifted north.

But at least when the People met before the Great Cave, they could sit comfortably, loosely clad, talk and listen and make their decisions. The holy fire leaped red, yellow, blue. Where it had not blackened the cliff behind it, the paintings stood boldly forth, those creatures that were the life of their hunters. The early dusk was setting in, the first stars glimmered out of utter, blue-violet clarity. A tingling chill was in the breezes that wandered across the range.

After Hawk Talon had called upon him, Thunder Horse went to take stance beside the blaze. He folded his arms and looked over the seated ranks of the People. When his gaze reached Laughing Up The Morning, it lingered.

He drew a long breath, which seemed to carry an odor of distances, before he said: "Some of you have already heard my tale, but

I will tell it again for the rest, and for the thinking of us all. You know that I fared south in hopes of finding us a new and better home. I failed. Hear how this was."

In brief words he related what had happened, and saw the horror that had now faded in him break out afresh amidst his listeners. Raising a hand to calm them, he finished: "Aye, it is truth. If we sought to the Forest, we must needs change more than our quarry and our means of taking it. We must become one with its Folk, under its god.

"My venture was not for nothing. Without it, we might always have wondered whether we were denying something splendid to our children and children's children.

"Now I can tell you, O brothers and sisters, that we will do right to follow the reindeer north. Let us therefore go with whole spirits. We may become poor, but we will remain free."

Johannes V.
Jensen

Although I have done my best to be accurate, within the limits of what is known about its period, the foregoing tale may appear to climax on a note of fantasy. You can read it that way if you like; or you can reflect that panic attacks do come upon people, and that it is told from the viewpoint of a primitive man, who makes less distinction than we do between what is inside and what is outside his skin.

It has been well said that the past is another country. The further back we go, the more foreign it becomes. Modern narrative techniques begin to fail us in conveying some sense of eras as remote in spirit as they are in time. Myth has more power, but very few writers can handle it. I'd like to tell you about one who could.

ONCE AT THE VERNAL equinox this year, when the weather went like an ocean over the city, whining in the telephone wires, I lay asleep and heard the wet wind crying hilariously in all the doorways, drunk with hope, crazy with wanderlust, and while I slept I imagined how the countryside now lay out there under the spring storm, open to its wild caresses, where the blue-black snow water in plowed fields traveled with shivers first of sun and then of gust, and how the crows pressed themselves flat on the green, thin rye and shunned the wind with their backs. . . .

Yes, the leaves have begun to fall. They have sat the whole summer on the trees, now they all want to be something in their own right, and God have mercy on them. They turn brittle in their stems from desire for independence, and do not know that the new, biting life is the work of the night cold; it is no longer fashionable to be green, now every leaf has to be yellow and never suspects that that is to die. Withered and on your own, that is the watchword. Hoo heigh, they stream from the trees, they move away, no, they emigrate, they say, for that is supposed to be more violent, and still it is only the wind that drives them.

It was late and the streets were totally deserted. The frosty moon hung as if in a white crypt over the rimed roofs, the city filled the horizon like a stiffened field of nothing but strange lifeless things, from which there came a fine tone, a shrilling of the frost, as if the whole earth were a sphere of crystalline ice, which grew still colder and sang from it. But from farther out, from space itself came a dark whistling; it was the bird Roc, which lay on its wings in great circles among the extinguished globes. If it should sweep in over the city now and break only the spire off one of the towers, the whole outstretched city would at once collapse to the finest ice-powder. . . .

A fragile music resounded high up in the air, a harping sound old as the Flood, but more springlike than anything else in the world, and in the silver-white moon-glimmer could be seen a flock of wild geese, which passed in a wedge over the ruin and vanished in the violet-blue night.

These poor translations of mine, from four different pieces by the Danish writer Johannes V. Jensen, may perhaps convey to you a little of the reason why I rank him among the giants. It has been said that a writer who belongs to a small country has the choice of being buried alive in his own language or mutilated in somebody else's. But if he happens to be a genius, the world at large will be the richer for having even a crude and partial knowledge of his achievement. If the remarks that follow persuade you to look up English versions of the books I shall mainly be discussing, they will have served their purpose.

The literary history of Scandinavia goes back a thousand years, to the Eddic poems. Not very long afterward, the Icelandic sagas were written down. Little that was noteworthy came out of the later Middle Ages, except for the Danish folk ballads, which are fully as colorful as the Scottish. A revival that began in the Reformation era became brilliant in the eighteenth century, whose master figures are the playwright and scholar Ludvig Holberg and the poet Carl Michael Bellman. The Romantic movement produced several more, as good as their English and German contemporaries. Hans Christian Andersen speaks to the whole human race—though foreigners are apt to present him in watered-down versions that omit his occasional grimness and do scant justice to his basic realism. That same realism brought fame to Henrik Ibsen and August Strindberg. In the North as elsewhere, it took firm hold during the nineteenth century. Around the beginning of the twentieth, important new writers were appearing, some of whose names are also well known abroad—to give a few random examples, the Swedes Selma Lagerlöf, Verner von Heidenstam, and Frans Bengtsson; the Norwegians Sigrid Undset, Knut Hamsun, and Johan Bojer; the Icelanders Gunnar Gunnarsson and (later) Halldor Laxness; the Danes Henrik Pontoppidan, Martin Andersen-Nexø, and Isak Dinesen. This high performance continued till the Second World War, though a number of its leaders were poets, such as the marvelously melodious Hans Hartvig Seedorff Pedersen, and have therefore seldom been translated. Since the war, Scandinavia seems once again to be in literary eclipse, for whatever reason; its people speak of a "culture pause," though half a century seems like a long time for catching one's breath. About the only surviving luminary from the 1930s is Piet Hein, who has himself put many of his delightful "grooks" into English.

Johannes V(ilhelm) Jensen (1873–1950) was a towering part of that milieu, and it is he with whom we shall be dealing.

In calling him and most of his contemporaries "realists," I do not mean that they were "naturalists" in the technical sense. Indeed, they were in revolt against established naturalism, which confines itself—often narrowly—to what the author takes for observed facts—often grubby. The school has produced works of great stature, but it does not have the sole possible approach to writing; and the new generation around 1900 wanted to deal with other aspects of life: fun, fantasy, feeling. Yet this was not a neo-Romantic movement. These writers were quite uninterested in grand generalities, long odes, or stage heroics.

Their realism expressed itself in sharp observation of the details that can tell of a larger whole; in awareness of the findings of modern science, the accomplishments of modern technology, and the implications of these for the future; in a sense of the shortness of life, the frailty of happiness, and still of how wonderful a world this is. Nowhere was it more robustly embodied than in the work of Johannes V. Jensen.

He was born in a country town in Jutland, the son of a veterinarian. In his *Himmerland Stories* (1898) and some subsequent pieces, he has described the land as it was then and the old peasant society of which he saw the last remnant, as vividly as Mark Twain described life on the Mississippi. Having studied medicine but gone into journalism, he began to write for himself on the side. Popular success soon let him become a free lance, which he remained for the rest of his days. His travels took him over Europe, to Africa,

China, Southeast Asia, and the United States, about all of which he wrote. Those books, essays, and poems are a joy to read, lyrical, richly sensuous, often breaking into wild humor. Who else could speak of Memphis, Tennessee, on a dismal rainy morning at the railway station as "sphinx-forsaken Memphis"?

At home he was enormously influential. He has been called the greatest reformer of the Danish language since Holberg, and certain it is that in his hands it became an instrument strong and supple. He invented a whole new literary form for himself, the "myth"—a sketch which in a few pages, whether of straightforward description, fiction, or fantasy conveys an intensely personal impression of something, someplace, or somebody. The quotations with which this review opens are from four of these.

Like Kipling, whom he admired and about whom he wrote a book, Jensen was keenly interested in science and technology. In his case, this interest concentrated itself on evolutionary biology, which he saw as endlessly working on man as well as in nature. That led him to views which are probably not tenable any more and are definitely in disrepute nowadays. He felt that natural selection had shaped the human species within historical time; different stages of society were the result of genetics as well as of environment, and so was the success of one social class vis-à-vis another. In fact, I can't deny that he was a racist, albeit of a mild, humane sort. He did not hold with oppressing those breeds of men that he felt were less highly evolved than others—especially since, in his philosophy, they had an evolutionary future ahead of them, and might well in time take over leadership from worn-out stocks. On the whole, he was always a friend of freedom.

With this much preliminary, let me go on to recommend two books available in English, out of print but surely in many a library, which are tremendous fantasies and one of which is also a kind of science fiction.

The older, *The Fall of the King* (*Kongens Fald*, 1899–1902), is primarily a historical novel. It takes place mostly in Scandinavia during the upheavals of the early Reformation period. The king is Christian II of Denmark. I advise you to look him and his times up in an encyclopedia before you read the story. Otherwise you are apt to feel confused; and anyway, it's a fascinating if terrible era. The protagonist of the book is Mikkel Thøgersen, whom we first meet as a student in Copenhagen. Expelled, he becomes a mercenary soldier, and so is present at many events, such as the bloodbath of Stockholm, a peasant revolt, and the deposition and long imprisonment of the king. This is no mere travelogue, though it does bring its setting wholly alive. It is a tale of youth and the loss of youth, love and the loss of love, cruelty, kindness, despair, death, and life that goes on heedless of those who have fallen.

The fantasy element lies in a few scattered chapters. They need not be taken literally; they could be visions that someone is having, or simply mood music. Nevertheless they are some of the most powerful imaginative writing ever done. In one, Death rides forth across winter ice; in another, based on a medieval ballad, a dead man rises from his grave to try fruitlessly to comfort his grieving beloved; in the third, the aged Mikkel lies dying and thinks he hears the song of the elemental giantesses who swing the quern that grinds forth all creation. ("—We grind you sun, moon, and stars runaway around the world. Day and night shall change in a blink, white and black, and heaven shall go like a wheel. We grind you summer and winter like fever; heat shall fly upon you and flee again from cold.—")

And Jensen completed this before he was thirty!

Fantasy is not peripheral to *The Long Journey* (*Den Lange Rejse*, 1909–1920). Rather, that mighty work is a fantasy throughout, an epic of man's faring through time and space from primordial forest to the uttermost ends of the earth. As such, it can also be reckoned science fiction, despite numerous sheerly mythic passages—but science fiction of the symbolic kind, not meant to be exact any more than Ray Bradbury's Mars stories are.

The sciences on which Jensen drew are evolutionary biology (again), anthropology, and archaeology. Even at the time he was writing, his interpretations of these must have been controversial, and surely no prehistorian would admit that events could have gone just as he said. It doesn't matter, in the way that the anachronisms in Shakespeare don't matter. *The Long Journey*, too, can claim the license given to great poetry.

After all, its very structure is poetic rather than novelistic. While there are individual persons in it, several of them unforgettable, whose entire lives we follow, hardly any of their conversation appears, unless we count their songs and occasional spoken verses. Scenes, happenings, and everyday tasks often get long descriptions simply for

the sake of describing them. This is never dull when the words go
so flowingly, with frequent bits that leap right out of the page into
your eye.

The Long Journey was published as six separate books, not in
chronological order, over a period of eleven years. The one-volume
English translation I have seen—not a bad one—arranges them
somewhat differently and omits "The Ship." In summarizing the
whole, I will go by the original plan.

"The Lost Country" tells of the vast warm forest that covered
Europe before the Ice Age. Life swarms, wild cattle, wild horses,
wolves, elephants, tigers, monkeys, early humans. Those last are naked, almost mute, gatherers of food where they can find it, without
fire or tools, roaming in tiny bands each dominated by its Old Man,
living hardly differently from the apes, yet already feeling themselves
somehow unlike. Brooding over the landscape stands the volcano
Gunung Api, "its black, scarred head reared above the clouds," which
sometimes casts forth flame that kindles the wilderness beneath. In
giving the mountain this Malay name, Jensen probably sought to
strengthen the impression of a tropical land; at the same time, he
may have been hinting at an origin of the Eddic myth of Ginnun-
gagap, the abyss from which the earliest gods arose.

One man, Fyr, born during a conflagration, ascends the volcano,
spends years in the company of its fire, and at last brings back a
burning branch—he a Prometheus who, in the end, pays for his gift
with his life. First, however, he has followed the stars in their courses
through the year and has begun to shape stones and tie them to
handles. Thus he stands for the countless generations who in actuality—we suppose—took these slow steps toward full humanness. A
while after his death, a chill creeps into the weather, and one morning hunters see on top of now silent Gunung Api a strange whiteness,
the harbinger of the Ice.

"The Glacier" is the title of the next book. It opens on a night
of cold, wind, and rain. Winter has come to the world, and life must
either flee south or change itself to survive. A youth named Dreng
is tending a fire and raging at the relentless worsening of things. (The
English version makes his name Carl, to convey the same archaic
meaning: a strong man.) He sets forth to seek out and kill the evil
being that must be causing this, fails, and returns to discover he is
outcast because he let the fire die. From then on he must dwell in

exile, while the glacier marches south through the years until it overwhelms the forest. Beginning as a hermit and a cannibal, Dreng becomes the first man to make really good tools, the first to light fire by striking stones together. The mate whom he finds becomes the first true wife, partner to her husband, inventor of the simpler household arts. Together they become the leaders and saviors of the people. Dreng's indomitability reveals him as an archetype of the sheer will by which man finally mastered hostile nature. His loss of an eye suggests that he was remembered as the god Odin.

His remote descendant, the hammer-wielding charioteer White Bear, likewise recalls Thor. By then the Northern folk have settled down into a static, priest-ruled existence as hunters. But the glacier is receding. Disastrous floods and changing landscape spell a new doom, which nobody can bring himself to see. Like his ancestor, White Bear gets into trouble, departs, and copes by using his head and hands. He makes the first wheel and the first ship; his woman thinks to plant seeds; at the close of his stormy life, the glacier has withdrawn toward the Pole and the Neolithic Age is dawning.

Of course we know none of this could have happened so fast. Jensen did too. He was writing a myth. In it, Northern man keeps a racial memory of the Lost Country, the forest before the Ice, as a paradise to be forever sought. Like an instinct, it expresses itself in inchoate yearnings, religious faiths, and the drive to seek out the unknown.

"Norna-Gest" (spelled somewhat differently in Danish) derives from a legend about the missionary King Olaf Trygvason of Norway, to whom came a man of that name who had lived for three hundred years. Jensen boldly set his birth ten times as far back, in the Stone Age of Denmark.

By 1900, researchers had come to a good understanding of that period. Hence the writer must now respect a large body of fact. It did not hem him in. Rather, he drew on it to create a lavishly full picture of life at the time, on the whole a gentle picture aglow with his love for the Danish land. Fantasy enters in the persons of the Norns, three traveling witch-wives, who become angry with Gest's mother and lay on her infant the curse that he will live no longer than a candle burning in her hut. The mother snuffs it out at once and, when her son is older, gives it to him to carry.

During the centuries that follow, Gest sometimes grows weary and lights the candle; but each time until the last he puts it out and awakens elsewhere, further aged. Thus he sees the coming of bronze and afterward of iron, the ever-changing ways of the Northern people, their eternal longing for a realm of bliss which must lie somewhere beyond the horizon. He makes himself a wandering skald, always welcome for his songs and tales. Finally he reaches the court of King Olaf, is baptized, and lets his candle burn down; for with the foreign faith, the old North will be no more, and he held the spirit of it.

Some readers will notice that I drew on the same legend for a chapter in *The Boat of a Million Years*. This was explicitly an act of homage to Jensen.

In "The Trek of the Cimbrians" Norna-Gest is still alive, since it takes place about a hundred years before Christ. Most of it is factual. The Cimbrians were driven out of Jutland by a long succession of bad years. With other barbarian tribes for allies, they invaded the South, destroyed three Roman armies sent against them, threw Rome into terror when they entered Italy, but there met defeat. In Jensen's telling, Norna-Gest tries vainly to warn them against leaving their homeland. Not only hunger, but the vision of the lost country is too strong in them. While most of them perish in battle or, worse, in slavery, one girl has a happier fate. She is found and bought by a Greek sculptor who, earlier, has been a captive in the North, and who becomes her loving husband. Their children are the first in that renewal of life which later Germanic immigrants will bring to the civilized lands. We do not have to believe that that was really the case, which it scarcely was, in order to appreciate the extraordinary visualization of a vanished age, the horror, and the beauty in "The Trek of the Cimbrians."

"The Ship" deals with the Vikings—specifically, a raid into the Mediterranean (recorded in a medieval chronicle). Out of curiosity and an idle generosity, on their way home they give passage to a Christian missionary, a humble monk who ends his days as archbishop in a Denmark where church bells are ringing everywhere. Again Jensen telescopes the work of many generations into one, yet does not seem to do harm to the truth behind the facts. He concludes with a remarkable piece of symbolism, an account of how the Danish forest arose and evolved after the glacier departed; it is like the rise and fall and rebirth of human dreams.

"Christopher Columbus" is the culminating book. It begins with a hunter in the early Iron Age, who runs beyond space and time; then recasts the story of St. Christopher, a ferryman who helps the Longobards on their way south; and then evokes a great cathedral as an emblem in stone of both the vanished forests and the ship in which men seek them. Mute longing finally bursts forth into action in the deeds of Columbus, heir of Cimbrian, Viking, and Longobard, who gives the Europeans back their lost country—which they do not recognize.

The core of the book describes his first voyage across the Atlantic, the dread as well as the triumph, the pettiness as well as the heroism. Ultimately Columbus' victory is a defeat for him; he does not find the Earthly Paradise for which he was searching. His death, forsaken in a narrow room, is heartbreakingly related. Afterward fantasy re-enters, for his is the ghost that must sail unresting at the bottom of the world.

This does not end *The Long Journey*. Half a planet lies waiting. The Spanish conquest of Mexico is told of with a gusto that in places gets uproariously funny—but later we see it from the side of the Indians. In North America, the Northern peoples build new nations wherein the soul of their race can grow. Meanwhile Charles Darwin, voyaging aboard the *Beagle*, begins to understand man's kinship with the whole of nature. At the end, Columbus wins release; he and his phantom ship dissolve into the living world. The last brief chapter is a hymn to life herself.

Elsewhere I have written: "*The Long Journey* is big enough to overshadow its own faults, as a mountain overshadows gravel and brush at its foot. Above, we find huge outlooks, stern cliffs, fresh winds—and beautiful small flowers where spring water comes forth. We owe Johannes V. Jensen many thanks for leading us out onto those heights he knew so well."

Fortune Hunter

He, who so loved the living world, did not live to see it menaced as we do—menaced and corrupted by ourselves. I cannot help but be glad of that.

He knew better than to believe in a nice, harmonious "ecology" presided over by a politically correct Mother Goddess. No such thing ever existed. The wilderness was not only once the home of humans, it was also often their terrible enemy, while they were from the beginning, by birthright, technologists and, yes, scientists. If today it is the victim, that is because of technology misused and science misunderstood. This has not been inevitable, and the hour is not yet too late. Through research, thought, and action, we can still save and restore that which is, after all, a part of our souls, and surely unique in the universe. I hope this tale is not predictive but only cautionary.

A FTER CLEANING UP INDOORS, I stepped outside for a look at the evening. I'd only moved here a few days ago. Before, I'd been down in the woods. Now I was above timberline, and there'd just been time to make my body at home—reassemble the cabin and its furnishings, explore the area, deploy the pickups, let lungs acquire a taste for thinner air. My soul was still busy settling in.

I missed sun-flecks spattered like gold on soft shadow-brown duff, male ruggedness and woman-sweet odor of pines and their green that speared into heaven, a brook that glittered and sang, bird calls, a splendidly antlered wapiti who'd become my friend and took food from my hand. (He was especially fond of cucumber peels. I dubbed him Charlie.) You don't live six months in a place, from the blaze of autumn through the iron and white of winter, being reborn with the land when spring breathes over it—you don't do this and not keep some of that place ever afterward inside your bones.

Nevertheless, I'd kept remembering high country, and when Jo Modzeleski said she'd failed to get my time extended further, I decided to go up for what remained of it. That was part of my plan; she loved the whole wilderness as much as I did, but she kept her heart on its peaks and they ought to help make her mood right. However, I myself was happy to return.

And as I walked out of the cabin, past my skeletal flitter, so that nothing human-made was between me and the world, suddenly the whole of me was again altogether belonging where I was.

This base stood on an alpine meadow. Grass grew thick and

moist, springy underfoot, daisy-starred. Here and there bulked boulders the size of houses, grayness scored by a glacier which had once gouged out the little lake rippling and sparkling not far away: a sign to me that I also was included in eternity. Everywhere around, the Wind River Mountains lifted snow crowns and the darker blues of their rock, into a dizzyingly tall heaven where an eagle hovered. He caught on his wings the sunlight which slanted out of the west. Those beams seemed to fill the chilliness, turning it somehow molten; and the heights were alive with shadows.

I smelled growth, more austere than in the forest but not the less strong. A fish leaped; I saw the brief gleam and an instant later, very faintly through quietness, heard the water clink. Though there was no real breeze, my face felt the air kiss it.

I buttoned my mackinaw, reached for smoking gear, and peered about. A couple of times already, I'd spied a bear. I knew better than to try a Charlie-type relationship with such a beast, but surely we could share the territory amicably, and if I could learn enough of his ways to plant pickups where they could record his life—or hers, in which case she'd be having cubs—

No. You're bound back to civilization at the end of this week. Remember?

Oh, but I may be returning.

As if in answer to my thought, I heard a whirr aloft. It grew, till another flitter hove into sight. Jo was taking me up on my invitation at an earlier hour than I'd expected when I said, "Come for dinner about sundown." Earlier than I'd hoped? My heart knocked. I stuck pipe and tobacco pouch back in my pockets and walked fast to greet her.

She landed and sprang out of the bubble before the airpad motors were silent. She always had been quick and graceful on her feet. Otherwise she wasn't much to look at: short, stocky, pug nose, pale round eyes under close-cropped black hair. For this occasion she'd left off the ranger's uniform in favor of an iridescent clingsuit; but it couldn't have done a lot for her even if she had known how to wear it.

"Welcome," I said, took both her hands and gave her my biggest smile.

"Hi." She sounded breathless. Color came and went across her cheeks. "How are you?"

"Okay. Sad at leaving, naturally." I turned the smile wry, so as not to seem self-pitiful.

She glanced away. "You'll be going back to your wife, though."

Don't push too hard. "You're ahead of yourself, Jo. I meant to have drinks and snacks ready in advance. Now you'll have to come in and watch me work."

"I'll help."

"Never, when you're my guest. Sit down, relax." I took her arm and guided her toward the cabin.

She uttered an uncertain laugh. "Are you afraid I'll get in your way, Pete? No worries. I know these knockdown units—I'd better, after three years—"

I was here for four, and that followed half a dozen years in and out of other wildernesses, before I decided that this was the one I wanted to record in depth, it being for me the loveliest of the lovely.

"—and they only have one practical place to stow any given kind of thing," she was saying. Then she stopped, which made me do likewise, turned her head from side to side, drank deep of air and sun-glow. "Please, don't let me hurry you. This is such a beautiful evening. You were out to enjoy it."

Unspoken: And you haven't many left, Pete. The documentation project ended officially last year. You're the last of the very few mediamen who got special permission to stay on and finish their sequences; and now, no more stalling, no more extra time, the word is Everybody Out.

My unspoken reply: Except you rangers. A handful of you, holding degrees in ecology and soil biotics and whatnot—a handful who won in competition against a horde—does that give you the right to lord it over all this?

"Well, yes," I said, and segued to: "I'll enjoy it especially in present company."

"Thank you, kind sir." She failed to sound cheery.

I squeezed her arm. "You know, I am going to miss you, Jo. Miss you like hell." This past year, as my plan grew within me, I'd been cultivating her. Not just card games and long conversations over the sensiphone; no, in-the-flesh get-togethers for hikes, rambles, picnics, fishing, birdwatching, deerwatching, starwatching. A mediaman gets good at the cultivation of people, and although this past decade had given me scant need to use that skill, it hadn't died. As easy as breathing, I could show interest in her rather banal remarks, her rather sappy-sentimental opinions. . . . "Come see me when you get a vacation."

"Oh, I'll—I'll call you up . . . now and then . . . if Marie won't . . . mind."

"I mean come in person. Holographic image, stereo sound, even scent and temperature and every other kind of circuit a person might pay for the use of—a phone isn't the same as having a friend right there."

She winced. "You'll be in the city."

"It isn't so bad," I said in my bravest style. "Pretty fair-sized apartment, a lot bigger than that plastic shack yonder. Soundproofed. Filtered and conditioned air. The whole conurb fully screened and policed. Armored vehicles available when you sally forth."

"And a mask for my nose and mouth!" She nearly gagged.

"No, no, that hasn't been needed for a long while. They've gotten the dust, monoxide, and carcinogens down to a level, at least in my city, which—"

"The stinks. The tastes. No, Pete, I'm sorry, I'm no delicate flower but the visits to Boswash I make in line of duty are the limit of what I can take . . . after getting to know this land."

"I'm thinking of moving into the country myself," I said. "Rent a cottage in an agrarea, do most of my business by phone, no need to go downtown except when I get an assignment to document something there."

She grimaced. "I often think the agrareas are worse than any 'tropolis."

"Huh?" It surprised me that she could still surprise me.

"Oh, cleaner, quieter, less dangerous, residents not jammed elbow to elbow, true," she admitted. "But at least those snarling, grasping, frenetic city folk have a certain freedom, a certain . . . *life* to them. It may be the life of a ratpack, but it's real, it has a bit of structure and spontaneity and— In the hinterlands, not only nature is regimented. The people are."

Well, I don't know how else you could organize things to feed a world population of fifteen billion.

"All right," I said. "I understand. But this is a depressing subject. Let's saunter for a while. I've found some gentian blooming."

"So early in the season? Is it in walking distance? I'd like to see."

"Too far for now, I'm afraid. I've been tramping some mighty long days. However, let me show you the local blueberry patch. It should be well worth a visit, come late summer."

As I took her arm again, she said, in her awkward fashion, "You've become an expert, haven't you, Pete?"

"Hard to avoid that," I grunted. "Ten years, collecting sensie material on the Wilderness System."

"Ten years. . . . I was in high school when you began. I only knew the regular parks, where we stood in line on a paved path to see a redwood or a geyser, and we reserved swimming rights a month in advance. While you—" Her fingers closed around mine, hard and warm. "It doesn't seem fair to end your stay."

"Life never was fair."

Too damn much human life. Too little of any other kind. And we have to keep a few wildernesses, a necessary reserve for what's left of the planet's ecology; a source of knowledge for researchers who're trying to learn enough about that ecology to shore it up before it collapses altogether; never mentioned, but present in every thinking head, the fact that if collapse does come, the wildernesses will be Earth's last seedbeds of hope.

"I mean," Jo plodded, "of course areas like this were being destroyed by crowds—loved to death, as somebody wrote—so the only thing to do was close them to everybody except a few caretakers and scientists, and that was politically impossible unless 'everybody' meant *everybody*." Ah, yes, she was back to her habit of thumbing smooth-worn clichés. "And after all, the sensie documentaries that artists like you have been making, they'll be available and—" The smoothness vanished. "*You* can't come back, Pete! Not ever again!"

Her fingers remembered where they were and let go of me. Mine followed them and squeezed, a measured gentleness. Meanwhile my pulse fluttered. It was as well that words didn't seem indicated at the moment, because my mouth was dry.

A mediaman should be more confident. But such a God damn lot was riding on this particular bet. I'd gotten Jo to care about me, not just in the benevolent way of her colleagues, isolated from mankind so they can afford benevolence, but about me, this Pete-atom that wanted to spend the rest of its flickering days in the Wind River Mountains. Only how deeply did she care?

We walked around the lake. The sun dropped under the peaks—for minutes, the eastern snows were afire—and shadows welled up. I heard an owl hoot to his love. In royal blue, Venus kindled. The air sharpened, making blood run faster.

"Br-r-r!" Jo laughed. "Now I do want that drink."

I couldn't see her features through the dusk. The first stars stood forth infinitely clear. But Jo was a blur, a warmth, a solidness, no more. She might almost have been Marie.

If she had been! Marie was beautiful and bright and sexy and— Sure, she took lovers while I was gone for months on end; we'd agreed that the reserves were my mistresses. She'd had no thought for them on my returns. . . . Oh, if only we could have shared it all!

Soon the sky would hold more stars than darkness, the Milky Way would be a white cataract, the lake would lie aglow with them, and when Jupiter rose there would be a perfect glade across the water. I'd stayed out half of last night to watch that.

Already the shining was such that we didn't need a penflash to find the entrance to my cabin. The insulation layer yielded under my touch. We stepped through, I zipped the door and closed the main switch, fluoros awoke as softly as the ventilation.

Jo was correct: those portables don't lend themselves to individuality. (She had a permanent cabin, built of wood and full of things dear to her.) Except for a few books and the like, my one room was strictly functional. True, the phone could bring me the illusion of almost anything or anybody, anywhere in the world, that I might want. We city folk learn to travel light. This interior was well-proportioned, pleasingly tinted, snug; a step outside was that alpine meadow. What more did I need?

Out of hard-earned habit, I checked the nucleo gauge—ample power—before taking dinner from the freezer and setting it to cook. Thereafter I fetched nibblies, rum, and fruit juice, and mixed drinks the way Jo liked them. She didn't try to help after all, but settled back into the airchair. Neither of us had said much while we walked. I'd expected chatter out of her—a bit nervous, a bit too fast and blithe—once we were here. Instead, her stocky frame hunched in its mother-of-pearl suit that wasn't meant for it, and she stared at the hands in her lap.

No longer cold, I shucked my mackinaw and carried her drink over to her. "Revelry, not reverie!" I ordered. She took it. I clinked glasses. My other hand being then free, I reached thumb and fore-finger to twitch her lips at the corners. "Hey, you, smile. This is supposed to be a jolly party."

"Is it?" The eyes she raised to me were afloat in tears.

"Sure, I hate to go—"

"Where's Marie's picture?"

That rocked me back. I hadn't expected so blunt a question. "Why, uh—" *Okay. Events are moving faster than you'd planned on, Peter. Move with them.* I took a swallow, squared my shoulders, and said manfully: "I didn't want to unload my troubles on you, Jo. The fact is, Marie and I have broken up. Nothing's left but the formali-ties."

"What?"

Her mouth is open, her look lost in mine; she spills some of her drink and doesn't notice— Have I really got it made? This soon?

I shrugged. "Yeah. The notice of intent to dissolve relationship arrived yesterday. I'd seen it coming, of course. She'd grown tired of waiting around."

"Oh, Pete!" She reached for me.

I was totally aware—walls, crowded shelves, night in a window, murmur and warm gusting from the heat unit, monitor lamp on the radionic oven and meat fragrances seeping out of it, this woman whom I must learn to desire—and thought quickly that at the present stage of things, I'd better pretend not to notice her gesture. "No sympathy cards," I said in a flat tone. "To be quite honest, I'm more relieved than otherwise."

"I thought—" she whispered. "I thought you two were happy."

Which we have been, my dear, Marie and I: though a sophis-ticated mediaman does suspect that considerable of our happiness, as opposed to contentment, has been due to my long absences this past decade. They've added spice. That's something you'll always lack, whatever happens, Jo. Yet a man can't live only on spices.

"It didn't last," I said as per plan. "She's found someone more compatible. I'm glad of that."

"You, Pete?"

"I'll manage. C'mon, drink your drink. I insist that we be merry."

She gulped. "I'll try."

After a minute: "You haven't even anyone to come home to!"

" 'Home' doesn't mean a lot to a city man, Jo. One apartment is like another; and we move through a big total of 'em in a lifetime." The liquor must have touched me a bit, since I rushed matters: "Quite different from, say, these mountains. Each patch of them is absolutely unique. A man could spend all his years getting to know a single one, growing into it— Well."

I touched a switch and the airchair expanded, making room for me to settle down beside her. "Care for some background music?" I asked.

"No." Her gaze dropped—she had stubby lashes—and she blushed—blotchily—but she got her words out with a stubbornness I had come to admire. Somebody who had that kind of guts wouldn't be too bad a partner. "At least, I'd not hear it. This is just about my last chance to talk ... really talk ... to you, Pete. Isn't it?"

"I hope not." *More passion in that voice, boy.* "Lord, I hope not!"

"We have had awfully good times together. My colleagues are fine, you know, but—" She blinked hard. "You've been special."

"Same as you to me."

She was shivering a bit, meeting my eyes now, lips a bare few centimeters away. Since she seldom drank alcohol, I guessed that what I'd more or less forced on her had gotten a good strong hold, under these circumstances. *Remember, she's no urbanite who'll hop into bed and scarcely remember it two days later. She went directly from a small town to a tough university to here, and may actually be a virgin. However, you've worked toward this moment for months, Pete, old chum. Get started!*

It was the gentlest kiss I think I have ever taken.

"I've been, well, afraid to speak," I murmured into her hair, which held an upland sunniness. "Maybe I still am. Only I don't, don't, don't want to lose you, Jo."

Half crying, half laughing, she came back to my mouth. She didn't really know how, but she held herself hard against me, and I thought: *May she end up sleeping with me, already this night?*

No matter, either way. What does count is, the Wilderness Administration allows qualified husband-and-wife teams to live together on the job; and she's a ranger and I, being skilled in using monitoring devices, would be an acceptable research assistant.

And then-n-n:

I didn't know, I don't know to this day what went wrong. We'd had two or three more drinks, and a good deal of joyous tussling, and her clothes were partly off her and dinner was beginning to scorch in the oven when

I was too hasty

she was too awkward and/or backward-holding, and I got impatient and she felt it

I breathed out one of those special words which people say to each other only, and she being a bit terrified anyway decided it wasn't mere habit-accident but I was pretending she was Marie because in fact my eyes were shut

she wasn't as naive as she, quite innocently, had led me to believe, and in one of those moments which (contrary to fantasy) are forever coming upon lovers, asked herself, "Hey, what the hell is really going on?"

or whatever. It makes no difference. Suddenly she wanted to phone Marie.

"If, if, if things are as you say, Pete, she'll be glad to learn—"

"Wait a minute! Wait one damn minute! Don't you trust me?"

"Oh, Pete, darling, of course I do, but—"

"But nothing." I drew apart to register offense.

Instead of coming after me, she asked, as quietly as the night outside: "Don't you trust *me?*"

Never mind. A person can't answer a question like that. We both tried, and shouldn't have. All I truly remember is seeing her out the door. A smell of charred meat pursued us. Beyond the cabin, the air was cold and altogether pure, sky wild with stars, peaks aglow. I watched her stumble to her flitter. The galaxy lit her path. She cried the whole way. But she went.

However disappointed, I felt some relief, too. It would have been a shabby trick to play on Marie, who had considerable love invested in me. And our apartment is quite pleasant, once it's battened down against the surroundings; I belong to the fortunate small minority. We had an appropriate reunion. She even babbled about applying for a childbearing permit. I kept enough sense to switch that kind of talk off immediately.

Next evening there was a rally which we couldn't well get out of attending. The commissioners may be right as far as most citizens go. "A sensiphone, regardless of how many circuits are tuned in, is no substitute for the physical togetherness of human beings uniting under their leaders for our glorious mass purposes." We, though, didn't get anything out of it except headaches, ears ringing from the cadenced cheers, lungs full of air that had passed through thousands of other lungs, and skins which felt greasy as well as gritty. Home-bound, we encountered smog so thick it confused our vehicle. Thus we got stopped on the fringes of a riot and saw a machine gun cut a man in two before the militia let us move on. It was a huge relief to pass security check at our conurb and take a transporter which didn't fail even once, up and across to our own place.

There we shared a shower, using an extravagant percentage of our monthly water ration, and dried each other off, and I slipped into a robe and Marie into something filmy; we had a drink and a toke while Haydn lilted, and got relaxed to the point where she shook her long tresses over her shoulders and her whisper tickled my ear: "Aw, c'mon, hero, the computers've got to've edited your last year's coverage by now. I've looked forward all this while."

I thought fleetingly of Jo. Well, she wouldn't appear in a strictly wilderness-experience public-record documentary; and I myself was curious about what I had actually produced, and didn't think a revisit in an electronic dream would pain me, even this soon afterward.

I was wrong.

What hurt most was the shoddiness. Oh, yes, decent reproduction of a primrose nodding in the breeze, a hawk a-swoop, spuming whiteness and earthquake rumble of a distant avalanche, fallen leaves brown and baking under the sun, their smell and crackle, the laughter of a gust which flirted with my hair, suppleness incarnate in a snake or a cougar, flamboyance at sunset and shyness at dawn—a competent show. Yet it wasn't real, it wasn't what I had loved.

Marie said, slowly, in the darkness where we sat, "You did better before. Kruger, Matto Grosso, Baikal, your earlier stays in this region—I almost felt I was at your side. You weren't a recorder there, you were an artist, a great artist. Why is this different?"

"I don't know," I mumbled. "My presentation is kind of mechanical, I admit. I suppose I was tired."

"In that case—" she sat very straight, half a meter from me, fingers gripped together "—you didn't have to stay on. You could have come home to me long before you did."

But I wasn't tired, rammed through my head. *No, now is when I'm drained; then, there, life flowed into me.*

That gentian Jo wanted to see . . . it grows where the land suddenly drops. Right at the cliff edge those flowers grow, oh, blue, blue, blue against grass green and daisy white and the strong gray of stone; a streamlet runs past, leaps downward, ringing, cold, tasting of glaciers, rocks, turf, the air which also blows everywhere around me, around the high and holy peaks beyond. . . .

"Lay off!" I yelled. My fist struck the chair arm. The fabric clung and cloyed. A shade calmer, I said, "Okay, maybe I got too taken up in the reality and lost the necessary degree of detachment." *I lie, Marie, I lie like Judas. My mind was never busier, planning how to use Jo and discard you.* "Darling, those sensies, I'll have nothing but them for the rest of my life." *And none of the gentians. I was too busy with my scheme to bother with anything small and gentle and blue.* "Isn't that penalty enough?"

"No. You did have the reality. And you did not bring it back." Her voice was like a wind across the snows of upland winter.

Wolfram

Upon its first appearance, I wrote of this little piece that it "involves a science and contains a fiction. Therefore it is science fiction. Right?"

At least it offers a change of pace.

ADMIRING THE ADS IN *Scientific American* a while back—they are always a potent source of wonder—I was pleased to see that the General Dynamics Corporation still refers to element number 74 as tungsten. I strongly disapprove of the arbitrary and high-handed 1949 decree of the International Union of Chemistry, that hereafter everybody shall call it wolfram. Admittedly this squares with the symbol, W. But damn it, "tungsten" was what I learned, and what they make light bulbs with, and if it was good enough for Scheele it's good enough for the International Union of Chemistry. They're probably just an affiliate of the Teamsters anyway. Aye, tear that tattered ensign down!

I growled some such remark to my wife over an evening beer, and she asked where the name "wolfram" came from. Well, I said, it's the German word for tungsten—no harm in that, if only the Germans wouldn't be so aggressive about it—and comes from wolframite, the principal ore. So what's wolframite named for, she wanted to know. I suppose some chemist named Wolfram, who first described it, I shrugged, and got down the American College Encyclopedic Dictionary. It gave the mineral derivation as expected, but said that "wolfram" was of uncert. orig.

I was astonished. Turning to Webster, I found G. *wolf*, meaning "wolf," and *rahm*, meaning "cream, soot." Wolf cream? Wolf soot? Try as I might, I couldn't make sense of it. Webster evidently feels the same way, because his etymology reads "said to be fr.," etc. In other words, he's passing on this ridiculous bit of folklore for lack of anything better, but disclaiming all responsibility. In fact, he's rather badly shaken by the whole episode, so much so that he has forgotten to capitalize the German nouns.

By far the most believable theory is that there was a Wolfram, whose pioneer study of this material won him the honor of having his name bestowed upon it, but who fell into deep posthumous obscurity. Had Webster ransacked enough archives, he would surely have discovered the reference. However, since Wolfram was not a professional chemist (had he been, his name would have gotten into the histories that Webster presumably did consult, if only as a footnote) it's hard to know a priori just where to begin looking.

Nevertheless, I can see him quite clearly, this humble worker in the vineyard of science, altogether overshadowed by his gigantic contemporaries but, perhaps on that very account, shining across time's abyss with a luster of simple humanity and mixed metaphors. Karl Georg Johann Friedrich Augustus Wolfram, born and died in the eighteenth century, court librarian to the Margrave of Oberhaus-Blickstein or whatever the place was called, who occupied his leisure with walks through the countryside and brought back samples of outcroppings in his pockets, to be pored over until the candles guttered low. . . .

He cannot have been even of petty noble birth, or the histories would have paid him some attention. Nor can Oberhaus-Blickstein have been one of the brilliant and intensively studied principalities of that era, like Brandenburg. No, it was undoubtedly a backwater, peaceful, prosperous, a little smug and complacent, inhabited by peasants who tugged their forelocks and said, *"Jawohl, Herr Rittergutsbesitzer"* when the squire told them what to do and then went ahead and did the right thing anyway, by artisans and shopkeepers in the villages, and by the bourgeoisie of Schickenburg-am-Pfaff. This sleepy old town probably boasted a brick warehouse at the dock where the river barges left cargo twice a month; a pleasant though undistinguished cathedral said, on no very reliable evidence, to have been begun by Henry the Lion; several fine mansions; and of course a small palace.

Even in this idyllic setting there must have been an occasional bit of scandal, especially at court. Not that it mattered if the present Margrave was given to pinching servant girls and spent too much on imported fanciments, notably wine. (Since he really didn't know a thing about wine, the French shippers cheated him shamelessly; in the regional idiom, they took him by the nose and swung him around their heads. But nobody ever told the Margrave, so little harm was done.) Such things were acceptable. In fact, a Margrave with no minor vices would have seemed unnatural. However, in his youth this one had spent a year in Paris and become a liberal. Not too many years ago he had actually corresponded with Voltaire.

Luckily, the phase passed. Voltaire did nothing to encourage the correspondence—the Margrave's letters were incredibly dull—and so his enthusiasm petered out. He settled down to being as cultivated a gentleman as his limited means, his excessive distance from the centers of world civilization, and his not very sharp wits would allow. On the whole he was a good Margrave, well liked by his people. Not at all like his mad grandfather, the one who built that curious castle on the Hochhügel, where the moat was inside the walls to keep the swans safe.

The duties of his librarian were not onerous. Karl Georg Johann Friedrich Augustus Wolfram needed only take care of a generations-old collection of astoundingly unimportant books and documents, work desultorily at cataloging them, and recommend new acquisitions, which his master dutifully ordered but, as a rule, fell asleep over. The pay was not high, but not niggardly either; he could maintain a modest, comfortable house, a couple of servants, and six children. And he had social standing, attended court functions, enjoyed the friendship of other intellectuals like the Kapellmeister. A more dubious privilege was that of playing chess with the Margrave. It took skill and concentration to lose those games, particularly since they had to look hard-fought. Still, this was no major nuisance; and when the Kapellmeister visited the Wolframs, well, then they played real chess, with blood and iron in it.

Altogether, court librarian was quite an eminence for the fourth son of a shopkeeper to have reached. Of course, once when he was a boy, and the schoolmaster said that Karl Georg was the most brilliant Latin pupil he had ever had, and there was talk of sending him to Berlin to study— But that was long ago. Nothing had come of it. Best be content with what God has given one. This is not so little. A secure position; a good, sensible, if somewhat barrel-shaped wife; six fine living children; and, certainly, one's correspondence, one's contacts with the great world beyond the banks of the Pfaff. . . .

Few Schickenburgers had any inkling of their court librarian's other life. The Margrave did, but never really appreciated its significance; the Kapellmeister did, but was never in a position to do anything about it. Outwardly the Herr Hofbibliothekar Karl Georg Johann Friedrich Augustus Wolfram was the most staid and ordinary of men. You could set your watch by the time at which his stocky figure mounted the palace steps on workdays. His clothes were conservative, even a trifle old-fashioned—for Schickenburg, that is, which would have made them ludicrously out-of-date in Paris—and reasonably neat (albeit his wife was once heard to mutter that he was the only man she knew of who could get gravy on his wig). He was a kindly paterfamilias, a bit pompous but not unduly strict by the standards of that day and age; in the evenings he often gathered his family about him and read aloud from edifying books. Every Sunday morning saw him in church, every Sunday early afternoon seated at a gargantuan dinner, every Sunday late afternoon fast asleep. He allowed himself one pipeful of tobacco per diem, though to be sure it was a very large pipe, whose bowl stood on the floor. Alcohol was limited to a little beer or wine, except during Fasching, when he sometimes got mildly tiddly and recited Latin anacreontics. He did not make financial speculations, frequent the taverns, or pinch servant girls.

As for his nature rambles and his interest in the sciences, that was nothing unusual in the eighteenth century. What Oberhaus-Blickstein did not realize was the considerable actual and the possibly very great potential stature of the man. He corresponded regularly with Linnaeus, and it seems quite probable that the suggestions he made, out of his orderly catalog-oriented mind, had much to do with the evolution of the Swedish master's taxonomy. In his later years he became a corresponding member of the Royal Society. There were men in Paris and London who had never heard of Oberhaus-Blickstein but who, if the name Wolfram was mentioned, would nod and say, "Oh, yes, didn't he do something about minerals?"

We have seen that his description of wolframite, summarizing every reference in the literature and adding keen original observations by which it could instantly be identified, was honored by the bestowal of his name upon it. Hitherto every local set of rustics in Europe, if they noticed the stuff at all, had given it some loutish name of their own, like "wolf cream," and Chaos was king. But now, once and forever, scientists around the world could know exactly what ore was meant and what properties to expect.

His interests were not confined to mineralogy and natural history. Indeed, he himself considered these his minor hobbies. He was quite musical, playing both the violin and the harpsichord with some skill. A rather charming little hymn, sung locally to this day on the Eve of St. Odo, is attributed to Wolfram. He had connections with Leipzig, and one of the lesser-known Bach sonatas is dedicated to him. (Not *the* Bach—a fourth cousin twice removed.) Much of his time was spent on a ponderous compilation of regional folklore, with commentaries, which he regarded as his life's masterwork. Unfortunately, it is written in so crabbed a style, and is based on so erroneous an identification of every figure in every *Märchen* with something in Classical mythology, that not even Max Müller was able to make any use of it. By contrast, Wolfram's letters are fluent, brilliantly reasoned, lightened by flashes of a wit that few people today are sufficiently well-educated to savor.

His life had a normal share of disappointments and blunders. Though he angled for decades to get a patent of nobility, so he might inscribe that magical "von" in front of his name, he never mustered enough influence. In 1768 a young Frenchman wrote to him about certain ideas he had conceived in the field of chemistry. The reply was so disparaging that Lavoisier made no attempt at further correspondence. Wolfram admitted his mistake afterward, in a communication to Linnaeus, but pleaded that the gout which had bothered him of late years had made him irritable that day.

He was quite an old man when Goethe passed through Oberhaus-Blickstein and was the Margrave's guest for a night. Wolfram looked forward to this encounter for months. The diary of his friend the Kapellmeister relates how he spent days rehearsing what he would say, the questions, the comments, the little aphorisms out of a long experience to offer the young titan. He bought an entire new set of clothes, including shoes and wig, for the occasion, though medical bills had been so heavy that he could ill afford to.

Yes, Goethe came; and there was an interminable reception line, followed by an interminable banquet, after which the party repaired to the concert hall and heard a recital by the Margrave's oldest granddaughter and an original composition for voice and wind instruments by the Margrave himself. Goethe's eyes were closed and his head sunken onto his chest throughout this entertainment, doubtless so he could concentrate better. Immediately afterward he excused himself, since he must rise betimes to continue his journey in the morning. (However, at the banquet he had sat next to the youngest niece of the Margrave, who was then a widower, and been at his most charming, just beyond earshot of the court librarian. No one inquired where she spent the night.)

As for the Herr Hofbibliothekar Wolfram, he was introduced at the reception, bowed, said, "I am Your Excellency's very admiring servant," and moved on with the line.

He died peacefully just before the Estates General met at Versailles. It was a mercy. His admiration had never extended to the liberal ideas current in his time. Humane by nature, he nonetheless expected nothing but trouble from any upset of a social order which, at least in Oberhaus-Blickstein, worked so well. He would have known his forebodings confirmed, had he lived to witness that last scene of pitiful gallantry, when his old blind Margrave rode forth at the head of the principality's men to meet Napoleon and surrender. Sleep well, Karl Georg Johann Friedrich Augustus Wolfram.

You wouldn't have tried to steal the name off tungsten.

The Visitor

In gathering the stories for this book, I have tried to have them all show aspects of the exploration of the space-time universe by science. For that reason, their premises do not violate (I hope!) any well-established principles such as the conservation laws of physics; and two standard science fiction motifs, time travel and travel faster than light, are conspicuous by their absence.

Yet it would be foolhardy and, indeed, unscientific to claim that we today have learned everything important about the basics of the cosmos. Science *is* an exploration. As a matter of fact, recent work on the frontiers of relativity theory suggests that travel through time or faster than light may—emphasize "may"—not be quite impossible. Likewise, research into quantum mechanics shows us ever more powerfully how little we know for certain. In that spirit, I have included a couple of stories about alternate universes. Maybe, maybe.

The clutch of miscellaneous notions loosely grouped together as "psionics" is actually less radical. Very few of its advocates believe that anything occult is involved. The question is simply whether the phenomena are real and, if they are, how to account for them. I have described how John Campbell showed me what appeared to be conduit dowsing in action, and I wish someone would investigate it rigorously. There are similar reasons to look into water dowsing and various other abilities that are claimed to exist. My personal guess is that, if they do, they result from hitherto unmeasured sensitivities to variations in such quantities as terrestrial magnetism and local gravity. I should think it would be worth knowing something like that about our nervous systems—or else disproving it once for all.

Telepathy is trickier still, with no straightforward explanation to hand, wherefore I am quite skeptical. Nevertheless, when we haven't even reached agreement on what the conscious mind is or how it works, we are presumptuous to lay down limits it must always and forever observe. Some reports of telepathy may have some truth. Fugitive occurrences (wave function resonances, perhaps?) are conceivable, more or less within the bounds of accepted physics. Again, we need proper study. If that should give a positive result, well, science has already presented us with much greater surprises.

Meanwhile, telepathy as a fictional device allows us to see, or at least imagine, human minds in a special way.

A S WE DROVE UP between lawns and trees, Ferrier warned me, "Don't be shocked at his appearance."

"You haven't told me anything about him," I answered. "Not to mention."

"For good reason," Ferrier said. "This can never be a properly controlled experiment, but we can at least try to keep down the wild variables." He drummed fingers on the steering wheel. "I'll say this much. He's an important man in his field, investment counseling and brokerage."

"Oh, you mean he's a partner in— Why, I've done some business with them myself. But I never met him."

"He doesn't see clientele. Or very many people ever. He works the research end. Mail, telephone, teletype, and reads a lot."

"Why aren't we meeting in his office?"

"I'm not ready to explain that." Ferrier parked the car and we left it.

The hospital stood well out of town. It was a tall clean block of glass and metal which somehow fitted the Ohio countryside rolling away on every side, green, green, and green, here and there a white-sided house, red-sided barn, blue-blooming flax field, motley of cattle, to break the corn and woodlots, fence lines and toning telephone wires. A warm wind soughed through birches and flickered their leaves; it bore scents of a rose bed where bees querned.

Leading me up the stairs to the main entrance, Ferrier said, "Why, there he is." A man in a worn and outdated brown suit waited for us at the top of the flight.

No doubt I failed to hide my reaction, but no doubt he was used to it, for his handclasp was ordinary. I couldn't read his face. Surgeons must have expended a great deal of time and skill, but they could only tame the gashes and fill in the holes, not restore an absolute ruin. That scar tissue would never move in human fashion. His hair did, a thin flutter of gray in the breeze; and so did his eyes, which were blue behind glasses. I thought they looked trapped, those eyes, but it could be only a fancy of mine.

When Ferrier had introduced me, the scarred man said, "I've arranged for a room where we can talk." He saw a bit of surprise on me and his tone flattened. "I'm pretty well known here." His glance went to Ferrier. "You haven't told me what this is all about, Carl. But"—his voice dropped—"considering the place—"

The tension in my friend had hardened to sternness. "Please, let me handle this my way," he said.

When we entered, the receptionist smiled at our guide. The interior was cool, dim, carbolic. Down a hall I glimpsed somebody carrying flowers. We took an elevator to the uppermost floor.

There were the offices, one of which we borrowed. Ferrier sat down behind the desk, the scarred man and I took chairs confronting him. Though steel filing cabinets enclosed us, a window at Ferrier's back stood open for summer to blow in. From this level I overlooked the old highway, nowadays a mere picturesque side road. Occasional cars flung sunlight at me.

Ferrier became busy with pipe and tobacco. I shifted about. The scarred man waited. He had surely had experience in waiting.

"Well," Ferrier began. "I apologize to both you gentlemen. This mysteriousness. I hope that when you have the facts, you'll agree it was necessary. You see, I don't want to predispose your judgments or . . . or imaginations. We're dealing with an extraordinarily subtle matter."

He forced a chuckle. "Or maybe with nothing. I give no promises, not even to myself. Parapsychological phenomena at best are"— he paused to search—"fugitive."

"I know you've made a hobby of them," the scarred man said. "I don't know much more."

Ferrier scowled. He got his pipe going before he replied: "I wouldn't call it a hobby. Can serious research only be done for an organization? I'm convinced there's a, well, a reality involved. But

solid data are damnably hard to come by." He nodded at me. "If my
friend here hadn't happened to be in on one of my projects, his whole
experience might as well never have been. It'd have seemed like just
another dream."

A strangeness walked along my spine. "Probably that's all it
was," I said low. "Is."

The not-face turned toward me, the eyes inquired; then suddenly hands gripped tight the arms of the chair, as they do when the
doctor warns he must give pain. I didn't know why. It made my voice
awkward:

"I don't claim sensitivity, I can't read minds or guess Rhine
cards, nothing of that sort works for me. Still, I do often have pretty
detailed and, uh, coherent dreams. Carl's talked me into describing
them on a tape recorder, first thing when I wake up, before I forget
them. He's trying to check on Dunne's theory that dreams can fore-
tell the future." Now I must attempt a joke. "No such luck, so far,
or I'd be rich. However, when he learned about one I had a few
nights ago—"

The scarred man shuddered. "And you happened to know *me*,
Carl," broke from him.

The lines deepened around Ferrier's mouth. "Go on," he directed me, "tell your story, quick," and cannonaded smoke.

I sought from them both to the serenity beyond these walls, and
I also spoke fast:

"Well, you see, I'd been alone at home for several days. My wife
had taken our kid on a visit to her mother. I won't deny, Carl's
hooked me on this ESP. I'm not a true believer, but I agree with
him the evidence justifies looking further, and into curious places,
too. So I was in bed, reading myself sleepy with . . . Berdyaev, to be
exact, because I'd been reading Lenau earlier, and he's wild, sad,
crazy, you may know he died insane; nothing to go to sleep on. Did
he linger anyhow, at the bottom of my mind?"

I was in a formlessness which writhed. Nor had it color, or heat or
cold. Through it went a steady sound, whether a whine or drone I
cannot be sure. Unreasonably sorrowful, I walked, though there was
nothing under my feet, no forward or backward, no purpose in travel
except that I could not weep.

The monsters did when they came. Their eyes melted and ran

down the blobby heads in slow tears, while matter bubbled from within to renew that stare. They flopped as they floated, having no bones. They wavered around me and their lips made gibbering motions.

I was not afraid of attack, but a horror dragged through me of being forever followed by them and their misery. For now I knew that the nature of hell lies in that it goes on. I slogged, and they circled and rippled and sobbed, while the single noise was that which dwelt in the nothing, and time was not because none of this could change.

Time was reborn in a voice and a splash of light. Both were small. She was barely six years old, I guessed, my daughter's age. Brown hair in pigtails tied by red bows, and a staunch way of walking, also reminded me of Alice. She was more slender (elven, I thought) and more neat than my child—starched white flowerbud-patterned dress, white socks, shiny shoes, no trace of dirt on knees or tip-tilted face. But the giant teddy bear she held, arms straining around it, was comfortably shabby.

I thought I saw ghosts of road and tree behind her, but could not be certain. The mourning was still upon me.

She stopped. Her own eyes widened and widened. They were the color of earliest dusk. The monsters roiled. Then: "Mister!" she cried. The tone was thin but sweet. It cut straight across the hum of emptiness. "Oh, Mister!"

The tumorous beings mouthed at her. They did not wish to leave me, who carried some of their woe. She dropped the bear and pointed. "Go 'way!" I heard. "Scat!" They shivered backward, resurged, clustered close. "Go 'way, I want!" She stamped her foot, but silence responded and I felt the defiance of the monsters. "All right," she said grimly. "Edward, you make them go."

The bear got up on his hind legs and stumped toward me. He was only a teddy, the fur on him worn off in patches by much hugging, a rip in his stomach carefully mended. I never imagined he was alive the way the girl and I were; she just sent him. Nevertheless he had taken a great hammer, which he swung in a fingerless paw, and become the hero who rescues people.

The monsters flapped stickily about. They didn't dare make a stand. As the bear drew close, they trailed off sullenly crying. The sound left us too. We stood in an honest hush and a fog full of sunglow.

"Mister, Mister, Mister!" The girl came running, her arms out wide. I hunkered down to catch her. She struck me in a tumult and joy exploded. We embraced till I lifted her on high, made to drop her, caught her again, over and over, while her laughter chimed.

Finally, breathless, I let her down. She gathered the bear under an elbow, which caused his feet to drag. Her free hand clung to mine. "I'm so glad you're here," she said. "Thank you, thank you. Can you stay?"

"I don't know," I answered. "Are you all by yourself?"

"Yes. 'Cept for Edward and—" Her words died out. At the time I supposed she had the monsters in mind and didn't care to speak of them.

"What's your name, dear?"

"Judy."

"You know, I have a little girl at home, a lot like you. Her name's Alice."

Judy stood mute for a while and a while. At last she whispered, "Could she come play?"

My throat wouldn't let me answer.

Yet Judy was not too dashed. "Well," she said, "I didn't 'spect you, and you came." Happiness rekindled in her and caught in me. Could my presence be so overwhelmingly enough? Now I felt at peace, as though every one of the rat-fears which ride in each of us had fled me. "Come on to my house," she added, a shy invitation, a royal command.

We walked. Edward bumped along after us. The mist vanished and we were on a lane between low hedges. Elsewhere reached hills, their green a palette for the emerald or silver of coppices. Cows grazed, horses galloped, across miles. Closer, birds flitted and sparkled, a robin redbreast, a chickadee, a mockingbird who poured brook-trills from a branch, a hummingbird bejeweled among bumblebees in a surge of honeysuckle. The air was vivid with odors, growth, fragrance, the friendly smell of the beasts. Overhead lifted an enormous blue where clouds wandered.

This wasn't my country. The colors were too intense, crayon-brilliant, and a person could drown in the scents. Birds, bees, butterflies, dragonflies somehow seemed gigantic, while cattle and horses were somehow unreachably far off, forever cropping or galloping. The clouds made real castles and sailing ships. Yet there was rightness as well as brightness. I felt—maybe not at home, but very welcome.

Oh, infinitely welcome.

Judy chattered, no, caroled. "I'll show you my garden an' my books an', an' the whole house. Even where Hoo Boy lives. Would you push me in the swing? I only can pump myself. I pretend Edward is pushing me, an' he says, 'High, high, up in the sky, Judy fly, I wonder why,' like Daddy would, but it's only pretend, like when I play with my dolls or my Noah's ark animals an' make them talk. Would you play with me?" Wistfulness crossed her. "I'm not so good at making up ad-adventures for them. Can you?" She turned merry again and skipped a few steps. "We'll have dinner in the living room if you make a fire. I'm not s'posed to make fire, I remember Daddy said, 'cept I can use the stove. I'll cook us dinner. Do you like tea? We have lots of different kinds. You look, an' tell me what kind you want. I'll make biscuits an' we'll put butter an' maple syrup on them like Grandmother does. An' we'll sit in front of the fire an' tell stories, okay?" And on and on.

The lane was now a street, shaded by big old elms; but it was empty save for the dappling of the sunlight, and the houses had a flatness about them, as if nothing lay behind their fronts. Wind mumbled in leaves. We reached a gate in a picket fence, which creaked when Judy opened it.

The lawn beyond was quite real, aside from improbably tall hollyhocks and bright roses and pansies along the edges. So was this single house. I saw where paint had peeled and curtains faded, the least bit, as will happen to any building. (Its neighbors stood flawless.) A leftover from the turn of the century, it rambled in scale-shaped shingles, bays, turrets, and gingerbread. The porch was a cool cavern that resounded beneath our feet. A brass knocker bore the grinning face of a gnome.

Judy pointed to it. "I call him Billy Bungalow because he goes bung when he comes down low," she said. "Do you want to use him? Daddy always did, an' made him go a lot louder than I can. Please. He's waited such a long time." I have too, she didn't add.

I rattled the metal satisfactorily. She clapped her hands in glee. My ears were more aware of stillness behind the little noise. "Do you really live alone, brighteyes?" I asked.

"Sort of," she answered, abruptly going solemn.

"Not even a pet?"

"We had a cat, we called her Elizabeth, but she died an' . . . we was going to get another."

I lifted my brows. "We?"

"Daddy an' Mother an' me. C'mon inside!" She hastened to twist the doorknob.

We found an entry where a Tiffany window threw rainbows onto hardwood flooring. Hat rack and umbrella stand flanked a coat closet, opposite a grandfather clock which broke into triumphant booms on our arrival: for the hour instantly was six o'clock of a summer's evening. Ahead of us swept a staircase; right and left, doorways gave on a parlor converted to a sewing room, and on a living room where I glimpsed a fine stone fireplace. Corridors went high-ceilinged beyond them.

"Such a big house for one small girl," I said. "Didn't you mention, uh, Hoo Boy?"

Both arms hugged Edward close to her. I could barely hear: "He's 'maginary. They all are."

It never occurred to me to inquire further. It doesn't in dreams.

"But *you're* here, Mister!" Judy cried, and the house was no longer hollow.

She clattered down the hall ahead of me, up the stairs, through chamber after chamber, basement, attic, a tiny space she had found beneath the witch-hat roof of a turret and assigned to Hoo Boy; she must show me everything. The place was bright and cheerful, didn't even echo much as we went around. The furniture was meant for comfort. Down in the basement stood shelves of jelly her mother had put up and a workshop for her father. She showed me a half-finished toy sailboat he had been making for her. Her personal room bulged with the usual possessions of a child, including books I remembered well from years agone. (The library had a large collection too, but shadowy, a part of that home which I cannot catalog.) Good pictures hung on the walls. She had taken the liberty of pinning clippings almost everywhere, cut from the stacks of magazines which a household will accumulate. They mostly showed animals or children.

In the living room I noticed a cabinet-model radio-phonograph, though no television set. "Do you ever use that?" I asked.

She shook her head. "No, nothing comes out of it anymore. I sing for myself a lot." She put Edward on the sofa. "You stay an' be the lord of the manor," she ordered him. "I will be the lady making dinner, an' Mister will be the faithful knight bringing firewood." She went timid. "Will you, please, Mister?"

"Sounds great to me," I smiled, and saw her wriggle for delight. "Quick!" She grabbed me anew and we ran back to the kitchen. Our footfalls applauded.

The larder was well stocked. Judy showed me her teas and asked my preference. I confessed I hadn't heard of several kinds; evidently her parents were connoisseurs. "So'm I," Judy said after I explained that word. "Then I'll pick. An' you tell me, me an' Edward, a story while we eat, okay?"

"Fair enough," I agreed.

She opened a door. Steps led down to the backyard. Unlike the closely trimmed front, this was a wilderness of assorted toys, her swing, and fever-gaudy flowers. I had to laugh. "You do your own gardening, do you?"

She nodded. "I'm not very expert. But Mother promised I could have a garden here." She pointed to a shed at the far end of the grounds. "The firewood's in that. I got to get busy." However firm her tone, the fingers trembled which squeezed mine. "I'm so happy," she whispered.

I closed the door behind me and picked a route among her blossoms. Windows stood wide to a mild air full of sunset, and I heard her start singing.

> "The little red pony ran over the hill
> And galloped and galloped away . . ."

The horses in those meadows came back to me, and suddenly I stood alone, somewhere, while one of them who was my Alice fled from me for always; and I could not call out to her.

After a time, walking became possible again. But I wouldn't enter the shed at once; I hadn't the guts, when Judy's song had ended, leaving me here by myself. Instead, I brushed on past it for a look at whatever might lie behind for my comfort.

That was the same countryside as before, but long-shadowed under the falling sun and most quiet. A blackbird sat on a blackberry tangle, watched me and made pecking motions. From the yard, straight southward through the land, ran a yellow brick road.

I stepped onto it and took a few strides. In this light the pavement was the hue of molten gold, strong under my feet; here was the kind of highway which draws you ahead one more mile to see what's over the next hill, so you may forget the pony that galloped. After all, don't yellow brick roads lead to Oz?

"Mister!" screamed at my back. "No, stop, stop!"

I turned around. Judy stood at the border. She shuddered inside the pretty dress as she reached toward me. Her face was stretched quite out of shape. "Not yonder, Mister!"

Of course I made haste. When we were safely in the yard, I held her close while the dread went out of her in a burst of tears. Stroking her hair and murmuring, at last I dared ask, "But where does it go?"

She jammed her head into the curve of my shoulder and gripped me. "T-t-to Grandmother's."

"Why, is that bad? You're making us biscuits like hers, remember?"

"We can't *ever* go there," Judy gasped. Her hands on my neck were cold.

"Well, now, well, now." Disengaging, while still squatted to be at her height, I clasped her shoulder and chucked her chin and assured her the world was fine; look what a lovely evening, and we'd soon dine with Edward, but first I'd better build our fire, so could she help me bring in the wood? Secretly through me went another song I know, Swedish, the meaning of it:

"Children are a mysterious folk, and they live in a wholly strange world . . ."

Before long she was glad once more. As we left, I cast a final glance down the highway, and then caught a breath of what she felt: less horror than unending loss and grief, somewhere on that horizon. It made me be extra jocular while we took armloads of fuel to the living room.

Thereafter Judy trotted between me and the kitchen, attending to her duties. She left predictable chaos, heaped dishes, scorched pan, strewn flour, smeared butter and syrup and Lord knows what else. I forbore to raise the subject of cleanup. No doubt we'd tackle that tomorrow. I didn't mind.

Later we sat cross-legged under the sofa where Edward presided, ate our biscuits and drank our tea with plenty of milk, and laughed a great deal. Judy had humor. She told me of a Fourth of July celebration she had been at, where there were so many people "I bet just their toes weighed a hundred pounds." That led to a picnic which had been rained out, and—she must have listened to adult talk—she insisted that in any properly regulated universe, Samuel Gompers would have invented rubber boots. The flames whirled red, yellow, blue, and talked back to the ticking, booming clock; shadows played tag across walls; outside stood a night of gigantic stars.

"Tell me another story," she demanded and snuggled into my lap, the calculating minx. Borrowing from what I had done for Alice, I spun a long yarn about a girl named Judy, who lived in the forest with her friends Edward T. Bear and Billy Bungalow and Hoo Boy, until they built a candy-striped balloon and departed on all sorts of explorations; and her twilight-colored eyes got wider and wider.

They drooped at last, though. "I think we'd better turn in," I suggested. "We can carry on in the morning."

She nodded. "Yesterday they said today was tomorrow," she observed, "but today they know better."

I expected that after those fireside hours the electrics would be harsh to us; but they weren't. We went upstairs, Judy on my right shoulder, Edward on my left. She guided me to a guest room, pattered off, and brought back a set of pajamas. "Daddy wouldn't mind," she said.

"Would you like me to tuck you in?" I asked.

"Oh—" For a moment she radiated. Then the seriousness came upon her. She put finger to chin, frowning, before she shook her head. "No, thanks. I don't think you're s'posed for that."

"All right." My privilege is to see Alice to her bed; but each family has its own tradition. Judy must have sensed my disappointment, because she touched me and smiled at me, and when I stooped she caught me and breathed, "You're really real, Mister. I love you," and ran down the hall.

My room resembled the others, well and unpretentiously furnished. The wallpaper showed willows and lakes and Chinese castles which I had seen in the clouds. Gauzy white curtains, aflutter in easy airs, veiled away those lantern-big stars. Above the bed Judy had pinned a picture of a galloping pony.

I thought of a trip to the bathroom, but felt no need. Besides, I might disturb my hostess; I had no doubt she brushed her teeth, being such a generally dutiful person. Did she say prayers too? In spite of Alice, I don't really understand little girls, any more than I understand how a mortal could write "Jesu, Joy of Man's Desiring." Boys are different; it's true about the slugs and snails and puppy dogs' tails. I've been there and I know.

I got into the pajamas, lay down in the bed and the breeze, turned off the light, and was quickly asleep.

Sometimes we remember a night's sleep. I spent this one being happy about tomorrow.

Maybe that was why I woke early, in a clear, shadowless gray, cool as the air. The curtains rippled and blew, but there was no sound whatsoever.

Or . . . a rustle? I lay half awake, eyes half open and peace behind them. Someone moved about. She was very tall, I knew, and she was tidying the house. I did not try, then, to look upon her. In my drowsiness, she might as well have been the wind.

After she had finished in this chamber, I came fully to myself, and saw how bureau and chair and the bulge of blankets that my feet made were strangers in the dusk which runs before the sun. I swung legs across bedside, felt hardwood under my soles. My lungs drank odors of grass. Oh, Judy will snooze for hours yet, I thought, but I'll go peek in at her before I pop downstairs and start a surprise breakfast.

When dressed, I followed the hallway to her room. Its door wasn't shut. Beyond, I spied a window full of daybreak.

I stopped. A woman was singing.

She didn't use real words. You often don't, over a small bed. She sang well-worn nonsense,

"Cloddledy loldy boldy boo,
Cloddledy lol-dy bol-dy boo-oo,"

to the tenderest melody I have ever heard. I think that tune was what drew me on helpless, till I stood in the entrance.

And she stood above Judy. I couldn't truly see her: a blue shadow, maybe? Judy was as clear to me as she is this minute, curled in a prim nightgown, one arm under her cheek (how long the lashes and stray brown hair), the other around Edward, while on a shelf overhead, Noah's animals kept watch.

The presence grew aware of me.

She turned and straightened, taller than heaven. Why have you looked? she asked me in boundless gentleness. Now you must go, and never come back.

No, I begged. Please.

When even I may do no more than this, she sighed, you cannot stay or ever return, who looked beyond the Edge.

I covered my eyes.

I'm sorry, she said; and I believe she touched my head as she passed from us.

Judy awakened. "Mister—" She lifted her arms, wanting me to come and be hugged, but I didn't dare.

"I have to leave, sweetheart," I told her.

She bolted to her feet. "No, no, no," she said, not loud at all.

"I wish I could stay awhile," I answered. "Can you guess how much I wish it?"

Then she knew. "You . . . were awful kind . . . to come see me," she got out.

She went to me with the same resolute gait as when first we met, and took my hand, and we walked downstairs together and forth into the morning.

"Will you say hello to your daughter from me?" she requested once.

"Sure," I said. Hell, yes. Only how?

We went along the flat and empty street, toward the sun. Where a blackbird perched on an elm bough, and the leaves made darkness beneath, she halted. "Good-bye, you good Mister," she said.

She would have kissed me had I had the courage. "Will you remember me, Judy?"

"I'll play with my remembering of you. Always." She snapped after air; but her head was held bravely. "Thanks again. I do love you."

So she let me go, and I left her. A single time I turned around to wave. She waved back, where she stood under the sky all by herself.

The scarred man was crying. He wasn't skilled in it; he barked and hiccoughed.

Surgically, Ferrier addressed him. "The description of the house corresponds to your former home. Am I correct?"

The hideous head jerked a nod.

"And you're entirely unfamiliar with the place," Ferrier declared to me. "It's in a different town from yours."

"Right," I said. "I'd no reason before today to suppose I'd had anything more than a dream." Anger flickered. "Well, God damn your scientific caution, now I want some explanations."

"I can't give you those," Ferrier admitted. "Not when I've no idea how the phenomenon works. You're welcome to what few facts I have."

The scarred man toiled toward a measure of calm. "I, I, I apologize for the scene," he stuttered. "A blow, you realize. Or a hope?" His gaze ransacked me.

"Do you think we should go see her?" Ferrier suggested.

For reply, the scarred man led us out. We were silent in corridor and elevator. When we emerged on the third floor, the hospital smell struck hard. He regained more control over himself as we passed among rubber-tired nurses and views of occupied beds. But his gesture was rickety that, at last, beckoned us through a certain doorway.

Beyond lay several patients and a near-total hush. Abruptly I understood why he, important in the world, went ill-clad. Hospitals don't come cheap.

His voice grated: "Telepathy, or what? The brain isn't gone; not a flat EEG. Could you—" That went as far as he was able.

"No," I said, while my fingers struggled with each other. "It must have been a fluke. And since, I'm forbidden."

We had stopped at a cluster of machinery. "Tell him what happened," Ferrier said without any tone whatsoever.

The scarred man looked past us. His words came steady if a bit shrill. "We were on a trip, my wife and daughter and me. First we meant to visit my mother-in-law in Kentucky."

"You were southbound, then," I foreknew. "On a yellow brick road." They still have that kind, here and there in our part of the country.

"A drunk driver hit our car," he said. "My wife was killed. I became what you see. Judy—" He chopped a hand toward the long white form beneath us. "That was nineteen years ago," he ended.

Wellsprings
of Dream

Not only are minds wonderfully various, the ideas are that they bring forth. This is especially so when those ideas look outward, to other humans, work that can be done, discoveries that can be made, the sweep of time and the reach of space. Science fiction does not originate them, but at its best it draws inspiration from them and explores what their impact upon us may be.

A BOUT THIRTY YEARS AGO, at a party where most of the guests
were scientists and their spouses—several of whom were also
scientists—one complimented me on my work. Now I am not at all
humble, but I have known too many self-important jackasses to want
anybody numbering me among them. Therefore my answer was,
"Thank you. Actually, though, I'm just a barnacle on the ship of
science."

Shortly afterward, in a lecture at the Air Force Academy, I introduced a less modest metaphor for science fiction as a whole, calling it the tribal bard of science. As poets in heroic ages, from Homer
onward, celebrated great deeds, upheld ideals of courage and steadfastness, and fabled of wonders, so does science fiction do for the
adventures, discoveries, and achievements of science and technology—evoking the Scylla, Polyphemus, Lotophagoi, and Circe, as well
as the serene Phaeacia and triumph over evil, that are potential in
our future.*

On either occasion, I was trying to express the relationship of
science fiction to science and modern science-derived technology. It
is a dependency, which the two similes bracket. We writers are not
really barnacles, impeding progress. Some of what we do, especially
for the screen, might be so regarded; but as a rule we simply go

*Jerry Pournelle came up with the same figure of speech on his own. Likewise,
we both independently formulated the basic law of human effort, "Everything
takes longer and costs more." The First Law of the Sea was our joint discovery
while on a sailing cruise: "It's in the bilge!"

along on the voyage. Nor are we quite bards, necessary to the inspiring and immortalizing of accomplishments. Yet we do make these come alive for our readers, we do awaken dreams in many young people that lure them into such careers, and once in a rare while a story has actually sparked an idea in some worker.

Doubtless various of us will disavow this secondary status. At best, they will say, it was something we have outgrown. They will point to the fact that rather little science fiction has much, if anything, to do with real science; that a large part of what writers try to pass off as science is either gobbledygook—what Norman Spinrad more charitably calls "rubber science"—or outright false; and furthermore that this is not only the case today but has been from the beginning of the literature.

Others will claim that science fiction goes in the van of science, or that it is visionary in the way that the prophets of Israel were. They will recite long lists of inventions and events allegedly anticipated by it. With regard to pseudoscience, they will argue that we can never be sure we have found ultimate truth. The natural laws and phenomena we know may be special cases. Revelations may be awaiting us comparable to those of Galileo, Newton, Planck, Einstein. Then why shouldn't we, for story purposes, postulate hyperspace or psionics or whatever?

Why not indeed? I've done it often enough myself, besides writing my share of pure fantasies. Nor do I say anything against stories about social problems, individual *Angst*, or other motifs, including plain old-fashioned derring-do. Much fine work has been done in all these categories. The diversity of contemporary science fiction is perhaps its greatest strength.

Nevertheless I maintain that it has a direct and vital connection to science. Without this, it would have no particular reason to exist. It would soon fall into sterile self-imitation and presently wither away. There have been times in the past when that came near happening; but we were saved by writers who drew freshness by turning back to reality, especially to the realities of science and technology.

The space-time universe around us is infinitely more wonderful, complex, surprising—yes, imaginative—than our minds. You don't see anything new by looking in the mirror, but by looking out the window. The boldest, most exciting intellects in our world belong to practicing scientists. They were the ones who foresaw everything from space travel and nuclear power to bioengineering and ecological crisis. The role of science fiction, honorable but lesser, was to fill in flesh-and-blood details. As for visions, we writers have never matched the transcendence of what some scientists have beheld. Nor do I expect we ever shall. We can only hope for another Stapledon to put it into fictional terms, as he did the cosmology of his period. That will be no minor success.

These reflections were prompted by reading Freeman Dyson's recent book *From Eros to Gaia* (1992). A more obvious starting point might have been K. Eric Drexler's *Engines of Creation* (1986). However, his pioneering study of the nanotechnology soon to be ours, with all its promise and danger, has gotten plenty of attention. That bodes well for science fiction. True, many writers have misunderstood and misused the ideas, while for many others they have become merely the latest cliché. This was inevitable, and does not detract from those excellent stories that have been written and will be written by authors who do their homework.

Freeman Dyson's earlier books, *Disturbing the Universe* (1979) and *Infinite in All Directions* (1988), have already given source material to some among us. (*Weapons and Hope* (1984), though its most immediate concerns are happily outdated, remains a rich lode for the sociologically minded.) The Orion project on which he worked, a spacecraft to be propelled by atomic bombs, is one example. It led to my *Orion Shall Rise*, Larry Niven and Jerry Pournelle's *Footfall*, and probably more, in spite of the undertaking having long since been abandoned. Such is the force of a big idea.

The Dyson sphere offers a still more conspicuous instance. The concept is, essentially, that an advanced civilization in need of living space might dismantle the planets of its system—at any rate, the one or two largest—and englobe the sun at a suitable radius. It would not be with a continuous shell, gravitationally unstable and otherwise impractical, but with a cloud of small bodies in separate orbits. A sphere like this, capturing the whole output of the star for the benefit of its inhabitants, must reradiate the energy at infrared wavelengths. Dyson suggested that astronomers search for objects of that kind. Of course, he did not claim that any exist, nor that any infrared sources would necessarily be artifacts, only that the investigation was worthwhile for its own sake.

Larry Niven modified the image to create his *Ringworld* and its sequel. A few others have used it more directly. The story possibilities are by no means exhausted. Consider what a civilization so old and so mighty could be like; consider those swarming worldlets, each maybe unique; ask yourself how your characters get there, what the voyage is like, why the Builders have apparently never come to us; evoke something of the vastness and mystery of the cosmos.

Dyson deals with more than immensity. Kenneth Brower's *The Starship and the Canoe* (1978), a fascinating and moving book, seems to me to embody a fundamental mistake. It tells of the conflict between Dyson and his son, and their eventual reconciliation, as if the father were an archetypal high-tech zealot, opposing the younger man's return to a life in living nature. Actually Dyson's own writings make clear that he is intimate with the traditional humanities, feels as deeply about the natural world as anyone, seeks to learn what its troubles stem from, and has concrete proposals for mending matters while preserving liberty. Little or none of that is true of the Green politicians and the ecofascists, although of course it is true of his son and other reasonable people who care.

Illustrating this and going again beyond, I will draw mainly on *Infinite in All Directions*. *Disturbing the Universe* is primarily autobiographical; *From Eros to Gaia* is a miscellany, much of it about the extraordinary persons Dyson has encountered. Both still brim with ideas, which overflow and fountain from the first-named.

Let us, for instance, consider global warming through greenhouse effect. Dyson declines to join in the hysteria about it. Like most honest scientists, he points out that we have no hard evidence for or against its reality. What we have is merely some computer models of phenomena very poorly understood, and the conflicting predictions we get from them. That scarcely justifies radical measures of enormous cost and incalculable social consequences.

This becomes especially plain once we inquire whether a certain amount of global warming *is* undesirable. As Dyson observes, we have no cause to believe that Earth's present set of climates is optimal. The planet was in fact warmer a thousand years ago, when Norse settlers raised crops in Greenland, than it is now. Whatever the price of coping with such changes as a rise in sea level, quite likely it will be far lower than the price of cutting back the industries by which all but a tiny élite live.

Don't suppose Dyson is complacent. He raises some real questions. For one, our measurements account for only half the carbon dioxide that we know our activities are putting into the atmosphere. Where is the rest going? Into the oceans? Into the biosphere? We have no solid information. Without that, we flat-out cannot tell what we ought to do or stop doing. Our cures could prove catastrophically worse than the disease.

Meanwhile, for every carbon atom in the fuels we burn, two oxygen atoms are tied up, not to mention what combines in water and other oxides. What about the environmental effects of that? At the time Dyson was writing, efforts to measure this change were minuscule. They appeared to indicate that a significant oxygen depletion is going on. Again, we do not know what is actually happening—the balance between chemical reactions, or how they work—nor what could result from any policies we adopt. We desperately need more science: genuine science, not politically correct charades.

I should add that Dyson expresses himself less vehemently and more politely, which heightens the convincingness.

In short, his is a voice of both concern and reason. It is also a voice of imagination. He tells us that we can probably bring carbon dioxide and oxygen under control by extensive, worldwide reforestation. We can be certain this would be safe. Ample land is available, not currently farmed or grazed. The program would, not so incidentally, make our planet again beautiful, pleasant, and life-full.

He remarks wryly that the environmentalists won't like it because it denies their gloom-and-doom scenarios and their Luddite ideals, while the conservatives won't like it because it requires large-scale government action. Here I beg to differ. Conservatives have nothing in principle against government action, if it be for worthy ends not otherwise attainable. Libertarians, among whom I count myself, ought not to perceive this one as a threat to freedom; on the contrary.

The politics of getting reforestation started, and the kind of society that ensues, could be the theme of a major science fiction novel.

Looking toward the next century, Dyson sees molecular biology and neurophysiology as two of its dominant endeavors. The third is spacefaring. Between them, they will transform the world and the human condition.

He spins off a dazzling array of possibilities. How about an energy tree, using sunlight to produce fuel which its roots then convey to the pipeline? How about a worm that mines ores or a turtle-like creature that scavenges and reprocesses waste materials? How about plants that can grow on Mars, not hypothetically terraformed but as it is? How about a vine that can grow on comets? How about the space butterfly, massing a kilogram or two, easily launched, which once in orbit metamorphoses, growing solar-sail energy-collector "wings," organs of locomotion and manipulation, and an artificial intelligence adequate for exploratory missions? How about humans comfortable when naked in raw vacuum and weightlessness? Further ahead, how about spores sent across the interstellar gulfs, designed to unfold as a new ecology and a new intelligence on the planets of other stars?

Some people will recoil from prospects like these. They will speak of Frankenstein, hubris, blasphemy. To Dyson, it is no more than a continuation of what life has been doing ever since it arose in the primeval waters of Earth. He foresees the greening of the Solar System, the galaxy, perhaps at last the universe. For my part, I think he makes us fiction writers look pretty tame and stodgy. We have a lot to learn from him and his kind.

Life, intelligence, has even a chance of outliving the stars. But let us backtrack a little before we go on to the utterly stupendous.

Hans Moravec, one of our foremost roboticists, surely adds his science and technology to Dyson's three leaders in the next hundred years. This implies no contradiction or rivalry. They are all ultimately about the same thing, the subtleties and complexities of matter-energy interaction, from the quantum level on upward. Our distinctions between organic and silicate, natural and artificial, life and machine, are disappearing. Like space and time, in Minkowski's famous statement about general relativity, from now onwards these classes sink to the position of mere shadows, and only a sort of union of them can claim an independent existence.

Moravec's book *Mind Children* (1988) gives an authoritative short history of his field to date, and goes on to enthusiastic forecasting. He sees artificial intelligence fully equal to the human in another 40 years or so. This optimism has its doubters, including me, but it may well prove true, and Isaac Asimov didn't use up the stories to be told about such a development occurring within the lifetimes of the majority now on Earth. Rather, his admirable tales will look as quaint as Kipling's great yarns, around 1910, about globe-girdling lighter-than-air craft. The entire world will have been transformed.

For a single aspect, think of virtual reality. At present it is a toy just beginning to become a tool, in a few specialized areas such as architecture. Moravec sees it taking over industry as the computer did and pervading everyday life as telephones and television do. Science fiction stories about whole societies of people hooked up addictively to their dream machines are old. They are also unbelievable. To the best of my limited knowledge, nobody has yet attempted a serious treatment of the effects.

This will be the more difficult to do because the forms and functions of the similarly pervasive robots are unpredictable, except that they will be legion. Moravec proposes a delightful, fractally dendritic "bush," but simply for an example. (I adapted this to an extraterrestrial sophont in *The Boat of a Million Years*. I steal only from the best sources.) The real significance will lie in the artificial intelligence itself, and its interplay with us.

Among other possibilities, Moravec discusses several different ways in which a human personality could be transferred to a computer matrix with a robot body. Some science fiction has employed this, but not in the depth that the subject warrants. What will personality, individuality, mean? What will be the new capabilities—and limitations? How must the mind change as its long years of existence pass by, and how can it? How must and can society change? What happens if the dead are "resurrected" as recreated minds, or if personalities are synthesized to order? What tales to tell!

Meanwhile, Moravec thinks, the artificial intelligences will rapidly improve themselves, and soon be incomprehensibly superior to the human. Again, this is a not uncommon theme in science fiction, but one not well explored. It seems unlikely to me that humankind will either go gently into that good night or settle down as parasites on the machines. The relationships that evolve ought to be multitudinous and mutable. Moravec gives some intriguing hints.

In the long run, though, he says, it is our "mind children" that will continue our heritage and carry it to heights unimaginable by us. Here we find his thought converging on Freeman Dyson's. Before going on in that direction, I will backtrack afresh, to another remarkable book.

This is *The Anthropic Cosmological Principle* (1986) by the British astronomer John D. Barrow and the American mathematical physicist Frank J. Tipler. Many readers will recognize these names, Barrow's for his popular accounts of science, Tipler's for some of the most amazing real-science concepts to come before us since the Big Bang.

As far as I know, Tipler was the first to demonstrate rigorously, almost 20 years ago, what has later been shown by other routes: that a sort of faster-than-light travel and a sort of time travel are not incompatible with general relativity. The requirements may be physically impossible to meet (Tipler slyly quoted Simon Newcomb on the subject of heavier-than-air craft) but they don't violate the laws or the mathematics. I was quick to seize upon this for *The Avatar*, and Larry Niven got an ingenious short story out of it, but few if any other writers seem to have noticed. That hardly matters by now, in view of what has been learned about such things as black holes and what Tipler has since been up to.

Why is reality as it is? In scientific terms, why do the important quantities of physics (the gravitational constant, the fine-structure constant, Planck's constant, the charges and masses of the elementary particles, the present size and age of the universe . . .) have the values they do? Is it fortuitous, arbitrary, or is there an underlying logic by which they must be what they are? *The Anthropic Cosmological Principle* attempts to find an answer.

In its weak form, the principle looks almost like a tautology. The universe that we perceive has the characteristics we perceive because if they were otherwise, we could not exist to observe it. Almost a tautology; not quite. As Barrow and Tipler declare, it restates a fundamental of science, "that it is necessary to take into account the limitations of one's measuring apparatus when interpreting one's observations." A writer who can't see story possibilities here, whether or not they are possibilities s/he cares to use, had better get out of the science fiction business.

More controversial is the Strong Anthropic Principle: "The universe must have those properties which allow life to develop within it at some stage in its history." The reasoning behind this claim involves quantum mechanics and the enigmatic relationship between observer and observed, experimenter and experiment. Indeed, the book gives a deep look into that area of physics.° It does the same for cosmology and even biology. The reader, though, must be willing to concentrate and think.

The Final Anthropic Principle goes further yet, and is admittedly a *non sequitur*: "Intelligent information-processing must come into existence in the universe, and once it comes into existence, it will never die out." Ah, but what if this should be true? The book culminates in a stunning exploration of what that could mean.

Nonetheless the authors set forth what amounts to a science fiction heresy. So much the better; we need heresies, to shake up and sometimes supplant our orthodoxies. Barrow and Tipler assert that intelligent life must be very rare. It may well be unique to Earth. Life itself may be.

As scientists, they argue from what we know, the single specimen we have, our planet. It seems there was nothing inevitable about the course, or rather courses, that evolution took. (In this brief review, I pass over an impressive amount of details.) True, such "inventions" as the eye and the wing were made repeatedly, independently, because they confer advantages. But only one lineage among countless others went in for intelligence, and only the hominids developed it highly. If anything, a big, energy-hungry brain is a biological handicap, akin to the overgrown antlers of the Irish elk. Special circumstances must have been needed for it to be viable. The whole progression was such a chain of improbabilities as to make vanishingly small the likelihood of anything analogous elsewhere.

Another argument against extraterrestrial intelligence is that we have no evidence for it, whereas we should if it exists. The authors examine Fermi's question—"Where are they?"—with a thoroughness that uncovers innumerable story plots. All it takes is one high-tech civilization, or just a few determined individuals within one, and a few million years; then, if nothing else, its von Neumann–type robots will be everywhere in the galaxy. If nobody has wanted to make this much of an effort, why don't we at least see attention-

°Likewise does Roger Penrose's *The Emperor's New Mind* (1989), also highly recommended, especially since Penrose disputes the algorithmic model of intelligence that Moravec, Barrow, and Tipler take for granted. A variety of opinions stimulates thought.

getting beacons? Any of several kinds would be cheap and easy to set up. The simplest explanation of the Great Silence is that nobody lives yonder.

The nonexistence or extreme rarity of alien minds also has cosmological implications, ruling out certain models, which provides a separate test of the statement. I don't have room to go into that, or into other marvelous concepts—most notably, perhaps, the many-worlds interpretation of quantum mechanics—that are discussed. Let me only say that here is the stuff of the scientific frontier, where writers should seek who hope to break new ground.

Obviously, I disagree with Barrow, and Tipler on a number of points, including the matter of nonhuman sophonts. Plenty of scenarios will accommodate their objections. But whether we accept or deny their picture of a universe in which we are essentially alone, we science fiction people have a lot of rethinking to do. We can't stay in our dear old conceptual cosmos—not if we want to go on calling ourselves pioneers. Fortunately, a number of us are already outbound, in a number of different directions.

However common or sparse it be, life is not necessarily an accident, an epiphenomenon, doomed to perish with the stars. Here we come to the point where Dyson, Moravec, Barrow, and Tipler meet. They are not the first to venture there. J. D. Bernal did in *The World, the Flesh and the Devil* (1929) and Olaf Stapledon, fictionally, in *Star Maker*. What we now have offered us is an eschatology for today. What we need is a genius who will make a story of it.

Granted, these thinkers do not see precisely the same future. Doubtless they would debate vigorously among each other about the form of it. None of them claims to be a prophet. Here are speculations, imaginings. Yet how well-timbered they are with genuine science, and how high-flung!

Rather than go over them point by point, which the authors do better anyway, let me give you a hasty overview of what they seem to me to have in common.

Intelligence expands through the future universe. It does this not by hyperspatial jumps nor, usually, by settling planets, but by relativistic conveyances and self-replication. There is ample time, billions upon billions of years. The intelligence is probably not embodied in what we would call life; but it is aware, it thinks and feels, dares, loves, sorrows, creates, and carries within it something of us, an inheritance, even a memory. Although its variousness becomes as enormous as its range, always there goes an undertone of communication—across parsecs, light-centuries, intergalactic distances, a little like us today reading the words of Homer or Confucius and their far-off descendants reading our words. Think how many stories lie in the mere five thousand–odd years of recorded history on this single globe, then think onward.

But meanwhile the universe ages. Stars flare up and gutter out; fewer and fewer new stars form; galaxies disintegrate; night advances. A quadrillion years from now, the last white dwarfs have cooled to black, and only proton decay (if protons do decay) keeps their temperatures a few degrees above absolute zero. Eventually nothing is left but electrons, neutrinos, and photons. The time for this as measured in years is counted by 1 followed by more than 100 zeroes; but it will come, it will come.

That is if the universe is open, continues expanding forever, whether or not the rate of expansion slows down to almost nothing. We today don't know. Perhaps it will reach some maximum size and collapse, back to the fire and then to the singularity in which it began, perhaps to rebound in a new cycle with every trace of the old obliterated. Perhaps. We don't know.

In either case, intelligence could live eternally. We cannot say that it will, but we can say that this is scientifically conceivable.

Dyson pictures an open universe in its deepening darkness, where beings make for themselves a succession of forms, finally changeable configurations of leptons. With energy ever less available, life and thought must go ever more slowly, but these minds remain wholly alert. In fact, to them communication across astronomical distances has become fast and easy; and thus they may at last join together in a oneness that continues through time without bound.

Barrow and Tipler consider this possibility. It does not violate any law of physics. They then look at the alternative, a closed, collapsing universe. They find that, although it will only last for a finite time, within that span an infinite number of events—thoughts, experiences—can occur. That includes the transmission of signals; and thereby the light-speed barrier is not broken, but transcended. So here, too, a single immortal intelligence may come to fill the cosmos, our whole universe and any others there be. Following Teilhard de Chardin, the authors call this the Omega Point.

They could almost as well call it God. Indeed, in later work of his own, Tipler draws overt parallels to theology. An Omega Point will be able to know everything about all that ever occurred, whether directly or by brute computational force. It can, if it chooses, resurrect us: you, me, everybody. That will be as computer programs, but we won't sense the difference, nor will it matter; we will live anew, perhaps made perfect. Tipler suggests that the Omega Point may do this not because it has to, which of course it doesn't, but because it loves us.

Sheer imagination, yes. I don't believe in it myself. But what an imagination! And not idle daydreaming. None of these concepts are. They spring from the ground of science as ballet does from the everyday dynamics of walking or myth did from everyday birth, life, love, death, mystery. From them, in turn, can spring some grand science fiction.

The Voortrekkers

And so, as promised, we are coming full circle. From outer space we went back to Earth, here and now, then to some of its possible futures and possible pasts, with excursions into nearer space, daydream, and nightmare, along the way pausing to salute a few of the giants who opened these ways for us. We end where we began, beyond this planet, not so far away as at first but—I hope—about to range more deeply and widely than before.

John Campbell used to say that nothing happens one at a time. All factors interact ever-changingly, throughout the universe and in that tiny department of it known as human affairs. If, somehow, a writer knew the future, s/he could not write a story set in it. There would be too much strangeness, too much explaining to do. (Think of yourself going back just a hundred years in time and trying to tell people what it was like up ahead.) And of course nobody can predict, or even venture much of a guess. It is inherently impossible. In the strict mathematical sense of the word, history is chaotic.

Still, we can make out certain regularities, we do know certain natural laws, and if we look around us we can see what some of the possibilities are. Using imagination and reason, we can bring them together as a hint of something that might conceivably come to pass. The cosmos *is* one, and stories of this kind celebrate that miracle.

—A ND HE SHALL SEE old planets change and alien stars arise—

So swift is resurrection that the words go on which had been in me when last I died. Only after pulsebeats does the strangeness raining through my senses reach my awareness, to make me know that four more decades, and almost nine light-years, have flowed between me and the poet.

Light-years. Light. Everywhere light. Once, a boy, I spent a night camped on a winter mountaintop. Then it entered my bones—and how can anyone who has done likewise ever believe otherwise?—that space is not dark. Maybe this was when the need was born in me, to go up and out into the sky.

I am in the sky now, and of it. Around me stars and stars and stars are crowding, until there is no room for blackness to be more than a crystal which holds them. They are all the colors of reality, from lightning through gold to the duskiest rose, but each one singingly keen. Nebulae are flung among them like veils and clouds, where great suns have died or new worlds are whirling to birth. The Milky Way is a cool torrent, here cloven by the thunderstorm masses of galactic center, there open a-glint toward endlessness. I magnify my vision and trace the spiral of our sister maelstrom, a million and a half light-years hence in Andromeda.

Sol is a small glow on the edge of Hercules. Brightest is Sirius, whose blue-white luminance casts shadows of fittings and housings across my hull. I seek and find its companion.

This is not done by optics. The dwarf is barely coming around the giant, lost in glare. What I see, through different sensors, is the X-radiation; what I snuff is a sharp breath of neutrinos mingled with the gale that streams from the other; I swim in an intricate interplay of force-fields, balancing, thrusting, while they caress me; I listen to the skirls and drones, the murmurs and melodies of a universe.

At first I do not hear Korene. If I was a little slow to leave Kipling for these heavens, so I am to leave them for her. Maybe it's more excusable. I must make certain at once, as much as possible, that we are not in danger. Probably we aren't, or the automatons would have restored us to existence before the scheduled moment. But automatons can only judge what they were designed and programmed to judge, by people nine light-years away from yonder mystery, people most likely dust, even as Korene and Joel are surely dust.

Joel, Joel! Korene calls from within me. *Are you there?*

I open my interior scanners. Her principal body, the one which houses her principal brain, is in motion, carefully testing every part after forty-three years of death. For the thousandth time, the beauty of this seat of her consciousness strikes me. Its darkly sheening shape is only humanlike in the way that an abstract sculpture might be on far, far Earth—those several arms, for instance, or the dragonfly head which is not really a head at all—and only this for functional reasons. But something about the slimness and grace of movement recalls Korene who is dust.

She has not yet made contact with any of the specialized auxiliary bodies around her. Instead she has joined a communication circuit to one of mine.

Hi, I flash, rather shakily, for in spite of studies and experiments and simulations, years of them, it is still too tremendous to comprehend, that we are actually approaching Sirius. *How are you?*

Fine. Everything okay?

Near's I can tell. Why didn't you use voice?

I did. No answer. I yelled. No answer. So I plugged in.

My joy gets tinged with embarrassment. *Sorry. I, uh, I guess I was too excited.*

She breaks the connection, since it is not ideally convenient, and says, "Quite something out there?"

"You wouldn't believe," I respond by my own speaker. "Take a look."

I activate the viewscreens for her. "O-o-o-ohh; O God," she breathes. Yes, breathes. Our artificial voices copy those which once were in our throats. Korene's is husky and musical; it was a pleasure to hear her sing at parties. Her friends often urged her to get into amateur theatricals, but she said she had neither the time nor the talent.

Maybe she was right, though Lord knows she was good at plenty of other things, her astronautical engineering, painting, cookery, sewing fancy clothes, throwing feasts, playing tennis and poker, ranging over hills, being a wife and mother, in her first life. (Well, we've both changed a lot since then.) On the other hand, that utterance of hers, when she sees the star before her, says everything for which I can only fumble.

From the beginning, when the first rockets roared into orbit, some people have called astronauts a prosaic lot, if they weren't calling us worse; and no doubt in some cases this was true. But I think mainly it's just that we grow tongue-tied in the presence of the Absolute.

"I wish—" I say, and energize an auxiliary of my own, a control-module maintainer, to lay an awkward touch upon her "—I wish you could sense it the way I do, Korene. Plug back in—full psychoneural—when I've finished my checkouts, and I'll try to convey a little."

"Thanks, my friend." She speaks with tenderness. "I knew you would. But don't worry about my missing something because of not being wired up like a ship. I'll be having a lot of experiences you can't, and wishing I could share them with you." She chuckles. "*Vive la différence.*"

Nonetheless I hear the flutter in her tone and, knowing her, am unsurprised when she asks anxiously, "Are there . . . by any chance . . . planets?"

"No trace. We're a long ways off yet, of course. I might be missing the indications. So far, though, it looks as if the astronomers were right" who declared minor bodies cannot condense around a star like Sirius. "Never mind, we'll both find enough to keep us out of mischief in the next several years. Already at this range, I'm noticing all kinds of phenomena which theory did not predict."

"Then you don't think we'll need organics?"

"No, 'fraid not. In fact, the radiation—"

"Sure. Understood. But damn, next trip I'm going to insist on a destination that'll probably call for them."

She told me once, back in the Solar System, after we had first practiced the creation of ourselves in flesh: "It's like making love again."

They had not been lovers in their original lives. He an American, she a European, they served the space agencies of their respective confederations and never chanced to be in the same cooperative venture. Thus they met only occasionally and casually, at professional conventions or celebrations. They were still young when the interstellar exploration project was founded. It was a joint undertaking of all countries—no one bloc could have gotten its taxpayers to bear the cost—but research and development must run for a generation before hardware would become available to the first true expeditions. Meanwhile there was nothing but a few unmanned probes, and the interplanetary studies wherein Joel and Korene took part.

She retired from these, to desk and laboratory, at an earlier age than he did, having married Olaf and wishing children. Olaf himself continued on the Lunar shuttle for a while. But that wasn't the same as standing on the peaks of Rhea beneath the rings of Saturn or pacing the million kilometers of a comet, as afire as the scientists themselves with what they were discovering. Presently he quit, and joined Korene on one of the engineering teams of the interstellar group. Together they made important contributions, until she accepted a managerial position. This interested her less in its own right; but she handled it ferociously well, because she saw it as a means to an end—authority, influence. Olaf stayed with the work he liked best. Their home life continued happy.

In that respect, Joel at first differed. Pilots on the major expeditions (and he got more berths than his share) could seldom hope to be family men. He tried, early in the game; but after he realized what very lonely kind of pain had driven a girl he had loved to divorce him, he settled for a succession of mistresses. He was always careful to explain to them that nothing and nobody could make him stop faring before he must.

This turned out to be not quite true. Reaching mandatory age for "the shelf," he might have finagled a few extra years skyside. But by then, cuts in funding for space were marrow-deep. Those who still felt that man had business beyond Earth agreed that what resources were left had better go mostly toward the stars. Like Korene, Joel saw that the same was true of him. He enrolled in the American part of the effort. Experience and natural talent equipped him uniquely to work on control and navigation.

In the course of this, he met Mary. He had known a good many female astronauts, and generally liked them as persons—often as bodies too, but long voyages and inevitable promiscuity were as discouraging to stable relationships for them as for him. Mary used her reflexes and spirit to test-pilot experimental vehicles near home.

This didn't mean that she failed to share the dream. Joel fell thoroughly in love with her. Their marriage likewise proved happy.

He was forty-eight, Korene sixty, when the word became official: The basic machinery for reaching the stars now existed. It needed merely several years' worth of refinement and a pair of qualified volunteers.

It *is* like making love again.

How my heart soared when first we saw that the second planet has air a human can breathe! Nothing can create that except life. Those months after Joel went into orbit around it and we observed, photographed, spectroanalyzed, measured, sampled, calculated, mainly reading what instruments recorded but sometimes linking ourselves directly to them and feeling the input as once we felt wind in our hair or surf around our skins—

Why do I think of hair, skin, heart, love, I who am embodied in metal and synthetics and ghostly electron-dance? Why do I remember Olaf with this knife sharpness?

I suppose he died well before Korene. Men usually do. (What does death have against women, anyway?) Then was her aftertime until she could follow him down; and in spite of faxes and diaries and every other crutch humankind has invented, I think he slowly became a blur, never altogether to be summoned forth except perhaps in sleep. At least, with this cryogenic recall of mine which is not programmed to lie, I remember how aging Korene one day realized, shocked, that she had nothing left except aging Olaf, that she could no longer see or feel young Olaf except as words.

Oh, she loved him-now, doubtless in a deeper fashion than she-then had been able to love him-then, after all their shared joy, grief, terror, toil, hope, merry little sillinesses which stayed more clear across the years than many of the big events—yes, their shared furies and frustrations with each other, their few and fleeting intense involvements with outsiders, which somehow also were always involvements between him and her—she loved her old husband, but she had lost her young one.

Whereas I have been given him back, in my flawless new memory. And given Joel as well, or instead, or— Why am I thinking this nonsense? Olaf is dust.

Tau Ceti is flame.

It's not the same kind of fire as Sol. It's cooler, yellower, something autumnal about it, even though it will outlive man's home star. I don't suppose the unlikenesses will appear so great to human eyes. I know the entire spectrum. (How much more does Joel sense! To me, every sun is a once-in-the-universe individual; to him, every sunspot is.) The organic body/mind is both more general and more specific than this . . . like me vis-à-vis Joel. (I remember, I remember: striding the Delphi road, muscle-play, boot-scrunch, spilling sunlight and baking warmth, bees at hum through wild thyme and rosemary, on my upper lip a taste of sweat, and that tremendous plunge down to the valley where Oedipus met his father. . . . Machine, I would not experience it in quite those terms. There would be too many other radiations, forces, shifts and subtleties which Oedipus never felt. But would it be less beautiful? Is a deaf man, suddenly cured, less alive because afterward his mind gives less time to his eyes?)

Well, we'll soon know how living flesh experiences the living planet of Tau Ceti.

It isn't the infinite blue and white of Earth. It has a greenish tinge, equally clear and marvelous, and two moons for the lovers whom I, sentimental old crone, keep imagining. The aliennesses may yet prove lethal. But Joel said, in his dear dry style:

"The latest readouts convince me. The tropics are a shirtsleeve environment." His mind grinned, I am sure, as formerly his face did. "Or a bare-ass environment. That remains to be seen. I'm certain, however, organic bodies can manage better down there than any of yours or mine."

Was I the one who continued to hesitate because I had been the one more eager for this? A kind of fear chilled me. "We already know they can't find everything they need to eat, in that biochemistry—"

"By the same token," the ship reminded, not from intellectual but emotional necessity, "nothing local, like germs, can make a lunch off them. The survival odds are excellent," given the concentrated dietary supplements, tools, and the rest of what we have for them. "Good Lord, Korene, you could get smashed in a rock storm, prospecting some wretched asteroid, or I could run into too much radiation for the screens and have my brain burned out. Or whatever. Do we mind?"

"No," I whispered. "Not unendurably."

"So *they* won't."

"True. I shouldn't let my conscience make a coward of me. Let's go right ahead."

After all, when I brought children into the world, long ago, I knew they might be given straight over to horror; or it might take them later on; or at best, they would be born to trouble as the sparks fly upward, and in an astonishingly few decades be dust. Yet I never took from them, while they lay innocent in my womb, their chance at life.

Thus Joel and I are bringing forth the children who will be ourselves.

He wheels like another moon around the world, and his sensors drink of it and his mind reasons about it. I, within him, send forth my auxiliary bodies to explore its air and waters and lands; through the laser channels, mine are their labors, triumphs, and—twice—deaths. But such things have become just a part of our existence, like the jobs from which we hurried home every day. (Though here job and home go on concurrently.) The rest of us, the most of us, is linked in those circuits that guide our children into being.

We share, we are a smile-pattern down the waves and wires, remembering how chaste the agency spokesman made it sound, in that first famous interview. Joel and I had scarcely met then, and followed it separately on television. He told me afterward that, having heard the spiels a thousand times before, both pro and con, he'd rather have gone fishing.

(Neither was especially likable, the commentator small and waspish, the spokesman large and Sincere. The latter directed his fleshy countenance at the camera and said:

"Let me summarize, please. I know it's familiar to you in the audience, but I want to spell out our problem.

"In the state of the art, we can send small spacecraft to the nearer stars, and back, at an average speed of about one-fifth light's. That means twenty-odd years to reach Alpha Centauri, the closest; and then there's the return trip; and, naturally, a manned expedition would make no sense unless it was prepared to spend a comparable time on the spot, learning those countless things which unmanned probes cannot. The trouble is, when I say small spacecraft, I mean small. Huge propulsion units but minimal hull and payload. No room or mass to spare for the protection and life support that even a single human would require: not to mention the fact that confinement and monotony would soon drive a crew insane."

"What about suspended animation?" asked the commentator.

The spokesman shook his head. "No, sir. Aside from the bulkiness of the equipment, radiation leakage would destroy too many cells en route. We can barely provide shielding for those essential items which are vulnerable." He beamed. "So we've got a choice. Either we stay with our inadequate probes, or we go over to the system being proposed."

"Or we abandon the whole boondoggle and spend the money on something useful," the commentator said.

The spokesman gave him a trained look of pained patience and replied: "The desirability of space exploration is a separate question, that I'll be glad to take up with you later. If you please, for the time being let's stick to the mechanics of it."

" 'Mechanics' may be a very good word, sir," the commentator insinuated. "Turning human beings into robots. Not exactly like Columbus, is it? Though I grant you, thinkers always did point out how machine-like the astronauts were . . . and are."

"If you please," the spokesman repeated, "value judgments aside, who's talking about making robots out of humans? Brains transplanted into machinery? Come! If a body couldn't survive the trip, why imagine that a brain in a tank might? No, we'll simply employ ultra-sophisticated computer-sensor-effector systems."

"With human minds."

"With human psychoneural patterns mapped in, sir. That is all." Smugly: "True, that's a mighty big 'all.' The pattern of an individual is complex beyond imagination, and dynamic rather than static; our math boys call it n-dimensional. We will have to develop methods for scanning it without harm to the subject, recording it, and transferring it to a different matrix, whether that matrix be photonic-electronic or molecular-organic." Drawing breath, then portentously: "Consider the benefits, right here on Earth, of having such a capability."

"I don't know about that," said the commentator. "Maybe you could plant a copy of my personality somewhere else; but I'd go on in this same old body, wouldn't I?"

"It would hardly be your exact personality anyhow," admitted the spokesman. "The particular matrix would . . . um . . . determine so much of the functioning. The important thing from the viewpoint of extrasolar exploration, is that this will give us machines which are not mere robots, but which have such human qualities as motivation and self-programming.

"At the same time, they'll have the advantages of robots. For example, they can be switched off in transit; they won't experience those empty years between stars: they'll arrive sane."

"Some of us wonder if they'll have departed sane. But look," the commentator challenged, "if your machines that you imagine you can program to be people, if they're that good, then why have them manufacture artificial flesh-and-blood people at the end of a trip?"

"Only where circumstances justify it," said the spokesman. "Under some conditions, organic bodies will be preferable. Testing the habitability of a planet is just the most obvious possibility. Consider how your body heals its own wounds. In numerous respects it's actually stronger, more durable, than metal or plastic."

"Why give them the same minds—if I may speak of minds in this connection—the same as the machines?"

"A matter of saving mass." The spokesman smirked at his own wit. "We know the psychoneural scanner will be far too large and fragile to carry along. The apparatus which impresses a pattern on the androids will have to use pre-existent data banks. It can be made much lighter than would otherwise be necessary, if those are the same banks already in use."

He lifted a finger. "Besides, our psychologists think this will have a reinforcing effect. I'd hardly dare call the relationship, ha, ha, parental—"

"Nor I," said the commentator. "I'd call it something like obscene or ghastly.")

When Joel and I, together, month after month guide these chemistries to completion, and when—O climax outcrying the seven thunders!—we send ourselves into the sleeping bodies—maybe, for us at least, it is more than making love ever was.

Joel and Mary were on their honeymoon when he told her of his wish.

Astronauts and ranking engineers could afford to go where air and water were clean, trees grew instead of walls, birdsong resounded instead of traffic, and one's fellow man was sufficiently remote that one could feel benign toward him. Doubtless that was among the reasons why politicians got re-elected by gnawing at the space program.

This evening the west was a fountain of gold above a sea which far out shimmered purple, then broke upon the sands in white thunder. Behind, palms made traces on a blue where Venus had kindled. The air was mild, astir with odors of salt and jasmine.

They stood, arms around each other's waists, her head leaned against him, and watched the sun leave. But when he told her, she stepped from him and he saw terror.

"Hey, what's wrong, darling?" He seized her hands.

"No," she said. "You mustn't."

"What? Why ever not? You're working for it too!"

The sky-glow caught tears. "For somebody else to go, that's fine. It'd be like winning a war—a just war, a triumph—when somebody else's man got to do the dying. Not you," she pleaded.

"But . . . good Lord," he tried to laugh, "it won't be me, worse luck. My satisfaction will be strictly vicarious. Supposing I'm accepted, what do I sacrifice? Some time under a scanner; a few cells for chromosome templates. Why in the cosmos should you care?"

"I don't know. It'd be . . . oh, I never thought about it before, never realized the thing might strike home like this—" She swallowed. "I guess it's . . . I'd think, there's a Joel, locked for the rest of his existence inside a machine . . . and there's a Joel in the flesh, dying some gruesome death, or marooned forever."

Silence passed before he replied, slowly: "Why not think, instead, there's a Joel who's glad to pay the price and take the risk—" he let her go and swept a gesture around heaven "—for the sake of getting out yonder?"

She bit her lip. "He'd even abandon his wife."

"I hoped you'd apply also."

"No. I couldn't face it. I'm too much a, an Earthling. This is all too dear to me."

"Do you suppose I don't care for it? Or for you?" He drew her to him.

They were quite alone. On grass above the strand, they won to joy again.

"After all," he said later, "the question won't get serious for years and years."

I don't come back fast. They can't just ram a lifetime into a new body. That's the first real thought I have, as I drift from a cave where voices echoed on and on, and then slowly lights appeared, images, whole scenes, my touch on a control board, Dad lifting me to his shoulder which is way up in the sky, leaves above a brown secret pool, Mary's hair tickling my nose, a boy who stands on his head in the schoolyard, a rocket blastoff that shakes my bones with its sound and light, Mother giving me a fresh-baked ginger cookie, Mother laid out dead and the awful strangeness of her and Mary holding my hand very tight, Mary, Mary, Mary.

No, that's not her voice, it's another woman's, whose, yes, Korene's, and I'm being stroked and cuddled more gently than I ever knew could be. I blink to full consciousness, free-fall afloat in the arms of a robot.

"Joel," she murmurs. "Welcome."

It crashes in on me. No matter the slow awakening: suddenly this. I've taken the anesthetic before they wheel me to the scanner, I'm drowsing dizzily off, then *now* I have no weight, metal and machinery cram everywhere in around me, those are not eyes I look into but glowing optical sensors, "Oh, my God," I say, "it happened to me."

This me. Only I'm Joel! Exactly Joel, nobody else.

I stare down the nude length of my body and know that's not true. The scars, the paunch, the white hairs here and there on the chest are gone. I'm smooth, twenty years in age, though with half a century inside me. I snap after breath.

"Be calm," says Korene.

And the ship speaks with my voice: "Hi, there. Take it easy, pal. You've got a lot of treatment and exercise ahead, you know, before you're ready for action."

"Where are we?" breaks from me.

"Sigma Draconis," Korene says. "In orbit around the most marvelous planet—intelligent life, friendly, and their art is beyond describing, 'beautiful' is such a weak little word—"

"How are things at home?" I interrupt. "I mean, how were they when you . . . we . . . left?"

"You and Mary were still going strong, you at age seventy," she assures me. "Likewise the children and grandchildren." *Ninety years ago.*

I went under, in the laboratory, knowing a single one of me would rouse on Earth and return to her. I am not the one.

I didn't know how hard that would lash.

Korene holds me close. It's typical of her not to be in any hurry to pass on the last news she had of her own self. I suppose, through the hollowness and the trying to cry in her machine arms, I suppose that's why my body was programmed first. Hers can take this better.

"It's not too late yet," she begged him. "I can still swing the decision your way."

Olaf's grizzled head wove back and forth. "No. How many times must I tell you?"

"No more," she sighed. "The choices will be made within a month."

He rose from his armchair, went to her where she sat, and ran a big ropy-veined hand across her cheek. "I am sorry," he said. "You are sweet to want me along. I hate to hurt you." She could imagine the forced smile above her. "But truly, why would you want a possible millennium of my grouchiness?"

"Because you are Olaf," Korene answered.

She got up likewise, stepped to a window, and stood looking out. It was a winter night. Snow lay hoar on roofs across the old city, spires pierced an uneasy glow, a few stars glimmered. Frost put shrillness into the rumble of traffic and machines. The room, its warmth and small treasures, felt besieged.

She broke her word by saying, "Can't you see, a personality

inside a cybernet isn't a castrated cripple? In a way, we're the ones caged, in these ape bodies and senses. There's a whole new universe to become part of. Including a universe of new closenesses to me."

He joined her. "Call me a reactionary," he growled, "or a professional ape. I've often explained that I like being what I am, too much to start over as something else."

She turned to him and said low: "You'd also start over as what you were. We both would. Over and over."

"No. We'd have these aged minds."

She laughed forlornly. " 'If youth knew, if age could.' "

"We'd be sterile."

"Of necessity. No way to raise children on any likely planet. Otherwise— Olaf, if you refuse, I'm going regardless. With another man. I'll always wish he were you."

He lifted a fist. "All right, God damn it!" he shouted. "All right! I'll tell you the real reason why I won't go under your bloody scanner! I'd die too envious!"

It is fair here beyond foretelling: beyond understanding, until slowly we grow into our planet.

For it isn't Earth. Earth we have forever laid behind us, Joel and I. The sun is molten amber, large in a violet heaven. At this season its companion has risen about noon, a gold-bright star which will drench night with witchery under the constellations and three swift moons. Now, toward the end of day, the hues around us— intensely green hills, tall blue-plumed trees, rainbows in wings which jubilate overhead—are become so rich that they fill the air; the whole world glows. Off across the valley, a herd of beasts catches the shiningness on their horns.

We took off our boots when we came back to camp. The turf, not grass nor moss, is springy underfoot, cool between the toes. The nearby forest breathes out fragrances; one of them recalls rosemary. Closer is smoke from the fire Korene built while we were exploring. It speaks to my nostrils and the most ancient parts of my brain: of autumn leaves burning, of blazes after dark in what few high solitudes remained on Earth, of hearths where I sat at Christmastime with the children.

"Hello, dears," says my voice out of the machine. (It isn't the slim fleet body she uses aboard ship; it's built for sturdiness, is the only awkward sight in all the landscape.) "You seem to have had a pleasant day."

"Oh, my, oh, my!" Arms uplifted, I dance. "We *must* find a name for this planet. Thirty-Six Ophiuchi B Two is ridiculous."

"We will," says Joel in my ear. His palm falls on my flank. It feels like a torch.

"I'm on the channel too," says the speaker with his voice. "Uh, look, kids, fun's fun, but we've got to get busy. I want you properly housed and supplied long before winter. And while we ferry the stuff, do the carpentering, et cetera, I want more samples for us to analyze. So far you've just found some fruits and such that're safe to eat. You need meat as well."

"I hate to think of killing," I say, when I am altogether happy.

"Oh, I reckon I've got enough hunter instinct for both of us," says Joel, my Joel. Breath gusts from him, across me. "Christ! I never guessed how good elbow room and freedom would feel."

"Plus a large job," Korene reminds: the study of a world, that she and her Joel may signal our discoveries back to a Sol we can no longer see with our eyes alone; that in the end, they may carry back what we have gathered, to an Earth that perhaps will no longer want it.

"Sure. I expect to love every minute." His clasp on me tightens. Waves shudder outward, through me. "Speaking of love—"

The machine grows still. A shadow has lengthened across its metal, where firelight weaves reflected. The flames talk merrily. A flying creature cries like a trumpet.

"So you have come to that," says Korene at last, a benediction.

"Today," I declare from our glory.

There is another quietness.

"Well, congratulations," says Korene's Joel. "We, uh, we were planning a little wedding present for you, but you've caught us by surprise." Mechanical tendrils reach out. Joel releases me to take them in his fingers. "All the best, both of you. Couldn't happen to two nicer people, even if I am one of them myself, sort of. Uh, well, we'll break contact now, Korene and I. See you in the morning?"

"Oh, no, oh, no," I stammer, between weeping and laughter, and cast myself on my knees to embrace this body whose two spirits brought us to life and will someday bury us. "Stay. We want you here, Joel and I. You, you are us." *And more than us and pitifully less than us.* "We want to share with you."

The priest mounted to his pulpit. Tall in white robes, he waited there against the shadows of the sanctuary; candles picked him out and made a halo around his hood. When silence was total in the temple, he leaned forward. His words tolled forth to the faces and the cameras:

"Thou shalt have none other gods but me, said the Lord unto the children of Israel. Thou shalt love thy neighbor as thyself, said Christ unto the world. And sages and seers of every age and every faith warned against *hubris*, that overweening pride which brings down upon us immortal anger.

"The Tower of Babel and the Flood of Noah may be myths. But in myth lies a wisdom of the race which goes infinitely beyond the peerings and posturings of science. Behold our sins today and tremble.

"Idolatry: man's worship of what he alone has made. Uncharity: man's neglect, yes, forsaking of his brother in that brother's need, to whore after mere adventure. *Hubris*: man's declaration that he can better the work of God.

"You know what I mean. While the wretched of Earth groan in their billions for succor, treasure is spewed into the barrenness of outer space. Little do the lords of lunacy care for their fellow mortals. Nothing do they care for God.

" 'To follow knowledge like a sinking star, Beyond the utmost bound of human thought' is a pair of lines much quoted these days. Ulysses, the eternal seeker. May I remind you, those lines do not refer to Homer's wanderer, but to Dante's, who was in hell for breaking every constraint which divine Providence had ordained.

"And yet how small, how warm and understandable was his sin! His was not that icy arrogance which today the faceless engineers of the interstellar project urge upon us. Theirs is the final contempt for God and for man. In order that we may violate the harmony of the stars, we are to create, in metal and chemicals, dirty caricatures of a holy work; we are actually to believe that by our electronic trickery we can breathe into them souls."

∗   ∘   ∘

Nat the rhesus monkey runs free. The laboratory half of the cabin is barred to him; the living quarters, simply and sturdily equipped, don't hold much he can harm. He isn't terribly mischievous anyway. Outdoors are unlimited space and trees where he can be joyful. So, when at home with Korene and Joel, he almost always observes the restrictions they have taught him.

His wish to please may stem from memory of loneliness. It was a weary while he was caged on the surface, after he had been grown in the tank. (His body has, in fact, existed longer than the two human ones.) He had no company save rats, guinea pigs, tissue cultures, and the like—and, of course, the machine which tended and tested him. That that robot often spoke, petted, and played games was what saved his monkey sanity. When at last living flesh hugged his own, what hollow within him was suddenly filled?

What hollow in the others? He skips before their feet, he rides on their shoulders, at night he shares their bed.

But today is the third of cold autumn rains. Though Korene has given to this planet of Eighty-Two Eridani the name Gloria, it has its seasons, and now spins toward a darker time. The couple have stayed inside, and Nat gets restless. No doubt, as well, the change in his friends arouses an unease.

There ought to be cheer. The cabin is amply large for two persons. It is more than snug, it is lovely in the flowing grain of its timbers and the crystal-glittering stones of its fireplace. Flames dance on the hearth; they laugh; a bit of their smoke escapes to scent the air like cinnamon; through the brightness of fluorescent panels, their light shimmers off furnishings and earthenware which Joel and Korene made together in the summer which is past—off the racked reels of an audiovisual library and a few beloved pictures—off twilit panes where rain sluices downward. Beyond a closed door, wind goes *brroo-oom*.

Joel sits hunched at his desk. He hasn't bathed or shaved lately, his hair is unkempt, his coverall begrimed and sour. Korene has maintained herself better; it is dust in the corners and unwashed dishes in a basin which bespeak what she has neglected while he was trying to hunt. She sprawls on the bed and listens to music, though the ringing in her ears makes that hard.

Both have grown gaunt. Their eyes are sunken, their mouths

and tongues are sore. Upon the dried skin of hands and faces, a rash has appeared.

Joel casts down his calculator. "Damn, I can't think!" he nearly shouts. "Screw those analyses! What good are they?"

Korene's reply is sharp. "They just might show what's gone wrong with us and how to fix it."

"Judas! When I can't even sleep right—" He twists about on his chair to confront the inactive robot. "You! You damned smug machines, where are you? What're you doing?"

A tic goes ugly along Korene's lip. "They're busy, yonder in orbit," she says. "I suggest you follow their example."

"Yah! Same as you?"

"Quite—anytime you'll help me keep our household running, Sir Self-Appointed Biochemist." She starts to lift herself but abandons the effort. Tears of self-pity trickle forth. "Olaf wouldn't have turned hysterical like you."

"And Mary wouldn't lie flopped-out useless," he says. However, the sting she has given sends him back to his labor. Interpreting the results of gas chromatography on unknown compounds is difficult at best. When he has begun to hallucinate—when the graphs he has drawn slide around and intertwine as if they were worms—

A crash resounds from the pantry. Korene exclaims. Joel jerks erect. Flour and the shards of a crock go in a tide across the floor. After them bounds Nat. He stops amidst the wreckage and gives his people a look of amazed innocence. Dear me, he all but says, how did this happen?

"You lousy little sneak!" Joel screams. "You know you're not allowed on the shelves!" He storms over to stand above the creature. "How often—" Stooping, he snatches Nat up by the scruff of the neck. A thin tone of pain and terror slips between his fingers.

Korene rises. "Let him be," she says.

"So he can finish the . . . the havoc?" Joel hurls the monkey against the wall. The impact is audible. Nat lies twisted and wailing.

Silence brims the room, inside the wind. Korene gazes at Joel, and he at his hands, as if they confronted these things for the first time. When at last she speaks, it is altogether without tone. "Get out. Devil. Go."

"But," he stammers. "But. I didn't mean."

Still she stares. He retreats into new anger. "That pest's been driving me out of my skull! You know he has! We may be dead because of him, and yet you gush over him till I could puke!"

"Right. Blame him for staying healthy when we didn't. I find depths in you I never suspected before."

"And I in you," he jeers. "He's your baby, isn't he? The baby you've been tailored never to bear yourself. Your spoiled brat."

She brushes past him and kneels beside the animal.

Joel utters a raw kind of bark. He lurches to the door, hauls it open, disappears as if the dusk has eaten him. Rain and chill blow in.

Korene doesn't notice. She examines Nat, who pants, whimpers, watches her with eyes that are both wild and dimming. Blood mats his fur. It becomes clear that his back is broken.

"My pretty, my sweet, my bouncy-boy, please don't hurt. Please," she sobs as she lifts the small form. She carries him into the laboratory, prepares an injection, cradles him and sings a lullaby while it does its work.

Afterward she brings the body back to the living room, lies down holding it, and cries herself into a half-sleep full of nightmares.

—Her voice rouses her, out of the metal which has rested in a corner. She never truly remembers, later, what next goes on between her selves. Words, yes; touch; a potion for her to drink; then the blessing of nothingness. When she awakens, it is day and the remnant of Nat is gone from her.

So is the robot. It returns while she is leaving the bed. She would weep some more if she had the strength; but at least, through a headache she can think.

The door swings wide. Rain has ended. The world gleams. Here too are fall colors, beneath a lucent sky where wander-songs drift from wings beating southward. The carpet of the land has turned to sallow gold, the forest to bronze and red and a purple which bears tiny flecks like mica. Coolness streams around her.

Joel enters, half leaning on the machine, half upheld by it. Released, he crumples at her feet. From the throat which is not a throat, his voice begs:

"Be kind to him, will you? He spent the night stumbling around the woods till he caved in. Might've died, if a chemosensor of ours hadn't gotten the spoor."

"I wanted to," mumbles the man on the floor. "After what I did."

"Not his fault," says the ship anxiously, as if his identity were also involved and must clear itself of guilt. "He wasn't in his right mind."

The female sound continues: "An environmental factor, you see. We have finally identified it. You weren't rational either, girl. But never blame yourself, or him." Hesitation. "You'll be all right when we've taken you away from here."

Korene doesn't observe how unsteady the talking was, nor think about its implications. Instead, she sinks down to embrace Joel.

"How could I do it?" he gasps upon her breast.

"It wasn't you that did," says Korene in the robot, while Korene in the woman holds him close and murmurs.

—They are back aboard ship, harnessed weightless. Thus far they haven't asked for explanations. It was enough that their spirits were again together, that the sadness and the demons were leaving them, that they slept unhaunted and woke to serenity. But now the soothing drugs have worn off and healing bodies have, afresh, generated good minds.

They look at each other, whisper, and clasp hands. Joel says aloud, into the metal which encloses them: "Hey. You two."

His fellow self does not answer. Does it not dare? Part of a minute goes by before the older Korene speaks. "How are you, my dears?"

"Not bad," he states. "Physically."

How quiet it grows.

Until the second Korene gives challenge. "Hard news for us. Isn't that so?"

"Yes," her voice sighs back.

They stiffen. "Go on," she demands.

The answer is hasty. "You were suffering from pellagra. That was something we'd never encountered before; not too simple to diagnose, either, especially in its early stages. We had to ransack our whole medical data bank before we got a clue as to what to look for in the cell and blood samples we took. It's a deficiency disease, caused by lack of niacin, a B vitamin."

Protest breaks from Joel. "But hell, we knew the Glorian biochemistry doesn't include B complex! We took our pills."

"Yes, of course. That was one of the things which misled us, along with the fact that the animals throve on the same diet as yours. But we've found a substance in the native food—all native food; it's as integral to life as ATP is on Earth—a material that seemed harmless when we made the original analyses"—pain shrills forth—"when we decided we could create you—"

"It acts with a strictly human-type gene," the ship adds roughly. "We've determined which one, and don't see how to block the process. The upshot is release of an enzyme which destroys niacin in the bloodstream. Your pills disguised the situation at first, because the concentration of antagonist built up slowly. But equilibrium has been reached at last, and you'd get no measurable help from swallowing extra doses; they'd break down before you could metabolize them."

"Mental disturbances are one symptom," Korene says from the speaker. "The physical effects in advanced cases are equally horrible. Don't worry. You'll get well and stay well. Your systems have eliminated the chemical, and here is a lifetime supply of niacin."

She does not need to tell them that here is very little which those systems can use as fuel, nor any means of refining the meats and fruits on which they counted.

The ship gropes for words. "Uh, you know, this is the kind of basic discovery, I think, the kind of discovery we had to go into space to make. A piece of genetic information we'd never have guessed in a million years, staying home. Who knows what it'll be a clue to? Immortality?"

"Hush," warns his companion. To the pair in the cabin she says low, "We'll withdraw, leave you alone. Come out in the passageway when you want us.... Peace." A machine cannot cry, can it?

For a long while, the man and the woman are mute. Finally, flatly, he declares, "What rations we've got should keep us, oh, I'd guess a month."

"We can be thankful for that." When she nods, the tresses float around her brow and cheekbones.

"Thankful! Under a death sentence?"

"We knew ... our selves on Earth knew, some of us would die young. I went to the scanner prepared for it. Surely you did likewise."

"Yes. In a way. Except it's happening to me." He snaps after air. "And you, which is worse. This you, the only Korene that this I will ever have. Why us?"

She gazes before her, then astonishes him with a smile. "The question which nobody escapes. We've been granted a month."

He catches her to him and pleads, "Help me. Give me the guts to be glad."

—The sun called Eighty-Two Eridani rises in white-gold radiance over the great blue rim of the planet. That is a blue as deep as the ocean of its winds and weather, the ocean of its tides and waves, surging aloft into flame and roses. The ship orbits on toward day. Clouds come aglow with morning light. Later they swirl in purity above summer lands and winter lands, storm and calm, forest, prairie, valley, height, river, sea, the flocks upon flocks which are nourished by this world their mother.

Korene and Joel watch it through an hour, side by side and hand in hand before a screen, afloat in the crowdedness of machinery. The robot and the ship have kept silence. A blower whirrs its breeze across their bare skins, mingling for them their scents of woman and man. Often their free hands caress, or they kiss; but they have made their love and are now making their peace.

The ship swings back into night. Opposite, stars bloom uncountable and splendid. She stirs. "Let us," she says.

"Yes," he replies.

"You could wait," says the ship. His voice need not be so harsh; but he does not think to control it. "Days longer."

"No," the man tells him. "That'd be no good," seeing Korene starve to death; for the last food is gone. "Damn near as bad as staying down there," and watching her mind rot while her flesh corrupts and withers.

"You're right," the ship agrees humbly. "Oh, Christ, if we'd thought!"

"You couldn't have, darling," says the robot with measureless gentleness. "No one could have."

The woman strokes a bulkhead, tenderly as if it were her man, and touches her lips to the metal.

He shakes himself. "Please, no more things we've talked out a million times," he says. "Just goodbye."

The robot enfolds him in her clasp. The woman joins them. The ship knows what they want, it being his wish too, and "Sheep May Safely Graze" brightens the air.

The humans float together. "I want to say," his words stumble,

"I never stopped loving Mary, and missing her, but I love you as much, Korene, and, and thanks for being what you'ye been.

"I wish I could say it better," he finishes.

"You don't need to," she answers, and signals the robot.

They hardly feel the needle. As they float embraced, toward darkness, he calls drowsily, "Don't grieve too long, you there. Don't ever be afraid o' making more lives. The universe'll always surprise us."

"Yes." She laughs a little through the sleep which is gathering her in. "Wasn't that good of God?"

We fare across the light-years and the centuries, life after life, death after death. Space is our single home. Earth has become more strange to us than the outermost comet of the farthest star.

For to Earth we have given:

Minds opened upon endlessness, which therefore hold their own world, and the beings upon it, very precious.

A knowledge of natural law whereby men may cross the abyss in the bodies their mothers gave them, short years from sun to sun, and planets unpeopled for their taking, so that their kind will endure as long as the cosmos.

A knowledge of natural law whereby they have stopped nature's casual torturing of them through sickness, madness, and age.

The arts, histories, philosophies and faiths and things once undreamable, of a hundred sentient races; and out of these, an ongoing renaissance which does not look as if it will ever die.

From our gifts have sprung material wealth at each man's fingertips, beyond the grasp of any whole Earthbound nation; withal, a growing calm and wisdom, learned from the manyfoldedness of reality. Each time we return, strife seems less and fewer seem to hate their brothers or themselves.

But does our pride on behalf of them beguile us? They have become shining enigmas who greet us graciously, neither thrust us forth again nor seek to hold us against our wills. Though finally each of us never comes back, they make no others. Do they need our gifts any longer? Is it we the wanderers who can change and grow no more?

Well, we have served; and one service will remain to the end. Two in the deeps, two and two on the worlds, we alone remember those who lived, and those who died, and Olaf and Mary.